~ It Really IS Rocket Science ~
"Rock 'N' Roll Fantasy"

Volume One

by
Brad H Branham ("Vexx")

Copyright 2013 by Brad H Branham

Congratulations!
Hope you enjoy the ride.
Brad H Branham

~1~ *"People Are Strange"* - The Doors

Blar stepped out of a light rail commuter car onto the station platform. The weather had turned nasty, the first snowstorm of the winter just weeks before Christmas. Portland was known for its quick changes in Pacific Northwest weather. This particular change made it difficult to see across the public brick-surfaced plaza that marked the center of the downtown shopping district. The city's holiday tree, nearly eighty feet high, dominated the center of the large open space. Its festive lighting reflected off of the falling snow illuminating the plaza in a rainbow hue of lights.

He slung his day pack over one shoulder, made sure his coat was buttoned and began trudging towards the coffee shop on the other side of the square. The cloud-covered sky was a uniform dark steel color except for the vaguely lighter region dipping near the western hills. The natives cynically called that lighter region the Sun for all the six or seven hours it appeared at this time of year. The combination of the holiday lights and the sparse remaining daylight entertained Blar with an surrealistic view of the buildings and the commuters milling around him, many of whom had been caught unprepared and were poorly dressed for the storm.

The average pedestrian would glimpse Blar appear out of the snowy gloom as a tall, imposing man with broad shoulders and shoulder-length shaggy dark hair streaked with flecks of gray. His face was lined with an old "chopper" style mustache and looked as it might have spent one too many nights in smoky bars. Piercing hazel eyes peered out at the path ahead, shaded behind an old fashioned pair of tinted round sunglasses. Blar was dressed in a dark trench coat, harness-style heavy boots, and carried a shoulder pack. Somewhat reflecting the cultural quirkiness of Portland, he also sported an old beat up top hat.

People were stepping aside as Blar passed, clutching their purse or briefcase a bit tighter. He was, bluntly, scary looking. He knew it. He had long ago adopted a fatalistic resignation to that fear. Blar thought of himself as the sort to jump to help if anyone needed assistance, but things were what they were. The public judged on superficial stereotypes and myths. Blar knew they only saw the modern version of a viking marauder or other medieval fantasy villain. Stay away. Don't make eye contact. Keep out of range. He had actually used his image to his advantage in his profession over the years.

Blar continued hiking towards the coffee shop. It was a locally owned place, his favorite, and it had large frame windows for people watching. Blar had a habit of sizing up the people in any establishment before he went in. As he did so this time, he caught a flash of a pair of fiery eyes, pale skin, black lace, and red bows in one of the windows. The view disappeared quickly as their feminine owner sat down.

The sighting snagged his attention with an imperative jerk, like a fish with a tasty lure in sight. Blar stepped just inside the door onto the entry grate and shook off the rather sizable amount of snow that had accumulated in the short walk from the train. As he removed his shades, the coffee barista behind the counter waved at him in greeting,

"The usual, Mr. U?!"

Blar nodded pleasantly and added himself to the queue of waiting customers.

As he waited, Blar tried to spot the owner of the lovely pair of eyes without luck. His search faded away, leaving him staring off into melancholy nothingness, the seconds ticking by until it was his turn at the counter. The barista handed him his drink and whispered, "This one is on me if you sign a cup. I have a friend that doesn't believe I know you." Blar cocked an eyebrow and a mild smile crossed his lips.

"Do I get an extra shot of espresso if I spell it right? Hey! No, I was just kidding. Here you go. Rock on, eh?"

Blar signed the paper mug with a flourish and it back. "Hey, instead of a free drink? Do this for me. I could swear I saw a heart-stopping frilly sweet treat here in the shop? A darkly cute woman with lacy bows? I saw her through the window. Did you see …?"

The barista interrupted with a nod and grin as he pointed with his eyes, "Over that way. Last booth. She's really something, isn't she? Started coming in here a couple of days ago. She's a spectacular little goth with lightning in her eyes. I think she's new in town, doesn't seem to have picked up the local chant yet, if you catch my meaning. She signs her cup *"Tsika"*. She is exquisite. Beautiful accent, too. I melt into a blithering idiot when she places her order. Now you've been briefed. I'll disavow any knowledge of your mission. Good luck!"

Blar nodded his thanks and took his coffee. The shop grew increasingly crowded as the storm outside worsened, so there wasn't any place to sit that he could spot. He took a spot at one of the standing tables, mildly alarming the businessman occupying it. Blar smirked and broke the ice by asking the suited man if he followed energy stocks and what he thought about the day's news on one of the local wind turbine companies. This soothed the nervous fellow and he started bantering about sustainable energy futures. Blar pretended to listen as he scanned the back half of the establishment.

Ah hah! That has got to be her. Or at least her hair. Wow, the hair. Keep an eye in that direction.

Two magnificent cascades of raven black hair secured by red bows were draped over a booth wall. Blar marveled at how the hair reflected the light and how intensely curly it was. He looked back at the businessman and realized he'd lost track of the poor sod's conversation. Time for diplomatic dancing.

"I'm sorry, what did you say about the new Vestas turbines? It's very loud in here."

The businessman got more amiable and animated, clearly thinking Blar was actually paying attention to his wisdom. Unfortunately for the poor fellow, Blar's perception of time had just slammed to a dead stop. Blar was experiencing what he sometimes called a perfect moment in time.

The twin cascades of hair rose and turned, revealing their owner. Calling the young woman exquisite had been a massive understatement by the barista, in Blar's opinion. She had a fine boned porcelain face with ruby red lips, flamboyant black eyebrows, and large eyes with brilliant amber pupils.

Blar had heard the term 'living doll' many times in his life but this was the first time he had ever felt the description actually applied so well. The pixie could not have cleared five feet in height and he could hear the click of high heels. She was dressed in a full-length embroidered black Victorian style dress trimmed with blood red bows and a black lace fitted corset. Blar was pretty sure the embroidery design portrayed spider webs.

Her garb, makeup, and hairstyle was a smoking hot example of the goth fashion popular in Japan and Europe. Her particular interpretation had a catchy hard-edged quality that went well with her tough expression. At first sight of her, Blar initially shifted quickly into depression. It seemed a fair chance she was a teenager with delicate features. He added more brakes on his intense attraction to her. He certainly didn't need that kind of problem in his life.

Closer examination of her face and figure relieved him of that dilemma, letting him up-shift again. There were curves to her figure, hints in the way she held herself, and much more maturity in her face than he had initially guessed. Blar estimated her age somewhere in the early to middle twenties. Definitely an adult but likely to be carded by bartenders for many years to come due to her small size and elfin features.

Okay, good. I haven't turned into a pervert. I really hope I'm guessing well because I am enthralled by her.

The little princess of darkness stepped regally towards the front door of the establishment. Blar could see she knew a lot of eyes were on her. She didn't look left or right but simply radiated remarkable stage presence as she subtly strutted for her audience. She wasn't being egotistical, she was actually giving a performance of a kind simply by existing. Impressive skill in execution, Blar thought. Fantastic stage presence.

Before Blar could avert his eyes, the young woman glanced his way and made eye contact. Blar was trapped by the gaze. One eyebrow flickered into an arch of inquisitive curiosity at him and he captured a bare hint of an impish smile. It seemed the briefest of instants and then her eyes shifted elsewhere. Blar guessed he had amused her simply by looking the way he did. Just outside the door, she opened a Japanese-style parasol to ward off the snowfall and vanished into the gloom.

Blar's mental gears were stripping their teeth. He knew he didn't have many to spare at this point in his life. He found her enchanting and felt absolutely compelled to follow. Blar turned to the businessman and made excuses.

"Oh crud! I just remembered I left my office unlocked. Sorry got to run thanks for the chat!" Blar abandoned his coffee and legged it out the door in pursuit, hurriedly buttoning his trench coat. Outside, Blar realized his first challenge. He knew how he stood out in a crowd and she had seen him. He could hope he was already a forgotten sighting. Fat chance.

Should I simply walk up to her and introduce myself? She made eye contact with me. Her reaction seemed positive. Am I about to make a fool of myself? Will I end up on the news in a 911 situation?

Blar, for the first time in nearly ten years of self-imposed social exile, found himself completely riveted by a woman and lost about what to do.

He decided to take his hat off for starters. Watching her walk away, Blar stood transfixed by the way the young woman moved. She really was a faerie, almost weightless, barely touching the ground. Her walk reminded him of something he had seen before, a prance to her gait that demanded attention.

"Can't ... let ... her ... get away. Don't screw up!"

Blar's first step ignited a screw up. He collided with a couple trying to step around him. Panic ensued until Blar calmed the pair as he repeatedly apologized for being distracted. He moved away as quickly as he politely could. Seconds later, Blar squinted into the thickening gloom and realized he had lost sight of the young woman in what now was a fullblown snow storm. A little panic of his own ensued as he scanned the plaza for her.

He took off jogging, then stopped short when he spotted her Japanese parasol at the edge of the square. She was standing at the intersection curb, waiting for the crosswalk light. Blar realized he was breathing hard and took a few measured breaths to calm himself.

How do I do this? Am I nuts? I haven't had this feeling about someone in … since dear Aina. I'll frighten her if I don't do this right. Is this stalking? I don't want to come off as creepy. I am stalking. This is bad. Maybe I should have someone track her down? Ugh, that's no better. Still stalking. I could wait at the coffee shop tomorrow. What if she never comes back? Augh! Who IS she? Tsika. The barista said her name was Tsika. Hmm, that sounds Russian. Maybe Ukrainian? Slav? By the gods, she is so pretty.

The light changed and the young enchantress crossed the street. Blar followed at a distance, mesmerized by her movement. She turned onto the street where Blar lived, an avenue of many tall condominiums. As the little goth made her way through the deepening storm, the snow kept piling up. At some spots the drifts were already more than a foot deep. The sidewalks were icing up as well. The storm was turning remarkably nasty as darkness began to take the city.

One block. Two blocks. Blar followed. His guilt piled up much faster than the falling snow.

Following people, following young women especially, was a ticket to ending up on the news these days. Blar simply didn't know what else to do. Just watching such attractiveness made Blar happy, an unusual feeling for him. Blar relished each second as he worshiped her existence in the world. Such a lovely walk she had, the way her two impressively long pigtails framed the swish of her hips. They swayed like dual metronomes, swinging with each step.

Her hair wasn't just long, it was quite thick and voluminous, simply an enormous quantity of hair for such a small body. So black, so curly, tight spirals from end to end, both tails extending down almost to her waist. Her hair was a such a striking feature that people passing the opposite way would stop to look back. Blar had to slow down several times so as not to alert other pedestrians that he was indeed following her.

That tactic didn't help his guilt at all. At this point, there was no other word for it – the scary thug was stalking the young tasty treat. His only excuse? It had simply been so long since Blar had felt this way about someone and he didn't want to let her slip out of his world. But how to make the first contact?

As he followed, Blar saw her slipping more frequently on the increasingly icy pavement. Each time she would gracefully recover her footing. She was quite agile. Blar thought the moves had a gymnastic quality in the movement.

Her small stature … oh! Duh! She's using the exact same walk gymnast women use on television! Time to slap myself for my lightning intellect. She's about the right size. She is almost certainly a gymnast or had been when she was younger. Had to have been. Whoa, she slipped pretty hard that time. Great recovery, like a cat.

Those antique lace up boots are probably smooth soled. They are very pretty but worse than useless in this icy stuff. Huh. She's walking right by my place. That might make it easier to figure out how to naturally introduce myself to her at some point if not today. I can't justify following past my home, even to myself. And whoa! Ouch! That was spectacular!

Blar's fascination shrieked something in a language he couldn't quite catch and disappeared in a large cloudburst of snow. The small side street next to the building Blar called home had become completely buried in snow. The bewitching but unfortunate creature had discovered the street by tripping off the hidden curb and landing face down in a snowdrift, completely vanishing into it. Blar heard a high-pitched angry squeal followed by some extremely imaginative and lurid cursing in at least four or five languages, only a few of which he could actually identify. Blar ran to her without thinking.

"Are you okay?! Gods, let me help! Here, I'm here! I'm helping!" The snowdrift puffed and exploded as she thrashed about inside. After a few seconds of Blar clearing snow, her head popped out of the drift as she sat up. Her entire body, face, and hair was caked in wet clingy snow. The poor sprite couldn't see a thing and she was wailing.

No, not wailing. Not crying. Howling. An impressively angry visceral howl. It was hair-raising. Blar half expected a pack of wolves to appear at her command. It was actually quite awesome to listen to.

"I don't know! I … I can't see! Ankle hurts!" She followed up with more utterances of clearly evil damnation in several languages. Blar could pick out phrases that were Russian or Ukrainian but also a few snatches of what sounded like Chinese and he had no idea what else.

"Okay, miss. Um … be still, please. Sorry, I need to put my hands on you to get this snow off of you." Blar got down on his knees. He took his scarf and wiped her face gently, steadying the young woman by cupping the back of her neck with his free hand. She stopped thrashing and sat very still. She seemed to be processing the size of his hand as it cradled her head.

What delicate shoulders and a fine little neck. Crap. I have no idea why small boned petite women fascinate me! With one very distinct exception in my life, I always have been fascinated by such creatures. Probably better not to analyze the reasons for attraction too closely. Therein lies madness. Focus on helping.

Several pedestrians had run over to see, but as they got closer and got a better look at Blar and the young goth, they hesitated and backed away. Blar sighed and rolled his eyes.

"It's okay, I've got her. I think she'll be okay. Thanks anyway."

Blar muttered under his breath as they scurried away. "Jackasses."

"They ran, didn't they? Stupids … like to gawk but when it counts they fear," a small voice quietly lamented.

She was shivering. Blar carefully blotted at her face with his scarf trying not to smear her precisely applied makeup. He wasn't doing very well. Her long lashes had picked up a good coating of frozen snow and she still couldn't see. He dabbed at her lashes gently, trying to get her eyes functional again.

"Wow. Rescuing hero has really big hands," she noted quietly. She had a heavy Russian lilt in her voice that was musical to Blar. He loved foreign regional accents, the more unusual the better. Where he had grown up, there was no such variety in language.

Her shivering was fairly violent now. The wet snow had soaked her clothing. Small slender fingers gripped Blar's sleeve and he could hear her teeth chattering. Time for very quick introductions because he needed to get her out of the frigid weather. The temperature was still dropping and it was getting dark.

"Hey, my name is Blar. Look, we need to get you out of this mess and somewhere warmer. You can put my coat on 'til we …."

Blar was helping her stand up as he spoke. She shrieked and fell again. Blar managed to catch her before she vanished back into the snowdrift, cradling her with both arms. The elfin doll rubbed her eyes and finally got a good look at Blar as he held her. She got very still again, gazing into his eyes. All Blar could see was entrancing beauty was just a few inches away. Unfortunately, he knew he was not getting the same appraisal.

Blar for the umpteenth time in his life lamented his threatening appearance. At one point he'd even cut his hair and shaved his face but it had still been like this. People thought he was scary. He'd given up and gone back to wearing long hair, growing his mustache, and wearing the kind of clothing he liked. Screw them all.

"I'm sorry, ma'am. Didn't want you to hit the ground again and you're shivering like crazy. Here, take my coat 'til we get you dried off." He stood her up again and started to take his coat off, but she howled something horrible in Chinese and fell against him.

"Dammit fuck shit hell! God damned ankle! Ow! Fuck! Fuck! Oh, fuck!" Blar held her close and just stood still.

He couldn't help smirking at the juxtaposition of such beauty and so much profane language. He could be pretty salty himself but she was priceless. The little potty-mouthed princess fell into silence as the snow fell on them. She clutched him tightly. At first Blar thought it was for support but she suddenly acknowledged there were other reasons.

"You're very warm and being so good with helping. Thank you." Enormous black-lined eyes looked up at him. Blar marveled at her skin color, made even paler in contrast to her blood red lipstick. Those pretty lips spoke.

"My name is Tsika."

"Tsika. That's a lovely name. Tsika, can you lean on this sill?" Blar's condo building had wide window sills for seating. She nodded and he was able to maneuver her onto one. Success.

"Good! Let me give you my coat before you freeze." Blar draped his coat around her and pulled it closed to shield her from the wind. Half of the coat trailed on the ground.

Tsika's new fashion motif was now 'tiny jail bait'. She really was quite small next to Blar and his loaned trench coat just emphasized the size difference between them. Blar rolled his eyes at the sliding slope of doom he was creating for himself.

"Oh fabulous. That will attract the wrong kind of attention at me. Ogre scampers off with lovely elf. Film at eleven."

Tsika laughed softly at his words as she shivered. "Not ogre! V-Viking marauder maybe! You're much warmer than your coat ... I'd rather stay close to you and ...," she stopped as a violent shudder took her.

"Bart? Er, Blar? Your coat. It isn't helping, Am so cold! Wet to skin." Blar heard an odd sound from inside his lent coat and Tsika's eyes got even wider. "Ow! What the fuck was that? What? Is going on? OH! Oh, you little piece of shit! OH! NO! NO! Not YOU, Blar! Sorry! My corset! The stiffening material ... I think it's warping! It ... ow! ... fucking thing is stabbing me!"

"Warping? They do that? That sounds really ungood. Can you unhook it?"

Blar just concentrated on keeping her bundled in the coat and supporting her. Alarmingly, he could hear the corset making cracking noises now. The phrase "DO NOT IMMERSE IN WATER! EVER!" danced through his head.

"No, idiot!" Her expression morphed from anger to regretful. "Sorry! Oh, I'm sorry I said that! But ... no! I can't get it off without Glycerin's help! She helps me put it on! It has lacing ... in ... the back. I can't ... reach."

Tsika was now breathing a bit raggedly. Her teeth were chattering and she was shivering so hard she was having trouble controlling her movements. She leaned against Blar for support and warmth. The cursing began anew.

"Shit! Whole week is shit sucking!! I told my Mouse she tied it too fuck tight this morn! Nothing going right!"

Tsika was jerking her eyes in different directions in a mixture of anger and panic. Blar could see tears in her eyes. With the temperature dipping below well below freezing now, even crying was not a good idea. Blar gritted his teeth and thought his options out. This was going to go wrong in so many ways from any fantasy hopes he might have had, but he certainly wasn't going to abandon her.

"Tsika. I live in this condo building. Right here. Let me offer my place to get out of the storm and dry off. I want to help. There's no graceful way to say this and not sound weird but … you need to get out of those clothes. I promise you'll be safe. I'll introduce you to the doorman, Jack. I'm well known around here. You will be safe. You can call your friends. It'll be okay."

Tsika responded with the frightened expression Blar had been resignedly expecting, but then she looked at the building she was leaning on before focusing more closely at Blar.

"You live in THIS building? Wow. Expensive. Ow! Ah … I can't breathe … it hurts … and …." She was trembling violently now and taking short ragged breaths. She stared at the sky and then scanned Blar intently, especially his eyes. Good girl, Blar thought, she's calculating the risk.

"Yes, Tsika. I agree. It looks risky. I know what I look like. I'd be wary myself. But I can't think of any other option at the moment unless my doorman comes up with something. At least let's get you into the lobby. I can not abandon you in this mess. Whatever you decide you want to do I'll help, but staying in this weather soaking wet is bad and your corset is making some scary noises. You will be safe. Scout's Honor!"

Tsika searched Blar's eyes again, clearly frightened but intent with purpose. She made her decision.

"H'okay! Will take … action! I … I decide to trust you! But I can't walk … or breathe … and …," one gorgeous eyebrow arched up skeptically. "Really?

Scout Honor? Hah! Is comedy gold! Large bear is boy scout? You even did … the salute thing!"

Tsika managed to get some laughter out between her short breaths. Blar really had unconsciously put his hand up in a Scout's three-fingered salute and left it there. He blushed and dropped the salute.

Blar made sure his coat was wrapped around her, then picked her up in his arms in one motion. He grabbed her parasol as he did so. The sweeping movement generated a very short stifled squeal out of her. Tsika was surprisingly light even caked in all that wet snow.

"Okay, Tsika. If you say it's okay, we'll go. Hot chocolate and dry clothes ahead. I promise. And yes, I really was an Eagle Scout when I was a teenager. So yes, really."

"Now I should be … making with etiquette. Nice t-to m-meet you, Blar." Tsika's teeth were chattering and she wasn't hanging on to him. She simply curled up shivering in his arms.

Blar carried Tsika over to the condo doorway where the doorman ran out to greet them with a concerned look. He had a rough voice that sounded of many years in smoky bars drinking the hard stuff.

"Hey, Blar! Wow! Scored a little dark angel? Are they falling out of the sky down at – ?"

Blar interrupted. "Hi, Jack. This lassie fell and is a wet mess. We need to get her dry and warm. Rescue time."

The uniformed doorman nodded. "Absolutely, yes, Blar … uh, Mr. U! Tragically, I can not offer anything here in the lobby. I'm freezing here myself and all I have are band-aids and a cardiac jump-starter. We'll shoot you up to your place. Give me a yell for anything she needs, I'm here until midnight. Just need her name for the guest log."

Tsika was gripping Blar's shirt like a clamp with both hands now. She gave Jack a curious look and then looked up at Blar. She managed to speak in between short breaths.

"Eh? Why does name sound familiar? And … the face? Um … yeah … ow! Hi, Jack … hi … name … is Tsika ... Tsika Tsarinkov." Her breathing was worsening by the second.

"Good enough, we can chat it up later! I'll be up in a jiff when you ring me, Blar! Let me get the elevator for you, uh damn! … Mr. U! Setting it for warp drive to your floor, no stops!"

The doorman sprinted for the elevator with Blar close behind carrying Tsika in his arms. Blar vaguely realized he had lost his top hat – again. So many times he had lost and replaced that hat.

- - - - - -

Blar reached the door of his apartment cradling Tsika while fishing for his keys.

"Большой парень! Big guy … sorry, I got you all … soaked, too. Owwww!" She gasped and gripped his shirt. "This shitty cheap god damned fuck corset … is … is … skewering me! Will burn crappy thing in fire!"

Tsika sounded like she was delivering a baby. She was very focused and panting in short rapid breaths in between outbursts of shivering. She gripped his shirt tighter and buried her face in his shoulder. It was obvious to Blar that Tsika was unable to control her shivering at all at this point as she blew through her energy points.

"We're there. Don't pass out on me, eh?" Blar sidled in the door to avoid bumping her head or feet. It closed automatically behind him He turned smoothly into his kitchen, setting Tsika on the counter with her back to the counter bar. Blar unwrapped his trench coat off of her and tossed the snow-soaked thing back into the entry way. She sat staring at nothing as she panted. Tsika gave off the impression of a small black cat just rescued out of a storm – soaked, miserable, and violently shivering.

"Quick, let me see your back before this thing finishes you off like a python." Tsika swiveled for him. "Freaking cat's cradle! This will take at least five minutes to untie all these knots!. Maybe I should just throw you in the shower under warm water?"

Tsika nodded, "Yeah ... hah. No, let's not. More water. But ... ow ... good guess ... that's ... hah ... how long ... it takes ... Gly- ...." She never finished the sentence. Blar leaned close and made eye contact, looking closely at Tsika's face. She was definitely much more blue than porcelain now.

"See me? Hear me? Nod! Good. I'm going to cut the lacing. You're way past uncomfortable now, you look like you're in real trouble. This is suffocating you and you've lost far too much body heat. We need to get you warm quick." Tsika looked Blar in the eyes. She had a few tears running down her face and was slipping into a fatal look. She nodded meekly as she panted.

Blar grabbed a kitchen knife and slipped it under her corset lacing. Blar steadied her with his hand on her shoulder. Tsika put one of her hands on his and squeezed it in a death grip.

Blar began slicing the strings from the top down. As the laces fell away, her breathing improved gradually, resuming a normal pattern. Her grip on Blar's hand lessened. As the laces fell away, Blar heard a deep breath, soft whimpering, and then her shoulders began shuddering. She was crying and cursing now.

"Fuck ... fuck fuck fuck! Crossed my mind that I was going to die! Then Saint Peter kicks me to Hell from Pearly Gates laughing because STUPID Russian bitch was too cheap! Bought this piece of SHIT instead of proper clothing. God damn it, god ... damn me. *Я глупая сука!*"

Blar cut the last string and gently removed the corset revealing a sopping wet black blouse beneath it. He tossed the corset into the entry to join his coat on the floor. Tsika was alternately muttering curses and sniffling. Blar was intrigued by her vast creativity in cursing.

Blar instinctively started massaging her shoulders, both to calm her and to start warming her. The drenched blouse was nearly transparent. As he massaged, he couldn't miss a lovely pair of dark tribal style wings tattooed on the pale skin of her back. The black ink art stretched across both shoulder blades.

Time for a soft soothing voice. Blar shifted her to face him and gently hugged her, patting her back as she pressed her face into his shirt.

"You're okay. Shh, Tsika. You're obviously new in town. The weather is mercurial. Okay, it sucks like a black hole sometimes. It's okay. You're safe. Shh, it's okay. I'll buy you a proper corset. Shh. Just ... breathe ... breathe."

Tsika's muffled noises subsided and she straightened up. Blar backed up and watched the young woman begin to take stock of where she was. Sitting on a kitchen counter top in a stranger's apartment, who had just used a knife to remove her top and had just been hugging her. Blar could only imagine he was on razor thin ice. Tread very lightly.

On the upside of his sudden adventure, the more Blar stood near the little beauty on his counter the more enchanted he became. Her raven hair, pale moonlight skin, and blood red lips contributed to his overall impression of a tiny wild goth version of Snow White. Blar couldn't help abusing the word 'delicate'. She was heart stopping in his eyes.

"Little pixie, you're still drenched and shivering. I'm worried you're going to catch pneumonia next. My guest bathroom is over there. It has a lock. Take a hot shower and there are some spare clothes in there you can wear while your outfit dries. Or ... you can call your friend and have them bring clothes over? Give your friend a call, eh?" Blar handed Tsika her cell phone, it had ended up in his shirt pocket at some point in the rescue.

"I dropped this, too? Fuck me to hell. Almost deserve not to make it through day alive!"

Tsika's amber eyes flared and then her little storm subsided.

"Thanks, thank you, yes, okay. I get it. I am much lucky that large rescuing marauder is Honorable Scout. боже мой , this place of yours is so big and nice. Does not look like home of evil intent."

Her eyes searched his face. Again. Blar knew he was being scanned by the sensors of a scared nervous young woman. Make her feel safe. Blar kept repeating that mantra in his head. That much he remembered from so long ago.

Blar wasn't entirely on edge. Tsika did seem to be sending him subtle signals she found him interesting, perhaps even attractive. Her expressions, tone of voice, choice of words all seemed encouraging. She was rightfully being very cautious though.

She slid off the counter top, winced and nearly fell again. Blar caught her. Tsika clung to his arm and examined his hands as they supported her.

"Damn, you have really big hands! Uh yeah, stupid bitch keeps saying that. Ignore my babbling. I am enormously stupid today it seems." An involuntary shiver interrupted her chatter. "Maybe more stupid than stupid blonde. Glad she isn't here to make fun of me."

After that cryptic remark delivered in a heavier Russian accent, Tsika looked up into Blar's eyes for what seemed to him like centuries, examining, searching. Once again Blar wished he didn't look like a thug from a bad motorcycle gang movie. He simply tried to smile gently and wait. She seemed terribly small as she analyzed his lumbering self.

"Okay. It is good, I hope. Help me to your shower, please. I can hop around once I get there."

Blar left Tsika sitting on the guest bathroom toilet seat getting her stockings off. He closed the door and returned to the kitchen. A minute later, he heard her talking on her cellphone as he started the promised hot chocolate.

He rummaged in his refrigerator, grimacing at the choices. He decided to warm up some left-over noodle soup from his favorite restaurant down the block. Blar knew he ate out entirely too much, it just wasn't a lot of fun cooking for one. The soup still smelled pretty good.

Blar wasn't exactly eavesdropping, but with the guest bathroom right across from the kitchen it was impossible not to hear Tsika chattering through the door.

"Hi, Glyc! … No, I am not lost! … Yes, dear, I know you worry … Sorry … I had an accident … No I am not dying! I fell off curb in damned storm and twisted my ankle … Nyet! … Got buried in snow and soaked to skin! Then! Then god damned corset tried to crush me like snake! "

Blar could hear her shedding clothing as he prepared the leftovers. Each sound made him twitch – just a little.

Try not to think about that lovely visual image, doofus. Focus on helping. I want her to feel safe. That used to work with wooing women anyway. Definitely want to get to know her.

"This большой медведь saved me and is letting me clean up at his place … No! Glycca! He is not rapist! … I have good radar, Mouse! He is being very nice … yes, I think he is very interes – … yes, he seems to be finding me desira – … no, darling Mouse, there isn't a torture room … Glyyyyc! Shhhh! … Nyet! Do not try to come get me! I will not have my precious Mouse dying in this fucking storm … Yes! You are right! No one told us this happened here! They said oh yeah it rains a lot it's cloudy, blah blah … bunch of shit fuck waste of … yes, Glycca. Yes, I should not curse so much. I am sorry."

Blar wondered who this 'Glyc' friend was. The one-sided conversation was kind of fascinating.

"Anyway, he is very nice helping man and the doorman knows my name and that I'm here … yes, there's a doorman … yes, it is extravagantly nice place … Glyc, have an extra drink for me, okay?"

Blar heard a huge sigh and the sound of a waterlogged embroidered dress hitting the floor.

"You and Kpau practice! Is there any sign of Sashiko? … Her ass is so fired! … Yes, I know I already fired her. But I figured she would regain sanity and beg apologies! … Why couldn't crazy woodpecker just do what she needed to do? … Yes, she is still our dear Sashi, always our dear Sashi. But, we need a new … Yeah, yeah, sure, sure. Augh! I sound like Kpau just then! Infected with her babbles! I am good, Mouse. I have my cell, battery has enough dots. I'll see you tomorrow noon at the club for practice if the weather lets up. See you then! *Zàijiàn, Glycca*! I love you, big Mouse. Night!"

Blar heard Tsika start the shower as he decided the soup needed some seasoning help and searched for spices.

That was interesting. She seems to assume she's staying here overnight during the storm. Well, it was a practical and astute guess on her part given the deepening storm and her sodden clothes. That dress did not look like it was meant to be beaten by a mere dryer.

Blar had no objection to the idea. He wanted to get to know her. His place had a guest bedroom. He was forcefully rejecting any personal fantasies right now about other possibilities. He wanted to chat with Tsika, just converse with the lovely little doll.

I want this to be something serious. I hate flings. Idiot. I am still assuming Tsika is actually interested. Meh.

Blar decided to straighten up the living room. He also made the decision while getting his own wet clothing off that his usual ragged shorts were not a good evening wear choice. He selected dry jeans and a tank top. Blar queued up some instrumental jazz tracks and opened the curtains. It was snowing so hard he couldn't even see the lights of the building across the street. Time for a deep breath.

Okay. I have a beautiful little goddess in my flat. Nothing less than a stroke of luck and a malfunctioning corset got her here. She's in my shower. I notice she didn't bother to lock the door, so maybe she trusts me. Go slow. Somewhere out there in the dark is a locomotive with the lights off bearing down on me – quite likely driven by my dearest Aina. Bitterly laughing and yelling I deserved to be run over … shut up, brain. Just focus on being helpful and friendly.

As Blar finished setting up his poor excuse for a meal, he heard the bathroom doorknob turn and glanced up. Tsika was leaning against the door frame, standing on one foot to favor her injured ankle.

She had found one of his old button collar dress shirts to wear. Between that article of clothing and the towel struggling to control her hair, Blar was pretty sure the little princess had nothing else on. The bathroom lighting was providing some translucent unintended confirmation via her silhouette in the shirt. What she had found was enough though. The borrowed shirt came all the way down to her knees and the rolled up sleeves covered her arms down to her fingertips. With a belt, it would have been a very modest dress.

Tsika's makeup had disappeared down the shower drain. Blar thought she was quite fetching without it. Gone was the artfully painted goth vampire who had graced the apartment. In her place was a sublime translucent forest nymph. Tsika's twin tails had vanished, disassembled before the shower. Now her mane was a single erupting tangle of glossy black curly hair lassoed by an inadequate towel.

Blar plead guilty – he was now completely smitten by the existence of a small impossibly beautiful flower of the species Tsika. Blar could feel his liquified brains oozing down into his gut.

Unbearably cute. Exquisite bone structure. The shirt clinging in just the right places ... oh, she's talking ... oh, um, yelling. Oops.

"HEY! A little help?! Stupid-head! Ehhh, err ... please?" She seemed abashed at her outburst. There seemed to be regular cycles of outburst and apology with this delicate flower.

"Am sorry, Blar! This one is just ... I'm not a nice person sometimes. My friends just smile and nod agreeably 'til my ranting storms fade out. I'm really sorry." Tsika blushed – the first hint he had seen in her skin that she had blood.

Blar moved quickly. He scooped her up in his arms, eliciting a surprised yelp out of her. He deposited Tsika on a bar stool where the meal awaited. He silently noted she smelled like his soap now. That was good for more mental twitches.

"Okay, pretty pixie. Here's hot chocolate as promised and here's some leftover *udon* I warmed up. Figured speed and warmth took precedence over quality."

Tsika gazed at Blar intently for several seconds before tasting her drink and snatching a bit of chicken with the chopsticks. He had forgotten to ask if she used chopsticks but she seemed quite adept. She kept her eyes on him. Blar guessed she was still analyzing him, wary and nervous he would suddenly turn into the sort of monster the mysterious Glyc worried about. Then she spoke and blew that theory to shreds.

"I was right. You did follow me from the coffee shop. I remember because I noticed you and your amusing top hat in there. Took me a while to add it up because you didn't have the hat when you came to my aid." Her big eyes narrowed at him as she slurped noodles out of the bowl.

Blar slumped his shoulders. The stalking was outed. He sighed. "Yeah. You got me. I think my hat is lost in the storm, though. Yes. I saw you at the coffee shop. I freely admit … I found you … fascinating. I meant no harm. You happened to be walking towards my home anyway so I was just enjoying your existence in the world and trying to figure out how to introduce myself."

Blar felt morose. Well, that was it, he'd blown any chance to get to know her. An older guy stalking younger women. Good job, idiot. Just fix her up and send her on her way. So much for waking up after all those years. Probably better to go back to the darkness quietly.

A small hand intruded into Blar's blossoming depression by stroking his arm.

"Thank you, Blar. I do not think anyone else out there would have stopped to help me. It is obvious we both generate our own kind of 'stay away' force fields. Large man looks like some scary, heh, um, Viking? Motorcycle hooligan? Whereas, I ... well ... I look like … a vampire or ghoul to the muggles. At least those are the labels that beloved stupid blonde ladles on me!"

She chuckled at her own self assessment. Blar wondered who this stupid blonde was that she kept mentioning. It didn't seem to be the one she had spoken to called Glyc. The attitude toward each was very different.

Wait. Is Tsika saying she is okay with my interest in her? I think she just did. What the hell? Bullet dodged?

Tsika sipped on her hot chocolate as she continued to regard him with those beautiful large eyes. Blar wasn't sure she had blinked once since she had started eating.

"If it comforts you, Blar, it must be revealed. I found the large bear with amusing hat … um, intriguing in the coffee shop as well. Was planning to just keep an eye out for you over several days. Thought I would see if you were regular there, see if anyone knew you, then find some way to strike up conversation. I … I just liked your eyes and expression in your looking at me." Tsika blushed. So there definitely was blood in her veins. She giggled nervously at her revelation that she had found him interesting as well.

"So! Both scary people are stalkers! Just different ways of stalking prey! Yes?"

Tsika quietly regarded Blar as she continued sipping her drink. Blar was somewhat flummoxed that she had been attracted to him in the coffee shop but he sensed she was still wary, feeling vulnerable.

"Am glad you followed else I would be much more miserable now. So! Large

Bear … you said I was fascinating. What does fascination look like now? Without all my makeup, decoration, and gift wrappings?"

She stared down at her drink as if preparing for bad news. Blar found the idea of someone saying something negative about her unadorned appearance incomprehensible.

Clue bat. Important question just asked. Her shields are coming down to let me answer.

"I see … a delicate snowflake of a faerie … um, wearing my shirt better than it ever looked on me … a fantastically beautiful tangle of hair … I … can't take my eyes off of you."

Blar's voice caught several times as he tried to be smooth. He was so out of practice. Utter fail. That was such maudlin cheesy crap! Terrible lyrics!

Tsika's face pinked up, "Ah! I … I like those words a lot better than other options! Like … skinny damp waif with Medusa hair … or … blood-sucking cave shrimp waiting chance to mesmerize large oaf and feast on much blood!" She quietly giggled and took a larger swig of her hot chocolate, finishing it off.

Wow. How did I manage to avoid utter disaster just then with her? I feel like I'm playing chess with dice.

Blar took a breath and drained his drink as well. "Want some Kahlua in the next round of chocolate? You're so lightweight I wasn't sure what your tolerance was and I did not want to be accused of drugging pretty fluff."

Tsika laughed huskily. "Silly Bear! Snowflake faerie drinks like a fucking pirate! Yes, Kahlua. Lots please."

"Do you have another preference for drinks? I have a pretty well stocked bar."

"One more chocolate with Kahlua then maybe … do you have makings for vodka tonic? Is comfort drink."

She held her cup up with both of those delicate hands as she swung her legs in the bar stool. Blar was loving her Russian accent. It varied in intensity depending on her mood. He had heard a number of different languages out of her in the last couple of hours. She seemed to be multilingual though so far most of it seemed to circle around black curses, probably all instant kill spells. Blar wondered what "большой медведь" meant. He couldn't even pronounce it. She had called him that in the phone call to her friend.

"Yup, I even have the authentic potato kind instead of grain vodka." Blar poured them both refills of hot chocolate and added a liberal helping of Kahlua this time.

Tsika took a drink, "Mmmm. Half and half is good mix! This will make my ankle feel better. No lectures about self-medication issues, please."

Blar wolfed down his portion of the left-overs. Time to talk. "So! How long have you and your friends been in town? I thought I heard you say you were practicing? Are you part of a gymnastics team?"

"Gymnast?! Ah! Haha! Funny! But large Bear has good eyes. I did do gymnastics for a while at boarding school! But not reason for being in this city! Friends and I are band! The music kind of band! Is great excuse for dressing such as this … or rather that over there?" She nodded at her pile of wet clothes visible through the bathroom door.

Blar growled, smacked his forehead and got up. Snagging his cell phone, he punched a single digit in. "Hey, Jack. Hi! … Yeah she's doing great … yes, she is pretty tough for a delicate angel. Hey Jack, can we get you to pick up her clothing for a cleanup job? … yeah, the one next door, they have my tab on file. I think they're open late for drop off. … really? Wow … okay, keep me posted. Thanks!" He looked back at Tsika as he set his phone back down.

Tsika was blinking in a small show of horror. "Oogh, cleaning will cost a fortune, just hang them up to dry!"

Blar shrugged. "I'm not bright about clothing but I suspect that wouldn't be good for that quality of dress. We'll have your clothes fixed up, though it's likely to be overnight. No big deal. There is no telling what you rolled on in that alley. Jack just told me the weather has turned to utter shit down at street level and the police are telling people not to drive."

He braced himself. He had to offer Tsika an escape clause. "I ... I can pay for a cab to get you home. I don't know if they are still running and I don't feel very comfortable sending you out without proper clothes. Um ... I have a guest room you can camp out in if you like. "

She sat silent for a few seconds, her eyes analyzing him. "Thank you for offering shelter. Nice scoutly thing for large Bear to offer. Seems ... practical ... to accept. I had already assumed I might need such extravagant offer with clothes such a mess and weather so shitty."

Still visibly nervous. She must really be sensitive to being in vulnerable situations. Times have changed?

Blar shrugged, trying to appear relaxed. "I want you to be safe and feel safe so I'll do whatever you want."

Keep her mind off of scary thoughts. Talk about other things.

"So! You're a musician! What kind of band is this you and your friends have?"

Keep the conversation going, make her feel safe. Just keep thinking that way. But Blar wasn't feigning interest now. He was really quite curious. What were the odds he and she would have similar career interests?

Tsika brightened up and nibbled at her food, "Well. Right now we poorly market ourselves as a rock punk girly cover band. We call ourselves "The Lost Girls". It turns out to be ironically apt name because we are not really going anywhere and cannot find our niche. Could not get more than a toe into music scene down in Los Angeles. Just random gigs accompanied with lecherous club managers. Much of the music wanted by the few fans we did have isn't what we want to play. They want really bubblegum pop stuff. I find such noises icky ... though precious Glycerin really likes them, poor thing. Anyways ... after much frustration, I researched and thought we try up here in frozen wasteland of Portland and Seattle."

Tsika rolled her eyes. "Now we just tell peoples we are mixed genre. Each of us has wildly different tastes in music anyway so we rotate through styles ... but ... the music we all agree on and really like ... rock, metal, punk ... well, sometimes – sometimes it just needs a guy at vocals. No matter how much I drink and inhale bar smoke, I can not do justice to rugged rock like a *Pearl Jam* or *AC/DC* tune. I do a fair cover of nu-metal tunes by such groups as *Evanescence*, melodic punk as *Joan Jett*, or any tune that is good for contralto voice. Can do a bit of opera actually, is my Russian upbringing. Sashiko did most of our rough hard-core vocals and she's gone now. She has really special unique voice. She split yesterday and has not come back, damn her!"

Tsika sulked on that as a noodle vanished between her lips. Blar thought it was amusing the little musician just assumed he knew what she was talking about and the groups she was mentioning. He actually did know them. Quite well. Some personally even. Her assumptions revealed she spent all her time burrowed in music culture. Tsika growled as she continued her halfhearted rant.

"Sashi has unique exceptional voice. She makes great stab at male vocals. Bad ass growly! Lots of energy! But she spent more time drunk and fighting than practicing. Personal issues, personality clashes. She missed too many gigs, let us down, and I finally canned her ass the other day. Hoped that would get her attention and she would shape up. Instead, she left. It hurt. A lot. She is a close friend to us from when we were in college but … no discipline at all."

More noodles vanished between those lips.

"So! We are kind of in Plan B at the moment. We are getting a few gigs here in Portland. But club managers, they mostly drool and sign pretty women on looks alone. Then they think they have license to touch. We are lucky with latest one. He is like nice grandpa. We'll have to knock them out come showtime though because I cringe at notion of just being a pinup sexy band. We are musicians … goddamn good ones!"

Tsika sighed and poured herself more Kahlua in her drink. Blar estimated the drink was mostly Kahlua by now.

"Do you have a website I could look at?"

Tsika looked up curiously at Blar's sudden businesslike inquisitive tone. He wanted to see more of what this group was about. While watching the little princess wave her hands as she ranted, he had noticed her fingers. They had very definite guitar string calluses. The way she moved as she talked was a clue. Blar was getting a vibe, a good one. He wanted to see more.

"Yes, where is your computer?" Tsika slipped off the bar stool and winced. She wobbled but stayed vertical as she scanned the room. The small beauty had tied a knot in the back of Blar's borrowed dress shirt and it accentuated her slim curves. Tsika turned to face him. Blar struggled to focus on those large amber eyes but couldn't help noticing a faint outline through the shirt's material just below her collarbone. She had a large dark spider tattoo inked just above her left breast. He chivalrously avoided looking farther down. Blar didn't want to be accused of any bad behavior and he desperately wanted this time with Tsika to be more than a transient moment.

"I have several computers. Come over to the couch, let me help … steady … there's a laptop." Tsika curled up on the couch. Blar grabbed the couch blanket and draped it on Tsika before sitting next to her with his laptop. The blanket chivalry made her smile. She adjusted it to let some of his warmth in. The next half hour they spent browsing her band's website. It was extensive but hadn't been updated in months.

During Tsika's narrative, Jack appeared at the door and was handed a bag of Tsika's wet clothing which he scampered off with. When Blar returned from the clothing hand off, he brought along a vodka tonic for her and a whiskey for himself. Tsika had pulled up a page of candid band snapshots for him to see.

"Here's your drink. So, these are your band mates ... long time friends?" Blar looked at the women in the photos. They were all quite striking in appearance, especially the tall one."Yes, drooling lecherous Bear! Ha! Spotted the looking! Large Bear is leering at delectable morsels!"

Tsika chuckled as Blar sputtered. He took a mild elbow to the ribs as she continued. "Is okay! Just messing with you. This is Kpau. She is drummer and jack-of-all-trades. She can sing, she can handle a bass guitar competently and she doesn't hurl her guts on lead guitar as long as melody is simple. She knows how to fix and build things. Very creative in odd ways. We met her in college the first year. She kind of latched onto us like puppy needing home. That's when we coined the name of our group. We call ourselves 'The Lost Girls' for very good reasons."

Tsika's face shifted to a more solemn expression. "The short story is we are all orphans. Lost our parents when we were young, boarding school, foster care, blah blah. Mine is a sob story that can wait 'til I am flaming drunk. The other stories belong to each of my friends to tell themselves."

Blar silently flinched at that revelation. His life problems were minor in comparison. He stared at the fuzzy image of a short tanned blonde named Kpau. "I'm gonna guess Kpau is the … stupid blonde … you keep mentioning?"

Tsika blinked. "What? Oh! I guess I have invoked her in vain that way. She really isn't stupid at all. We have many ill-mannered pet names for each other. She calls me vampire and other names. We do pick at each other in jest."

Tsika laughed but then returned to a solemn face as she pointed at a short-haired redhead with a freckled face and enough ear piercings to short out a metal detector.

"This is Sashiko, our former band mate as of the other day. She tagged in with us by way of introduction from Kpau our freshman year. Kicks ass at singing punk and metal. But she does not stay sober and she is a bitch when she drinks. I am sure she does occasional drugs but never really out of hand, mostly the drinking. Sad times there. Maybe crazy woodpecker will grow up on her own. I wouldn't mind having her back if she did."

Tsika looked more sad than angry as she flipped to the next web page for more photos. Then her expression transformed to a happy glow. "And this! This tall wonder is my precious friend for life, Glycerin! My sweet big Mouse. We've known each other since primary boarding school. I began learning bass guitar after she picked up guitar as her musical instrument … so I could stay close to her. We originally met when I saved her shy cowardly butt from some bullies at school."

Blar chuckled, "She's, what, twice your height? And you saved her?"

"It is comedy, yes? Some call me small fury from hell and that is using nice words! She is statuesque fatally shy wallflower. Is strange, though. Glycerin changes when she gets a guitar in her hands. Then she is wild whirling dervish of dance. It is awesome to watch. It blew me away the first time I saw her transform. She was passionate even early on about the art. She is compelled to dance when she plays guitar, like she is channeling something from gods."

Tsika sipped her vodka. Blar noticed her head wasn't quite steady now and decided any further drinks should be weaker. The sprite smiled sadly and continued.

"Should warn you. Glyc is terrified of guys in most situations. Am not overstating at all – she is petrified of men in general. Bad history. She can get by if one of us is near for support. It has gotten better since teen years."

Tsika bit at the inside of her cheek. "Though … she can get used to men individually. I have seen that. Kpau likes to joke that given Glyc's wild abandon in her music-making, stupid blonde thinks if Glyc ever does feel safe with a guy inside her panic perimeter she'd probably be under him like a wild animal in heat … annnnnnd I shouldn't have said that about my pure innocent Glycca. Christ on a stick. Time out! Is the drinks talking now!"

Tsika sat silent watching Blar as he played a few of the audio clips on the site. There was no video. They had a really good raw sound but Blar felt like he needed to see them perform live. Maybe he had a win-win situation here, a band he could give some assistance with and a sexy little sprite to court.

"Hmm. Your group sounds amazingly sharp technically. I can hear stellar licks in there, the drumming has flair, and the vibe just communicates you all clearly love playing together … but … yeah, some kind of repackaging might be good. Something to twist it around the bend, stand out a little more."

Blar realized that Tsika had curled up against his ribs under his arm, sucking warmth from him. Little creature probably had a lot of trouble staying warm even on warm days. She leaned over into his face and cocked an eyebrow.

"You sound like you have some ... experience in this line of work? I am saying this out loud now. Why do I keep feeling like I know you? That I've even spent a lot of time with you? You seem familiar to me, which is impossible of course! Are you ... someone I might know? Professionally?"

Blar sighed heavily and looked out the window at the snowstorm. No use concealing anything.

"Cripes. The storm isn't going away is it?" He looked down to find Tsika was now nose-to-nose with him, staring up at him with her large eyes. She was breathing a bit huskily and her cheeks were flushed.

The cute little liar was a lightweight drinker after all, or maybe she was just exhausted and that made it easy.

"You are such a nice man ... and warm ... with big comforting hands. I like that. I rarely meet nice men."

She kissed him lightly on the lips and then blushed as she snapped out of her haze. "Ah! Fuck! Another time out! Sorry! I am drunk! Please play like I did not do that! I am good girl! Really!"

She looked so abashed, almost distraught. It had Blar hoping she was wanting to make a quality impression on him as well. It made him want to stroke her head to comfort her. He memorized the kiss though. Salty Kahlua.

She slipped off the couch leaving the blanket behind and took a few tentative steps. He watched her small shapely hips and back. His brain just kept locking up every few moments with Tsika, like he could die right now and it would be okay. He knew she existed and that was enough.

"This little kitty is going to check out the landscape of your kingdom while she gets her head straight. Any safety tips? Landmines?"

"Ah ... no, not really. In fact, I was going to give you the house tour because it would explain why I was so interested in your band." Blar sensed a minor opportunity had slipped by. It didn't seem to be a critical miss. For a brief instant, he thought of all the video games he had played where he would save the game status just before taking a chance. No game saves in real life.

Tsika was limping but she made her way down the hall unassisted with Blar narrating as he followed behind her. Every time she took a step and flinched, he flinched.

"Master bedroom to the right. Marvel at my mounds of books and wall art. To our left, the guest room I mentioned you can camp out in. It is boring but comfy. Full of Asian art and sculpture. I have spent a fair amount of time in Japan and points east, blah blah boring stories. This room on the left is my work office. No windows so I'll stay focused. Be amazed at the amount of computing power of which I use about ten percent for actual work – the rest for gaming and mucking about. Now. Here is the room I think you need to see so that everything I'm about to say will make sense. I think you are going to appreciate this."

Blar pointed to the door that capped the end of the hallway. It looked different than the other doors. It was larger and carved in an ornate Japanese woodblock style. Tsika stopped, leaning against the wall for support. She was having difficulty maneuvering. Blar could sense her increasing exhaustion. She looked up at Blar, uncertainty flickering across her face. Her breathing edged into ragged again and her eyes dampened.

"This … isn't the … torture sex slave room ... is it? Glycca was sure … you had one." Her lip quivered as she made a pretense of humor.

She was clearly really scared. Her expression filled Blar with depression. He was still on a tight rope with her. Keep her feeling safe. He smiled gently, "No, little Tsika. There's absolutely nothing in there that can hurt you. Glycca need not worry. Unless a guitar string breaks I guess."

Tsika's eyebrows crinkled quizzically. Blar swung the door open. The lights came on automatically and Tsika curiously, and in Blar's mind quite bravely, stepped into the room.

It was a large area, arranged for entertaining. There was an imposing but snow-muted view of the city on one end provided by large plate windows. To a new visitor, there was too much to take in at once. In a quick glance, one might spot a large drum set, several guitars, amplifier stacks, some wall elements that had plaques with circular metal disks, sound suppression panels on walls and ceiling, and a number of framed wall posters. Tsika limped up to the closest plaque and stood reading the inscription. She had her back to Blar so he just relaxed and waited by the door, enjoying his view of her. Tsika got very still. Very still.

"This ... this is a platinum record. A real one! It ... It is for the band *Gothic Fire*. This ... this band. It is like Glycerin's favorite band of her life. When we were kids, um, teens. Precious girl would make me listen to them over and over. We would pick out the bass and lead lines. We would practice them 'til our fingers bled."

She limped over to other plaques. Despite her limp, she moved faster as she examined each artifact. Blar could tell she was around the bend, so exhausted. Between the cold exposure, the stress, the pain of her ankle, her fear, and the alcohol, he was impressed she had not passed out. Tsika kept wobbling, yawning and rubbing her eyes but the room was fascinating her. "This is like a museum for the band. You are quite a collector! This is amazing. You and Glyc might have things to talk about! This is ...."

Tsika stopped at a poster. It was a large framed picture of the *Gothic Fire* band members on stage at the end of their performance at a concert held eleven years before.

"God damn it to hell! Fuck me! That is why I feel like I know you! You are the fucking drummer! You are fucking Christ man Blar Umlaut! You are fucking rock god! One of Glycerin's gods! Poor Glycca would be barfing up her guts if she were here. You were the biggest thing in her world when we were teens! In many ways, you saved her. You! Aina the keyboardist! Especially Aina! Torsten the bassist! Asgeir! The others!"

She looked at Blar in disbelief.

"You know exactly what it is like for band such as mine to be where it is at starting gate. How scary it is facing into oblivion. Heh, I am ... blown away. I am standing in house of Blar Umlaut!"

Tsika smiled weakly. Blar was approaching awe in marveling that she was coherent anymore. She was so tired her eyes weren't tracking together. Then

Tsika suddenly wheeled about, her eyes riveted by a particular display case. She limped over to investigate.

The display contained a bass guitar. A custom bass guitar with the body carved in the shape of a bat wing and finished off in an iridescent blood red. It looked expensive because it was hideously expensive.

"I … those pickups … bridge … frets … all look handcrafted. This is … beautiful to look at. I have never seen anything like it." Her small hands touched the glass. Blar broke out of his reverie of just watching her body erotically shift and flex his borrowed shirt.

"Here, want to try it? It was made right before we retired. Torsten didn't want it after we split. Bad memories for him. Never got used in public. I don't think anyone has touched this little jewel in several years now."

Blar opened the display case and took the guitar out. The base of the display had a practice amp cleverly built in and he activated it as he plugged the bass guitar in. Blar helped Tsika strap it on, enjoying his touch of her shoulders, neck, and back as he held her hair up so it wouldn't get tangled in the strap. Tsika stroked the finish and then flicked the low string. She stood transfixed, feeling the note resonate through her. She checked the tuning and then ran through a quick series of scales and arpeggios. Blar liked the skill he was hearing. Even ignoring her looks, the audio she produced was highly impressive.

"This is … godly. So light to the touch. Perfect frets." Tsika began riffing through a piece that Blar immediately recognized. The renowned bassist Flea used it as his primary refrain in "Dani California", a classic Red Hot Chili Peppers tune. She spread her legs out for stability and her hips swayed gently as she played. Riveting movement to go with marvelous skill.

Blar moved in front of her to watch her play. Tsika was amazing to watch, especially considering her hands were so small. She used some clever tricks to handle the long spans needed for certain aspects of bass play. She was at least as good as any studio musician he could recall working with and he had a feeling she wasn't even trying very hard.

Blar thought about the guitar sitting as it had been, mostly unused for almost a decade. He made a decision that he thought brilliant. His imagined silent train in the dark closed in for the kill. Later, Blar would wonder if Aina had awakened in her bed at that moment giggling at his blunder.

"Tsika, I think that guitar would be much happier with you than sitting here gathering dust. You take it. Something to get you rolling. For you."

Tsika froze mid-lick but Blar continued without noticing her face. He was staring into a far distance. "Yeah, that's the ticket. It fits you perfectly both in looks and skill. Very tasty combo that will open the right doors."

Tsika trembled and put the guitar back on its stand. She stroked it softly, running her fingers along the neck. Then she turned back to Blar. Blar was befuddled at her expression. It had become fearful with a glimmer of tears and disappointment.

"Oh. Okay. I can add. I … I get it now. Where this is going. I was … being childish and naive. This is grownup time … I … know how the music world works. Nothing for free … except chicks." Her eyes were flashing anger but she continued to sniffle and wipe her nose. "I need to … to … with you … for the guitar and your connections. Nothing ... unusual. I do want it so much. We … do desperately need … a way inside."

Tsika stood straighter. She started to unbutton the shirt she was wearing as her hands trembled. The spider tattoo in all its black widow glory appeared, the soft curve between her breasts. She was talking fast, almost babbling, trying to sound light and casual, but a tear ran down her cheek.

"I'm … I'm a big girl. I've read the biographies. How it goes with getting breaks. This ... not so bad. You're not, like ... fat and ugly. You're the Blar Umlaut! I should be honored. You've been ... very nice to me. I will … I will be a good girl if it helps. Not … not like I can get away anyway!"

More tears followed that last sentence.

Blar was in some shock. What the hell? He flailed in his head trying to figure out how he had triggered this. Worst scenario, the god damned train wreck. How the hell, what, where did she get that idea out of this? What had he done? Had he come off like one of those slimy record industry jackasses who demand sex for giving a band a chance? Aina used to call it 'rape for airplay'. Blar had beaten the crap out of one for going after Aina once. They formed their own label after that. She still ran it. Blar got regular checks in the mail from it.

Tired. Maybe Tsika was that tired. Or that scared. Given her situation, he could barely imagine what it might be like to be so vulnerable, how easy it would be to misread someone's intent. Move now. Quick.

Blar dropped to one knee in front of Tsika as fast as he could move. He grabbed her wrists to stop her from unbuttoning any more and looked directly into her eyes.

"Stop! No, that wasn't my intention at all! No. Please, please stop. Let me back up and try this again, please, please. Not how or what I wanted at all. I said or did something that was unclear. Please listen to me, Tsika."

Tsika's sniffles trailed off but the tears continued. Now she looked back and forth from Blar's eyes to his huge hands gripping her tiny wrists.

Fear.

Blar gently released those lovely little wrists and began re-buttoning her shirt. Back into hiding went the gentle curves, the spider, the fine collarbone. When he was done, Blar rested his fingertips on her shoulders as gently as he could.

"Please. Hear me. I do not nor have I ever wanted to do that to a woman, to make them feel like they have no choice. To me, it's just a kind of rape and an abominable dirty part of the business. I want nothing to do with it."

Blar sucked in a quick breath. I'm pleading here, I hope you're still listening, little flower.

"Somehow, I have fucked up and said something wrong. Let me try again. Please."

Blar was morose and he could feel his eyes wetting up. "I want to be your friend. I want to get to know you. And then, one day? If we're friends and you want? Maybe? If it feels right? I'll tell you right now I'm smitten with you. You enthrall me. But the only way I want to be with a woman is if she trusts me. That we are together as equals. In a way she feels safe, only with her permission. I absolutely hate the idea of women as property. It makes me ill. There is no price for this gift. None. The guitar simply needed someone who will use it and love it. I think that it needs to be yours."

Tsika took several deep breaths as she darted her eyes around, avoiding Blar's gaze initially. She blushed deeply and dug her toe into the carpet. Then she looked straight at him and whispered softly as she put her hands on his as they touched her shoulders.

"No, you didn't mess up, Honorable Scout. I think I fucked up just now. I … I am exhausted, full of fear and stupid. I ignored all the good guy signals you've been sending all evening and I went straight for Big Bad Wolf story in my head."

Tsika took a huge breath. "My bad. Really … I was just … I was just putting up a brave front for Glyc because I have been scared out of my wits since you carried me up here. It is hard not to think the kind of awful thoughts my Glycca always has. Normally, I can take care of myself. I really can be quite lethal. I have a long history of terrible moments. But ankle, fatigue … you're so big. I would have no chance if you were Bad Wolf."

She looked carefully at Blar while she wiped her eyes and sniffled. "I am still scared, large Bear. But not for an evil reason now."

Tsika moved to sit on Blar's still bended knee. She put her arms around his neck, resting her head on his shoulder. She took a huge breath and her voice quavered as she spoke.

"I am scared because I am going to let the honorable large Bear in. A new person inside my shields. I decide. I decide I will trust you. It is … okay now. You are honest in your motives."

Tsika went silent briefly.

"It is weird. Just a second ago, I felt trapped, big scariness. It was … terrifying. I really am more dangerous than you think but you are so big. I am damaged, weak. And you could hold key to my future, much power over me."

"But now. Now is like happy light is on. Even though I do the almost exact same thing I would be doing other way. Letting the large man touch me. But happy light is on. It feels … really nice instead of awful. And … and I do admit attraction to you. To the large comforting bear. Attraction is primal, not rational."

Blar was breathing his way back from utter mortification. Huge breath. Maybe a monastery wasn't a bad idea.

"In my head, Tsika, it's all about you giving the permissions. I am so much not perfect at life but if I can read the signs I follow them." Blar rubbed his face and tried to stifle a yawn. He'd forgotten how stressful it could be getting closer to someone. So tired now.

Tsika involuntarily yawned back. A huge yawn. Hellooooo tonsils! Her face flushed.

"Sorry! Bad manners and probably bad breath! I'm … I'm really really tired, honorable Bear … *большой медведъ*" Her Russian lilt had gotten quite thick during her speech.

Blar heaved a huge sigh of relief.

This is like disarming a nuclear bomb. I am so out of practice with women.

He stroked her head. She didn't flinch. In fact, she rolled into the stroke like a cat would.

"I'll crash on the couch. You can have my bed. That room has a lock on it."

Tsika lifted her head and stared into Blar's eyes. He could feel her breath on his face and her cheeks were still blushing.

"My turn to make move in this tragic comedy! I will … I will stay with you on the couch? I … I get it. I need to use practical sense. As I admit, there is mutual attraction. You … I find you exciting and not because of your name. Is exciting just because you are large comforting Bear. But I don't feel quite comfortable yet saying come to bed with me. I'm … stupid old fashioned in some ways."

Tsika smiled bashfully. "Bear needs to court me first!"

She looked down and touched her forehead to his. "But ... I want you to be close and I need someone to snuggle up with after all this stress. My Glycca isn't around tonight for snuggling." Blar thought about that notion. It both excited him and sounded psychologically painful. So it goes.

"Argh ... I won't deny it might not wreck my head, but on my honor ... whatever you need. I can do that."

Blar stopped in confusion as he processed Tsika's remarks. "What? Wait. Snuggle with Glyc -- are Glycerin and you? Have I misread something?" Blar looked baffled as he drew a line from Tsika to the room's window and back.

"Oh no, silly!" Tsika laughed softly and nuzzled into his neck. "We're not lesbians! She's just a great snuggle pillow when we're exhausted. And ... I think ... I think ... I need you to carry me to the couch. I like it when you carry me. My ankle is aching and I am burned Russian rye toast after too much excitement."

Blar scooped up Tsika as she yawned again. He carried her back down the hall to settle in back on the couch. Blar retrieved the couch blanket and drew it over her. Tsika snuggled up in Blar's lap and flipped the blanket over him to share. She buried her head in his neck and purred.

"You really are nice man ... small vampire will eat you last after we survive plane crash." She snorted cutely in the middle of the musical laughter that followed.

Blar looked down to reply but Tsika was already lightly snoring. Blar had nearly forgotten what it was like to have a soft pretty woman to cuddle up with. Later when asked, Blar would say that night was both the best and worst night of his life. Heaven and hell simultaneously. Damn scout's honor but there it was. He'd given it.

~3~ "I'm Still Alive" – Pearl Jam

The murky light of a cloudy Pacific Northwest morning shone through the curtains into an unusually eclectic but well-appointed living room. Quiet jazz drifted through the air along with the sounds of soft rumbling snoring. On the couch was a blanket, under which a rough looking bear and a small ghostly princess slept.

Tsika fluttered her eyes open and pushed some of her long curly black hair off her face. She was seriously disoriented. She couldn't quite focus her eyes. Tsika felt toasty warm and it slowly registered to her sputtering brain that she was curled up on the chest of a man whose large arms were protectively wrapped around her.

H'okay! Where the hell am I and do I still have both of my kidneys? When did I sign up to be kept woman of fearsome motorcycle gang lord? No, that doesn't ring right. Wait. Shitty snowstorm. I fell. Ankle hurt. Very wet. Then nice man rescuing. Scary moments. But he was so nice, trying so hard to help. The guitar. I got scared but then it was really nice. Blar Umlaut. Oh! I'm a damned idiot. Need coffee. Lots of coffee to ward off alcohol poisons.

Tsika turned her head to look at the man she was curled up with. His snore shifted to a milder noise.

Fuck me to hell. I have just spent the night curled up on THE Blar Umlaut. The drummer for legendary rock band *Gothic Fire*. Glycca will upchuck her spleen when she finds out! Such a pathetic fan girl, dear thing. He followed me because I fascinated him. I cast a spell on him without even knowing. But he was a perfect gentleman behind his scary legend! Scary legend is a god damned boy scout!

Tsika stretched out and snuggled against Blar. It was hard not to giggle at the disparity between the two of them. Her face was nuzzling his neck and her toes barely cleared his knees. As she lay on him, his hands drifted down until they settled on her butt. He was still asleep.

Such large hands! He is so warm! Damn it! Man lights my engines up! I have never even thought about being with a guy this big. He must weigh over twice my pittance. What would it be like? To have this man make love to me?

Tsika's hair fell into Blar's face and his snore derailed into a choking sound. Blar sputtered and awoke staring up into an enormous pile of minty darkness.

"I appear to have succumbed to the wiles of a gorgeous faerie princess who has me pinned. Okay. I concede that this is an exquisite morning present. Probably the best present I've had in a decade. I have a question, though, little pixie. How long does it take you get all this hair under control in the morning?"

Tsika lightly dug her nails into his chest. "That is why the pixie, as you keep calling me, arranges her hair into twin tails, you ginormous Bear. Flick and a flick! Wah ha! I am done! Worn it in twin tails as far back as I can remember. Imagine small, giggling, shrieking child running with twin exhaust smoke trails behind her. Seriously. As you can see, my hair is quite thick and impossibly curly. I could use it for concertina wire. The poor brushes! They scream and leap off of the mortal coil to the toilet when I reach for them!"

Tsika stretched her whole body while she used Blar's shoulders to pull herself up so she could be nose-to-nose with him. The feel of her body slipping up his chest made the man twitch. This did not go unnoticed by Tsika.

"The vampire has large Bear's attention?" Tsika's foxy seductress smile crashed into a blush. "I am sorry. That was mean. I slept great! First time in many nights. So warm and toasty. Large man fed my pathetic neediness nicely. I guess I probably made you crazy. I kind of hope it did, I guess?"

Tsika bit her lip. "Just … let me get to know the real you better and I might be a naughty girl for you. H'okay?"

She fluttered her eyelashes and ran her finger along Blar's mustache. Her eyebrows wrinkled as something curious occurred to her. "Is your name really Blar Umlaut? Is really a wacky name when I think about it!" She couldn't avoid making a goofy face at the way his name sounded.

Blar laughed. Tsika liked the way that felt and she loved the way his hands felt on her butt. She was such a total sucker for big hands. At the moment, it was hard for her to think about anything else.

"No, it isn't. Well, yes it is – now. I wasn't born with that name but had it legally changed. It was just easier after the band hit it big. Should I guess that Tsika isn't your real name either? It does SOUND Russian but I've never heard the name before."

Tsika growled and sat up on his lap. She raised her hands up over her head to start arranging her hair while keeping her eyes on Blar. He had a fascinated expression and had a nice grip with both hands on her hips. She could tell he was relishing every little move her hips made.

That made her blush. He seemed so awed by her, almost mesmerized. Tsika felt just brave enough that she arched her back a bit, making it appear to be an artless moment. The move tightened her borrowed shirt up against her small pert breasts. His eyes moved from her eyes to those treats as they pressed against the shirt.

Really? He really likes my body? The way I look? Without all my paint, fashion, bows, and decoration? I'm not sure I know what to do with that idea. No gift wrapping and he seems to not care less.

"No, big Bear. Long long ago, a stupid-head administrator misspelled my name and then mangled the pronunciation. The class thought it was hilarious and took to calling me that. It stuck. I've looked it up, there's some island in Africa with the same name. My real name is Tsarina, which means 'little princess' in Russian but don't you dare use my real name. I'm known to gut people for calling me that." Tsika flicked her head, sending her enormous tangled mass of hair spraying behind her.

Blar gave her that odd little mild smile she had already noticed he used a lot. He moved his hands from her hips up to her ribs in a stroking move, then lifted her as if she were weightless. Tsika sucked in her breath and stifled the noises trying to escape her mouth.

His hands gripping my ribs like that! So close to my … he is such a clueless bear! Oh gods, that feels so good!

Tsika felt her nipples tingle and harden in response to his grip on her ribs. She grasped his arms as he lifted. She blushed, harder because she saw he was aware of her breasts responding. Blar sat up on the couch and settled Tsika on his lap. She curled up and burrowed her toes in between his legs. She was just small enough she could tuck her shoulder under his armpit. Blar ran his hand up and down her spine and began massaging her back. He kissed her forehead. Tsika felt herself crumbling, melting to his caresses. She shivered and leaned her head back exposing her pale throat for him.

Blar growled mildly and bent over, kissing her throat. Tsika relaxed and turned towards him slightly so her breasts brushed against his chest. She found herself tantalized with the possibility he might drift down with his mouth and tend to those. Her legs relaxed and hinted at no resistance to the man.

Damn me! I can't even pretend to play hard to get! I must be desperately needy from all the stress we're under.

Tsika's breathing grew edgier as Blar ran his other hand across her collarbone, then down her side tracing each rib. He stopped at her hip and lightly squeezed it as he withdrew from tasting her neck. Tsika was gasping in short shallow bursts and her eyelids fluttered as she came out of her trance.

I … I need to shift the gears or the game is going to be over before I even know him and we will be here the rest of the day. Such a prospect sounds so delightful! But, no! No, I need to know he won't run away! I won't have that happen again. It is too painful. Get to know him. Kpau's way isn't my way!

"Big Bear? Darling Bear? Is there time for breakfast? I'm supposed to meet the band at noon." Tsika let her accent roll thickly while she traced the outline of his collarbone with her finger.

"Going for the embarrassing endearments already? I think I like that." Blar scratched her head behind her ears as she watched him take measured breaths to calm back down.

So nice! He is willing to back down at my request. That is very good sign!

"Yes! Whew! I will scramble us up some eggs and sausage. Oh! I need to check on your clothes. Your corset is trashed, I'm pretty sure. There's no fixing that. I'll find something you can tie up to wear over your blouse. It may sound weird but there are a few pieces of women's clothing in the house. Probably very out of date though."

Tsika brushed his cheek with her nose. "Hey! Who started out calling me 'Little Pixie' before he even knew my name while I am face down in snow? Is okay, Blar. This vampire will have Glyc warm some clothes for me at the club. And! The little vampire will fix you breakfast if you hunt down my clothes, Honorable Scout."

Tsika ramped up to a thick Russian accent, "It is stupefying, large Bear, but vampire princess can actually cook despite appearance she only drinks blood!" She slipped back into her milder normal accent. "Now I need to see how my ankle is doing. It doesn't hurt so much today."

Tsika reluctantly threw the blanket aside and gingerly stood up, using Blar's hand for support. She winced at first but felt fairly confident she could bluster her way forward.

"I think I will ask the Bear to be a gentleman and walk arm-in-arm with me outside for support. But once inside at Hans' club we .... Oh! Wait! I am making horrible assumption! Do you have anywhere you're supposed to be today? I just ... assumed you could come ... see band and meet friends?"

Damn and derpiness! I just assumed Bear was fabulously rich and doesn't work. He might actually have a job he must attend to. Retired from Glycerin's favorite band of all time did not automatically mean wealthy.

Tsika watched Blar grab his cellphone and punch buttons for a few minutes. "There, I now have no appointments at all today. I'd love to meet your band and see what transpires. I think I simply have to meet your Glycerin just to see what happens. It might be fun."

Tsika glared at Blar with her fiery amber eyes and returned to her heavy Russian accent. She jabbed a finger at him. "You will not damage my friend.

You will not cause my friend to splort her internal organs all over floor. Go! Find the grim pixie her clothes! While you do so, pixie will burn the fetal chickens on the altar of sacrifice! Warning you now that I shall raise hellfire if there is not real bacon to be used in ritual!"

Blar got up and bowed, kissing Tsika's hand. She couldn't stop the stupid little girl giggle that blundered out of her mouth. Blar waved his hand as if he were a swashbuckler.

"The princess must be obeyed. But the little princess shouldn't get too cocky. I might pick her up and duct tape her up on the wall for some lengthy amusement." Blar smiled and turned away as he began his call down to the doorman.

Tsika had no doubt now – the large scary looking man would never harm her on purpose. He was making the stupid parts of her brain glow. Now it was time to impress him with her culinary sorcery.

- - - - - -

"Dearest Bear, I didn't mean to set your kitchen on fire. I really do know how to cook."

Tsika sat glumly in the taxi next to Blar as it merged with the street traffic. Blar shook his head, very amused by the events of the preceding hour.

"It is entirely okay. Despite the fact I had several packs of bacon, you invoked hellfire anyway just to prove you could. We put it out, little damage, and we got to eat what you cooked, so it's good. I'm just glad to see you don't freeze up in a crisis. That will be important when the zombie invasion starts."

They were heading to the club where Tsika's band was staying. Tsika had informed Blar during breakfast that Kpau had charmed the old man who ran the club, offering to do the first show for free if he let them practice there. The old man had done even better and loaned them a room above the bar to sleep in and store their equipment. Tsika said she suspected Hans just liked having the cloud of fluffy girls around, but in any event Kpau's flirt magic seemed to have done the trick.

Blar remembered passing by the club occasionally on his way to parts further north in town. It was near the local Chinatown district off of Burnside Street. A real hole in the wall, sandwiched between pole-dancing bars, drag queen clubs, and very sketchy bars. Despite that, it gave him the vibe of being a fun place, a bit of a throwback to older days of scrubby rock bars.

The snowdrifts from the storm of the previous day had mostly melted in the temperamental weather. The temperature was back to what the locals called shirtsleeve weather. Tsika nonetheless pronounced the weather conditions a "frozen god damned hell".

Tsika stroked Blar's arm for attention. "I have told others that I am bringing someone who could be very important for us. Nothing else. I thought it would be fun to let them stew in their juices for a short time." Tsika rocked and smiled. Apparently she enjoyed the consternation she imagined was happening.

Just as the cab rolled to a stop near the club, Tsika sat up straight, unbuckled her seat belt, and quickly turned to Blar.

"I just realized … I haven't really done this yet and you deserve reward for being such honorable scout to me."

She grabbed his jacket collar with both hands, pulled herself up to his face and proceeded to kiss him deeply and thoroughly. When she was done, Blar sat stunned while the cab driver whistled and clapped. "You folks can do that show in my cab any time, better than tip!! But tip is still appreciated, yes!"

- - - - - -

At roughly the same instant, above the bar in an ill-kept room, an exceptionally tall slender young woman circled back and forth. She had to step around luggage, mattress pads, band equipment, and random female garments, making her pacing erratic. She kept wringing her hands and looking out the second floor window on each pass. An observer would note her hint of Asian features, long silky black hair with bangs framing exotic lavender eyes. When she spoke, she had a strong British lilt in her voice though she was stammering so hard it could be missed.

"She's hurt! D-Dead! I … I just know it! Bloody hell, we just know … it. I-I sh-should have … should have g-gone after her. Bollocks! What will I do if she d-d-doesn't come back?!"

Watching her with a sympathetic but mildly impatient expression was a much shorter woman with platinum blonde hair streaked with a variety of colors. She had thick blonde eyebrows that stood out against her deeply tanned island girl skin. The blonde was gathering drum set pieces in a more productive way while waving a magazine at the tall worrier.

"Glycerin! Ohhhhh, Glycerin! Glycca! Glycca, help me get this downstairs. Pay attention! Tsika called this morning. She's not dead, she sounded quite perky. She told us to be ready. We're not ready. This mystery person … the little ghoul is messing with us. Too mysterious! Boo! Hopefully, it is a new singer … but it might be a new boyfriend! That would be nice. I hope. She needs someone who won't freak out when she transforms."

Glycerin nodded but kept pacing. Exasperated, the glittery blonde threw the magazine at her. It caught Glycerin on the back of the head.

"Ow! Kpau! That h-hurt! What?! B-Boyfriend?! S-S-Surely n-not! I thought she was done with those! Uh … oh. Oh, okay. G-Get the pre-amp, gots it, we gots it." Glycerin blushed and picked up the equipment Kpau pointed at. She meekly followed the young blonde out the door and down the stairs to the club stage.

Blar and Tsika exited the cab and made their way to the club entrance. Tsika was leaning on Blar heavily for support and grimacing with each step. It was easy to see it hurt more than she was admitting. They stepped inside to silence. The bar was rather dark except for the stage area. It strongly reminded Blar of his band's earliest days, especially the smell. It reeked of whiskey, smoke, and other things best not mentioned. The little goth faerie took charge of the situation.

"Blar. You stand over there by the bar where it is dark. Say hello to the

owner. His name is Hans. Stay in the shadows, h'okay? It is show time!"
Tsika took a deep breath and let go of Blar, striding over to the stage area
without a misstep as if her ankle was just fine. Blar mused it must be her
gymnastics training kicking in.

She called out to Glycerin by several variations on the woman's name. Blar
thought it was rather fascinating that her tall friend seemed to have so many
nicknames. At Tsika's calls, Glycerin stepped out of a backstage door onto
the platform. Blar stifled a whistle at his first real life view of Tsika's friend.

He instantly realized the website had done exceptionally poor justice in
communicating Glycerin's looks. Blar guessed she was his height or just a
hair shorter, probably six foot without heels on. Tsika had told him Glycerin
was half-Chinese, the result of a union between a British expatriate and a
Hong Kong woman. Obviously Glycerin had been doused with the tall genes
from everywhere they lurked in her family tree.

On the website images, Glycerin had sported shaggy unkempt hair that
covered most of her face. That was seriously out of date. Her black silky
straight hair now was shoulder-length and she had cut straight bangs over
her eyes in a classic Asian style. If Asia had produced *Cleopatra*, Blar would
have voted for Glycerin to be cast in the lead role.

Blar knew he had hit the outlier of the kind of woman that riveted his
attention. Normally, small and petite was his standard default reference for
what he found attractive but Glycerin was enchanting. The young lady
obviously liked purple. It was her thematic color. She had a makeup style
that Blar silently labeled as "sci-fi dystopian-mod", reminiscent of Stanley
Kubrick's classic movie *Clockwork Orange* or perhaps Ridley Scott's *Blade
Runner.* The effect gave her a sad pretty clown demeanor. At the moment,
she was sporting red leather jeans, a purple tank top, and was barefoot.

Tsika had warned him that Glycerin was catastrophically shy. Therefore Blar
found it tremendously interesting that someone supposedly so shy sported
an extensive array of vibrant colorful tattoos. Her arms were largely covered
from wrists to shoulders with bright vibrant ink. Her chest was un-inked
except for one centerpiece of art in the form of one very large snake tattoo

peeking out of the tank top between her breasts. Then there was the way she moved. She had a stride that managed to be both gangly and graceful at the same time, a beautiful giraffe of the human kind.

Glycerin reacted to Tsika's arrival not with words but by dropping everything she was carrying as she pounced on the smaller woman. She hugged Tsika, lifting the small woman off the floor as the pixie squeaked. She kept checking Tsika for damage as the small woman's legs dangled a foot off the ground. Glycerin began cooing unintelligible endearments to her. It was obvious that Glycerin was positive terrible things had been done to Tsika during the night. Blar was having more than a little trouble understanding the tall lassie between her British accent and the odd sing-song stammer she spoke with.

While that was going on, the other member of the band entered the stage. Kpau was carrying a cymbal kit and a snare drum. Blar had to stifle another whistle. Again, the website hadn't done justice. Kpau simply waved to Tsika and went to work assembling gear. She was wearing slashed jeans and what appeared to be a bikini top under a denim jacket.

Kpau wasn't much taller than Tsika, perhaps five foot two by Blar's guess. Her tan was iconic Southern California or even Polynesian. She was dark enough it looked artificial compared with the mushroom skin tint so common in the Pacific Northwest. Kpau radiated Los Angeles beach fashion chic. Deviating from the typical stereotype, the surfer girl look came with a hint of Asian heritage in her eyes. Blar guessed she was getting some natural assistance with her skin tone from her ancestry. Her DNA seemed to have rolled the dice wildly in different directions because her hair was platinum blonde and her eyebrows were the same color. Tsika had informed him Kpau's blonde color was natural. She had added a rainbow of highlights to it with a result that reminded him of a prism under the stage lights.

Her eye makeup carried the rainbow motif further. It was a nifty little glam effect giving Blar the sketchy impression Kpau was fond of the ko-gal fashion fad popular in Japan, some aspects of which he knew had leaked over to the Los Angeles club scene.

According to Tsika, Kpau was indeed the blonde's real name – not a stage name. The name still made Blar chuckle. Quite a fitting name for a drummer. Ka-pow.

Blar had been informed that it was a Cambodian family name she had been tagged with in honor of an Asian grandmother. According to Tsika, Kpau was the real wild child of the group. Blar was told he should not be surprised at any level of suggestive flirting Kpau might fire up on a whim. Kpau was a real heart breaker with the guys. According to Tsika, the blonde's view of life was just being in the moment. No attachments for her, she ran from clingy boys like they were toxic.

While all the hugging and squealing was going on, Blar noticed an older man behind the bar staring at him. He introduced himself quietly to the club owner. Hans had already recognized Blar and began talking excitedly. Blar shushed him quickly.

"I'm here scouting the band. I met Tsika yesterday and I'm very interested in seeing what they can do. Tsika wants me to stay secret until she introduces me." Blar smirked and held his finger to his lips.

Hans chortled quietly. "Dat Tsika, she's a prankster. Hey if dis works out I could get a bounce off of it, yah? I mix you drink. Whiskey? On the house."

Blar nodded his thanks and turned back to hear Tsika talking as he lurked in the shadows.

- - - - - -

Tsika freed herself from Glycerin's frantic hug and strode to her bass guitar, strapping it on as she chattered. The little Russian cursed and winced when she spun around on her heel. Blar flinched. Glycerin spotted Tsika's pain and leaped into nightmare fantasies of doom.

"O g-god! The man hurt you?! Are you raped?! We need to get y-you help!"

"Shut up, darling Mouse. We discussed this! I twisted my ankle. That's all. He was a perfect gentleman! Glycca! Focus on right now! My guest wants to hear us play something live. Something fun. How about a cover of Joan Jett's

"*Fake Friends*"? We usually warm up with that."

Kpau looked up from her drum kit. "But … WHY … are we doing this? I'm confused. From the phone call, I thought you were bringing a new vocalist for us to interview. Shouldn't she be trying out for our benefit?"

Tsika stewed a moment. "Well …. um … actually, I've brought my rescuing gentleman. HE might be interested in providing some help. Maybe INVESTMENT and … maybe management? He … I don't know, I hadn't thought about that … he might be interested in being in … yeah, he can definitely sing." Tsika glanced over to the bar and bit her lip.

It was obvious to Blar she hadn't thought about him joining the band as a member. He hadn't thought about the idea either, simply assuming they wanted to be an all female band. They were the *Lost Girls* after all. Blar's mental gears started recomputing the possibilities.

Tsika continued. "But he wants to hear us live. H'okay? After that, I'll introduce him and it all will make sense."

Kpau had visibly perked up at the first real admission a male was involved. "A guy? For the band? Really? Ooooh …. I am liking this notion!"

Glycerin had been tuning her guitar. Her reaction to that same admission was to freeze and lose all the color in her face. "A … mannnnn guy? Oh?! Um … I thought … maybe …. s-someone to re-re-replace Sashiko. Sashi … Sashi left-left for home to N-N-New J-Jersey out of the air-airport today. I … I said bye to her for us."

Glycerin's expression kept flickering between fear, sadness, and panic, along with a bit of nausea as her face pallor started shifting to green. Tsika gripped Glycerin's hands and kissed them. She looked up into Glycerin's eyes and said, "Just play the notes, my precious Mouse. Don't think. Play."

Glycerin nodded with a desperately bleak look.

Blar was completely taken aback by Glycerin's behavior. She wasn't just shy, she was pathological. He couldn't imagine how she played lead guitar with that kind of handicap.

After a sound check with the amplifiers, Tsika spoke into her microphone. "Okay. This is a favorite warm up cover tune. *"Fake Friends"*, courtesy of a personal hero of mine, Joan Jett."

Blar sat back and put on his professional musician ears and eyes. The music started.

- - - - - -

By the time Glycerin had finished her guitar solo in the latter part of the song, Blar was completely hooked. Tsika could flick serious bass. The little Russian's contralto voice was powerful – something he might describe as a musical love-child of names like Pat Benatar, Joan Jett, Annie Lennox, and maybe Grace Slick with a seasoning of Bif Naked or Amy Lee. Blar had to admit some personal bias as he watched her small hips weave with the music and her delicious mouth move, but he was fiercely trying to corral that. He had to look at this professionally.

Kpau's drumming was primal and solid with a lot of flair and energy. He chuckled, she reminded him of a puppet named Animal, the drummer in the band from the old Muppet series – wild and crazy. That brilliant hair flew in all directions as she smashed, staccato'd, and thumped. She had a huge grin on her face, happy and free in her art. Her skills looked self taught to Blar but smashing good in a Keith Moon kind of alarming way.

But the centerpiece of the band was Glycerin. Tsika had not exaggerated. The lanky woman was transcendent, an incarnation of a goddess of music with a guitar. Blar made a bet with himself that Glycerin did not remember her performances, only the feelings of rapture. She danced as she played. She twirled, she swayed. She executed amazing jumps and moves with her long legs. No wonder the band was arranged on stage the way it was. She was a whirling Shiva of destruction for anything in her dance zone. Yet in all that pulsing energy of dance, she was hitting every note and scorching the riffs. Blar felt sad when the music faded away. He could listen and watch them all day.

That's the way you want your audience to feel. Happy that you witnessed it as it happened and sad that it is over. Okay, time to drop the mystery and walk out of the shadows. Tsika has had enough fun.

Glycerin saw him immediately. She locked eyes with Blar and froze. It wasn't hyperbole, she utterly froze, even her breath stopped. Kpau stood up trying to see him as she blinked from the stage lights. She looked a bit unimpressed with no hint of recognition. Tsika put her guitar down and limped towards Blar.

"Ladies. Glyc. Kpau. This is …," Tsika was interrupted by Glycerin, who had spiraled into a wretched shade of green and was shaking so hard her hair was vibrating. She had the enormous eyes of a doomed deer in the road that has, too late, spotted the oncoming eighteen-wheeler truck.

"B- B- Bl- Blar … B-b-blar!" She started hiccuping. "Blar Umlau- … Blar … Goth … Goth … gah … guh …!"

Blar found her reaction to him alarming. Between the hiccups, the stuttering, the accent, and the hair-raising keening wail she was weaving through the mixture, the poor girl was nearly incoherent.

She was having some kind of panic attack. Blar did recognize that. He knew he needed to defuse it quickly, but was at a loss. What to do? Run outside? Get out of her field of view? Time to wing it. He trotted behind Glycerin and put his hands on her shoulders and began massaging them as he leaned her back against him. Gently. She was incredibly tense and spitting out random noises now as she gasped.

"Breathe. Come on, Glycerin. Keep breathing. Breathing is good. Like a metronome, keep breathing. Breathe." Blar kept his voice low and soft. He was trying his best to sound like a meditation video.

Kpau scrunched up her face as she watched the small spectacle unfolding. She seemed relatively unalarmed by Glycerin's behavior. It must not be unusual.

"Wait. Wasn't that some band when I was a kid? Oh! Oh! I get it! Tsika! Those tunes you two play all the time when ya'll are goofing around? That band! This is … the leader? What was it? Blarrrrr?? Wait. I'm catching on, hang on. I remember now! Blar was the drummer!" Her face took on the expression of mild alarm. "Um, hey ... am I fired, too? Was it one of my jokes?"

Blar kept stroking Glycerin's shoulders and neck. The tall beauty seemed to have gone catatonic now. Blar glanced at Kpau with a bemused expression. "Hi, Kpau. Nice to meet you! No, you are definitely not fired. That would be insane because you're damn good. Maybe if you want to sing up front occasionally, maybe I can help with that. But I haven't been asked to JOIN the band. I just wanted to see what I could do to help you guys out. What I saw on your website piqued my interest but I wanted to hear you perform live before I went further."

Blar took Glycerin's guitar off of her. Tsika watched silently with an awed expression, but Kpau calmly uttered what Tsika must have been thinking. "Wow. Glycerin is letting a guy touch her. Color me amazed. She is totally malfunctioning though."

Tsika moved in and stroked Glycerin's arm, talking in a sweet cooing voice. "Glycca. Say hello to the nice man. He's Blar Umlaut. I feel safe with him! He won't eat you. After all, you're his fiercest fan girl."

Glycerin's mouth moved but no sound emerged.

Blar put his mouth near Glycerin's ear. His hair brushed against her cheek. She started hiccuping more frequently. "Glycerin? I'd love to hear you say hello."

She made a small dolphin-like shriek ending with a hiccup.

"Uh, okay. I'll take that as good. Hi, Glycerin. I'm Blar, like Tsika says. I'm very happy to meet you. You're quite pretty and you play that guitar crazy good."

Another dolphin-like shriek emerged. Glycerin finally got some coherent sounds out – all shrieks.

"Tsika!!! Gothi- … I … it's … Fire!!! Blar! I … I'm … throw up!" Green-faced and in tears, Glycerin bolted from the room to the backstage hallway.

Tsika sighed, "Well, she didn't pass out. Got through that gate, big Bear. You get a gold star! I'll go check on her and do repairs while you fill Kpau in."

~4~ *"Breathe" – Pink Floyd*

Blar found Kpau to be a lot smarter than she pretended, as Tsika had noted. She had a knack for cutting through cruft to the important stuff. As they talked, he explained how his initial notion was to provide some investment support and connections to help give the band a jump start. The idea of Blar being part of the band hadn't occurred to either him or Tsika until just now. Kpau's response was direct.

"Either way, this is great! This is like a winning Kickstart moment! But, what's in it for you? Besides having a hard-on for Tsika?" Kpau hooted as Blar stuttered that wasn't it at all. "Or … are you thinking you wanna do all of us, big guy?"

Blar found himself babbling as badly as Glycerin. "B-but I really do want this to be p-professional! I won't lie … I'm mesmerized by Tsika. I won't lie about that! But the sound you all make … I know what sells and you've … you've all got it! I just want to help!"

Kpau laughed and put her hand on his stomach. "I am messing with you, ya dork! Or … what did Tsika call you? Big Bear?" She laughed wildly at Blar's obvious discomfort. "It is probably a bad idea to dick around with the guy who might grease us a break in our career. But it is deeply obvious she turns you on and it is equally obvious our littlest vampire is brimming with wet fire back at you." She looked at Blar contemplatively. "And, you ARE hot in a scary way," she tapped his nose, "I never rule out anything."

Blar decided that this was simply Kpau's normal behavior. Best plan was to simply ignore it and stay on topic. He looked around at the stage, the equipment everywhere, took a sniff of the air. "Frankly, little chicklet? I was dead. I was bored with my life. But I didn't realize it until I bumped into Tsika … and now you and Glycerin."

He ran his fingers through his hair. "I am having VERY good vibes and it isn't JUST because you're all damn cute. There's an array of technical expertise and wizardry behind that cuteness curtain. But! There's that nasty word – BUT. You know what I mean – there's a thousand great bands out there so you need something to stand out. Right place, right time, catch the right escalator kind of luck. I don't know, maybe a trio of naughty jailbait school girls with a sketchy looking teacher kicking rock ass could generate some very naughty buzz? The kind that makes parents march around with signs and newspapers write scathing editorials?"

Kpau's eyes widened and she laughed, "Ooooh!!! I like being told I still look illegal! I wouldn't ride with that too long though. Inside Extra Crapola infotainment demands ever evolving scandals. What's a newspaper? Is that like Reddit?!"

Kpau blinked her eyes at him intentionally as she coupled that with a goofy grin. This girl was a seriously goofy prankster. He was liking her attitude more and more. Bands needed humor to prick nasty trends of being serious or snooty.

Like any good drummer, the little blonde was already tapping on every surface near her as she talked.

"Tsika may have given you the band spiel already, but we have some crazy different tastes in music. We're together firstly because we're friends and secondly because we love music. So, we're mixed genre. We rotate doing the kinds of tunes we each like and we're always looking for new stuff. We haven't really written much original stuff yet outside of composition done for college classes and diddling around. I'm excited to see YOU mostly because … if you sing for us, we can do the rocking stuff I REALLY like to play. I like loud, noisy, and hard. Sashi hitting the road makes that harder, maybe you can keep it hard! The harder the better, she snickered! Hah!"

Obviously no pun, no matter how awful, was to be left behind in Kpau's world. She's merciless.

Kpau took her jacket off and draped it on her drum stool, revealing she was wearing only a bikini top. It marked off a finely toned set of abs and drummer muscled arms. There was no doubt any more to Blar. She should be the official archetype of the classic L.A. Beach surfing girl. The twist was her voice had a Texas twang lurking under the Southern California accent. She posed for Blar with a gleaming smile and twirled, revealing a pair of lacy wing tattoos on her back.

So, Blar thought, all the girls have tattoo wings on their back. He had noticed Glycerin's intricate tattoo wings earlier while rubbing her shoulders. Blar guessed that the band had made the trip to the tattoo parlor all at the same time for a bonding tattoo session. Kpau turned and poked his chest with her drum stick.

"This here body ... is the original reason I started drumming. You know how it works, I can see that! Those are some yummy pecs and abs I see under that shirt, dude! No love handles either – most excellent! Drumming burns calories like crazy and I get to be psycho wild when I play. And yes, big Bear ... haha! I'm flirty luring you to join our fun. I have to think of a different nickname to torture you with, though. I don't like hijacking the vampire's endearment."

Kpau blinked her eyes at Blar again and leered at him. "I'm not beautiful, but I'm cute and I'm fun." She had a gleam Blar sometimes saw in the eyes of serious drummers. "But I, at least, want the old guy to prove something. Can YOU can still kick ass? You've been vanished for, like what, ten years? If we can reboot Glycerin back there, I'd like us to jam with you. Maybe some of those bits from *Gothic Fire* that Tee and Gee play. I've done them so often I dream the drum line."

Blar had already decided he quite liked Kpau. She was completely deluded about not being beautiful. He deemed her quite pretty. Low self-esteem warning flags went up in his head. All these women seemed quite self-deprecating. Answers to that might surface later. Maybe that was just standard for twenty-somethings these days? He was out of touch from spending so long in his little self-sealed box.

Blar spoke more with Kpau about her other skills, especially her guitar skills. As it turned out, the striking blonde was able to plod through music or guitar notation but really needed to learn tunes by ear. In other words, she could plink her way through written music but she really needed to hear someone else play it first to get it right. Kpau considered herself competent but nothing remotely approaching Glycerin's skill level.

"With stringed instruments, I fake almost everything. Fortunately, when we can get Glyc to sing at all she likes tunes I can muddle through easily. She loves to sing butterflies and unicorns, puppy music. Blegh! But our darling demented dancer has never sung onstage. She just seizes up when it is even mentioned. I'm only good for chorus on drums … maybe hot panting and heavy breathing. Tsika, as you saw, can sing and play but she really shines when she can focus on her bass guitar."

Blar strapped on Tsika's bass guitar as Kpau's thoughts scampered out of her mouth in random factoids. He handed Kpau the guitar Glycerin had been playing. They jammed for a few minutes, just riffing around as they spoke. Her Cheshire Cat grin kept expanding as Blar spoke to her about singing up front. Kpau expressed very loudly her drummer's lament about being at the back of the stage. She was stoking up on the idea of being able to strut around as she sang. After a few more minutes of banter and musical dueling, Blar put the bass down.

"Should we go check on them?"

Kpau shook her head. "You go, big lug. No, that nick doesn't sound right either. I'll nail something that works. Anyway, I'll stay out here and watch our stuff. My drums need care and feeding. Also, we do have some occasional thieving from outsiders so I need to stand guard."

"You could just call me Blar, you know. But you carry on with your new hobby."

Kpau giggled as Blar went backstage. The two women weren't hard to find. He just followed the sound of Glycerin gagging and retching. Tsika's melodic voice was consoling her. He found the employee restroom where Glycerin was cradling the toilet. Tsika was holding the poor girl's long beautiful hair and stroking her back. Glycerin kept trying to lecture Tsika in between her nausea bouts.

Blar's silently observed that Glycerin could make some awe-inspiring noises while throwing up.

"Tsika!" Glycerin stopped to throw up. "You sh-should have TOLD me! "

Pathetic coughing noises danced in between the other noises. "So … *** … I could … cou-" More throwing up. "… prepare! Now B-Blar, he thinks - thinks … my idol th-thinks … I'm … useless!"

Glycerin started crying. The sheer number of different noises Glycerin seemed to be able to make at the same time was astounding. "I … I'm so embarr- …"

Cute British accent, sniffles, retching, coughing, beauty, hiccups, embarrassment, shyness, and stammering. Blar could feel all his protective hormones igniting and swamping any rational notion to run away. The woman just radiated a magical field that demanded "love me, protect me". It must have Tsika deep under its sway. Tsika made cooing noises at Glycerin and kept stroking her, but to Blar's interest, Tsika thumped her tall friend on the head.

"Glycca! He thinks you play wonderfully! His eyes were locked on you the entire song. Just rest a bit and …." Tsika looked up and noticed Blar standing just outside the door. She blinked quizzically.

Blar put his finger to his lips and motioned Tsika to move. Tsika arched her eyebrow skeptically, but nodded and got up. Blar took her place by Glycerin. Tsika smirked and waved, mouthing silently that she was heading back to Kpau. She finished that with a thumbs up gesture, turned and walked back down the hall.

He carefully gathered Glycerin's lovely silky black hair to hold it out of the way. It was long enough to reach below her shoulder blades when she was standing so there was quite a lot of it to manage.

Blar used the opportunity to take a closer look at Glycerin's colorful tattoo work on her arms. Up close, they were even more dramatic. Combinations of tropical flowers, snakes, bugs, vines – and then Blar noticed they weren't just decorative. Many of the tattoos concealed scars, some fairly traumatic looking. Her arms weren't entirely smooth. Some of the scars were bad enough they were ridged, those had been painted into leafy vines or snakes. Injury accident? Some horrific self-destructive moments?

Glycerin was still utterly self-absorbed with her nausea. She was mostly just working her way through dry heaves at this point. Blar decided to try something that his mother had done for him when he was young and sick. He put his finger tips on her back, two fingers on each side of her spine. Starting at her waist, he pressed down and traced her spine up to her neck and back in a smooth repeating motion. Glycerin's back relaxed quickly. They stayed that way for several minutes, Blar holding her hair, stroking her spine, and she coughing sporadically.

"That's ... really ... n-nice, Tsika. Where did you learn ...?" Glycerin must have spotted Blar's boot at that moment. She jerked straight up, still on her knees but staring into Blar's eyes. Blar released her hair and closed his hand gently around the back of her neck. He grabbed the small wet towel Tsika had prepared and began softly wiping Glycerin's face and lips.

Glycerin didn't move, her eyes remained locked on Blar's eyes. Her eye color was really almost purple, not just sapphire blue as he had thought earlier. He'd never seen that eye color before. Some sort of mutation? Her lips were quivering as if he were a large carnivore who had snagged her as a tasty meal.

As Blar looked into her eyes, he found them even stranger. Her pupils were unsynchronized. They dilated separately and erratically regardless of the light on them. Blar had never seen that before either, even watching someone on drugs. The effect made it seem each eye were being independently driven. One pupil would shrink while the other dilated without apparent cause. Glycerin didn't seem to be drugged up so Blar put it off to her sheer terror. She was drowning in panic. Time to talk, but very softly.

"You're a charming lovely young woman, Glycerin. You play amazing guitar. It's obvious you love Tsika. I like her, too. I hope you and I can be friends. I'm here because I want to give your band some help. Yes, you're right. I'm THE Blar Umlaut from *Gothic Fire*. I'm also just a regular person ... like you, I like making music."

Blar paused and just breathed smoothly and regularly. He smiled a bit as he watched her breath start to synchronize with his.

Heh! That worked in martial arts class and it worked here. Synchronized breathing for calming meditation.

"Would you like to go get a drink of water? That might help you feel better. Get the taste out of your mouth?"

He could feel her neck muscles relaxing into his hand. Her face softened. "Ye … Y-Y-Yes."

Glycerin blinked and nodded slightly, flinching as she spoke to him. Blar held his other hand out and she very slowly put a shaky slender hand in it. Blar stood up and provided support as she stood up with him.

He couldn't help it. The more arm tattoos he examined the more faded scarring he spotted under the bright colors. Scars on top of older scars. What had happened to this treasure?

"I … I-I …," she hiccuped, "I thought … I thought you'd be … taller?" Blar wondered if she always stammered or if it just got much worse around men. Questions for Tsika later, but her query made him grin.

"I WAS taller when you were a thirteen year old girl. But now you're a quite beautiful woman. Statuesque and delightful. One who plays guitar like nothing I've seen in a long time. Come with me, I'd like to play some music with you."

Glycerin eyes got wider but she managed an affirmative shudder. Walking back, Blar kept her hand in his and quietly slipped his other hand around her waist. He could feel her breath catching at his touch, but she was otherwise silent, her eyes staring straight ahead. Blar thought of the descriptions he had read of Marie Antoinette marching to the guillotine and sighed. No matter what, at this point he was already on some kind of ride with this trio. They were all fascinating to him.

- - - - - -

When they got back to the stage, Kpau was practicing a drum riff. Blar recognized it because he had written it. Meanwhile, Tsika was flicking out some bass notes he knew by heart, because his old band mate Torsten had written those as well, about twelve years ago. Obviously, Kpau was keen on playing some classic *Gothic Fire* tunes and testing him. Good for her – though he was a bit uncertain how much he remembered.

Tsika looked up from her guitar play at Blar and Glycerin as they stepped onto the stage. Blar was instantly and keenly aware of Tsika's fiery eyes locking onto Glycerin's hand in his. The little Russian darted her eyes to his other hand around Glycerin's waist. Blar grimaced but then confusion reigned. Tsika's reaction was to be immensely happy. What an alien response. Aina would have been throwing bricks at him.

Kpau noticed the lack of music from Tsika's guitar and glanced up.

"Yay! Drama done! Let's play!" Kpau smashed out a rhythmic blast on her drums and stuck her sticks in the air like they were flags.

Tsika helped Glycerin strap on her guitar while Blar got a glass of water. He returned and handed it to the still ashen faced woman. Her hands were shaking so badly Blar worried she was going to spill it on her guitar. But finally Glycerin sipped on the water and then nodded as she handed the cup back. She still looked like she'd just seen her death in the tarot cards. The only sounds out of her were tiny hiccups and fast breathing.

"Okay", Blar grabbed the mike and the spare guitar, "I'll play rhythm guitar and do vocals because it looks like Kpau desperately wants to burn off some energy." Kpau was spinning around on her drum stool. "It sounds like you two have already picked a tune."

Tsika was getting Glycerin's attention away from staring bleakly at Blar, "Glycca. We're going to play *"Icy Plains of Tartarus"*. One of your favorites!" Glycerin hiccuped more fiercely and nodded. Blar didn't think Glycerin's eyes could possibly widen any farther.

They tuned and prepped for a few minutes. Blar kept expecting Glycerin to hyperventilate or throw up every time he spoke or got near her. Tsika appeared to be very well practiced at keeping Glycerin's eyes on her, cooing calming noises, and smiling sweetly – that seemed to help immensely. The lanky beauty appeared to depend almost completely on the little princess.

Finally, Tsika looked at everyone expectantly and said, "Ready? Yes? Okay, 1 ... 2 ... 3!" Tsika broke into the frigid dark refrains of the opening bass line and they played.

- - - - - -

By the time the foursome rolled out the last notes of the fourth tune they tried, there were twenty or more people who had come to hear them in the bar. Some were just listening and watching, a few were dancing, and many were calling or texting to their friends about the band. One of Portland's special breed of hipster was recording video with his phone.

Glycerin was still stuttering and flinching every time Blar looked at her but she was positively glowing, looking happy enough to burst. Blar looked over to give Tsika a thumbs up. However, Tsika had eyes only for Glycerin and an ecstatic smile on her face. Blar took that as an indirect cue he had 'done good'.

Blar signaled for a break and thanked the small crowd. He told them to keep an eye out in the local newspaper and the club sign for real performance dates. The group retreated to the kitchen. Kpau was jumping like a pogo stick as she spoke.

"I don't care ... if we make .... any money ... that was ... fuck ing fun!"

Tsika had both Glycerin's hands and was dancing gently with her. Glycerin still looked shell-shocked. "Glycerin! My Mouse! They were coming in off the street to listen! They liked us!"

Blar could just barely hear Glycerin's whispered response as she managed to glance at him. "Bl-bloody hell. We ... we al-almost w-whizzed m-me knickers. I just played m-m-m-music with B-B-Blar Uml-l-laut."

Blar, meanwhile, was silent and contemplative. Tsika stopped dancing and looked at him inquisitively. After pulling on his mustache for a few seconds, Blar spoke.

"Okay, you three. What do you think about this idea? It is up to you, this is your band. You let that buzz we just generated percolate for a day or so on the streets. Let Hans do his advertising. Thursday night we play a selection of tunes that everyone is very comfortable with, some of yours and some of mine. I want to do some thinking and accounting. In my head it works but I want to run the numbers and make some calls."

Blar paused to make sure he believed the words he was about to say.

"I'd like to take you all on a retreat. There's a place down near Big Sur where *Gothic Fire* used to hide out to rejuvenate and write music. I think it is still there. That's where we can really see if this is something that works. We write original music there, bring the results back and play several key spots in town. See what happens."

Blar paused a second. "But! And this is a huge but. I want to keep in mind you might need one more member, female, primarily vocalist and rhythm guitar or keyboards. We seem to sync up nice musically … but I may not be the best addition for the group from a market perspective. In that case, I'd just hover, support, and wear a manager hat for you guys. How does that sound? I'll put together something more formal if you nod."

Silence. Wow, that went over like a stun grenade.

Tsika was the first to break silence. She said quietly, "Blar, I'm … I'm amazed you seem to believe in us. That sounds huge, so lovely, but we can't afford that. We can't even afford a place to live right now."

Blar grumbled. "That is where I can help. I am confident enough in what I've seen and heard that I'm going to pull the trigger on my notion of investing in your band. I have retirement investments I can cash out. Money issues should not be stopping talent like you all have. It would be a god damned crime to let it stop you."

Blar stared up at the ceiling. "You know, I'd rather take the risk in doing something I believe in like this than piddle out my years walking a stupid rat dog in the park. I'll liquidate everything, except I'll keep the condo."

Blar stopped and squinted as he hesitated. "We … we could use that as your base and you all can stay there if you want. That will cut living expenses tremendously. I have a big place. There is enough room for privacy with some re-arranging. I think I just kicked myself out of my bedroom. Tsika has been there, she can fill you in on how big the place is. The master suite has its own bathroom. I'd punt myself to the guest bed and bath. That way you have privacy and I won't die waiting my turn with a house full of female room mates."

The girls looked at each other. There was silence. Kpau coughed, "Seriously? You barely know us! Okay, I mean, I trust you already. You're THE Blar Umlaut, not some sleazy candy man in a van. You brought back our Tsika squeaky happy and in one piece. So I'm not worried about evil things. We'll need to huddle and think this over between us girls before Tsika says a word! Yeah, I see you bouncing at the idea, little ghoul, but we need to do our own calculations."

Blar thought it was illuminating to watch how Kpau took charge in a guarded tactical stance as she intercepted Tsika's nodding agreement.

"Seriously, Kpau. I approve of that kind of wariness – it is essential in the nasty business side of music. You three talk on your own."

Kpau stuck her drumstick in Blar's navel. "But you! You are throwing yourself into a potential fiery crash off of one afternoon of us goofing off? Is that how it works where you're from? Snap decisions and major life change on a whim? I am being lured just by shiny fascination! And here I thought little ol' ME was a leaf on the wind!"

Blar leaned back against the butcher block table. "I'll call this my mid-life crisis. Well, a very EARLY mid-life crisis. I'm only thirty three! But it is unlikely I'll get another chance to take this ride again later in life. I can't think of a better way to burn my money than to spend it helping people who love to make music get a lift up."

Blar sniffed the air. It smelled nicely of German sausages and sauerkraut. "But seriously, I've got vibes I haven't had since the day Torsten and I named our band when we signed Aina on with us. What I don't know yet … and I'll keep this centered in my head, is whether Blar Umlaut is the right addition for your band. I need to talk to some people on the marketing side. I can do that while you huddle."

Blar rubbed his scalp, leaving his hair in disarray. "Women rock bands are very popular on the international level. That may be the best niche for you anyway given your looks and style. They have a rougher time staying in the spotlight here in the US. There are some exceptions … *The Donnas*, *JOANovARC* in the UK, or the *Dixie Chicks*. The most enduring groups I can think or are a woman fronting a group of guys. People like Joan, Pat, Debbie, Amy, and such. Some groups have a female bassist, like the *Talking Heads* or *White Zombie*. This combination would be quite unusual. I can't decide if that is good or bad yet but … I'm having a hell of a time recalling any band with this guy-to-women ratio. If it isn't clear by now, I'm way past the music issue – I think your music will sell even if all you ever do is covers. You put your own twists on them, make them your own anyway."

He straightened up and clapped his hands. "So! It isn't a snap decision at all. I'm just saying let's start. You three talk about my proposal. There are other solutions but this seems practical, safer, and cheap. It's pretty much what *Gothic Fire* did when we started. We kind of just took over a boarding house, separate bedrooms, one common area. Heck, I even have a music studio. Back then we just practiced in the garage, to the horror of the neighborhood."

Kpau giggled, "I'm not against the idea of getting a safe place to sleep, just let us roll it around in our heads a smidge. Whatever the case, you are crazy like an armadillo on crack! I like you! Oh! We would need a new name! We're *The Lost Girls*. You're certainly not a Lost Girl!"

Blar smirked. "Glad that's noticeable. I'll leave that to you three. For now, let me take you all out to dinner. There's a Japanese restaurant a few blocks from here I eat at so much they leave a table reserved. Let's put your gear up and go talk details. Then we'll start planning how this 'secret performance' of a new band flows. Where did Glycerin go?"

Tsika emitted a small bat-like shriek. Glycerin was down on her knees with her head tucked between them on the floor. She had passed out but with just enough sense to drop gracefully.

- - - - - -

Glycerin was toast. Dinner was out. Hans cooked them some bar fried randoms. Blar learned Hans could actually cook. The food was tasty if not healthy, some kind of deep fried German sausages, sauerkraut, and beer. Glycerin had been put to bed with Tsika tending to her. Blar observed that tending to Glycerin consisted largely of talking her down from from her hysteria.

Kpau and Blar jammed on a variety of instruments while they chatted about what tunes they might play. Full practice was a loss for the day with Glycerin incapacitated, so they'd have to cram it in the next day and on the day of the performance.

Blar kept marveling at his new drummer friend, not just for professional reasons. Besides being very good with the drumsticks, Kpau just seemed to be a natural unconscious flirt. Just standing near her gave the sense she was making love to him in a teasing giggling way. It was clear that it wasn't something conscious she did. She just loved the idea of swimming in the moment. It was easy for Blar to see how younger guys would be misled by her antics. He readily admitted he was enjoying Kpau brushing up against him as they'd discuss drum kit mechanics. Blar took the opportunity to get some back story from the little blonde. By now, Blar had audio proof Kpau really did have a Texas twang simmering under her Southern California accent. She hid it fairly well, but to a man from Alabama it was noticeable.

"So the three of you attended college together?"

"Eyup! University of Southern California Thornton School of Music. Trojans all! Fight on! Tee and Gee both have a trust fund from their parent's estates that covered expenses. They're theoretically wealthy little bugs if they can ever get their hands on it. I was on scholarship and benefits as my parents didn't have that much stashed away when they died. So was Sashiko. You might get to meet the crazy woodpecker if she cleans her act up and grovels to Tsika." Kpau paused and her eyebrow cocked. "You know that's why we call ourselves *The Lost Girls*, right? All of us were orphaned as young kids."

"Tsika mentioned it but I don't know any details." Blar felt a strong blast of sadness from her. It added reinforcement to his sketchy theory that Kpau's eyes, face, and smiles were shields for the concealment rather than expression of inner feelings.

"Yeah, I was in the car with mine … at least I got to say bye. Neither of those two got that chance. They both ended up in British boarding schools and that's where they met in … oh, I call it junior high. I don't know the proper Brit term. I didn't meet the two of them until freshman year at the university. As soon as I saw them and heard their stories, I just latched onto them. I just knew I had to be around them."

Kpau stopped to drum out a short sequence that Blar recognized as a classic *AC/DC* drum riff. She had quite the drumming vocabulary in her head. She rarely repeated a sequence when she was just beating around.

"Tsika and Glycerin are really tight. It took them quite a while before they naturally started thinking us as a trio then as a foursome. But I love them." Her face lost its Cheshire Cat grin completely for a moment.

Wow, now there was an undisguised blast of loneliness. Time to shift gears.

"So did you all graduate? Musicians … aren't always the best finishers." Blar smiled in what he hoped was a bonding way. Kpau chortled.

"Actually, as a matter of fact we did. I got out by the skin of my teeth, but Glycerin graduated with honors. We had to get her drunk before she could walk the stage and shake hands with the dean though. Tsika double majored in Chinese dialects and music. No doubt you've heard her lurid curses in Martian talk. Her grades were better in languages than in music. We started out by opening a shop to teach music."

Kpau beat on the drums briefly as she pursed her lips and bobbed her head.

"But that sucked." More drum beats. "Really sucked." She added a cymbal to her pattern while she talked. "So we started playing gigs. We didn't do …," she paused to slap the bass drum in her pattern, "… terrible but finding the audience was hit and miss. So we decided to head up here." She finished her drumming in a flourish.

"There's just a huge number of little music bars and clubs here and it was cheaper than Seattle."

More evidence she's an intrinsic drummer, thought Blar. Even without sticks, she'd be slapping her hands on anything that resonated. They jammed for a while longer and then called it a night.

"Okay, you three stew on my offer. Tsika can describe the place to you or you can come tour it before you decide. Otherwise, I could put you up in something separate – but that just makes my accounting and logistics brain grumble as it doubles cost of living. I want my investment to pay off after all."

"Roger, roger, Old Man … bleh, that sounds insulting and you're too tasty looking to call old. Usually I nail a nickname immediately. I'm finding the Very Large Umlaut challenging to tag with a good nickname. Don't worry, I'll nail something to torture you with!"

Blar did have some minor work to do on an investment contract he needed to finish. He told Kpau to tell Tsika and Glyc good night and that he'd see everyone the next day. He whispered to Kpau he had an instrument to bring that belonged to Tsika and something Glycerin might like. Kpau flashed her bright grin and waved him on.

- - - - - -

Blar decided to walk home. The snowfall was light, the sunshine a distant memory now. Blar just liked slogging through snow at night. The sound of the snow crunching under his boots was calming. He was thinking about the women, the music, whether he had gone nuts, and whether he was thinking with his brain or something else.

Blar easily admitted he was very much infatuated with Tsika. The conundrum was that Blar now couldn't think of Tsika without thinking of Glycerin. And Kpau flittered around in that mental image as well.

Glycerin had other-worldly alien charm -- well, when she wasn't throwing up, passing out, or hiccuping. Now there's a challenge. He thought her stuttering was very cute in an odd way though it may have been the British accent that topped it off. There was just something really different going on in that pretty head, very mysterious. Those amazing eyes.

Kpau. Heh, he just liked saying her name. Kpau. He connected with her as one drummer to another. He could imagine being with her as a companion. He could far too easily imagine that. Somehow though, he figured it would always be at some emotional arms length. He wasn't sure seeing one's parents die violently was better than just being told they were dead. Both his parents were dead but they'd gotten to live their lives and see Blar become temporarily famous.

"Cripes, if I'm going to be in a professional relationship with them the band has to come first, not my testosterone fantasies," he said out loud to the air. Yeah, just keep thinking that. Idiot.

Reaching his condo building, he waved to the doorman, Jack, and updated him on Tsika's well-being. He also let Jack know that he'd probably be getting regular visits from her and a couple of her friends. The doorman laughed appreciatively.

"Still the rock star, Blar? Heh, no problem. I'd like to see more pretty glitter coming through our doors. Mostly old people here now as you well know from those building owner meetings you love so much."

Blar made his way to his home on the top floor and looked around. There was a lot of re-arranging to do if the women decided to move in. He decided to start the project by passing out on the couch for the night.

~5~ "Heart Breaker" – Pat Benatar

Glycerin opened her eyes as her sense of self fluttered into the mirror maze she called consciousness. Immediate mind-wrenching disoriented panic obliterated any thoughts. A few gasping breaths later, she established that she was on a mattress staring at the ceiling of a little room above a rock club in the Pacific Northwest.

No life obliterating waves. No snakes. No torrential rain. No rotting bodies. No smell.

Right-o. There is the smell of whiskey and smoke, sort of a jolly pub smell. We'll take that, won't we?

Glycerin closed her eyes and focused on her breathing and began relaxing. Then recollection flashed and she had a real reason to consider panic. She sat up abruptly on the mattress in horror.

"Re-remember? Yes, we remember! They … th-they were talking about … m … mov … moving in with him!" The hiccuping started, interleaved with short gasps. "B-B-B-Blar! The … the Blar … my … my Blar."

Between her hiccups and muffled shrieks, Glycerin beat her fists on her thighs as she tried to stabilize herself. She took long breaths, most of which failed, shredding into ragged gasps.

Calm. Yoga breath. Calm. We can do it. Shhh. Bloody safe here. Tsika is near. Our little dove Kpau is near.

Glycerin forced herself to recall her *Gothic Fire* wall posters she had stored away down in Los Angeles. Images of Blar's old band at the height of their fame. She knew the names of all core members and every fact about them she could scour off of the Internet – all committed to memory: Blar, Torsten, Asgeir, and Aina.

She especially idolized Aina, the flamboyant female keyboardist of the group. Glycerin had taken up keyboards in boarding school because of her worship of the silver-haired goddess. The pathologically shy and fearful young girl had dreamed of becoming a glittering assertive Scandinavian ice goddess like Aina. Glycerin thought she was so beautiful!

Sadly, Glycerin had realized early on that such was impossible for her. Her hair was jet black, her eyes were shaped differently, and her skin almond tinted. Worse, she quickly discovered that sitting still at a keyboard was intolerable. The slender girl felt trapped, claustrophobic, and suffered anxiety attacks behind a keyboard. Just more motive to join her family in oblivion.

One day a few months after Glycerin had met and befriended Tsika, she discovered the electric guitar was her instrument. Glycerin could stand, sit, and move with the stringed instrument. She could dance with her guitar and she did. Her music and dance became utter escape, transcendent bliss like the whirling dervishes of Turkey.

Poor Tsika! Glycerin's little princess warrior had picked up the bass guitar out of desperation. The dangerous little creature just wanted to be near Glycerin. But fairly quickly, Tsika became just as driven as Glycerin. She loved music and wanted to make it a career so she and Glycerin could be together. And now?

Glycerin surveyed the drab little second floor room, cluttered with mattresses, clothing, musical gear, and suitcases. She was alone. Tsika and Kpau were likely already grabbing breakfast downstairs in the bar's kitchen. Glycerin stood up on her mattress and began stripping down as she made her way down the hall to the wretched excuse for a shower the women used. It was actually a maintenance shower in a janitor's closet but at least the door closed. She stepped in and turned the handle. The shower head's burst of spray did an excellent job of cleaning out Glycerin's navel.

Bollocks. My little Tsika must have been last in the shower. She never remembers to move the shower head back up, poor dear.

Glycerin adjusted it up to pound water on her forehead while she tried not to think. There was little luck with that effort. The thoughts came skittering through,richocheting about in her shattered mind.

Blar ... oh ... my ... god, bloody hell. Blar! We're thinking about ... we might be living together! A man! This man! One of my music idols!

Glycerin groaned and beat the shower wall with her fist. She wanted to stop being afraid so badly. It was so unfair. Glycerin knew what she had been told to do to cope by those so-called experts. Yet she failed over and over again at conquering her fears. When Blar had appeared the previous day, Glycerin erupted in one of the worst panic attacks she could remember. She cried quietly.

My idol. Hero. My Blar. Right there, right in front of us and we choked – no, it was worse. We had hurled our guts up. Vomited in technicolor! And then we passed out!

"But … he … he held our hair!" Glycerin hiccuped. "He cleaned our face up. He was so nice ... trying so hard not to be scary. He's not like … his videos or his scary image on stage at all." She hyperventilated again. To cope she stuck her head under the hot spray of water and stared at her feet.

Big feet. Not small and delicate like Tsika's. He likes Tsika, we guesses. We don't haves a chance, do we? Hush. I know you don't care. Shhhh, it is okay. Sleep, love. One day you may get your way. But out here, out here I care.

The shower's warmth helped level her. As Glycerin toweled off, she stared into the mirror. The pupils of her eyes fluttered periodically as she muttered, half-thinking half-talking.

Glycerin rummaged in her suitcase. What to wear? She chose her ragged capri jeans and her button-down shirt. She tied the shirt off above her waist for comfort, then froze at her appearance in the room's mirror.

Oh! Oh … oh gods, Blar is going to be here today. Is this enough? It doesn't seem enough!

Glycerin hiccuped as she tried to decide if she had enough clothing on. She took a long deep breath and put on her favorite cap, a school girl's cap from her boarding school days. Somehow that made the outfit okay. She smirked at her snake tattoo as it peeked out of her shirt. Underneath, its tail spiraled down to her navel.

"You're mostly covered, love. At least you can hide. I'm st-stuck out here."
Deep breath. "Bloody well right! Please? No strange men in the b-bar 'til Blar
gets here. I want to do better today, we needs to show him we can."

Hans is okay, he's like a grandpapa. Is he? I think? Don't remember my
grandparents. Off we go! Spit spot!

- - - - - -

Glycerin peeked around the door into the main room of the club. No
strangers in sight. She relaxed and followed the smell of eggs and bacon into
the kitchen where Hans was cooking up breakfast. The old gentleman
seemed to be enjoying having a temporary family of daughters. Hans had
told them when they had met him that he had two grown daughters. He
sounded a little sad when he told them they lived on the east coast so he
rarely got to see them. It wasn't hard to see he enjoyed them being around.

Glycerin smiled weakly at Tsika as she rounded the corner. Kpau waved and
grunted at Glycerin with a mouth full of eggs. Hans was chatting up a storm
as he cooked.

"You girls did good connecting up wit Blar! Dat guy, he is going to do good
things for you. He got connections. It is only been a week since you got here
but I already missing you. You remember Hans when you make it big, yah."
He grinned as he handed Glycerin her breakfast. She stammered her thanks
to him and settled in to eat.

Tsika talked through a piece of bacon dangling out of her mouth. "Glyc!
Kpauf sath Blarm is gunna bring," she paused to choke her bacon down,
"bring you a present! How cool is that, my gorgeous Mouse?!"

Glycerin got visibly paler. "I ... I ... d-d-d-don't ... h-have anything t-t-to give
him in return!"

Kpau rolled her eyes. "Glyc, he doesn't EXPECT anything back. When we're
all rich and famous, we can get him a pony. Eat your breakfast. I want it
digested in you before Blar shows up, so you can't throw it up. Egg upchuck
is ... ewwwww!"

Glycerin blushed as she peppered her eggs, then began morosely chewing on her food. Tsika sipped on her coffee and watched Glycerin closely. "Glycerin, darling. What do you think of Blar so far?"

Glycerin put her fork down and sat looking at her hands. "He's … he's … he's not as tall as I thought he'd be. But he's still taller than me. That's … um, that's rare for anyone … to be t-taller than me. And he's … he's so big! His … his arms! I just n-never thought about it even though I know so much about him and the others! I think he has bigger muscles now than he d-d-did in my *Gothic Fire* posters."

Glycerin looked up into Tsika's precious amber eyes. She couldn't help the little flutter of excitement those eyes gave her. "And! A-And he's got some gray in his hair! I … I … I like that! He … h-h-h-he has nice eyes, I like it when he looks at me. I … I feel safe and terrified at the same time!" She knew she was blushing deeply.

Tsika grinned perversely. "Oh ho! My trembling Mouse made eye contact! That's really good, Glycerin! Sounds like you really checked him out!"

Glycerin looked shocked. "No! No, I wasn't! After all, it's … it's … it's you and …," Glycerin looked morosely at her bacon. Tsika's face had an expression that Glycerin couldn't quite decipher. Tsika patted her lips with the napkin and folded it neatly on her plate.

"No one owns anyone, Glycca. We're a team, we're friends, we're the *Lost Girls*. We're going to be a real band now, I think. I hope. And it will be you and me … and Kpau together for it. No matter what. It is just that now we have a new friend who wants to help us. To be part of the adventure." Tsika leaned over and hugged Glycerin. Kpau gulped the last of her egg as she watched with a goofy smile.

"You two, seriously. Ya'll should just get married and adopt me so I can eat Glyc's cooking. No offense, Hans! But you really ought to let Glyc cook for you once." Hans just smiled and continued his clean up.

"Sorry, Kpau, I know we … I'm sorry, I never mean to make you feel like a third wheel. You know you are just as much a *Lost Girl* as either of us. Hell, you named us even." Tsika smiled as Kpau fired back with a goofy face and motorboat noises. She turned back to Glycerin.

"Seriously, Glycerin. Yes, I'm already very fond of Blar. He seems really easy to be fond of. I want you to be fond of him, too. Get to know him, get comfortable around him, it looks like we're going to be together a lot. I think Blar is going to be really good for you. So let us focus on the band. We need to talk about his offer to share his condo with us."

Kpau got up. "Let's not have an official meeting. Let the fuzzy thoughts roll out and we'll pro and con it. I'm having trouble thinking of any cons unless it blows up in some maudlin soap opera about how toothpaste should be rolled. Just makes money sense even to my addled head. Anyway, I'm off to do my morning stretches, Glycerin. Come on, you need 'em, too." The two women cleaned up, thanked Hans, and headed back upstairs leaving Tsika contemplating her coffee. She still wore an indecipherable expression.

- - - - - -

After their exercises, Glycerin and Kpau began setting up the equipment. Kpau looked towards the kitchen. "Tsika got a bit odd there. I wonder up what is up with that?"

Glycerin blushed. "I ... I don't know. Normally, we feel ... I feel quite in tune with her." Glycerin was still doing her deep breathing she'd learned in her yoga classes. She knew Blar was going to arrive any minute and wanted to be braced for it. "I hope I didn't ... say something wrong."

Glycerin started doing a sound check on her guitar. She was fretful. She had just assumed that Blar and Tsika were already a pair, that Glycerin's little princess had made love with the big man that night despite Tsika's assertion that he was a "boy scout".

The thought that Tsika hadn't done any such thing made her brood and she wasn't sure why. Glycerin got so introspective she didn't notice when Blar lumbered into the club carrying two large instrument cases.

She had just put her guitar down when she was enveloped from behind in large strong arms. Glycerin sucked her breath in sharply and had a shriek started when she recognized Blar's cologne from the day before. He was giving her a bear hug. Her shriek collapsed into short ragged breaths. Blar was standing perfectly still, letting her collect herself while he just gently hugged her.

"Sorry, little dancer. After yesterday, I figured it was better not to let you spiral into panic if you saw me coming. I hope this was better. Was it better?"

Glycerin automatically tuned into his breathing and used that as a metronome for her own breathing. Blar wasn't holding her tightly, but in the cold room she felt blissfully warm in his arms. It was such a comforting feeling. So nice. She could get used to that – she jumped away and turned.

"H-H-H-H-Hi! Yes. Y-Yes, it w-was." Glycerin mustered a quirky half-demented smile and looked down at his chest while she turned beet red. "I … I …," she gasped, "I promise I won't get bloody sick today." Glycerin hugged herself as Blar watched her curiously.

I did it! I got a whole sentence out! Keep breathing! We can be near him! We can!

Glycerin's eyes flickered and she quickly scuttled over to Kpau before she did anything weird in front of Blar. She began assisting the little blonde with her drum kit assembly. Blar watched her a little longer with a quizzical expression, then wandered off, presumably to find Tsika. Glycerin took short quick breaths as she helped Kpau align the bass drum.

"K-Kpau. I did it. I s-s-said a whole sentence to him!" Kpau grinned at her. "He's …. so warm." Glycerin could feel her face flushing as Kpau's grin got bigger. She wanted to smack Kpau with a cymbal. It was so easy for her with guys.

Kpau has a prankster's grin on her face now! What is she thinking? She's going to tease us, we wager.

The glittery blonde leaned over and whispered. "Glyc, are you thinking about being Blar's woman? If we move in with him, it would be so easy! Being his personal groupie curling up with him at night? Serious aspirations for a fan girl of a rock star."

Glycerin nearly dropped the cymbal. "No! No … no no no. He's … Tsika … they're … no, that would be wrong … no I couldn't do … no."

I am trying to be casual about her teasing! Why do I feel like I am tearing my guts out? Breathe. Breathe slower!

"I just think … I just think … it is nice to know Blar as a person after being in awe of what he seemed like on stage when I was little. He's really very gentle … and he was so scary in his videos! When I w-was little, I wanted to be-be-be like his friend Aina, a f-fallen angel with feathery wings so gr-graceful at the keyboards. I wonder if he still talks to her?"

Kpau twisted a lug tight on the bass drum and pointed her wrench at Glycerin. "Guess what?! I bet we're going to find out. I'm jumping with glee! Whether or not we make it, crash or fly, it's going to be a VERY interesting roller coaster ride! It's like we haz won the lottery and the first thing they did was give us a book of day passes to Knott's Berry Farm! Roller coasters all day!!! Woohoo!!"

Glycerin's stomach knotted up at the thought of roller coasters. Blar had come back out of the kitchen with Tsika. They were laughing and Blar was giving Tsika a neck rub with one hand under her hair. That was so nice to watch. Glycerin briefly regretted pulling away from Blar and then shoved that thought back into the basement of her mind. Blar is speaking to us now! We must listens!

"I already gave Tsika a kickstart present but hadn't brought it over yet. So I went rummaging through my storage while thinking about how you play guitar, Little Dancer."

Bloody hell, I'm blushing again! He's going to call us "Little Dancer" all the time, isn't he? Someone who calls me little! That's so bloomin' sweet. How did he know being tall bothered me? Did Tsika tell him? Oh god, we hopes not! Ah! He's still talking to us! Listen!

"Here. I want you to try this guitar out today and see how it sits with you. It's very light so you can move easily and it's had considerable work done on the pickups, bridge, and electronics. Here." Blar lifted the guitar out of the case and presented it to her horizontally as he would have presented a sword. Glycerin blinked. It was a glossy black Ibanez brand axe with a lot of customization. An outstanding axe for a metal rock guitarist. It dripped evil forces of violence. She could picture a cloud of malevolence oozing out of it. It was beautiful.

"C-c-c-c … can … we … t-touches … it?" Glycerin cursed herself for trembling so badly.

"I want you to take it and play it today. If you like it, keep it." Blar held the guitar closer to her. She was sure she had misheard him. This was stunning. She had no idea how much this guitar cost. Her guitar was one she had carried around since high school. Hers was a nice guitar, a lesser Fender Stratocaster, but it was very heavy. Glycerin had spent many nights nursing an aching back and shoulders thanks to it. She timidly put her hands out.

Oh bloody twisted knickers! I really am shaking like I'm having a seizure!

Glycerin quickly gripped the neck, if only to stop the shaking.

"It … it hardly weighs … a-anything. H-How is the s-sound?"

"You try it out and see what you think. I have a few others lurking about if that one doesn't work out." Blar turned to Tsika. "And Tsika, this guitar has already chosen you. It just needed a ride over this morning."

Glycerin watched as Blar pulled out a guitar that glistened like fresh blood. She got the impression of a swooping bat wing and then her eyes resolved it as a low slung bass guitar, completely scratch-built with custom electronics. Blar handed it to Tsika. Tsika's eyes were moist but she had on her tough chick face as she took it and cradled it in her arms. Glycerin couldn't imagine a more perfect looking bass guitar for her little doll.

Kpau sat back on her heels with her eyebrows raised. "Wow. O' Great Wizard! I bet there's nothing in that little black bag for me. It's too small."

Blar's face took on a pained expression over Kpau's theft of movie dialog. Glycerin softly smiled behind her hand. Blar understood Kpau's joke! That was nice! Her little Kpau was a walking storehouse of popular culture references. The blonde had a quote from books or movies for almost any occasion. Glycerin knew she herself missed half of the joking references because of her isolated past. Blar continued to talk to Kpau.

"I do have some more guitars and we can talk custom drum kits. Drum kits are deeply personal things, so I figured you could rummage around my storage room and cannibalize something as you saw fit before we went shopping."

Kpau hooted as she bounced up onto her feet. "Yay, dungeon crawling date! You charmer, you!"

Glycerin was staring at the guitar in her hands. It made her feel like she could kick ass and take names, though she knew better. It looked like a weapon to cleave a monster in half. Glycerin heard Blar talking to her again.

"Yeah, I can tell it isn't your favorite color, Little Dancer. If it works out for you, we can have it refinished in whatever color you like. That ought to freak out some purist Ibanez fanboys, heh."

Glycerin strapped it on. "I … I w-will … will try. Yes. See … if … thanks … well … if it works … for us."

Kpau made a face at Tsika and Glycerin. "I think we girls need to do some clothes shopping if those guitars are a reflection of things to come. I feel like I ought to put on my good clothes just to be in the same room with them. Can we practice now? Can we? Can we?"

Glycerin nodded. It was going to be a nice day. She realized she was standing right next to Blar, even brushing shoulders with him. She was breathing quite normally. She tried to avoid crying and wasn't really sure whether the looming tears were from fear or a feeling of victory.

Well! I'm doing splendidly! Blar Umlaut! He's just this guy, you know!

- - - - - -

Her nice day feeling lasted about an hour. Glycerin kept working with the guitar. There was nothing technically wrong with it. It was clearly a high caliber instrument. She was just not getting the sounds that she wanted. Her internal dialog of doom began revving up.

He gave this to me. He must know more than I do. I'm … I'm just not getting something. It must be something I'm doing wrong. No, it's not you. You're behaving splendidly today. Even paying attention! Hush, dear. It's me.

She knew she was just beating herself up but she couldn't stop the cloud of doom strangling her thoughts. On a break, she collared Tsika off to one side.

"Tsika! I … I … it doesn't … I'm doing something wrong. We can't get-get … the bloody sounds … I want. All cocked up. But … he gave it … gave it to … us. What d-do I do!?" Glycerin was wringing her hands and sniffling.

Tsika held a finger up. "First. Sweet Glycca, calm down. Breathe. It's just me."

She stared at Glycerin a moment until Glycerin stabilized herself. "Good. Yes, my Mouse, I noticed the cloud of doom you were engulfed in. It's really simple, just tell him it's not working out and he'll find you another one. He said exactly this – play with it. IF you like it, keep it."

"I … I just don't want to … dis … disappoint him." Glycerin felt very forlorn and started hiccuping.

Tsika sighed and put her arms around her and cooed at the trembling woman. "Just do it. I promise it won't be bad. He was very sweet to you yesterday. Not at all like most guys who think they want to get close to you, don't you think? You said you felt safe with him! You've hardly ever said that about a guy! Just keep that in mind."

Glycerin nodded glumly and turned towards Blar, who was chatting with Kpau over by the drums. The hyperventilating started. Glyc gripped the neck of the guitar hard and forced herself towards him. Her feet felt like boat anchors. Why does this have to be so hard for me? By the time she got near Blar, she had no color left in her face at all and she was shaking like a buzzer. Blar looked up and smiled.

"You've decided it isn't working for you, haven't you?"

Glycerin made a small piping shriek noise and then nodded hard. "I … I …

I," she sighed, "I tried. It must be m-me … I …." Her heart felt shredded from grieving inside.

"Little Dancer, it isn't you. Guitars are very personal things. I just picked up the lightest guitar I had. Tell you what! I have some catalogs in that case. Go through them and give me an idea of what you want and we'll go shopping. There's three or four very good guitar shops within a few miles of here. For now, use your own guitar. It may be that we'll end up just having some work done on yours. Whatever works best for you is what we want here, Little Dancer."

"Okay! … O? … kay!"

He called me "Little Dancer" again! So full of happy from that! Oh my god! We just agreed to go out with Blar!

Glycerin started hiccuping and shaking as she headed back to Tsika over by the bar.

Tsika will go. Yes, that's it! She'll goes with us. Yes. It'll be bloody fine.

- - - - - -

"No, that's fine. You go with him, Glycca! Me and Kpau need to work out some drum/bass combos. We don't want to just do the old tunes note for note. It'll be fun! You and your rock star shopping for guitars!"

Glycerin clung to Tsika's hand desperately.

"But-t-t-t!" Glycerin was bleating little shrieks between every word. "But … I … I need you … what about ... you! You … and …!" Her head was filled with a terrified keening sound, a banshee wail echoing in her skull.

Tsika had an infuriating expression of innocence. "Glycca. The band. This is about the band. Go get those catalogs and think about guitars. Focus on that, Little Dancer!" Tsika giggled as she used Blar's nickname for Glycerin. She led the trembling woman to the stack of catalogs Blar had left out. Glycerin tried to read them but she kept thinking about Tsika and Blar. She felt she was drowning in fluster.

- - - - - -

"Little Dancer, we'll start with a guitar shop over in the Pearl District. That's just about ten blocks or so from here and we can hop the rail and trolley. I don't get the feeling you lot have seen much of the city anyway so it'll be like a little sightseeing trip." Blar was smiling at Glycerin, who had dropped the catalog when he spoke and locked eyes with him, a doomed rabbit. Blar wasn't entirely sure Glycerin had been reading the catalog at all.

"T-T-Tsika isn't ... coming! S-S-She ... she and ... Kpau ... they ... they!"

Glycerin coherent speech fell apart, leaving her to flutter her hands in their direction. She shivered as a December breeze leaked into the club. It had an effect on Glycerin that left Blar guiltily noticing the young woman was wearing no bra under her tightly knotted shirt. He tried to focus on her fascinating eyes, but the shirt loudly demanded he admire the contents. The implicit display of nipples and curves were delightful, but she wasn't so large as to need support. As the slender woman nervously tried to conjure some resemblence of chatter, he absentmindedly followed the line of the long curling python tattoo she sported with his eyes.

The tail started just above her navel. It looped its way under where Glycerin had knotted her shirt between her breasts and swirled up near her collarbone before dipping down to bite her – errrr, she's turning beet red, cancel that examination. My stupid brain needs a leash.

"Hey, Glyc, you probably need to put on more clothes to go outside. It's still chilly. Hustle, Little Dancer, so we have plenty of time to shop, okay?" He watched Glycerin nod jerkily and sprint off like a startled deer.

Great! Now we'll have to send someone to retrieve her from under a bed in a few minutes.

Tsika and Kpau were chatting and giggling as they drank at the bar so Blar walked over to join them.

"Tsika, are you ...? Is that a good idea to make Glycerin go by herself with me?"

Tsika looked up at Blar with the authoritative and imperious demeanor that small women seem to excel at projecting. "Yes. Definitely! Look! Darling

Bear, I've been helping dear Glycerin with her … um, special challenges … since we were fresh new teenagers."

She put her hands on Blar's chest and raised up on her tiptoes. "Glycerin is my best friend, my most important treasure. I'd do ANYTHING for her. I hope you grasp we're a kind of a package deal. You're the first guy I can EVER remember that she's been able to interact this well with. I think some of it is just from her being the Rock Star Blar Umlaut's fiercest fan girl, but much of it … well, you just seem to be fabulous at handling her quirks gently. It is amazing to watch!" Tsika looked deeply in his eyes. "You can't possibly know how much I appreciate that." She stretched up further and kissed him. Blar basked in her closeness. He glanced at Kpau, who had a crooked quirky smile as she watched.

Blar pretended to glare at the young blonde. "You look like Harley Quinn from Batman when you smile like that! I keep wondering when the butcher knife or the large pop gun will appear."

Kpau punched his arm and then grabbed it to pull it around her so she ended up under his armpit. With a devil's laugh, she pushed his hand down her shirt so it appeared he was groping her. Blar tried to detach himself looking a bit alarmed at Tsika, but the goth was just giggling at the antics.

"Hah!!! You should know I dressed up in cosplay as the psychotic Harley one Halloween!" She jumped away from Blar and struck a pose. "Yes, I'm a geek! Comics, movies, cosplay! I play computer games, too! Please, please, please tell me you play!"

Kpau was distracted by movement from the door by the stage before she waited for an answer. "Annnd, here comes Glyc. Oh, now THAT is interesting! The Mouse is dressed to kill. Going out with her rock star must have seeped down into that mysterious alien brain!" Kpau was appraising the clothing Glycerin had changed into.

Glycerin had changed to a suede leather miniskirt and boots. Blar couldn't quite stop gaping at her outfit. The boots were thigh-high leather platforms with buckle straps and laces all the way up. The combination of skirt and boots left just a few inches of delightfully exposed thighs. Little Dancer was going to part the pedestrian crowd like the Red Sea with that aspect of her outfit. He was certain Tsika and Kpau had helped her on shopping for it, dressing her up for the stage lights.

The blouse Glycerin had put on had clearly been hand-sewn just for her. Blar wondered who the seamstress of the group was. It was a long-sleeved black silk blouse with transparent gauze sleeves. There were additional transparent gauze panels across the shoulders and just above her breasts. It had clearly been constructed to display her rather extensive tattoo collection. Blar could see that snake peeking out in its last loop where the head looped around and down pointing towards her left breast. It was an eye-catching stage outfit.

Sadly, it was also obviously something designed for the sunny weather of Los Angeles. Blar couldn't quite stop marveling at Glycerin's bravery at possessing so many tattoos given her general state of terror she seemed to swim in. There had to be a story to go with that, likely intertwined with those scars lurking in the tattoos.

"That's spectacularly pretty, Little Dancer. But I think it still needs … oh what the hell. Put this on and let's go." Blar grabbed his jacket off of the stool he had draped it on. It was an old leather bomber jacket he had worn for more than a decade, his all-purpose outer wear.

Glycerin froze as he stepped behind her, positioning her arms to slip it on. It was, of course, several sizes too big but the visual effect with the boots and skirt was dramatic. Even Kpau dropped her jaw.

"Holy shit, Glycerin! You look like a Princess of Leather! They'll give you a guitar for free just for hanging out in their shop!" Glycerin turned a shade of red only she seemed to be able to accomplish but she was hugging herself and purring in the warmth of the jacket.

"It really isn't rocket science to see my precious Glycerin is now totally lost in fan girl land. Wearing idol's jacket!" Tsika patted the tall beauty on the arm. "Go! Have fun! Stay close to Blar so you won't get lost."

Blar smirked. "Yeah, speaking of leather, since all three of you seemed inclined, there's a quirky leather shop near Burnside that may warrant a visit for stage gear. Some of their stuff even makes me nervous but it's a useful destination. I'll take everyone there on a slow day. Okay, Little Dancer, let's go."

Glycerin looked at Tsika in despair but timidly took Blar's hand and meekly followed him out of the club. Kpau had one eyebrow arched as she watched them leave. She shook her head skeptically.

"Tsika? You might be playing with fire, you know. Tsika … Tsika? Oh, look! I'm talking to thin air. Where did you go, Short Round? Bah!" Alone in the room, Kpau returned to her drums and gave one of her cymbals a solid whack.

~6~ "Don't Stand So Close To Me" – The Police

It was warm for a Pacific Northwest winter's day so Blar felt very comfortable in his flannel shirt. He could see that Glycerin was appreciating his loaned jacket while possibly regretting her choice to wear a skirt. The suede leather miniskirt was heavy so wardrobe malfunction wasn't an issue but the cold winds whipping around and up pretty thighs were giving her the shivers. She hadn't let go of his hand though. Blar guessed she was more terrified of being separated than she was terrified of him.

As they walked towards the light rail stop, Blar pointed out a few shops he thought the women might be interested in. He also pointed out his condo building as it peeked over the nearer buildings. Blar got the distinct feeling he might as well have pointed out the gates of Mordor to Glycerin the way she looked fearfully in that direction.

Good grief, what happened to this girl before Tsika met her? Or had she been born this way?

"Glycerin, here's the rail stop. It's free in this part of town so all we have to do is get on." She nodded meekly and stood close to him, using his body to block the breezes. She was glancing about, probably gauging how many homicidal maniacs were close enough to strike. When Tsika had said they were a package deal, Blar had found that a curious statement but it was quite clear Glycerin simply wasn't functional without someone to shepherd her.

A light rail train pulled up. Glycerin stuttered out something about it reminding her of the metro in Los Angeles as they boarded the train car. It was fairly crowded but Blar was caught by surprise anyway when she turned to face him, nearly burying her face in his neck and gripping his shirt.

So there were a lot of things scarier than him, such as being in a crowd. Glad to find that out. They certainly had the attention of the other passengers. She was nearly six feet tall in bare feet, currently wearing heels. He was a bit over six feet himself, just a hair taller. Blar found that Pacific Northwest folk tended to run a bit short so between their height, her looks, and his "naturally rugged" scariness, Blar thought perhaps he should put out a tip jar for the passengers to fill.

Blar gently put his arms around her waist. Her initial reaction resembled rigor mortis, but then her muscles slowly relaxed and she melted against him. Glycerin kept her face burrowed under his ear. "Glycerin, it'll be about five stops and we'll get off. We'll walk the rest of the way." She nodded. He heard a tiny "meep" noise. He couldn't possibly guess what was going on inside that raven haired head.

By the time they reached their stop to get off, she was leaning into Blar so hard he wondered if Glycerin had fallen asleep, but she jerked to the ready when he whispered it was time to get off. Still gripping his hand like a lifeline, they stepped off the train.

Blar played tour guide just to fill the silence, pointing out some of the more iconic restaurants in the area as they neared the guitar shop. A lot of street people frequented this part of town but one of the few perks about looking the way he did is that the homeless tended to steer clear of him. He was able to navigate around panhandlers without being accosted. He imagined Glycerin wouldn't be able to cope with them at all.

They reached the front door of the musical intrument store. The shop was a big one, located on the corner of a major intersection. It was popular, having carved itself quickly into the music scene in the few years it had been there. Glycerin peered through one of its windows, still gripping Blar's hand like a shield of safety.

"Th-th-th-they have a lot … lot of …," she eventually nodded as if she had finished her pronouncement.

"They'll look even better inside the shop. Come on! Inside with you, young lady." He let her step inside first. He wanted to watch the reaction of the store personnel and customers. Blar got what he hoped for. The store literally came to a stop. She might have been the hero stepping into a saloon in a bad western cowboy movie. So it wasn't just his own quirky tastes. She was strikingly beautiful and a knockout in that leather – just very broken on the inside.

Ah well. Muddle on.

Blar adopted the smile of a cat with prey as the owner hurried over to greet Glycerin. The man suddenly noticed she had a companion, and then realized the companion was Blar. "OH! Hey there, Blar …," he looked around quickly as he dropped his voice. Blar had long ago requested prudence from places he liked to frequent on avoiding the use of his name.

"So! May I ask who this completely delightful creature is that you've brought us and what may we do for her?" He wasn't leering, the guy was just awestruck. Blar add ten more points to his "taking risk = good" column with the women. Stage impact was vitally important. Glycerin had it without even moving an eyelash.

"Hello, Taylor. This is Glycerin. She's a guitarist, plays hardcore rock and metal rock lead, new in town, and we're upgrading her gear. We'd like to see what you have." Glycerin blinked a few times and nodded to confirm Blar's words. She was going to have to let go of his hand sometime.

Taylor looked her over from head to toe. "Really? A LEAD guitarist? Good lord, I will definitely have to see you in action! Right this way!" Taylor headed towards the Ibanez guitar section until Blar waved him off.

"No, no. I had her try the XP300 series and it just wasn't her cup of tea. She has been using a Stratocaster, an older model. It's perfectly good but too heavy for the way she plays. My stupid drummer opinion is that she's looking for something much lighter, without a lot of superfluous pointy parts to interfere with movement. It needs electronics capable of handling the fastest shredding as well as clean power tones. Active pickups, fairly bright. Yeah, I know! Challenging. She may end up needing several guitars but lets see what we can do to start."

Glycerin just nodded again. She finally released Blar's hand and began wandering down the aisle away from the two men, touching guitars that caught her eye. Taylor leaned close to Blar and whispered.

"Does … does she talk? Speak English? She looks a bit Asian. So pretty! Man, those long legs!"

"She, hmmm. Best way to say it is that she has some speech difficulties. Very shy. Once she gets comfortable she might open up a bit. Just be patient with her. You will want to watch her play, believe me." Taylor nodded as he watched her, appreciating the swish of her skirt from the backside.

"It sounds like she will want something triangular, something she can put against those magnificent hips. Let me grab some of our customized Jackson line. I've done a lot of work power leveling them. Start with those." Taylor scuttled off. Blar knew the man knew his stuff and would likely strike gold for Glycerin quickly.

Blar found it pleasant to take up where Taylor left off watching the lovely swish of the skirt belonging to the "Princess of Leather" as she examined the long rack of guitars.

Glycerin looked back to see Blar smiling and watching her. She blushed and and jerked her eyes down but kept shopping. Taylor soon returned with three guitars. Blar looked them over and nodded. "I think you're as good as you've always been at first guesses. Lets see what the young lady thinks." Blar walked over to Glycerin and spoke quietly, "Glyc? The store owner has some guitars he thinks you might like. Let's have you give them a swing."

Glycerin glanced around nervously. "H-h-h-h-ere? W-w-w-won't it … be … loud?"

She was likely afraid of the attention her play tests would bring. Blar was perplexed at how she could be on stage fearlessly but be such a mouse everywhere else. She must be in one seriously happy place on stage playing her guitar.

"It'll be fine. The neighborhood expects loud noises out of this store. They have a special testing area over here. Lots of room for you." Blar led her over to the testing area and waited until Glycerin chose one of the guitars.

He helped her strap it on, holding her hair up out of the way and adjusting the buckles. That minor trivial process left Blar sweating. Glycerin was so coy and shy that touching her was incredibly sensual. The feeling was amplified by her soft accidental flashes of eye contact with him. She was trying to look at him without him noticing. Blar felt blasted by small continuous imperative waves that compelled him to keep her safe. He had never felt like this with any woman he could recall.

Glycerin did a quick sound check after Blar activated the amplifier. Blar had seen her play at the club, but mostly simpler tunes and he could tell she was holding back around him out of fear. Being able to stand close and watch her fingers dance up the strings in scales and tweaks of the guitar's control knobs was fascinating. Taylor had an effects pedal in place. The tall woman rapidly stepped through a number of filters to find the sound she wanted, so fast Blar knew he had missed identifying almost half of them as they flew by.

"How does it feel, Ms. Glycerin?" Taylor asked as he looked on expectantly from a short distance. Blar had warned the store manager that she was dangerous to be near when she played.

"I-i-i-it is very light. I …," she stopped and took a deep breath, "… I …," Blar watched her get angry at herself. Good, he thought. Glycerin clenched her teeth and forced out an entire sentence through them.

"I like the w-way I can p-prop it on my hip." She demonstrated, thrusting one hip out and bracing the inverted curve of the guitar's base on it. Blar stopped breathing. Gods bow down to her. Poster rock goddess material. He glanced to see if Taylor had fainted. Nope. He's made of strong stuff.

"Okay, Glyc! Let's hear you. Start with some power chords, try some riffs, and then some shredding. Do what you like. You're the pro here. Then we'll try the other ones doing the same thing again. I'm getting out of your way now. Close your eyes if you like and just listen for what you want. Good girl." Blar briefly stroked the back of her head and took cover.

Glycerin closed her eyes and stood still. The only movement was her sliding her fingers along the neck. It was unusual to Blar, but she was gathering a mental image of the fret locations. The other customers had all stopped to watch. He had a premonition he was about to experience another perfect moment. Her hands moved and the sound wasn't just a single power chord, it was a collection of them – the opening refrain to *The Kinks* classic tune, *"You Really Got Me"*. Taylor must have caught a whiff of the same premonition because he had set the volume to "11" on the amp circuit. The melodic progression was probably vibrating the innards of the diners across the street. She gently swayed as she played, her eyes still closed. Then she stopped.

Some of the customers started to clap. Blar threw his hand up in a silencing motion. He didn't want her to realize she had an audience. Glycerin moved closely to Blar as she unstrapped the guitar. It was clear she had mentally closed her world solely onto him just as she did with Tsika. It appeared to let her pretend to herself she was alone with either.

"A-a-a-a-al-al-al-most. I … I … try that one."

Glycerin frequently sounded like she was drowning when she tried to speak. It impressed Blar how hard she fought against whatever demons had her shackled. She shakily pointed to a variation on the guitar she had just tried. It had an additional pickup and a modified bridge.

Glycerin stopped to take off the jacket Blar had lent her, revealing her custom blouse and those vibrant tattoos. That elicited several appreciative remarks and a quiet whistle from the still growing crowd. Blar held his hand up for silence again. A minute later, she repeated the opening chords of the Kinks' tune. That impressed Blar, she had repeated the sequence perfectly. By his ears, it could have been a recording playback.

Was she some kind of idiot savant? Was that part of her mental state? More questions to discuss with Tsika.

She broke off from her rendition. Blar saw a tiny smile through the curtain of hair that hid most of her face. He looked at the guitar she was using. It wasn't terribly expensive by Blar's standards but Taylor had done some excellent work on it. Blar realized Glycerin wasn't done. She spread her legs for stability, raised her strumming hand into the air and started windmilling her arm, her pick lightly touching the strings, building up a massive power chord. She had it angled toward the amplifier, creating a powerful tightly controlled distorted feedback. Blar knew very few professionals who had the level of skill she was demonstrating with that kind of control.

Pete Townshend of *The Who* had popularized the windmill move decades before, but it wasn't a Who tune that erupted from her finger tips. Glycerin ripped into a free-spirited rendition of Joe Satriani's metal jazz tune "*Surfing With The Alien*". Blar blinked in astonishment. The woman was giving Joe a deadly serious run for the money on his own famous metal jazz tune and adding all sorts of her own twists on it. Nothing extraneous, every note seemed to belong exactly where she put it.

She was in stratospheric "Little Dancer" mode now, no holding back – twirling, hopping, strutting. Her long fingers were flying through the tune's melody. Blar was impressed that her eyes remained mostly closed as she danced, a hint of a smile on her face. The look seemed familiar to him, something religious.

At this point, people were crossing the street to get a better view through the large plate glass windows. One of Taylor's employees was making sure customers stayed back because she really was dangerous to be near now as she whirled about.

A display rack fell to her boot in one of her kicks, spinning as it spiraled off to a corner. Guitar strap packages scattered. Glycerin was oblivious to everything, playing faster now. She had arrived at the central part of the composition, pure jazz melodic noise shredding. Fast. She was so fast. Blar felt unworthy and held back a shudder. Why was he ever famous and she was still metaphorically struggling in a garage? The smile on her face was ecstatic now as she tore through the notes – Blar's heart pounded as he watched. Here was someone who literally became her music. Spiritually transcendent. A muse incarnate.

And then it was over. Blar could no longer think of Glycerin as anything but utterly beautiful, quirks, neuroses, and all. Glycerin opened her eyes. She was suddenly aware that she had a crowd shrieking, whistling, and clapping. Uh oh. Blar moved to her quickly.

"Glyc, how did you like that guitar?" He helped her unstrap, standing to block her view of the crowd.

She looked around at the noise, her face taking on that terrified rabbit expression she wore so often.

"Glyc, it is just like being on stage. Hold my hand and bow to the audience. Then we'll run to the back room."

She gripped his hand. He thought she was going to crush it. Glycerin faced the crowd and without actually focusing on them, bowed, and bestowed no one in particular with a half-mad terrified grin. She kept her grip on his hand as he grabbed his jacket and they fled to the back room.

"Do you want to try the other guitar?" She shook her head and buried her face in his neck. She was hiccuping. All Blar could process was intense feelings of a soft and warm body pressed against him as he stroked her back.

"It it it it … d-d-didn't have the … pickup positioning … like, I like. I … I like this one. This … I like this one."

Glycerin still had the guitar in her other hand as she stared at him with those big sad doe eyes. Taylor, the store owner, was following them. He had an enormously sympathetic expression. Once in the back room, they sat Glycerin in a chair where she quietly strummed and plucked the unplugged guitar. Blar and Taylor went to work out the details of the purchase at the other end of the storage room.

"Damn, Blar! I am totally blown away. Where did you FIND her? She's devastating! Brilliant … agonizingly fragile at the same time. It reminds me of … I have this cousin … she's autistic – plays the piano brilliantly. Not saying your girl is autistic but … wow. Her skill, stage presence and so shy. Just … wow." Taylor was clearly moved.

"She's part of a band. There's two more amazing women who have mad skills. They are a little band I'm giving some guidance to." Taylor silently mouthed another wow as he created the invoice.

"I'm going to just go twenty percent on my cut, Blar. I haven't been able to get that guitar out the door in months and certainly no one ever made it sound like she did. That little performance might even be on the news tonight. I saw some news media people I recognized lurking around by the end of her solo and there were cellphones up. Free advertising! Here. Give her this soda while I work up the invoice."

Blar ferried the soda to Glycerin. She gratefully took it and sipped. "Just a few more minutes, Glyc. He's cutting us a good deal you impressed him so much."

Glycerin was picking out the opening guitar refrain from the *Bon Jovi* tune "Wanted: Dead Or Alive" when Blar returned after he had completed the transaction.

"Hey, Little Dancer. It is yours. Here's the case for it with some bonus baubles. Taylor is going to let us slip out the back door. You seem to have attracted a news crew out by the front door."

Her strumming stopped. Glycerin cradled her new guitar and looked up at Blar. Her eyes were moist.

"Why? You're … being s-s-s-s-so nice to all of us. Why?"

Simple and direct. Blar couldn't think of nearly so simple an answer.

"I … I have a rational explanation. It really isn't the entire truth. Rationally? Rationally I see three women who I think can take it all the way to the top in this music business and stay there. Getting to the top could pay for whatever you wanted for the rest of your lives, build you safe places, go where you want. The selfish part is that by helping you, I end up in a safe place, too. That place I wanted to go but couldn't quite make it a permanent stay the first time. I … messed up that time."

Blar sat down close to Glycerin. She had stopped shaking. She was listening intently. "But that's my mask of rationalizing. The truth? Feelings. Irrationality. I saw Tsika in a snowstorm. She mesmerized me. I was utterly compelled to follow her."

Blar tentatively put his hand on her hand. It shivered but she didn't move it away. "Then I saw you yesterday. Or thought I did. I saw the real you today for the first time out there as you played Satriani's music. I'm enthralled by you. I find myself utterly compelled to keep you safe and help you reach your dreams. It would be an utterly immoral act in my mind not to do that.

You are lovely witchcraft."

Blar glanced at her. Her eyes were behind her curtain of hair but he could see she was actually looking at him.

"I could rationalize more. Nonsense like thinking how terrible it is for amazing talent to go untapped but the irrational is just basic. I just NEED to help. I can't stop myself. I like you, Glycerin. That word sucks. You stop my heart you're so adorable."

Blar blurted that out before he thought it through. Glycerin seemed to have an infinite scale of how deeply she could blush. Blar quickly continued to recover. "Tsika is adorable. Kpau is adorable. Each in your own different ways. Like I told Kpau, you three made me realize how dead I've been the last few years. I was effectively dead, just waiting for the dead cart to pick me up. My days are interesting again and I can thank you three for that. I'm just glad you three seem to be okay with me injecting myself into your world."

Glycerin was sniffling. She had lost eye contact, her eyes focused on his hand on hers. Blar wondered if he had said too much but then her other long slender hand slowly reached across to his sleeve and grasped it. Blar held his breath while Glycerin struggled to speak.

"I-I-I … We will bloody work hard. I want-want to. My friends … they … they are … so important … , " she was sniffling, hiccuping, and stammering all at once, "… We woulds be bollixy lost with-without them … w-without my p-precious Tsika. It … It's …. I'm … I'm scared. But she wants this so much and I so dearly want my d-doll to be happy." Glycerin stopped to gasp for air for a few breaths. "I'm h-happy. I'm … I'm glad …. I'm so glad … I got to meet you, Mr. B-Blar Um-Umlaut."

She leaned against him, laying her forehead on his shoulder. She was shaking and Blar had a feeling she was crying because his shirt was getting wet. He dearly wanted to hug her but feared blowing her last circuit.

"Okay, pretty Little Dancer. Let's get your new guitar into its case and sneak out of here. Are you hungry? There's a street vendor market not far from here. We can catch a bite there on the way back."

Glycerin looked up into Blar's eyes, making the briefest eye contact from under her bangs with a merest glimpse of a smile. Blar heart felt jolted, pierced as if by a spear. Damn it. He was not making anything up, she was adorable. Blar suppressed a shudder and forced himself to think about Tsika. Now. Think about the small exquisite goth. Think about her.

The pair quietly exited via the shipping door and scampered to safety. Glycerin was now clinging closely to his arm rather than just holding his hand at a distance. Blar hoped this was making Tsika a happy camper because the whole experience was totally rattling him.

~7~ "Flirting With Disaster" – Molly Hatchet

Kpau was generating an intense force field of chaotic tribal noise on her drums, weaving it above Tsika's rock-steady bass line. A sheen of sweat coated her tanned skin. Then a snort and a guttural growl, signifying no satisfaction with her product, preceded the blonde crashing to a stop as she slammed her cymbals and bells in a demonic cacophony. Tsika calmly unstrapped her bass guitar during the ruckus and set it down on her stool as drumsticks flew over her head.

"Kpau. Take a break, have a drink or two. I gotta go potty." Kpau made a crazy face at Tsika as the little twin-tailed imp scampered off. The bronze blonde clawed at the air as she stomped over to the bar and fumed as she poured scotch whiskey into a glass.

Tsika is either really focused on practice or she is doing a singular top class avoidance act. I have been trying to engage the little ghoul in a heart-to-heart chat since Blar left with Glycerin … what? Two hours ago?

Kpau snarled and mixed Tsika a drink as well, doubling the shots of alcohol in the drink intended for the small woman. Lubrication might be a good thing for the vampire's tight strings.

I'm not too worried about Glycerin. Blar can carry her if she passes out. I'm more concerned about Blar himself, in regard to my two friends. Blar isn't a terribly complicated guy by my reckoning. Tsika called him a boy scout. I have a strong suspicion that covers a lot more than not taking advantage of women in a rough spot. But I gotta be sure. He is something very suspicious to the terminally cynical like me – earnest and helpful.

She took a sip of her scotch. Glycerin easily attracted well-meaning sorts, but up before now the tall beauty had simply run shrieking away from them into Tsika's arms.

This was different. Those poor dudes hadn't been her rock idol. Kpau's internal alarms had gone off immediately when Blar had lent his jacket to Glycerin. The look on the Glycster's face radiated one massive crush on the big guy. That was something totally new. What really bothered Kpau is that

Tsika didn't seem to be considering the ramifications of pushing her new beau at her best friend.

"Oh, the problems we could see there could be for us three." Kpau chuckled. "Heh, that probably made Dr. Seuss flinch in his grave."

There was no doubt to Kpau that Tsika was excited about her new guy. The fact he was Blar Umlaut was irrelevant. It was the shape, scent, and touch of the man himself igniting Tsika's switches. Kpau could see Tsika's pupils dilating and her nostrils flare when she looked at Blar. No doubt other parts of her were firing up as well. Kpau stopped and put her drink down.

"Wow, I'm doing far more thinking than usual. That's alarming all by itself."

Kpau knew where she stood in life. She was the third wheel of *The Lost Girls*. It was just a fact of chronology. Nonetheless, she loved Tsika and Glycerin. They were literally the only family of any sort she had. She was going to protect that. Everything would be simpler if Blar were just a creep, she knew how to get rid of creeps. But he wasn't creepy at all once she got past his grim appearance. Adding more complication, Blar was their ticket out of the basement into adventure and lights. She needed to tread carefully no matter what.

And just for more spin to the ride, I already have Blar tagged as a great buddy. He actually talks TO me. He looks at my EYES! Dangerous. He somehow is managing to give off an air I find comfortable, safe, and even exciting. Gah! Whatever happens, all four of us need to have eyes wide open or this thrill ride will be short and nasty.

She realized she had finished her drink and poured herself some more scotch. Tsika returned as she was topping off her glass. Kpau waved her over, handing Tsika the drink mixed for the vampire – twin shots for twin tails. The wordplay in her head made Kpau smile.

"Kpau's Rule: Never drink alone. Here."

Tsika took a drink and raised her eyebrow. "Blonde woman's shot size measures are becoming seriously suspect. You should get famous BEFORE we have to have an intervention on you."

"Lubrication for drumming! All YOU have to do is stand there, darkly brood and sway with your bass." They both laughed.

"Look, Tsika. I'm gonna be quick and blunt for lack of time. You like Blar … a lot! Easy to see. Warning! Danger! Glycerin isn't just fan-girling on Blar. The shy flower has a big crush on him I can see a mile off and it probably spiked out there just now. Totally new territory for your big Mouse. Danger, Will Robinson."

Tsika looked down at her drink. Her lips formed a pout. "I … I don't own Blar! I've known him, what … three days? We're not even officially dating. No, you little minx, I see that look! He was a perfect gentleman that night. I even … I was even willing … well, he was very chivalrous. Besides, I expect to be courted and romanced by anyone with designs on me!"

Kpau's eyes narrowed. "You're sidestepping, widget. I'm not Glycerin, ya know."

Tsika's face flushed and her eyes flashed.

"What is most important to me is Glycerin! I want my Glycca to get better. To be able to function. To be with me because she WANTS to be with me, not because she's trapped by all those shackles in her head. That takes priority to me. If Blar can help her out of … out of those chains," Tsika's voice cracked and she kept her eyes down, "I'll deal with whatever is consequence of that."

Kpau put her hands on Tsika's shoulders and gently shook her. "Look. I know it's been ten plus years with Glycerin and painfully slow progress. But there is no need to rush to throw yourself under a train for her." Kpau paused to consider her next words. "You … you guys. You are my family. It's like the little Stitch says."

Kpau affected the voice of a certain little blue alien cartoon character. "You are my family. I found it … all on my own. It's little … and broken, but still good. Yeah - still good. Ohana stuff and happy follows!"

The blonde returned to her normal voice. "I want us all to be happy together. How about we all focus on the band and try to minimize drama? Make that our priority. We're the band! Everything should be filtered by how it helps the band! Maybe things will flow more naturally. Whatever happens later will be happy for all."

Tsika sniffed and nodded. Kpau rolled her eyes. Little tough girl is all gooey inside.

Tsika's cellphone lit up. It was a text from Glycerin, they were on their way back. She had a new guitar.

"Righteous! Now finish your damn drink and lets go make useful noise." Kpau patted Tsika's shoulders.

- - - - - -

Kpau and Tsika were goofing around with the bass and drum line from the Rammstein driving rugged metal tune "*Du Hast*" when Glycerin and Blar returned. The two women were being silly. Tsika was tipsy, head banging and growling. Both women had stripped down to their bikini tops and jeans. They were covered in sweat from the musical roughhousing. When Tsika and Kpau noticed the pair gaping at them, both women burst into laughter.

Blar shook his head as he smiled. "You two goblins laugh. We may do that tune and more variety of metal. I agree with mixed genre notion – bands are better off being versatile rather than being stuck in one niche."

Glycerin had set her new case down and was snapping the latches open. Kpau danced over to see what bauble Glycerin had garnered. Her eyes popped at the contents.

"Oooooh! That axe looks lethal! I won't even ask you how it plays cuz I know you're particular, Glyc!" A crooked Kpau smile appeared as she launched some friendly torture. She had a nickname for him now.

"Soooo? How was the date with PAPA BEAR?!" Kpau leered pornographically. Glycerin turned firetruck red. Score one! Blar looked aggrieved at Kpau's new nickname of him. Score two!

"Papa Bear?! Hey what the hell is that name?! I'm not ancient! I'm less than ten years older than you, Chicklet!"

"Ehhhhhhhh! You talk like an old man! You're getting better though, must be the new company you keep!" Kpau bounced over to Blar and leaned her bare back against his chest as if he were a wall, grinning like a hyena and generating a damp spot on Blar's shirt.

"You're playing with evil forces, Chicklet. I bite." Blar growled and held her away from him by her shoulders as she wiggled to rub up her sweaty body up against him. Glycerin was watching them and Kpau swore she saw a wistful look on the tall woman's face, like that sort of horseplay was something she wanted to do, too.

Hah! Scouting mission successful! Though it worryingly confirms we haz got potential issues brewing.

Tsika was standing by Glycerin, ignoring Kpau's antics and admiring the new guitar. "Oh, Glycca! Precious Mouse is going to be able to just dance your heart out with that! I can't wait to hear it." She took Glycerin's long slender hand in her small hands and caressed it, smiling at her friend.

Meanwhile, Blar was manhandling Kpau playfully while she was doing her best to climb up on him. Her goal was to perch on his shoulder but he was quick, too. She wasn't having much success outside of a great deal of skinship bonding.

"Guh! Chicklet, that's not glow that's sweat! Augh!" Blar kept trying to talk business as he wrestled to keep Kpau from clambering up on him. "Tsika? You might like to know your little Glyc did some advertising for us. There's street buzz now about the mystery girl shredder floating about. She handed the entire block a kick-ass rendition of Satriani's *"Surfing with the Alien"* on a whim."

Glycerin kept finding new colors of red to blush in as she floated in a happy haze of Blar's praise.

Kpau gave up her quest to perch on Blar's shoulder and flashed Glycerin a victory sign. "Outstanding, Glyc! But … it occurs to me. We haz a problem! We still gots no name! And I already veto '*Blar & the Lost Girls*' or any such concatenated mess."

Blar looked uncomfortable. "I don't know if I want to mess with that. The name *Lost Girls* has a much deeper meaning for you three than just a random name. I'm really wary of touching it."

Tsika smiled at the large man. Kpau watched tiny flashes of lust in the little goth's eyes. "We will always be *Lost Girls* even if we are inside another band or even different bands. Sashiko is still a *Lost Girl* even though we fired her. *Lost Girl* status is permanent. No leaving allowed."

Kpau waved her arms. "Focus! Group name!"

Glycerin looked thoughtful but remained mute. Tsika scowled and pointed at the bulletin board of local concert advertisements. "Well, it can not be horribly hard! Look at the wretched band names posted on this wall! Is not rocket science!"

Glycerin straightened up and she stuttered, "B-But, but, but … Tsika! It really IS r-rocket science!"

Silence. Three pairs of eyes focused on Glycerin as she shifted colors, turning ghostly pale from the attention.

Kpau spoke. "Glyc. That is fucking brilliant! Tsika is ALWAYS using that damned line about rocket science when she howls!"

Kpau looked at everyone. "Is it agreed? Glycerin just named the group? I mean, the announcer screams into the mike. 'AND NOW! IT REALLY **IS** ROCKET SCIENCE!' Cue crazed fans and huge bank accounts! For the win!" Kpau bounced around like a puppy.

Blar just laughed, "That is as oddball as anything I might come up with. It'll do for now. I'll tell Hans so he can update his sign. Good job, Glycerin."

Glycerin looked confused. "I … I … what? I was just … oh … OH! I get it!" Glycerin came as close to laughter as Kpau ever saw her muster. Tsika hugged the tall woman with a sweet smile and they went back to admiring Glycerin's new guitar as she held the treasure up for inspection.

Kpau stood back and took a deep breath as the other two women gushed at each other. She eyed the backside of Blar as he ambled off muttering about finding Hans. Kpau's crooked smile appeared again.

This may actually happen. We may be actually able to do this, as a family. My family … and maybe … maybe that big bear Blar is part of that family now. I still have some tests to run on that, some checking to do. Time for a solo mission. We have to decide whether to move in with the guy or not. So much to manage.

- - - - - -

The foursome practiced the remainder of the day, switching around between Blar's old music, some modern cover tunes, and a couple of short original musical pieces Tsika had written. Tsika and Kpau agreed Glycerin had made an excellent choice in guitars. It fit her playing style like a glove. Kpau sidled up to Glycerin during an extended break.

"So, Glyc! How many stores did you two have to visit?"

Glycerin stroked her guitar dreamily. "Just … just one." She looked at Kpau with clueless big doe eyes. Kpau got a gleam in her eye and sipped her latest glass of scotch.

"Sooooooo, what did you two DO for the rest of the time? Ehhhh?" Kpau shot a glance over at Tsika, who was over at the bar with Blar. The impish vampire was sitting in his lap and howling about something that had pissed her off so neither of that pair were paying any attention to her and Glyc. Time for fun. And score. Yet another color of blush on Glyc's face.

"We … Kpau! It wasn't bloody like that! You're always so … dirty minded! He w-was nice. Blar took us to find food afterward b-because I was hungry. We ate at a street v-vendor park. It was barmy weird -- they have whole blocks of them like a little permanent festival."

"Soooooooo, what did you talk abouuuuuut?" Kpau decided she shouldn't torture Glyc too much, she could sense the fragile woman's stress alarms going off.

"I … I didn't say much. It was so hard to talk to him. I was proud I w-was able to sit next to him. He talked about the city, ideas f-for the band. He was so kind to me. I know I am a bloody disaster to b-be with. He asked me about my-myself, but … I was stuttering so badly. I promised that one day we w-would tells him about myself eventually."

Glycerin looked vaguely morose then suddenly smiled. "Then we had to run and hide! The news crew w-was looking for us! That was exciting! I … I think … adventures are going to be fun with him! He's funny! My Blar is funny! I never knew that! He was always scary in his videos!"

Glycerin got a easily deciphered expression. She had a history of trying one-up Kpau in the teasing department. Kpau waited for Glycerin to try and pull off her tease.

"The way you two act, we guesses you likes Blar a lot, too?" Glycerin's lips were pouting again. Kpau thought the question had an interesting edge to it. She played her answer straight.

"Oh! Still checking it out, but I'm treating him like a long lost big brother with a slathering of incest."

Glycerin horrified expression caused Kpau to choke on her drink in laughter. Kpau started toweling off her sweat. "Glyc. You know I think of you and Tsika as my family. I want Blar to be part of that family, too. Wanna make sure he is someone I can trust, who will pull me out of shit I get into, whom I can cuddle up with on a bus like I do with you. Think about it, you big fangirl! We can even pile up like ferrets when we watch television!"

Glycerin look of horror now had an added component of intrigue. "Um … yeah … he has offered us his place to live. We're supposed to t-talk about it. It … it would be nice to have a real place with a door that locks."

Kpau blinked. Wow! That was different from the abject terror Glycerin initially expressed to the idea of living with him. "Soooo, you're okay with living with him? I figure Tsika is fine with it. Her little engines are redlining around the big oaf."

"It is-is sweet to w-watch her, isn't it? It … it makes practical s-sense. We … we're g-going to be to-together a lot. Gigs, travel … practice. Tsika says he has a recording st-studio in his place. We get our own bathroom. I don't mind sharing a bedroom with you and Tsika."

"Yeah, he told me he's having someone design the layout and do the re-arranging. All we have to do is decide before he triggers the project. Okay, I guess I'm doing the devil's advocate part here. I'll do some research. We don't want to get all entrenched and then find out it isn't going to work. That would just hurt feelings in all directions too early in the game. Tally Ho, I guess!"

- - - - - -

The day's practice was about to end when Kpau stuck her hand up, waving her stick around like a flag.

"Hey, hey! We're doing mostly easy tunes here. I want to see Glycerin rip a hole in space-time on her new guitar. Let's do "*Surfing*"! Burn some calories!"

Glycerin bit her lip. "Bloody hell, oh … oh, I'm f-fine with that. It will be fun w-with everyone playing."

Tsika screwed her face up in annoyance. "I … hmmm, it's been a while. H'okay, I might have to fake some of the bass line but I'm in." Tsika looked over at Blar with a quizzical expression.

"You three have fun. I'll watch." Blar put his guitar down and strolled over to the sound board.

Glycerin took a deep breath and got very still. She closed her eyes. Kpau grinned and waited. When she saw Glycerin nod slightly, Kpau tapped an energetic fast count with her sticks and the trio was off and running with Glyc taking over control of the pace. After listening to the opening bars, Blar cranked the master volume up. Kpau sensed that Blar wanted the street to hear it. She kept her eyes on Glycerin. Her friend from outer space was a whirling transcendent dervish floating just above the ground, her guitar seamlessly attached to her body. It was a beauty to watch. She loved watching Glycerin dive into her happy space.

Eventually the last notes faded out and Kpau put her sticks down to wave her arms and cheer. "I think THAT was an ass-kicking example of *Rocket Science*. Let's put this stuff up and eat. I am starved!" She stretched and leered at Blar. Kpau had spotted him appreciating her boobs as she raised her arms behind her head. She wiggled her torso and winked at him for emphasis. He stammered nonsense and looked away.

Good times!

- - - - - -

Blar stood in the middle of his condo looking pointlessly for his favorite tinted "Ozzie" style glasses. Nothing was where it should be. There were boxes on every horizontal surface. Piles and stacks created mazes. Furniture was stacked or not to be seen. Not even the gods likely knew where his television remote had landed. He only wanted his sunglasses, where were they?

Blar had decided in the interest of efficiency to go ahead and begin his condo overhaul project with some options. He wanted to change up his apartment anyway and get more day use out of the window side of his unit whether or not the trio of women moved in. He hadn't changed a thing in almost ten years. Change was good.

He had contracted with an interior designer he knew over in the Pearl District. Felicia had helped him set up the condo back when Blar first moved in. She jumped at his request for a re-do with a passion after he laid out the requirements. Blar insisted on keeping the Japanese-style decor despite her protestations that he needed to "update". He simply liked Asian décor and didn't care if it was in style or not. She grumbled and took the job anyway.

If the trio of women accepted his offer, they were to share what was formerly his master bedroom and large bathroom. If they declined and he found them other quarters, Blar was going to use that room as a war room for managing the band, big enough for meetings, white boards, and office space.

The guest room and its smaller bathroom would become his Fortress of Solitude. It had no window and all he did was sleep in his bedroom anyway. Where he slept could be one of those Japanese hotel room tubes for all he cared.

Blar's small office was being repurposed into a storage area for supplies, electronics, and he was putting his network servers in there. Duly labeled as an all purpose "toss things in here" room with a door to close.

The large museum room was being converted back to a recording studio and musical practice room. Blar was upgrading the soundproofing to the entire unit with his buddy Jack's assistance. Even after that, the band would have to play at partial power if Blar wanted to avoid a lynching by the building association.

The between-floor maintenance space was roomy enough that Blar and Jack had been able to do most of the soundproofing themselves rather quickly and quietly. Jack called those areas the building's 'Jefferies Tubes'. Blar figured Kpau would appreciate the *Star Trek* reference to the engineering crawl tubes in the series. No reason to ruin tea time for the condo's board of directors after all. Blar figured his band mates would be practicing there mostly during the daylight hours anyway.

Blar glanced through the invoices he was holding, doing quick summations in his head.

Yup. There went the first IRA cash out. I'm definitely on this ride now. I do hope they decide to move in. It would be kind of nice to have regular chatter in this place after all these years.

He finally spotted his sunglasses lurking next to the television. Best way to find something was to stop looking for it. The remodeling team had left for lunch so the condo was silent. Blar decided he might grab some Indian curry for the band and head over to the club for some stress release.

Blar sighed, thinking about his new sexy little goth obsession, Tsika. He couldn't believe how attracted he had gotten towards the dry humored witty little Russian doll. It had been so long since anyone had energized his interest. Tragically, other than that first night, he had managed only the random moment to spend with Tsika by herself. Her comment about the package deal was almost right. The band absorbed all time. Blar wondered if he'd made a strategic error and there simply wouldn't ever be time to romance the little thunderstorm. He growled at himself. Just enjoy the moments, let things percolate. Life was certainly a lot more interesting now. The doorman buzzer rang and Jack's voice burbled through the speaker unit.

"Good morning, Mr. Umlaut. Not having too much fun, I hope."

Blar grumbled, "Jack, you're just enjoying all the cute little decorator gnomes heading in and out of the building today. Bad news for you, I am pretty sure most of them are lesbian." The doorman chuckled lightly.

"Oh, it just got a thousand percent better, Blar. There's an incredible little cherry dessert standing in the lobby who says she's here to see you. Just calls herself Ka-pow. And I think Ka-pow describes her perfectly."

Blar knew Jack, the doorman and his buddy, from way back. Blar snared Jack the job he had now. The older man had been an enduring roadie for Blar back in the days of *Gothic Fire*. He ran into hard times when the economy crashed a few years before. Blar had snagged him this job before the bankruptcy demons got him.

"That's one of your potential new tenants. Her name is Kpau, work on that pronunciation, because whether she moves in or not you'll get to see her a lot soon. I don't know why she's here, but send her on up." Blar scratched his mustache and wondered what the mischievous moppet was up to.

A few minutes later, Blar's front door buzzed. He opened it to find Kpau sticking her tongue out.

She pouted, "Darn shuckies! I hoped you'd look through the peephole first." The young lady sauntered in, grinning like a little girl on her first day at school.

No wonder Jack had forgotten his professional demeanor. Kpau was dressed for a top flight man-eating kill. She was wearing little boots with glittery chains and a short plaid skirt adorned with belts, buckles, and dangles. A cute jacket with a fur trimmed hood topped it off, but once she removed that Blar found himself admiring the pink and black corset she sported. It added boost to her charming assets while leaving her arms, shoulders, and upper back bare. Blar had been impressed since Day One with Kpau's muscle tone. One thing Blar hadn't noticed before though – her legs. They were nicely sculpted works of art on their own. Kpau clearly did much more than just drum to keep herself fit. Her left thigh was adorned with a tattoo of a pair of cherries on stems. He didn't disguise his examination of them as Kpau grinned back at him like a hyena.

"Hah! Old man noticed my cherries? Yeah, that was the first tattoo I ever got. I was trying to be a tough girl near the end of high school and well, yeah, it seemed funny at the time. Ended my cheerleading career but I didn't care. It was already spring time senior year." She made a face and looked around at the carnage. "Well, normally I'd say 'nice place' but wow it looks like a bomb went off."

Blar headed to the kitchen, "I went ahead with a remodel that works whether or not you all move in. I figure you're going to be here a lot even if you don't live here. Felicia says they'll be done by Saturday. I no longer believe her. Care for a drink?" Kpau pointed to the bottle of scotch out of his collection of liquor. Blar poured her a glass, straight up. He had noticed that seemed to be her standard go-to drink of choice.

"You know you're awfully young to be drinking this stuff straight. Counting on liver cloning technology to save you?" Blar handed her the drink as they both leaned against the kitchen counter looking out into the living area.

Kpau sipped her glass, "Bah! See? That's old man talk! You're doing it again! If you're paying that much attention, you noticed I'm never actually drinking all that much at once. Just lots of sipping." She sidled close enough to him that her hip was against his leg and shook her head so her hair brushed him. She smelled like old-fashioned bubble gum.

After the last few days together, Blar had already figured out that Kpau just liked being close to people. She was always touching or close to everyone, male or female. He guessed it might be one key reason many guys misinterpreted her casualness for something serious.

Kpau surveyed the mess as she sipped and asked Blar a few questions about the layout of the living area. Her eyes focused on Blar's entertainment center and she trotted that way excitedly. "Oh, great! You have both a Playstation and an Xbox! I haven't been able to play since we left Los Angeles! You and me, we gotta play! Tsika plays some, but Glycerin mostly reads. Yippee Ki Yay! You gots the whole Borderlands series!"

She finished her drink, returned to the kitchen next to him, and blinked her eyes at him. Blar had an epiphany – this was how Kpau winked – with both eyes. She was one of those people unable to close just one eye. It wasn't too unusual a physical trait. His mother used to call it 'one string for both eyes'.

"Gonna give me a tour? I think I can visualize the grand design through the debris." Kpau put her hand on his arm and stroked the hair on it. Tough little drummer girl fingers, Blar thought.

"Come on, Chicklet. I'll let you do your spying before it's ready. No making fun of what isn't ready." Blar brushed behind her and ruffled her hair. She shivered and giggled, following him.

"So, where's this magical bedroom you say we can have if we join your herd, o moose-sized one?"

"Hush. You're gonna get the whole tour." Blar stood at the near end of the hallway. "I'm moving my butt into the guest room here. I use its bathroom most of the time anyway these days and I don't need a window to sleep. The room with two futures is this one. It will either be the lair of the *Lost Girls* or a band war room for meetings and management."

He led her into the master bedroom. She danced over to the wall of large plate windows.

"Wow, bigger than advertised and with a view! Hah! I can see the club from here!"

Blar rolled his eyes. He really did enjoy her frequent use or misuse of pop culture and movie quotes but his mind was running between curiosity and confusion. Why was Kpau really here? It seemed rather silly to walk all this way just for a look. Maybe she just wanted to walk back with him and chat? He moved some of the boxes on the bed and sat down while she checked the closet space out.

Blar kept talking just so he wouldn't feel awkward. "There's more storage space in the practice room and I have some deep storage, my dungeon as you called it. I think there's enough space here for everyone's clothing. I took a guess you three had not brought very much up from L.A."

Blar watched her butt and legs with a touch of amusement and lusty appreciation as she stretched behind the closet door checking the space out. Suddenly Kpau popped out with a girly magazine. Blar was positive he had boxed those up. She waved it like a flag and brought it over to him as he pretended to glare at the mischievous troublemaker.

She had an evil grin. "Oh Ho!" That was a terrible pun. "I see you have a fondness for Asian girls. That's hilarious! Three of us and you've latched onto the only one who lacks any Asian bits!" She sat down next to him and thumbed the magazine, pointing out women she thought were cute. Blar's mood shifted from being bemused to being mildly concerned by her antics. Is she ramping up to making a play or is this something else? Whatever. Let's just see where she goes with her game. He chose to growl at her comment about Tsika with a lament.

"I'm not exactly 'latched' onto Tsika. We haven't even had a date yet. I will not deny I'm smitten with her but we haven't even had a chance to compare favorite foods." Kpau scooted closer. At this point, she was about as close as she could get without being in his lap and she had slipped under his arm. She wasn't quite as small as Tsika but she was delightfully compact and her boot tip was tracing a pattern on the back of his calf. Blar found it really pleasant just watching her breathe and feeling her hair softly brushing against his arm. Dim alarm bells were going off in Blar's head but Kpau appeared mostly engrossed by the magazine rather than him.

"Oh, look. Now this outfit would be great stage wear! But … with those naughty bits covered!" She laughed and looked up at him with glittering eyes. Okay, now there was no question. Blar's internal alarms were all sounding for battle stations. She had fiery 'take me' eyes running at full power, her lips were moist and parted. She was openly giving him a delicious view of her cleavage. What the hell was going on?

"Kpau? Not that I am not utterly transfixed and enjoying you. But … what are you doing?" She held his gaze a few more seconds, searching his bemused eyes, and then she blinked and cast her eyes down as she dialed the heat back.

"I … I dunno sometimes. This time I wanted to see what you were like without the others around. How you'd react to my games. Stuff like that." Her smile was gone, replaced with an expression he found painfully sad. Is this another test? She didn't seem vindictive or catty to Blar. There had to be something else going on. No choice, time to save his 'game' for the next event.

Blar chose a path and put his arm around her shoulder, "Look. I think you're adorable. Gods, you're so adorable, little Chicklet. I love roughhousing with you and the way we poke and flirt with each other. I … I don't know what you're doing either. Some kind of test? I'm not really Tsika's guy yet -- so it's not exactly cheating to let you know I find you attractive. And you are attractive. But I don't want this to get complicated before the band even leaves the gate."

Kpau rested her head against him, "I think that's exactly what I needed to hear." She looked back up at him with the most genuine smile, maybe the first one that had been real for him. "Sorry, Papa Bear. I really was kind of doing weird experiments on you. I'll tell you why."

She put her arm around his back. Blar twitched because it just kept improving his view of her breasts and how pretty they were. He was beginning to hate corsets. She was gesturing with her other hand as she spoke.

"Tsika and Glycca. They are my only family of any sort and I'm very protective of them. You … are a new game in town and I already see a couple of danger signs. I don't think you're stupid … so you have likely noticed them as well."

"I have noticed some … possible complications. Yeah. Just recently. I was hoping it was just me hallucinating."

Kpau sighed. "But hey. Tsika knows I'm over here and she knows how I tick. I bet she already told you I'm a wild breeze, just a leaf in the wind! Believe me, if Tsika decides you be the one, she would not drop you even if I did pounce on you for some wet sticky cuddling fun. She knows me, how I'm wired. She's not about infantile jealousy shit at all, she's way deeper than that

… much deeper. Her priorities in life are very strongly aligned and not in ways some call normal. But you'll figure that out." Kpau stopped, obviously framing her next words.

"And, by the way ya dork, just to be coarse about it – casual wet sticky frolicking really IS a potential option with me in the right conditions. I'm really just not wired for considering sex any other way. I did say you were scary hot, Papa Bear. I sense it would be a great time with the Blar Umlaut dude. Very very good medicine. But it would have be the utterly right conditions in my book."

She winked with both eyes and curved her shoulders to accentuate her cleavage. Killer move. She continued.

"I have no intention of stealing you from anyone. I have no desire to be latched to anyone. I am just telling you I can be the best kind of drinking buddy. Don't go and catch any stupid smitten or lovey serious bug about me and we will be just fine. You might need me as a safety net some night, so don't forget it. I would kill to protect Tsika, but she can be … very complicated and challenging. You might really need a time out."

Blar had never encountered anyone who thought like Kpau claimed to think. Maybe he was getting to be an old man. He wasn't shocked – oh, scratch that, he was shocked. Damn.

"So! Let me try this summary. You and I are going to have a complicated friendship. Tsika won't disembowel me over it. You want to be my little sister and drinking buddy but there's a possibility we might decide to fuck each other into mush some night … but we are NOT in love and … you're standing with me as long as I'm protecting your family, that being Tsika and Glyc. Is that a fair summary?"

Kpau nodded and rewarded him with a kiss on the cheek and a loud 'mwah' sound. Blar stared in disbelief.

"Okay. My head hurts now. Does everyone's head hurt around you?"

"Probably! I dunno, the guys I try to play with rarely last more than a few days. They usually get stupid lovey serious and I have to send them on their way. Don't want it. I have a massively clear picture of just how … fragile life is. How brief … it can be."

Jesus, that wave of sadness under her happy glitter.

"You, despite being a curmudgeon of a moose, seem to get it, at least sometimes. Enjoy the moment you're in, every moment might be the last? Too many guys, they always get all chains and shackles forever. Meh on them. Now you've appeared and I am hoping you're our best roller coaster ride ever."

Kpau kissed him lightly on the cheek once more and stood up, hugging herself. "Now, real business! I wanna see the rest of this place! I think I am A-Okay with moving in with you. Tsika and Glyc are drooling at the idea I think but we should have a quick girl's meeting anyway just to cover the bases. You told me you had a dungeon. I want to go treasure crawling, Papa Bear. Chicklet needs new shinies!" Blar got a smile as bright as a xenon stage light from the quirky blonde.

~8~ *"Jukebox Hero" - Foreigner*

Kpau and Blar returned to the club together with two cases in tow. Kpau had decided to stick with her current drum kit for the week at least, but she had found a sculpted bass guitar and a transparent acrylic lead guitar she liked. She liked the showy stuff, saying she figured she wasn't good enough on guitars to worry about the sort of nuances Glycerin could pick out.

Blar had groused that the little blonde was going to need her own van at this rate but it was idle grumping. Kpau had been a total ray of sunshine after the bedroom conversation, chattering, stroking his arm, dancing and hopping alongside of him as she talked to him. Blar supposed he had gotten past the little gate guardian's test of fire and was in the temple, so to speak.

Tsika greeted them with an interrogative arched eyebrow and half-smile. "So, большой медведь , did Kpau give you a hard time?" She giggled. "Or did you give her a hard time?!" Blar ignored the terrible pun innuendo and wished he could just grab Tsika and run off for the evening to clear his head of confusion.

"As you can see, Kpau has added to her trove of shinies. She's checked out the condo and her assessment sounded positive – or at least she liked the view. You three should hurry up and huddle for a decision."

Tsika nodded. "I know, Blar. We just need to make sure this is right for us and that we're all on the same page."

Blar had a pretty good theory from Kpau's informative babbling on the way back that Tsika's main hesitation was Glycerin's well being. It wasn't clear the pathologically shy woman could cope with being in close quarters with a man twenty-four hours a day even if he was one of her rock idols.

"I'm not feeling hurt, if you're worried about saying no. It SHOULD be a big deal deciding to share living quarters with people, especially ones you work with. With *Gothic Fire*, we had a place right off the bat that gave everyone private space. Most bands just crash together because they're broke and if there's any rough edges it can get cranky fast."

Blar set the two guitar cases down and took the drink Tsika offered him. He finished it off quickly.

"I've found a couple of alternative apartments a few blocks away from my place. If you decide against, I'll send you over to them with my real estate agent. Either way, I have to rent a truck for your move so it would be nice if you three could work it out today. My designer has holds on two different sets of furniture and that clock is ticking. If you decline in the interests of sanity or whatever, I'd like to at least put you all in a hotel until we find something close that works."

Tsika was giving him a look that seemed bursting with happiness. He wasn't sure whether it was because he was being so careful in considering their needs or some other vibe he hadn't discerned.

"Whatever happens, it looks like the ribbon cutting will happen on Monday now unless the remodel team is superhuman. That might be better anyway if we end up playing an extra long performance Saturday night."

Kpau nodded in agreement, took her prizes and trotted off to find Glycerin. Blar was about to follow when a small hand tugged on his sleeve and a tiny soft plaintive voice stopped him in his tracks.

"Wait a sec, large comforting Bear." Blar looked down at large amber eyes and parted lips. Tsika stretched up with some dainty warm kisses on his mouth.

"Hmmmmm. I've been watching you look at me." She snuggled into his arms. "Yeah, we're busy as fuck and I appreciate your careful stepping around our sensitivities … but I haven't forgotten that morning. We'll find a way to … take up where we left off, you know?"

Tsika nuzzled his chest and then looked up at him with a devilish smile. She nearly snorted she was laughing so hard. Her small body shook from her mirth as she clutched onto him.

"Kpau tested you, didn't she? I can smell her on you!" Blar sputtered and gripped her tighter. Tsika just giggled. "Foolish Bear, I don't own your soul … yet. I just had a feeling Kpau was headed over there to run you through her glittery gauntlet. Apparently, you passed – since you're alive."

Tsika laid her head against Blar's chest. "Look. Despite how some may judge her morals, I assert Kpau is a good girl. I think she would murder an entire city to protect Glycerin and me."

Tsika was briefly silent. Then she quietly whispered, "Hey. Darling Bear. Whatever happens, don't be afraid to BE what Kpau needs when she needs it, okay? She likes to quote about family from that little blue Disney character, that alien Stitch. We're a family. We're broken – but good. I trust her with my precious things."

Tsika hugged him again and excused herself to retrieve the other women. Blar sat himself at the bar, poured a glass of scotch and proceeded to down it in as few gulps as possible. Kpau was right, Tsika was a deep conundrum to him. It seemed like the more dangerously he flirted with Glycerin and Kpau, the better she treated him. Blar finished his drink and got up.

Put that drama away, there is a performance to give tonight and socks to be knocked off. Okay, ladies and gentlemen, time to practice because tonight is show time.

- - - - - -

Hans and his staff were scurrying about, making sure they were ready for the evening. The band was executing final sound checks on the equipment and making sure every item needed for the performance was properly located. Blar's doorman, former roadie Jack, was off-duty and had shown up to play soundboard and light master. He was looking over the playlist and chatting about old times with Blar. Jack thought the lights were so simple he could handle them in his sleep even after all these years.

Blar took a moment to look over the new band he was part of. Glycerin had chosen to wear her plaid boarding school skirt and strapped high heeled boots. Topping that racy motif off, she had selected a fairly modest short sleeve blouse with a frilly bow tie and snugged the blouse up with a waist corset. This was over the objections of Kpau who kept pressing Glycerin to wear as little as possible to display all her glorious skin art.

Tsika quickly put brakes on Kpau's gameplay because Glyc was still having stress attacks over being on stage with Blar. In response, Kpau had run to Blar pouting loudly after she'd been lectured by Tsika about torturing Glycerin right before the performance.

Blar was getting the feeling he had a puppy more than a band mate in Kpau and that he was going to have a fairly complex role in this newly constructed 'family' as Kpau deemed it.

Kpau had glittered up almost as a taunt back at Tsika. She was sporting hot pants, fishnet hose under short stockings, her little boots, and her favorite leopard spotted pink bikini top. "I'd glitter my teeth and put glow mascara on my eyebrows if it weren't such a mess to clean up."

Tsika had dressed in a style she called 'perky goth'. She told Blar it had gotten her in trouble frequently at boarding school. Bare shoulders, lots of bows, lace, short skirt, thigh-high stockings, and bitten neck scarf; a mostly black theme with red highlights. The outfit had Blar's blood on fire in a way that had him worrying profusely once more over just what it was that attracted him to women like Tsika.

Blar had opted for – what he could find in his closet. He called it 'casual college professor'. Kpau called it 'nerdy dork' and gave it an 'F', arguing he should just take his shirt off. Blar promised to work on it. The women threatened to take him shopping if he didn't. Blar was quickly learning that he had hooked up with a band that liked to glam their looks up. Aina would likely be proud of them – and him. He thought about calling his former bandmate after he saw how the live performances went. It had been too long since they had talked.

Blar finished coordinating the engineering with Jack and surveyed the scene. Tsika and Kpau were test running some last minute bass and drum combinations. Glycerin was simply standing on her red 'X' with eyes half closed. Blar wondered if she had mentally crashed again. Should he go over? Would that make it worse, better?

Then he noticed Glycerin's fret hand was sliding up and down the guitar's neck, fingers moving rapidly. Oh. She was finding her happy place. He thought again that she probably never remembered her performances, only the state of bliss during them. Kpau sometimes called her a space alien. Watching Glycerin, it was obvious Kpau was merely describing her, no insult intended.

There was no other word to call the weather. It had gone to crap. The air was full of a snow and rain mix typical for December. However, this was Portland in the Pacific Northwest. People went out and had fun no matter what the conditions.

The crowd was filling the club, rowdy and excited. It was already bigger than Blar expected so early in the evening. Hans had pointedly made the connection in his advertising between the performance and the mystery girl who had musically shredded the streets earlier in the week. That seemed to have been a winning idea.

Blar recognized a few people in the audience, particularly a reporter from the local news rag who handled the music scene reporting. He went over and chatted the man up, giving him some back story about the new band. The reporter tried to hammer Blar for old *Gothic Fire* gossip about him and Aina, but Blar kept steering him back on track with *"It Really IS Rocket Science!"*.

Eventually, Jack signaled with his watch and Blar went back on stage. He signaled for a huddle. Glycerin took a rather long time to sidle up near him. She looked as terrified as the day he had first met her. Blar glanced inquisitively at Tsika who just shrugged and gave him a thumbs up.

"Okay, you three. We're not actually doing any rocket science tonight. Just easy tunes you all know. We'll let the crowd set the pace and react to them. Glycerin?" She jumped and hiccuped. Easy now, pretty girl.

"Little Dancer?" Smile. Shy eye contact. That was better. "Just find your wonderful happy place and stay there. We'll follow your lead. Okay? You are beautiful tonight." She blushed and stammered out a reply with short gasps for air.

"O-o-o-kay. I-I-I-I'm p-p-pretending … pre- … I'm pretending … the way …." She never finished the sentence. She smiled in a slightly demented terror-stricken way that Bar was convinced would get her sedated by an emergency medical team. Blar was in some level of silent panic himself as he watched her.

"That's … just great, Little Dancer. Go to it." She rushed back to her marked spot on the stage.

Blar looked at Tsika and Kpau in serious disbelief. "I am trusting you two little goblins with your goofy fanged grins that your fragile Glycerin can do this, you know."

Tsika and Kpau both nodded gleefully.

Tsika added embellishment. "Believe me, large Bear, once Kpau ticks off the beat, not a problem 'til the curtain call. Then fearless Bear might want to hold one hand of Mouse while I grab the other to be her shields."

Jack stood up, waved his arms to get the crowd's attention as he took the mike and cranked it up.

"Good evening all you night creatures! Thanks for coming, I'm sure you've all heard the street buzz. I won't waste your time … unless of course you haven't gotten your tasties from Hans' fine bar and kitchen crew over there. Then I'll glare at you until you do! This is all-ages time so – you old codgers! Behave over there! And now! For the first time anywhere! Let me present some of the finest noise I've ever heard in Portland! That's because … IT REALLY **IS** ROCKET SCIENCE!"

Jack flicked the lights down, put a spotlight on Kpau as she started her beat, and they were off. Kpau set the pace fast with a wild drum intro and they began with a cover of "*New Kid In School*" by the Donnas. Tsika was at vocals, her voice hard and sexy as she seduced the audience. For someone who wore the frilliest lace, ribbons, and little goth lolita outfits – the dichotomy with her snarling powerful voice was brilliant.

Glycerin initially was fairly static in her stage presence but on the first minor solo she kicked a long leg high in the air and glared at the audience. Blar was so caught by surprise, he lost his place in the music temporarily. The glare was a fabulous "fuck-you-all" look he had never seen out of the shy trembling creature. He experience a sharp sense Glycerin was channeling something from another dimension and it was in charge of her mood. After that, she was all over her part of the stage, twirling, diving, jumping – a combat ballerina with a guitar axe sharpened to eviscerate anything in her path.

Between Kpau, Tsika, and Glycerin – Blar realized he really did need to step up in his looks and stage presence just to keep the foursome balanced looking. Note to self, shop for eccentric glam. Blar jumped out of his comfort zone and started moving as he played backup guitar, trying to interact with Tsika without looking too awkward. He didn't feel like he should intrude on Glyceirn's whirling dervish space until she was a lot more comfortable with him.

The band played a five song set comprised of fast upbeat rock tunes from the last decade. The crowd was impressed if not totally blown away. Blar took the mike.

"Hi … I think a fair number of you recognize me from the pre-show noises I heard. Turns out I actually live here in Portland. Boo! I found these three lovely musicians just recently. You should pay the most attention to them as if I needed to tell you by now. Brief introductions, a quick break, and we'll give you some *Gothic Fire* flashback before refocusing on the modern times. To my right here, we have the little goth elf on bass guitar – Tsika."

Tsika was totally unprepared for being introduced. Blar had forgotten to tell them.

"De'Derp fuck! H'okay, uh, hello peoples!" She plucked a fast bass jazz riff to recover and glared at Blar. That was good for a few chuckles from the audience.

"The very aptly named Kpau on drums, yes, that's her real name." Kpau was ready, she bashed something that Blar realized was a classic Buddy Rich jazz drum riff, one of the greatest drummers of all time who had passed away years before the little fluff was born. He guessed music school was good for something after all.

"And finally, the person no one can take their eyes off of when she moves …

Glycerin on lead guitar, our alien shredder girl." Blar winced, having no idea what to expect.

Glycerin stood stone still for perhaps a second and a half, glaring at the audience with one eye. Her other eye was covered by her now disheveled hair, giving her the appearance of someone released too soon from the asylum. The visible eye darted to stare at Blar. Without moving any part of her body other than her hands, she fired off a sequence of notes faster than Blar had ever imagined could be made on a guitar. Each note was precise, clear, and damped out before the next one.

Blar couldn't help it. He just gaped at her and spoke out loud. "Oh my god. That's … fucking unbelievable. I'm not worthy."

Her glare vanished in a rosy blush and rapid blinking at his praise and the stunned applause from the audience. She bobbed her head bashfully. "I-I-I … 'ello, everyone."

Blar noticed Glycerin focused on Tsika as she spoke and kept her hair covering most of her face. She wasn't actually looking at people in the audience, just the lights, and her band mates on stage. Time to move attention off of her.

"Right! She's very shy – please give her space and she'll delight you with those fingers. Ah, that sounded sketchy! Anyway – short break, folks! We'll be back."

Blar herded them all backstage. He didn't want Glycerin exposed to the crowd.

"Okay … sorry, all. Obviously we have kinks to work out with audience repartee, especially given …." Blar bit his tongue. Praise. "Glycerin, that was the most astonishing little riff I've ever heard! How fast can you play?"

Glycerin was shaking like a leaf at Blar's attention. Tsika edged between them, obviously a practiced move by the little goth. "H'okay, Bear. She can play faster. It is frightening how fast. I video taped her once at high speed and played it back slow-motion. I think Kpau still has it on file. I cannot even pretend to match her ability to damp out note so it doesn't swamp the next note at that speed."

"Okay. I like her expression on stage. Don't lose that, Little Dancer. The glares, the ecstatic smiles – it's top notch. I agree with Tsika. Don't think, pretty girl, just play. You're gorgeous. I am in awe."

Glycerin was shifting shades of red faster than a cuttlefish but Blar could see that heartstopping little smile under her curtain of hair. At this point, she was actively using her hair to cover her face with those long slender fingers, gushing happiness at Blar's words.

Tsika stroked her shoulders and cooed comforting noises to her friend. "See, Glycca? He's not only Blar Umlaut, he is your new friend. One who loves you like we do. You are safe with him. You can relax."

Blar could hear little sniffles as Glycerin nodded. "I ... I ... I just c-can't believe that I'm st-standing here with him and he's s-s-saying what he's bl-bloody saying. Um-um-um, thank you, Blar."

Tsika punched Blar in the ribs. "And hey! Warn us that you are going to make with announcing schtick! But yes, we have been wholly focused on the music and not the stage performance. Is important to make connections with audience. Just glad we did not look like idiots! Maybe circus clowns."

Kpau, who had vanished, re-appeared with drinks for everyone. "Were we shiny?! Nah, I could tell! Man, cannot wait to show them the hard stuff! Drink! Drink! Let's get back out there while I'm jazzed! Woohoo!!"

"Okay, next the three *Gothic Fire* pieces and then we go punk/metal the rest of the night. No rush, Little Dancer, just sip your drink. Hans said he'd keep some food aside for us after the show. It's started off well! No one has left and the place is just getting more and more packed. I'd say we're off to a most excellent start. Party on!"

Blar clinked everyone's bottle with his and they raised them in a toast. Time to go back to work.

~9~ "Nothing But A Good Time" - Poison

Glycerin's mind flickered into one of her shards of consciousness. She thought about opening her eyelids but came to no decision on the matter. Dozing seemed like a nice option – she didn't sense any reason to panic yet.

What day was it? Um, Sunday? Sunday ... something about Sunday. She felt very warm and comfortable all over. Comfy warm pillow ... body pillow? Our body pillow is stored down in Los Angeles with our other things. Had Kpau crawled over in the night again? She does that. Sometimes we wakes up with Kpau curled up against us. Poor thing. Often crying in her sleep. Some kind of night terrors she won't talks to us about, though we knows it's about that last moment with her family. If we sing softly to her, the poor darling eventually settles back down and snuggles up.

Glycerin burrowed against the warmth and draped her arm over it.

So warm! Nice snuggle! Wait ... wait ... too much warm. Where are Kpau's boobs?

Glycerin's eyes flashed open. She was laying on Blar. She had one leg thrown over him and her arm flung across his chest. Her chin lay on his collarbone. Her nose was mere inches from his face. The broad shouldered man was snoring quietly. Her brain locked up. All she could muster was a rapid fire string of tiny wheezes.

What happened? Where? What is going on?

She was too terrified to move at first. Eventually, Glycerin slowly raised her head. She spotted Tsika's flowing explosion of hair across on Blar's other arm. Her little friend's body was curled up with ... blonde hair ... there's Kpau. Glycerin blinked and peered around her. The four of them were upstairs laying together on the mattresses in the room the girls bunked in. Glycerin's mind was grinding bare metal as she scrambled to recall events.

What do we do? What do we do? Stop gasping! Breathe. What happened?

She tried to remember the previous night, her thoughts flickering through her mirror maze of memories.

The performance ... oh, bloody hell! Saturday night, the last performance. So many people! Tsika fooled me! She made my drinks and lied about how strong they were. Sigh. We knows why Tsika does that ... so we can handles the attention. She could have asked us though. So many people were there! There were even people listening as they stood outside in the snow. Listening and dancing. They ... liked my music ... that makes us happy. Someone likes our sounds we makes.

B-B-B-B-But why? Why am I on B-Blar? Oh ... my ... god, I'm sleeping WITH ... my precious Blar! Him. On him. My Blar. I'm ... I'm ... I'm going to be bloody sick! Breathe. Long breath! It is so nice and ... so warm laying against him. Feels safe ... so safe.

Glyc watched Blar breathe. Her breath slowed and eventually paced his. She had become conscious over the last few days that matching her breath with his soothed her. She lay her head back down on his collarbone and watched his face, her eyes alert for the slightest move. Small tears ran down her face.

Don't wake up. Please don't wake up. I want to just lay here like this. For a little bit.

Why is this so nice and so scary at the same time? Augh! He has his arm around me! It's moving! Oh my god, his hand was on my bum! Oh, now it's ... sliding up my back. He's hugging me in his sleep!

She sniffled quietly and snuggled, her brain flipping between terror and joy.

What do I do when he wakes up? What? What?

Then she noticed his breathing pattern had changed. She looked up at his face. Blar was looking down at her. Such a kind face. Panic.

"You are okay, Glycerin. You can jump away if you need to. You fell asleep against me while we were all sitting together chatting. The two goblins over there insisted I not move. You're safe."

Glycerin's eyes changed from wide-eyed horror to a more teary-eyed look. She sniffled.

"I ... I ... HATE! I hate ... be-being ... a-a-afraid. C-c-can w-w-we just l-l-l-lay here ... a m-m-minute?" She trembled as she hammered out her syllables. Blar rubbed her trembling back gently with the hand that had recently been caressing her bum. He spoke softly. Glycerin wasn't sure if he was trying not to scare her or perhaps not wake the others. It was nice to be touched by him like this. Why was this different?

"I think Tsika has my other hand ... or Kpau does ... not sure ... they're so tangled up over there. We came up here last night with Jack, Hans, and the staff. Every one drank a lot. It was a good time. I hope everyone got home okay. I heard that you sang for some of the staff while I was downstairs. They said you had a lovely voice. I hope I get to hear it some time."

I ... I should just die. Yes. Die right now. I sang? For people? They heard me sing a song? Was it me? Or was it my other ...? Are you awake, love? Oh ... Blar's still bloody well talking to me.

"Do you know what today is, Little Dancer?"

Glycerin was consciously matching her breath with his. She forced herself to keep eye contact.

"S-S-Sunday? Something ... a-about ... Sunday."

Blar chuckled. She thought it felt nice against him when he laughed. Then she remembered.

"Moving Day!" She seized up, gripping his shirt like a vise. Blar grimaced.

O god, I pulled some of his chest hair!

She smoothed out his shirt. "S-S-S-Sor-- ... sorry! Y-Yes. We d-decided to move in with y-y-you!"

Blar stroked the back of her head. "I'm going to wake the others up. Are you okay?" Glycerin mustered the tiny smile of the doomed for him. She could see Blar untangling his hand from the other two. He started rubbing Tsika's back and stroking her head with his fingers.

He is so nice to my pretty doll! I ... I do loves laying like this. But my little doll, Tsika ... dearest Tsika, lucky Tsika ... he's going to be so good for her. She deserves that after all I've put her through.

Tsika growled and rolled over onto Blar's right side, her bright eyes snapping open. She came face-to-face with Glycerin, laughing and squeezing Glycerin's shoulder.

"Oh my! Seductive Glycca! What a pirate! He doesn't stand a chance against you!" Tsika's eyes glittered as she giggled.

Glycerin was appalled and flustered. "No! No, Tsika, that wasn't it!! My little doll, I w-was asleep! I thought it was Kpau!"

Kpau's head popped up out of Tsika's pile of hair. "You thought what?! That Papa Bear was me? I am way insulted! My boobs are cuddly! Way more curvy cuddly than his! He's just huge and lumpy! I'm not a big lump! Not much bigger than Short Round here!"

Glycerin started to feel panicky at Kpau and Tsika's teasing feedback. She knew they weren't being mean but she started sniffling. Then she felt Blar stroking her hair and rocking her. Her breathing slowed again and she stopped sniffling. Glycerin could see Tsika was watching Blar calm her. Her pretty doll kissed Blar lightly on the cheek and sat up to start managing her hair.

I want to sit up … but I'd … I'd have to … let go. I love being rocked by him!

Blar solved her dilemma for her. He sat up and pulled Glycerin along with him. He simply manhandled her as if she was a rag doll. When he was done, the tall brunette was cuddled up next to him with his arm over her shoulders.

How easily he lifted me! It's … it's like I'm not a lumbering giant at all!

Kpau crawled over and joined the pile. "Hey! Hey! Feeling left out here!" She curled up next to Glycerin and threw an arm around her slender waist. Kpau gently brushed Glycerin's hair out of the lanky girl's eyes. "Glyc! We're moving today! No more mattresses on the floor! Locking doors! There's a view! I've seen it!"

Blar nodded. "Yeah, it's true. I was positive Felicia wouldn't finish 'til tomorrow but apparently she worked all evening yesterday once you guys decided to move in. So, Little Dancer, we can move the goblins and you over this afternoon."

Tsika pulled away from the group hug and crossed her legs. She continued corralling her lovely mass of hair into its trademark twin tails. She lay her Russian accent on thick. "If no one minds, this goblin is going to skip shower 'til we reach new lair. I absolutely refuse to step into that shower down the hall one more time, darlings."

Glycerin agreed, nodding her head as firmly as Kpau was. They loved Hans for his charity but they had all quickly come to hate that poor excuse for a shower.

Blar wrinkled his nose. "Well, at least no one smells like barf."

Glycerin flinched, recalling her first encounter with Blar. Blar noticed and demurred. "That wasn't meant to poke at you, Glyc, but we all do smell like a rancid bar and several kinds of smoke."

Kpau and Tsika got up and assisted each other in adjusting their clothing back to presentable form. They headed downstairs chattering about the previous evening's antics. Glycerin was still firmly pressed against Blar's chest with his arm around her. Her eyes were down and her hands were pressed against Blar's chest. She could feel his heart beating under her fingertips. So warm and safe it felt. She had no memory of such a feeling.

We don't want to stop this moment. Is that ... good? ... bad? Does he knows what we're thinking?

Blar stroked her cheek and sat with her quietly for a few minutes. He kissed her forehead before gently untangling from her. She sighed and took Blar's offered hand to help her up. For a split second, she looked up at Blar and flashed a small smile. She noticed it had a palpable effect on him. His expression was very kind.

No, don't ... don't think. Don't wish! Just get my stuff ready. Eat first. Yes, Tsika is probably already starting breakfast. I should help.

Glycerin headed to the door and then looked back to see Blar standing and looking around at the room. "I-I-Is s-something w-wrong, Blar?"

Blar shook his head in response. "No, I'm just going to stack these mattresses to get them out of the way. I was just thinking back to days when my old group bunked up in places like this. Those memories are much better stories for later than when you're living in them. I'll be down in a second."

Glyc nodded and trotted down the stairs, hugging herself.

I … I … had a real normal conversation with him! About something besides music! Maybe … maybe I'm getting better!

She rounded the corner onto the stage and screeched to a halt. Several men were in the club talking to Hans. Glycerin nearly fell backwards to hide behind the corner. She quietly beat her forehead on the wall.

Why? Why is it okay to be watched by guys when I'm on stage or when Tsika holds my hand, but they terrify us when we're alone? Yes, we knows 'why' but it doesn't make any senses to us. Why can I talks to Blar? Is it … is it really just okay just because it's Blar? Yes, I know you don't know! No, dear. Not mad at you. I'm lost, too.

Glycerin looked up from her hiding place to see Kpau standing next to her with a concerned look.

"Ah! I figured as much, ya big Mouse. It is a little spooky out there. Hold my hand, Glyc. We'll scamper to the kitchen like demented school girls." Glycerin blushed but complied and off they went.

My shiny little dove Kpau. She teases but she is so good to us when it is important.

- - - - - -

Breakfast in the kitchen was drawing to a close, Glycerin was still picking at her food as she watched the others. Kpau had a mouthful of cinnamon roll while she chattered to Glycerin about the previous night. Blar, Tsika, and Hans were going over the club's performance receipts and tips. They were figuring up the band's share.

Glycerin wondered if the money actually meant anything to Blar. He must be fabulously wealthy, she thought. But he seemed to be quite involved, making sure that the band, the staff, and Hans were coming out of the accounting fair and square. She sporked up her last bit of ham and egg scramble and thoughtfully chewed, retreating into self-absorbed reflection.

She, Tsika, and Kpau had pooled all the money they could gather to come up to Portland. No one bought anything without checking with the others. She wondered if that would change. It would be nice not to have to dive for every coin she saw on the street.

Oh, bloody dog's breakfast, Kpau is waving her hands in front of our face.

"Glyyyyyyycca! Come on, lets go pack while they wrestle over that last nickel." Glycerin nodded and followed Kpau, holding her hand – just in case. They made their way up to the room and began packing the equipment first. The band had simply strewn everything about the night before. A half-hour later, Tsika and Blar appeared and began assisting with the packing. Blar made a call on his cell to ensure the truck would be on time.

"The truck should be here by lunch time. After we load it, we'll head straight over to the –," Blar was interrupted by Kpau.

"The Rocket Science Labs! I named it! I named it!," Kpau bounced and squealed. Glycerin couldn't help herself and snorted a giggle. That earned her a big smile from Blar.

Gah! Face blushing! So red now. Pack. Pack faster.

- - - - - -

Finally, all their belongings were boxed up. The truck had arrived and everyone grabbed boxes to load up. Tsika took point at guarding the truck. Glycerin carried some boxes but in most cases it was her working with Blar to maneuver bulky items down to the truck. She and Blar were roughly the same height so it was just easier. Glycerin didn't exactly push the opportunity away to work closely with him.

The two of them moved aside with the trunk they were carrying to let Kpau slip by with her load. Glycerin always marveled at Kpau's carrying capacity.

She'd have one speaker under each arm and more stuff wrapped over her neck humming a tune as if it were all weightless.

Tsika was chatting with Hans by the truck, assuring him that they'd play his club again after they came back from their working retreat that Blar had planned. Glycerin helped Blar in guiding the big clothing box into the truck as he did the heavy lifting. The work let her brush against Blar many times without him noticing. It wasn't just exciting to Glycerin, it really was helping her get used to having him near.

The tall Hong Kong Brit was pleased the sun had come out. She had started thinking the darkness of winter was going to seep into the deepest parts of her brain. Only Kpau seemed unaffected by the change from Los Angeles sunshine to the Pacific Northwest's damp darkness.

Hans was poking mild fun at Blar in the truck. "So, Mr. Blar, what mysterious place are you taking these young women to? Sounds sketchy and suspicious!" He grinned at Blar.

Blar smirked back at him. "It's a retreat resort down at Big Sur in California that my old band used to hide out at. Very zen, caters to musicians. The band would reboot our brains there, write, play, practice. It has recording studios among other diversions. Mostly it's isolated and the staff keeps the outside world out. This band of women needs original music and that's the best place I know to create it."

Hans nodded, "Sounds like good project for band! I'm going to be looking out for this week's Willamette Weekly to see how they reviewed the performances. Fingers crossed, yah – but the people seemed to like what you did."

Blar shrugged, "We gave them what they wanted. Some *Gothic Fire* oldies, some rocking cover tunes, and very very pretty girls."

Glycerin turned bright red as Blar winked at her, then she got even more embarrassed at her embarrassment.

Gods, can I never stop being a traffic light? Tsika just snorted a giggle! Bloody hell! She saw me blush!

Tsika patted out her skirt and cleared her throat. "Glyc, you were marvelous! The crowd loved you! But, must suggest fashion note, darling Mouse. You may want to wear longer skirts or pants if you're going to be flashing the audience when you jump and twirl. At least wear black panties, darling."

Glycerin couldn't stop herself. She uttered a piercing little dolphin shriek and nearly dropped her end of the box she and Blar were maneuvering.

"Hey, Glyc! Don't abandon me here!" Blar winced as the load shifted his way. Glycerin stammered apologetically but as soon they set the box down, she leaped out of the truck and ran back inside. She could hear Tsika trying to apologize to her. She knew Tsika meant well. It was just so embarrassing to talk about stuff like that in front of other people. She nearly ran into Kpau, who was carrying a stack of boxes in her arms so high the little blonde couldn't see in front of her.

"Hey! Watch out, Glyc! It's okay, I got it under control! There's one more stack and then we're done, kay?"

Glycerin helped straighten Kpau's load anyway. "O … okay!" Glycerin trotted upstairs and checked the bathroom one last time for any remaining items.

I am NOT going to miss that shower, eww. There's the stack … well, it is only two boxes, I can handle that!

She lifted them and started staggering back downstairs as she wondered what chunks of lead Kpau had stored in them. She took one last look at the room they had started their Portland adventure out in. What had Blar said? Better memories for later than actually living in them now? She had no disagreement with that notion.

- - - - - -

Tsika said she wanted to walk over to the condo since it was sunny, so the four of them set out after bidding adieu to Hans. Within half a block, Glycerin was aware that Blar had maneuvered her in between Tsika and him with Kpau leading the way in front of her.

He's like my darling Tsika! Always thinking about my bubble of feeling safe. All of them are so nice to watch out for me. They're so nice. We so don't deserve it. We shouldn't even exist. Should have finished out long ago.

Blar leaned over and whispered in Glycerin's ear, causing her to shiver. "I don't think Tsika realizes that we're going to be a bit of a spectacle in the daylight since we're all still dressed in our glammed up stage clothes."

Tsika was distracted by the display window of a clothing store that specialized in women's black formal wear. Kpau was up in front enjoying the pedestrians gawking at them as she danced and skipped.

Glycerin blushed. "S-S-She's used to it … I think … I th-think she … likes … d-disturbing … them. And! And … Kpau loves m-making a s-scene in a very different way." Long breath. Glycerin cheered to herself. Another whole sentence! Two sentences!

One young hipster walking in the other direction took a look at the women, at Blar, then back at the women and whistled, "Dude! You should share!"

Glycerin could feel her face turn crimson. She became aware she had grabbed Blar's hand when the stranger had spoken. Her idol interlocked his fingers with hers. That made her briefly happy but then she shot a worried look at Tsika, only to find Tsika smiling at her with big eyes and raised eyebrows. Tsika took Glycerin's other hand in hers and squeezed it.

Kpau glanced back at the trio and made a goofy face as she scanned all the linked hands. "Good grief! I feel like we should be singing *'Follow the Yellow Brick Road!'* but the question is … am I Dorothy or am I Toto? Hmmm." She twirled around, barked and panted, and started barking the old movie song in a cartoon dog voice. This drew even more attention from pedestrians.

The walking trip seemed like eons to Glycerin with Kpau's antics drawing stares and laughter, but they finally neared the condo. The building was much taller than she thought as she looked up at it. "H-how … What f-floor are we on?"

Blar pointed with his free hand, "Top floor, that corner. Fifteen floors up. Supposedly the building is ready for the Big One ... hope we don't have to test that claim any time soon." Glycerin knew he didn't mean to scare her but she had no luck driving the idea of being in an earthquake while fifteen stories in the air out of her head.

They saw Jack at the door waving at them. He wasn't even pretending to be professional. "Hello, you pretty looney toons … and also Blar! Your truck is at the shipping entrance and the freight elevator is open for use. I think it's the first time it has been used in months so it might squeak a bit. Just sayin'!"

Kpau clawed at the air in mock aggravation. "Argh, no rest for the wicked! Jack! Meet Glycerin! She's shy so give her space to get used to you! Really shy! Okay, introductions done! Lead the way, sir!" Jack bowed with a grand flourish to the young ladies and led them in.

- - - - - -

With the five of them, it didn't take long to empty the truck. Everyone was sprawled about in the living room but it was hard for Glycerin to see anyone else through all the boxes. Jack laughed as he exited, "I assume you all are in there somewhere. Have fun unpacking! Just leave the empty boxes folded up by the freight elevator. Give me a ring if you need anything. Good to meet you, Glycerin! Wherever you are in this mess."

Glycerin had taken refuge on a large chair near the window and was admiring her new view of the city. She could see the river that ran through downtown. Off in the distance loomed Mt. Hood, the iconic dormant volcano of the region. Kpau had told her there were ski resorts on it. Glycerin had never been skiing. She thought skiing might be scary but people always looked so happy doing it. She could just barely make out the blown remains of another volcano, Mount St. Helens off to the north, over in Washington State. She remembered reading before they had moved here that it had explosively erupted back in the nineteen eighties.

Her reverie was disturbed by a new sound. Glycerin's ears perked up. She could hear her precious Tsika snoring from wherever the little sprite had collapsed in their new home.

Kpau got up and flexed. "You all sit tight! I'm going to get the music equipment over to the practice room. That'll make it easier for us to arrange our mundane stuff." Blar started to get up and Kpau pushed him back down. "Sit, old Bear! You're going to throw your back out! Your lifting technique is terrible!"

Glycerin grinned, quietly watching the little blonde head move back and forth among the boxes, making them slowly disappear. So much energy.

Blar did get up and help Kpau with the large amplifiers. By then, Glycerin could see Tsika. The diminutive doll had passed out face down on a big bean bag. Glycerin got up and went over to her, laying down next to her precious friend. She stroked Tsika's hair as the small creature lay inert.

My pretty Tsika … always there for me.

The next thing Glycerin knew, Blar was gently shaking both her and Tsika. "Hey, you two. Kpau and I have moved all the boxes. I'm not going through your unmentionables, so you two need to start ripping your boxes open on your own."

Glycerin jerked up to a sitting position. "O god, … I-I-I … sorry! Oh, no, we'll … no. We'll do it!"

Tsika rubbed her eyes. "S'okay, Glyc. Gods, I didn't think I was so tired."

Kpau came dancing into the room and jumped up on Blar, hanging on his neck. He automatically scooped her into his arms just to save his spine. "Gah! Chicklet, I thought you were worried about my back!"

"Papa Bear, I'm hunnnnngry!" She kicked her feet, smiled and gave him her biggest blinking wink.

"You … you are a demon puppy, you know that?" Blar tossed Kpau onto the other bean bag, eliciting a happy squeal out of her as she flew. "Okay, what do people want? Thai, Japanese, Pizza, Korean, Indian …?"

The vote went for pizza. Glycerin thought Blar's expression was so funny.

"Argh! Right. Okay. Fine. Just tonight! We aren't doing pizza every night. Killing that idea right now, I'll do pizza tonight. I'll order if you tell me what you like but I'm going to strongly recommend we all take showers now?

Please?" Blar wrinkled his nose.

The girls circled for rock-paper-scissors. Glycerin won first dibs on the shower. She was always suspicious the other two rigged the game in her favor but didn't care this time. She retrieved her bag of essentials out of her suitcase and headed in to a new experience, her first shower in their new home.

Oh heavenly gods! A door that closes! And locks!

She stripped down as she examined her new bathroom. It was wonderful. No cracks in the wall, no holes in the floor. Two sinks. A mirror. There were two shower heads, one up at her height. She got in the shower and adjusted the water flow.

Omigod! Pressure! Real water pressure!!

She put her mouth in the water spray and gargled, then shook her head like a dog as she reveled in the intensity of the spray. She rotated with her arms up. She wondered why the silly hateful books that sent people like her to death didn't list this sort of thing as a mortal sin.

She reached for her lavender-scented liquid soap and lathered with it. She sang softly, she was so delighted. It was amazing what little things became so important in life sometimes.

~10~ "Skating Away (on the thin ice of a new day)" – *Jethro Tull*

Glycerin finished her last rinse of her hair and reached out – to an empty towel rack. She stuck her head out of the shower. Her eyes widened. Definitely no towel anywhere. She got out and checked drawers as she dripped. Nothing but toilet paper and cotton balls. Neither was a serious option for drying.

"Tsika?! Hello? Can you b-bring me a towel?" No answer. "Kpau?" No answer. Were the walls that soundproof? She called a few more times and muttered in frustration. Finally, she tried to shake herself off in the shower like a dog, then went to the door. Opening it slightly, she called out. "Kpau? … Tsika?" The voice she got back stopped her cold.

"Um, Little Dancer? Just me here. They went down for the pizza. What do you need?" Glycerin slammed the door shut. Fear. Panic. Nausea. Then she got angry at herself. Anger won.

It's … it is just Blar! He's … he's nice. We're safe with him. He'll help us.

She forced the door open and gritted her teeth. "B-B-Blar? I … I …," a small shriek got loose, "… I don't have any bloody towels! I need one for my h-h-hair and one for my … for my … for the r-rest of m-me!" She knew her face was beet red. She could hear him growl at himself.

"My fault, Glyc! Let me grab a set and I'll hand them to you, okay? Just don't slip. Or wait. Wait. Better idea! Get back in the shower, the glass is opaque. I'll put the towels on the counter and scamper back out. How's that?"

"I … I … okay, that … that will work. Th-Thank you, Blar." Her face felt fiery. Glycerin left the door open and got back in the shower. Blar was right, all she could see were vague outlines through the glass.

"Okay, C-c-c-come in!"

She turned and pressed her face against the wall of the shower. Then she got mad at herself again. Glycerin turned and forced herself to reach for the shower glass panel, cracking it open and dragging herself to lean over to peek out. Blar walked in with a large stack of towels. He placed them on the counter. He looked up at the mirror and noticed Glycerin's face peering out of the shower. She flinched but stayed, feeling her face flushing. Breathe. Regular breaths. Breathe.

"Thanks for trusting me, Glyc. You're very brave. I'll leave now and close the door, okay?"

Glycerin smiled at him. She knew it was her weird half-insane demented smile that scared people, but he only smiled back. She watched him leave and close the door.

Thank you, Blar.

- - - - - -

After drying, Glycerin pulled on her brief flannel shorts and wiggled into her over-sized tee shirt she liked to sleep in. She stepped out into the large bedroom. The first thing she realized was that no one had decided who would sleep where. She considered the three beds and decided to be bold. Make her own decision. Glycerin threw her stuff on the bed near the window farthest from the door.

Mine!

She wondered if Tsika and Kpau had returned. Without pausing to think, she sauntered out into the hallway and ran right into Blar. He had just come out of his own bedroom. Blar had on gym shorts and a tank top. They were both barefoot. They both still had wet hair. Inches from him, nose to nose. She stared into his eyes. He looked back. Neither moved.

Blar broke the silence. "Obviously, this is going to take a lot of getting used to. I've lived by myself here for quite a long time. I need to remember not to wander around under-dressed. I'm okay if you're okay. Are you okay?"

Glycerin was very proud of herself, she hadn't died on the spot. Her face was on fire. She was acutely aware she had no bra on and her night shirt was tight enough that it was obvious. Her shorts felt really short. Extremely short. Her legs felt so naked. He was so close. So big. Such broad shoulders.

"Yes. I can bloody do th-this. I'm splendid, Blar" Not too many shrieks that time.

She blinked, giving him another version of the demented goofy grin of terror that sometimes got her medicated.

"Nice tee shirt. I like the logo. *Gothic Fire!* I think I've heard of them!" Blar smiled at her.

Glycerin stopped herself from flinging her arms across her chest in terror.

He's … the man is trying to bloody joke with me! Treating me as if I were normal! That's so nice!

She took a couple of long deep breaths – then she realized that she was causing Blar to fail at something he was desperately and chivalrously trying to avoid – staring at her breasts. The t-shirt tightened hypnotically around them with each breath. Now. Now is a good time to just die.

Blar simply headed for the kitchen, "Want a drink? Non-alcoholic, promise." She meekly followed, nodding silently. She propped her derriere against the counter and watched him pour her a cola with ice and squirt a bit of cherry syrup in it. He plopped a maraschino cherry in the glass and presented it to her.

Glycerin couldn't help smiling at his effort. She dropped her eyes, automatically fluttering her lashes.

"T-t-t-thank you, Blar Umla-laut."

Blar leaned on the counter next to her and took a measured breath. "Damn it, Glyc. You are really pretty, especially when you smile like that. You're going to kill me."

Alarm. "Oh ... no, no you … no. I ... I should ... put more … on?" She looked at Blar with pained eyes."Tsika."

Blar got reflective. "Don't worry, Little Dancer. I'm just going to have to get used to you three pretty flowers floating around me. But that doesn't mean I can't appreciate my scenery." He smiled gently. Her brain was melting now.

He … He thinks we're pretty! Big, tall, gawky, clumsy, mousey, broken, crazy – very crazy, he thinks is pretty!

She heard the front door click and open. "Hey you two! We're back! The hunt was a success, though the pizza guy was not a prize. Alright! Wheeeee! Shower's open!"

Kpau bounced in with two pizzas, Tsika followed close behind her with two more.

Blar moved to take the pizzas from each of them. "You two hit the showers. Tsika, there's towels in the master bath. Use my shower so we can eat faster."

"Shower! Shower!" Kpau lit off into their new bedroom like a rocket.

Tsika lingered. She looked at Blar, looked Glycerin up and down from eyes to toes, silently appraising Glycerin's post-shower appearance. A devilishly impish grin and arched eyebrow appeared.

"You two darlings don't start without me, okay?" Tsika smiled cryptically and padded away in such a slinky manner that Glycerin had no doubt the little hip swish was frying Blar's head. Glyc couldn't help smiling, Tsika was really good at that. Glycerin loved to watch her gorgeous doll walk.

"She's so pretty, isn't she, Blar?" She watched Blar break out of his trance.

"Yeah, little Glyc, that she is. But … all three of you do that to me. I need to stay focused on what we're trying to do."

Glycerin sipped her drink, "I think ... I ... I think we all know we sh-should do that." She stared into her drink, not daring to make eye contact while she glowed in the notion she was standing next to one of her music idols and he had just made her a drink!

- - - - - -

The pizzas met their doom, ripped to pieces by ravenous mouths. The band was sprawled out around the living room comfortably miserable after over-eating. Blar was queuing up some of his favorite new age and jazz music to pass out to. Kpau was draped on a bean bag, stretching in her flannel pajamas. Blar was amused, they were covered in little images of the Disney character Stitch. How appropriate for her.

Tsika. Oh god, Tsika. Damn her, did that woman REALLY wear that to sleep in? It was a frilly black teddy lingerie with black spider lace and white bow trimming. Her trim pale white legs were curled up under her as she sat. Her curly black hair was unbound in a big spray around her face. Calendar pinup Princess of Darkness. Amazing. She was holding a drink to her lips and her big amber eyes were watching Glycerin nod off on the other bean bag next to Kpau.

Kpau yawned. "This ... is SOOOOOO much better. Now I don't have to sleep with one eye open for sneaky night thugs. Blar looks like a night thug but he probably couldn't sneak to save his life!"

Blar threw a pillow at Kpau, scoring a face hit. "I suppose we can all sleep in tomorrow. I have some calls to make in the afternoon to some industry people and then confirm our travel plans. There's some favors I want to pull but I need to start the preliminaries. When we come back, we're going to need to have demo recordings and some video to show fat thugs with cigars."

"Fuck ... it's snowing again!" Tsika growled at the window. "Big Sur isn't exactly warm but it's gotta be warmer than this arctic wasteland."

Kpau stared at the ceiling as she sank into the bean bag pillow, "I foresee ... I foresee us moving back south after we hit it big just so Tsika will stop whining and crabbing." Tsika rewarded Kpau with another pillow in the face.

Blar scratched his mustache. "Tsika, are you actually from Russia? Isn't this weather your natural habitat?"

Tsika shook her head, "No, Blar darling. My parents were international NGO workers. I was actually raised in Los Angeles. But they sent me to private school and I was surrounded by other Russian kids so we kept a lot of our accent and language. We went back to Russia once when I was six to meet my grandma for Christmas. I hated it. Never got above zero!"

Blar nodded. Ah, a little more of her story emerges. He needed to ask – he braced himself. "Do any of you have any living family?"

Kpau had been juggling the two pillows she'd been 'awarded' in the air. She stopped. "Not me. Both my parents were only children. Gramps died a few years ago right after I got into college." The pillow juggling didn't resume. Kpau just stared at the ceiling. Blar grimaced.

Tsika finished off her drink. "I have a cousin just outside of Moscow, but we haven't spoken since Grandma died." She stared out the window at the snow.

Good job, Blar. Way to kill the evening.

"Well, both my parents are dead. Dad died about four years ago and my mom died last year. I have a brother somewhere on the planet but he's in the Foreign Service. We spoke for a few minutes at Mom's funeral but nothing since then, just not much in common. Well, sorry, young ladies for killing the mood. You three seem to have evolved a thing here that works beautifully for companionship and it is very nice to watch."

Kpau jumped up and planted herself in Blar's lap, curling up like a Siamese cat. "You! You're part of that thing now, right? For the long haul? You're gonna be there?" She looked fiercely in his eyes. Gods, she was cuddly. Stupid brain. "Yes, Chicklet. I'm in. I'm not sure what you mean by the long haul as I can't predict past next week but I'm way in. I've already emptied one of my retirement accounts just getting this started."

The color drained out of Kpau's face. "I'm ... I'm sorry! I ... I thought ... guess I just thought ... you had millions or something!" Blar stroked her back and she burrowed her head under his chin.

"I'm not ... poor, but it is finite. We just need to produce, to make this work. I calculate we need to make positive cash flow within about 18 months barring any disasters or I'm broke. Earlier is better."

He could feel her relax a bit. "Oh! Well! Surely we'll at least be breaking even by then."

Money did not appear to be her strong suite, Blar surmised. Kpau rolled over and looked at Glycerin's inert body. "We should probably put ourselves to bed." She hopped up and started patting Glycerin's arm to wake her.

"Come on, sleepyhead! Go sleep in your new bed. We gotta finish unpacking tomorrow." Glycerin yawned and stretched. Blar was – well, he couldn't take his eyes off that. Good god, those long legs. That slender frame, those arms and fingers. And damn that shirt for being tight around her breasts. Glyc was stretching from head to toe until she saw Blar was looking at her. Her reaction was golden. She resembled one of those ferns that curl up into a tight ball when touched. Priceless comedy though he felt bad for her. She let Kpau lead her down the hall as she mumbled her good nights.

That left Tsika and Blar in the room. Blar admired the view but – so tired. "Want me to come over there, little Princess? That outfit is killer though I can't believe you actually sleep in it."

Tsika giggled wryly as she finished her drink. "Will admit truth, darling Bear. It's actually the top part of my 'spider mode' outfit. I need to figure out where my house robe is packed. Normally, a Princess of Darkness sleeps naked!" She looked at him with those big piercing eyes. Clearly wanted to see what he would do or say.

"You're an evil pixie. But Kpau is right, I tried really hard to throw my back out today. I'm toast. Off to medicate and sleep." He got up and bent over to kiss her. She reached up and put her arms around his neck to submit, rubbing his cheek with her nose and fondling his ear with her finger. He could feel her pert little breasts brushing against him.

"Good night, large Bear. Watch out for goblins." Blar headed to his new smaller bedroom and just flopped on his new bed.

Hmmm, smaller mattress now.

Blar flipped the light switch, leaving the room only illuminated by the dim blue light of his alarm clock. He faded out quickly.

- - - - - -

Blar opened his eyes. Still dark. He heard some movement. Oh yeah, other people live with me now. It's probably a drink of water they are after or something. He glanced at the clock. 1:17 AM. Painful. He rolled over.

There was something small and warm curling up against his back. It had glorious long curly hair and cold toes. And ... what was she wearing? Oh, a fuzzy house robe. She must have found it. He turned over and looked into Tsika's face, dimly illuminated by the blue clock light. She spoke in a very soft voice.

"I thought ... did I scare you?" Blar shook his head as he put his arms around her. She snuggled up against him.

"I ... I ... I keep promising to ... be a naughty little girl for the big bear. Just thought ... maybe ... tonight. " Blar stroked her neck and back. He kissed her nose.

"You sure you know me well enough yet, pretty pixie? You don't have to rush it." He kissed her cheek. She loosened her robe and pressed her body against him. No question that she had nothing under that house robe; she was a small loosely wrapped present with a fantastic prize inside. Delicate bones and so small. Soft breasts.

"It's nice just ... just laying here." Tsika whispered. She relaxed and put her face against his neck and her hands on his chest. They lay quietly as he just kept stroking her back and she nuzzled his chest and neck. Finally he slipped a hand further down to her delightful small butt and –

That's when Blar heard it. A tiny high pitched snore. Yup, no mistaking that. He rolled his eyes and resigned himself to his doom. "Could have seen that coming a mile off. We're all exhausted."

Oh well, this was nice anyway. Blar glanced at his alarm clock to ensure it was set. He'd just carry her back to her bed before dawn. Hopefully, the other two wouldn't suspect a thing and he'd save her some likely embarrassment. He had no doubt Kpau would have a field day ribbing Tsika if she knew. Blar made himself comfortable with the little candy mint in his arms and slowly passed out.

Blar thought life had certainly turned upside down in a good way if it was going to contain moments like this from now on.

~11~ "No Rain" – Blind Melon

It was still pitch dark when Blar thumped his insistent alarm clock into a coma. Six o'clock. December in Oregon meant no sunrise until almost eight o'clock. Blar murkily realized the time of year no longer mattered. His bedroom was now what used to be his guest room – no windows. Blar made a mental note to get one of those clocks that lit up the room slowly like a sunrise, otherwise he was doomed to miss appointments.

He rolled over and found something soft, minty, and small in bed with him. It was topped with cascades of thick curly hair.

Oh! There is one small task to take care of. This is really nice to wake up to, though.

Blar slipped his arms around Tsika and held her close to him. He listened to her soft regular breathing for a moment. He could feel her little heart beating. Blar really liked the smell of the mint soap Tsika used mixed with her natural scent. It was a shame he couldn't keep her there all morning. Bowing to the inevitable, Blar gathered the little woman up in his arms to sneak her back to her bed.

"Mmmmm, beg burr, mwanna steh." She really wasn't awake at all. Blar thanked the gods that his doors didn't squeak and slipped into the newly designated women's bedroom. He tucked Tsika into her bed in the darkness while listening to a mild snore coming from Glycerin's direction near the window. Blar slipped out, closing the door behind him. Mission accomplished.

Blar showered and dressed in his workout clothing, then tiptoed into the kitchen. He started coffee and made a bowl of warm cereal. Blar had long ago established a regular appointment every morning with the equipment upstairs in the building's gym facility. He slipped out of the front door and took the stairs up to the roof level.

The gym had a nice large plate glass view to the east. Outside that was a rooftop patio and a small outdoor pool where small events and parties could be held. This time of year that area was closed for the winter. On clear days,

Blar could work out in the gym and watch the sun rise over Mt. Hood from there. This time of the year, that kind of visibility was fairly unlikely and it was far too early to know about the weather for the day yet.

He stopped to listen as he entered the weight room. Sounds of clanks and sharp breaths made it clear the room was occupied. This was highly unusual. Blar was always the only one up here at this time of the morning and he was half convinced he was the only one in the building that used the place.

He rounded the corner and saw a splash of platinum blonde hair with shimmering highlights draped on the bench. Kpau. There was no mistaking that hair.

The compact blonde was doing bench presses, giving a rather large set of weights a lot of hell for someone her size. A little growl escaped her lips on each lift. Blar stood and watched her for a moment. She was fierce, like the weights themselves had committed some wrong and she was punishing them. The look on her face was unholy anger. Fury at the world.

Blar waited for her to pause at one of her rest phases and spoke up. "Good morning, Chicklet. Does this mean I'll have a regular partner in the mornings now?"

Kpau's face transformed to the bright smile he was more accustomed to seeing.

"Hi, Papa Bear! Yay! Someone to spot for me!"

She jumped up and gave him a sweaty hug. Kpau was dressed in gym shorts, sneakers, and a tank top. Blar was wincing as much from the free movement of the pleasant contents of her tank top as from the sweat she was covered in. Did none of these women wear bras? Was that fashion statement in now? Blar extricated himself and grabbed a towel.

"You just revel in covering me in your sweat, don't you, Chicklet?" Blar grumbled as he wiped himself off. Kpau stuck her tongue out.

"Meh, work on your timing and you might get to feel the best kind of sweat!" Blar decided not to pursue what that meant. He tossed his gym bag down and got on the running machine to warm up, setting it for a brisk jog.

Kpau moved to the chin up bar and jumped up to grip it. Blar couldn't take his eyes off of that. Watching her attack her chin ups was enthralling.

She was growling on each lift and providing quite a pleasant view of her tight muscle tone and delicious figure from behind. Blar was not getting any traction at all on his morning meditative mood.

Kpau paused after her first set and just hung there.

"Sooooooo, how did it go with Tsika last night? I didn't hear any noise and I always figured the little vampire would be a noisy little wildcat when she was properly fucked!"

Blar nearly fell off the jogging machine, banging his shin on a bar as he slid off.

"You … little … what the hell? Ow!" Blar sat down to nurse his shin. Kpau dropped off the bar and came over. She grabbed a cold pack out of her bag and got down to press it to his blossoming bruise.

The view down her tank top was splendid. Blar jerked his head up and looked straight out, only to be impressed by her shapely rear in the room's mirrored wall.

Maybe yoga down the street was a sanity-keeping option.

"I saw her sneak out of our room last night and not come back! Then I was awake when you brought her back in. Good thing she's portable, eh?!" Kpau grinned like a mad Cheshire Cat.

"Honest to god, Chicklet, she fell asleep right after she got in my bed. She was exhausted."

Kpau's grin vanished to be replaced with solemn sympathy. "Oh, hell! Poor little ghoul! She's really trying, ya know. My antennae say she wants to be your girl pretty bad."

Blar tried to relax. Maybe Kpau really did just want to be his buddy, comrade-in-arms, or whatever.

"Kpau, I keep telling her there's no rush. That she can take all the time she wants to check me out. I'm not really a very good … catch. I have serious flaws. I can be boring. I am about ten years older than she is. She has lots to consider."

Kpau stared at him with one eyebrow arched, "Wow, you sound really old when you talk like that." She laughed and then cut it short.

"Blar, seize the moment. Always … seize … the moment. There might not be other moments." There it was again, that flicker of something underneath her smile and behind those brown eyes. She checked his shin one last time and pronounced it survivable after she watched him put weight on it.

"Hey, Blar, can you spot me on the leg press? I want to push myself to exhaustion, my thighs and calves are falling apart."

Blar silently disagreed with her assessment. Kpau set the weights for what Blar guessed was four or five times her body weight and lay down on the machine.

Impressive. Blar rarely set it over three times his weight. He decided his new band mate had a potential second career as a fitness model. Blar positioned himself by the weight handles.

Kpau started her press sequence. Again, the fierceness. Her smile took on a death mask aspect, every bit of her focused on the lift. That growl on each press was a bit scary.

Blar was quickly honing a theory that everything Kpau did was about escaping from little demons in her head. She attacked everything as if monsters were right on her ass. Impressive results but it left him feeling a bit sad for her. Blar was left flipping back and forth emotionally between admiration and sympathy.

Kpau started faltering and Blar started picking up the slack. Finally, she let out a huge roar as her legs failed. Blar lowered the weights as Kpau just rolled off the bench and sprawled on the floor making small noises and gurgles.

"You alive down there, Chicklet?" A small but tough hand stuck up in the air. He took her wrist and lifted her up in the air until her toes were dangling. Kpau giggled and took half-hearted swings at him with her free hand. He set her down and she lightly punched his chest a number of times times in rapid fire.

"Got drummer's arms for sure to lift me like that! You can be awfully fun for an old man when you try! Don't ever lose that, Papa Bear. Need me to spot for you?" Kpau bounced from side to side on the balls of her feet boxing her fists at him.

"Stop calling me old, little girl. Thirty three! I don't know if you're good for much in the way of spotting after that little demonstration. But okay yes, I need to do some bench presses." Blar set the weights. Kpau made fun of him until he added twenty more pounds.

"Okay, my cell phone is on speed dial for the medics, you little blonde goblin." Blar lay down and gripped the barbells.

Kpau positioned herself as his spotter as Blar lifted. Looking up, Blar was beset with the sudden realization Kpau's tank top was not tucked in. He had a splendid view of a tanned belly button up to delightful breasts and beyond them all the way to her chin. He spluttered and down came the weights, Kpau guiding them just in time to their stand.

"Whoa, Papa Bear, are you okay?" She leaned over the weight bar at him with serious concern. That view was just as distracting.

"Dammit, Kpau?! Can you tuck your shirt in or something? I know we're getting close and friendly but that five-star goddess real estate you've got is making me insane down here!"

Kpau looked down at her tank top and nearly busted her gut laughing. "Sorrrrrrrry! Oh, I am! Really! Gosh, pervy Bear! I had decided my type wasn't even on your radar! Okay, okay!" She grabbed a stretch band out of her bag and made a makeshift belt.

Blar wasn't impressed by the attempt though he was still impressed by the figure it cut. Her breasts weren't large but they were just right for her surfer-girl body shape and muscle tone.

"Okay, all that does is accentuate the obvious but ... I can probably live with that. If we're going to keep doing this together, please get a sports bra, please?"

Kpau curled her lip, "Bleh! … okay ... for you, Papa Bear. Right, lets get our workout finished, I'm getting hungry."

- - - - - -

Kpau and Blar roughhoused all the way back to the condo unit. Blar kept watching the young woman's face for those flickers under the smiles, laughter, and guffaws – but she was remarkably good at keeping her shields up. By the time they entered the apartment, he had Kpau under his arm like a satchel. He simply tossed her onto one of the giant bean bag chairs while she squealed in delight for the duration of the flight.

Blar heard a hiccup and turned. Glycerin was in the kitchen. She had eggs and bacon going on the stove. Their boisterous entry had startled her. She fell back and automatically put her hands behind her to catch herself. Those critically vital hands. The hot grill.

"Grill!" Blar shouted abruptly. She jerked away from the stove, her eyes welling up in tears as she shrank down into a little ball. Blar felt terrible for scaring her. He gently stood her back up and rocked her in his arms.

"Oh gods, don't burn your hands, Glyc. You'd be on the sidelines for months." Glycerin was distraught but Blar didn't know how else to have warned her. He reached out and ruffled Glycerin's hair, trying his best to coo softly at her. "Sorry, Little Dancer. My real terror is that I'd have to cope with seeing you in pain. I have a feeling that would be unbearable. I feel awful enough just watching these tears."

Glycerin dropped her eyes and blushed. Didn't she ever run out of blush power? Blar wiped her cheeks with a hand towel and let her go after she nodded. He thought he might lend a hand and reached for a stack of plates to put on the table.

"I-I-I ... thank you. I'll b-be more c-careful, Blar." She spotted him reaching for the plates and then wrinkled her nose. She waved her hands in alarm to stop him from touching anything.

"Y-y-you two s-s-should take a shower." Glycerin's eyes widened more. "Oh! O-o-o-oh! I di-didn't m-mean t-t-t-together! I-I-I meant ...."

Kpau's head popped up from behind the bar counter top like a gopher, "Ah, Glyc! Great idea! It'd save water!"

Blar stood stone faced. "No. Not happening. Off with you, blonde goblin."

Kpau snorted and danced off. A few seconds later, they heard a horrified squeal from Tsika in the women's bedroom. Apparently, the little goth had still been in bed.

"Kpau! Get OFF me!! You're god damned sweaty! Augh!!!"

That was followed with more malevolent Kpau laughter which diminished as the source vanished into their bathroom.

Blar looked at Glycerin. "I've invited some horrific girl's dorm comedy into my home, haven't I?"

Glycerin just looked at him silently and then nodded with that twisted possibly demented grin she excelled at. The mysterious young woman turned back to her preparation of breakfast.

- - - - - -

 After Blar showered, he headed to the dining area where he found all three women eating. He found he rather enjoyed the sounds he was hearing. Clatter, chatter, and racket where there used to be silence.

Thank god, everyone is dressed in something that leaves my heart functioning. I may need drugs at this rate.

Tsika was the only one not smiling though. She was pointedly staring down at her coffee with pouting lips. Blar stopped before they noticed him and gazed sympathetically at her. He took a wild guess that she was not happy about passing out last night.

I need to find some reason for just her and I to go somewhere. Today.

Blar walked on in to a chorus of greetings and sat down to a pair of fried eggs, bacon, and fruit arranged in the shape of a happy face. He stared at it and silently added that information to his picture of Glycerin as she studiously avoided eye contact with him. Say something? Don't say something? Blar looked out the window, dark and cloudy but no rain or snow. He took a bite of the eggs and was surprised by the flavor.

"Is Glycerin the team chef? These eggs are really tasty." Glycerin blushed and mumbled something.

Kpau nodded vigorously with a mouthful of toast, "Shef coog etter than … than me by a long long shot. Tsika's pretty good, too. I'm more a 'hot dog and hamburger' short-order girl."

Blar watched Tsika out of the corner of his eye as she sank farther into her chair. He decided cracking a joke about the kitchen fire the previous week was a bad idea. Blar ate silently, listening to Kpau and Glycerin chatter and laugh. It was really mostly Kpau chattering while Glycerin responded with short stammered comments and giggling at Kpau's babbling antics. Charming to watch while Blar tried to concoct a reason for just he and Tsika to go out. He stared at the little goth's dainty throat choker absent-mindedly, admiring the small bats and alabaster skull decorating it.

Ah, maybe this will work. Gotta hope that Kpau gets the hint.

"Hey, Tsika. I've been listening to you complain for most of the week about your inventory of outfits. There's a shop I would like to take you to that specializes in goth apparel, culture, and fashion. I won't pretend to have a clue but I've been there and I do know it gets good Yelp. It's over on Burnside so we can walk or taxi as you like."

Tsika brightened up. "Yes, Blar. I'd like that very much." She pinked up, looking happier.

Kpau started to open her mouth excitedly. Blar cursed silently but put a brake on that mood as Kpau suddenly froze. Her computational gears were obviously grinding and percolating. Her brown eyes darted over to Glycerin.

The shy woman seemed to be gearing up to speak as well.

"Hey, Glyc! You and I need to grocery shop so we don't have to eat out! I can barely cook and even I can tell this guy's pantry sucks." Whatever Glycerin had been about to say – Kpau's pronouncement clearly succeeded in distracting her from her original thought.

"Eh? Oh! Yes, y-yes! It desperately needs to be p-properly st-stocked! That w-would be sw-sweet if y-you went along with me, little dove!"

Blar silently thanked Kpau and dedicated a beer to her later. Kpau looked Blar in the eye and blinked. She blinked again with a grin.

Oh! Right! That was her way of winking. Her one string for both eyes wink. Good girl.

Tsika excused herself to get ready. She said she had to be properly dressed to shop. She looked at Blar resignedly, "Blar, darling. Can … can you … wear something … something?"

She fluttered her hands at him as if the possibility of him dressing acceptably was beyond hope.

"Don't worry, I'll wear something pointedly dark. I've been in the shop before." Blar looked at Glycerin. "Glyc, I'll give you some cash so you can get whatever you need to cook as you like. They have kitchen supplies and there's also a nice kitchen shop just across from the book store."

Glycerin responded with her cute slightly daft smile and nodded. "Oh, that would … it would be … w-w-w-wonderful! I'll make something sp-sp-sp-special tonight f-f-for our own p-p-pers … sonal housewarming."

Jesus, that was a marvel. She got two whole long sentences out. Progress! Though – it is likely she's stopped thinking of me as a guy again. Many tiny little steps up that mountain.

- - - - - -

Blar walked out of his bedroom ready to go. Kpau nearly choked on her drink laughing so hard at him.

"What? What's wrong with this?" Blar had put on his black jeans, some urban boots, and a black silk dress shirt with a hint of ruffles. Over that was a black vest and he had a slightly rumpled black top hat with a poisonous looking green band. He'd put on his green-tinted round-lensed "ozzie" glasses. Blar had several colors of the frames and liked to rotate wearing them. However, Kpau was hooting her assessment as she held her sides.

"The hat! Omigod, the hat! You look like you jumped out from Alice's looking glass!"

"Well, that's … it's supposed to be a mild Van Helsing kind of Victorian vampire thing."

Kpau was still snorting and giggling. "Okay, if that's what you say! You certainly look dangerous, in a dorky run-out-of-medications-for-the-month way." More laughter ensued from the blonde faction in the room.

Then Tsika stepped out of her bedroom and Blar forgot all about Kpau. Her effect was as strong on Blar as the first time he had seen her in the coffee shop. The phrase "living doll" had to have been created with her in mind. Cliche but no exaggeration. The diminutive beauty was in a color scheme of black with red trimmed bows. Her calf-length dress had a Victorian air enhanced with spider web embroidery. The dress itself was shaped to accentuate her slim curves. Pointed boots with lacing embroidered to match the dress. The outfit contrasted dramatically with her pale white skin. Her skin set off her dark eye makeup and blood-red lipstick.

Now THAT was Van Helsing vampire material in spades. She was carrying the parasol that he had first spotted her with. What, that was only a week or two ago?

"Kpau, I don't think anyone on the street is going to be looking at me."

Kpau looked Tsika over and grinned madly. "You are right on the mark there, Papa Bear."

Tsika blushed. "Is my first time to this place. I must make sure they understand I am serious. I looked them up, they seem to be on the ball with the culture and not just silly gift shop half-assed pretense of goth."

Glycerin came out of the kitchen. She just glowed as she admired Tsika. Then Glycerin did something Blar found amazing, she growled at him.

"My little Tsika looks so b-beautiful! B-blar! You t-take bloody g-good care of my precious doll! She's precious to me!" Blar stared wide-eyed at Glycerin until she blushed and backed into the kitchen pantry. That was the first ferocity he had seen out of her since meeting her. He gathered he had better damn well take care of Glycerin's little doll.

Tsika was inspecting Blar. "Well … you're passable. And they've seen you before."

Kpau came back up for air after her giggle fit, "They'll just think he got lucky and you're going to fix him up." A thrown couch pillow from Blar headed her way but she ducked.

Blar growled, "Okay, Kpau and Glyc. You … Team Rocket people." The wretched Pokemon reference joke got a laugh from Kpau. "You know the way to the grocery store, right? Uh huh. If you get more than you can carry, they have vans that can bring you home for a small fee. Make Jack get off his duff and help you haul it up. He'll probably enjoy the scenery of you two anyway. We're off."

Blar held out his hand. Tsika put her gloved hand in it and smiled up at him. That look was worth almost any price. The couple made their way down to the sidewalk outside. Jack was off-duty and the doorman on duty was new. Blar didn't recognize him. The man simply stared at them with his mouth hanging open. Blar made a mental note to talk to Jack about him.

Tsika wanted to walk and Blar judged that the weather was likely to treat them nicely. The cloud covered sky didn't have that wet feeling and there was a light dry breeze. Tsika popped her parasol open and took Blar's arm.

Blar was happy, both because he was escorting such a lovely creature and because she seemed to have a knack for not poking his eye out with the parasol. As he predicted, a fair number of pedestrians just gawked at them. A few tourists took pictures. One elderly woman was brave enough to ask them to pose for a picture. As they continued down the sidewalk, Blar smiled down at Tsika. She was walking alongside him with her characteristic strutting gymnast walk. Blar had quietly figured out over the last few days that it was how Tsika kept up with people who had longer strides.

"You know, Tsika, until you came along, my sidewalk experience was mostly people grabbing their purses tightly and giving me a wide berth as I walked by." Blar smiled ruefully. Tsika offered him an aristocratic smile and patted his arm.

"Scary Bear, one thing I came to know long ago was that I was always on stage in some way by dressing as I do. Giving them a good show creates memories and stories for these "muggles" to tell at dinner."

She paused to step lightly around a street grate. "Sometimes I get mad at them but I try to remember I asked for the attention by stepping out of the rut of the mundane."

Tsika smiled graciously at a little girl who was jerking at her mother's dress and shouting, "Look mommy! A doll! A live doll! She's pretty!"

The girl let go of her mother and ran over to Tsika. "Mommy! Take my picture with her. She's not any bigger than I am!"

The mom's reaction wasn't so joyful, she got started to yell but Tsika interrupted in a really thick Russian accent. Blar couldn't help laughing as he thought of the old Rocky & Bullwinkle cartoons. Tsika could have easily voiced one of the characters in it, a Soviet spy named Natasha.

"Is okay, madam! I would not dress as this if I did not enjoy such attention. I am being delighted to be in picture with your darling daughter. What is your name, little girl?" Tsika posed by the excited girl while the mother got her cellphone out to take a picture. Blar decided to stay out of the shot. As the pictures were being snapped, several businessmen walking by recognized Blar and Tsika. They all spoke at once.

"Hey! It's …! It's the *Rocket Science* people!" "Outstanding show the other night!" "Hey, Blar, will you sign my flyer, I've still got it!" "Wow, this is the little bass player! She's even cuter up close!"

The little girl's mother seemed to grasp that the strangely dressed couple were local celebrities of some kind. Blar could sense the mother's suspicion ebbing away, replaced by embarrassment she might be out of touch.

Blar signed the flyer and then handed it and his pen to Tsika. Tsika took it and stared blankly at him.

"Tsika, sign it. It'll be more collectible later." Blar grinned at her. Tsika blushed, but signed the flyer and handed it back to her new fan.

"Tsi-ka … pretty name for a really pretty lady. I'll keep an eye out for the rest of your band." The young businessman was handling the flyer carefully now and slipped it in his brief.

Blar threw him a bone. "Well, if you hurry you might be able to catch the other two on the way over to Whole Foods grocery. They should be easy to spot since Glycerin is as tall as I am and Kpau's hair shines in the dark. Just a warning: Glyc is pretty shy, so approach Kpau first and nicely – that way Kpau won't break your face and Glyc won't faint." Blar laughed.

The man looked at his buddies, "We … are going to be late getting back. I gotta do this. Thanks, Blar … and … Tsi-ka." He smiled and took off with his coworkers.

The mom of the little girl seemed regretful about her initial suspicion, she apologized and thanked them for being nice to her daughter. Tsika waved at the young girl as she skipped off with her mom.

"One day … on day … a little girl would be nice to –." Tsika stopped short and glanced up at Blar. Her face almost beat Glycerin for the intense blush erupting on Tsika's cheeks as her eyes were transfixed by something on her boots.

Blar saved her. "Come on, little pixie, your shopping awaits."

After a couple of minutes spent walking, Tsika spoke again. "That was … really strange signing an autograph. Does it ever get … blase?"

"Nope. At least for me, it has always been a surreal moment. They think you're their best buddy … or lover. Sometimes it can get very weird or even creepy. Back in the day, the band was always punching out some jackass who thought they could take Aina home for a trophy. And … I've always kept John Lennon in mind. It only takes one crazy fan when you're off guard and the ride is over."

They continued to make their way through the shopping district. Blar started humming. He noticed Tsika watching him out of the corner of her eye and smiled.

"Do you know that tune, little pixie? One of my favorites from the Grunge Era and it always sticks in my head. It just seems to fit this town perfectly."

Tsika giggled. "Yes, I do! It is fun song because tune is so happy but the words are so … sad and reflective."

Blar started singing the lyrics. The tune was "No Rain", written and performed by a band called Blind Melon in the early '90s. After the opening stanza, Tsika joined in on harmony during the chorus. The pair slowed to a stop as they sang to each other.

At that point, people on the street around them had slowed to a halt to watch. Blar started a small dance step and Tsika danced-skipped with him. They continued harmonizing together as the lyrics spoke of rain, insanity, points of view, and sticking together no matter what. Tsika was glowing. Blar couldn't believe the happy aura emanating out of such a darkly cute little goth.

Blar put his hand on Tsika's back and spun her around him. He knew he wasn't a great dancer but he improvised with his stage moves. Her smile and expression was brilliant. They continued their song and dance as the crowd grew.

The couple faded the song out to finish and their impromptu audience erupted into applause. Tsika hadn't seemed aware of them. Her face flushed bright crimson. Blar just smiled and gave the crowd a big stage bow pulling Tsika along with him.

"Thank you! Thank you! No tip jar today! We'll be here all week, folks, thanks. Thank you."

They both jogged away as Tsika burst into a throaty laugh. "I … love... I love … I … love … I like … being with you, Blar. A lot. Whole lot!" Blar got a full blast of what Tsika was wanting to say from her big luminous eyes and parted lips. He squeezed her hand. He could also sense her fear – fear of being emotionally exposed and vulnerable.

Interesting. Kpau has her shields, Glycerin swims in constant introverted terror. Tsika seemed to be extremely wary of letting herself be vulnerable with anyone.

"I'd kiss that pretty mouth but it is probably a bad idea for me to mess up your makeup, little pixie. Our destination is on the next block." Tsika wrapped both her arms around his arm and squeezed tight as they walked.

- - - - - -

 As they approached the shop, Tsika got excited as she drew near and could see the displays in the windows. The little boutique shop "Alternate State of Mind" specialized in dark fashion, though Blar had told her that many other little shops in town also had little treasure chests of items for goth clothing stalkers. This shop made for an excellent first stop, nonetheless.

Blar let Tsika enter first. That tactic had gone over well with Glycerin at the guitar shop and it worked here in spades. The manager nearly leaped over the counter to greet Tsika before forcing himself back into his proper mellow dark mood.

Blar made himself invisible, not hard to do with Tsika to look at. He browsed the jackets with the idea of updating his rather untended wardrobe. Blar found a couple of potential pieces of stage wardrobe but decided he would let Tsika approve. Blar felt a little off balance about his own selection skill after Kpau had made such fun of him earlier.

Meanwhile, Tsika had charmed the manager sufficiently so that the man had skipped right past the "trash goods" and was bringing out the enchanted gear. Blar could feel his wallet moaning quietly in his pocket but he knew the good stuff was expensive, often handcrafted. She clearly knew what to look for and he dearly anticipated seeing her in anything she found.

Blar guessed that malfunctioning corset in the snow provided a sign of how close to the financial edge the *Lost Girls* were, how little money they had left. Blar silently praised that corset for providing the ignition to meet Tsika. He still had it in his closet, maybe he should have it framed.

As he browsed, Blar spotted the latest issue of a popular tattoo magazine. He browsed it and decided to pick the issue up for Glycerin. He rather liked watching the shy lassie blush when he gave her things anyway – but she did have some beautiful tattoos on her and she might want more.

Two hours later, Tsika was an immensely happy little goth camper with several bags, one of which contained a jacket for Blar. His top hat now sported a new silk band and had been freshened up, though he had rather liked its usual ratty ambiance. His wallet was now quite a bit lighter. He always tried to paid cash at independent shops but this time it had been especially painful. However, the direct result was a Tsika who was almost bubbly, definitely in an emotional state upside down from any Dark Brooding Princess of Darkness act.

Blar called Kpau on his cellphone as they started their walk back. She and Glycerin were already back at – home. Kpau announced to Blar that she was now calling the condo 'home'. The little blonde had a distinctly happy lift in her voice in making that pronouncement. She kept babbling to Blar over the phone as he walked with Tsika.

"Papa Bear! Someone … someone asked us for our autographs today! I thought I was going to have to pull Glyc out of a storm sewer! But his flyer had your signatures … wait! YOU told them where we were!"

"Yes, I did, Chicklet. And he walked over ten blocks to track you down. Be impressed."

Blar easily visualized little sprays of self-satisfied glitter and colored lights bursting out of his phone.

"We … got … FANS! See ya in a bit, Blar. Can't wait to see what Tsika scored!" Kpau giggled and hung up. Blar looked at Tsika, who was listening to the conversation with a seductive smirk.

"Kpau informs us we have fans. Film at eleven."

Tsika smiled serenely and handed Blar all her bags so she could open her parasol up.

- - - - - -

 Back at home, Blar was sitting on the couch looking over Glycerin's grocery bill. It wasn't cheap but she had an impressive knack for maximizing the results of what she spent. She even used coupons. He was glad he had called them while at he loitered while Tsika shopped and reminded them only to get perishable stock for the week. They would be out of town for a month at the retreat. Not much would last that long.

Glycerin was in the kitchen busy cooking. He could swear he heard her humming.

Humming? Out loud? Glycerin?

Kpau had already set the table. She now lay on the couch next to Blar upside down with her feet hanging over the backrest and her hair hanging off the seat. She was reading a copy of the local weekly newspaper. It contained a review of the band and their performances at Hans' club.

"Wow, four stars! The only thing he dinged us on was that we needed more of our own music." Kpau kept reading as she wiggled her feet. "I think he has a crush on Glycerin. This is almost erotic prose." Her eyebrows rose as she read further.

Blar leaned back. "Yes, Chicklet, and that is why we're heading out to a retreat. No, you little pervert, not to save Glycerin from a drooling reporter. We need to create the band a portfolio of its own music."

Blar looked over into the kitchen. He could swear Glycerin was singing now. What tune was that? He looked back down at Kpau, "I'd ask Glycerin what she's cooking, but I'll be damned if I'm going to burst that bubble of happy in there."

Kpau nodded approvingly. "She sings when she's drunk, too. Just sayin', you know." Kpau blinked her one-string wink.

Blar's mouth dropped open as he identified the tune. "Is … is she singing "*Break Me*"? That raunchy tune by *The Irresponsibles*?" Kpau gave Blar completely insincere innocent puppy eyes and nodded.

Blar marveled, "Kind of racy for the Mouse, isn't it?" Kpau simply nodded again. Blar added that into his mental picture of Glycerin as her lilting voice floated out of the kitchen. The song lyrics were full of rough sex, feeling good, being naughty, and wanton lust.

"This sounds wrong but, we … may have to be evil and get her drunk for some recordings in the studio. It is more than a little riveting to hear." Blar ruffled Kpau's hair absent-mindedly.

Kpau shivered and whispered, "Tsika has it down to sort of a science, some drunk but not too drunk. She's very protective of Glycerin as if you hadn't noticed, so she doesn't do it often. We've never gotten her to sing on a stage though. Only when it's just the girls." Blar added that tidbit to his growing pile of Glycerin knowledge.

Tsika wandered into the living room from the large bedroom. She had changed into shorts and an off shoulder sweatshirt long enough one might mistake her for having forgotten pants. Standing in front of Blar and Kpau, she crossed her arms and raised her eyebrows.

"Hey, why are you two hooligans not helping Glyc?"

Blar reluctantly took his eyes off of Tsika's moon-white bare shoulders and hint of cleavage. "I am NOT going to go into that kitchen and disturb that happy bubble. She's in there singing! She sings beautifully … and sexy! Why wasn't I told? It's awesome!"

Tsika listened to what Glycerin was singing and then put her fingers to her lips choking back a giggle.

"Okay, Blar is excused but both of you get to do the dishes." She cast an evil glance at Kpau, who was kicking her legs in the air in protest. Blar beat Kpau into submission with a couch pillow.

Tsika approved of the beating. "I'll go see what I can do to expedite dinner.

I'm starving." Tsika trotted off to the kitchen.

Kpau flipped into an upright position curled up on the couch, looking much like a wiggling ferret during the process. "Ah ha! The little princess is telling you what to do already. You should demand sacrifice for that privilege. Tie her up and have your way with her. She might like that, especially with silk ribbons. I have some if you want to borrow them!"

Blar halfheartedly tried to smother Kpau with the pillow.

"It was a good day today so I'll let you live, little minx. Tsika and I shall proceed at the speed that works for both of us, but the priority should be the band." Blar released Kpau.

"Dead serious agreement there, Papa Bear. Time out! Potty break." Kpau somersaulted out of the couch and bounded down the hall. Blar wondered if Kpau in his life was what having a little sister was like.

- - - - - -

Glycerin had concocted quite a meal. They sat down to a baked salmon dinner with stir-fried vegetables and wild rice. Wine and toasty bread topped it off. Blar thought it was good as anything the better restaurants in town could present and said so. Glycerin turned beet red and mumbled incoherently from behind the hair and fingers she often hid behind.

Kpau was no help. "I used to tell those two they should just get married and adopt me so I could eat Glycerin's food forever."

Tsika smiled at Glycerin. "Glycca, sweetie, don't forget the desert before we lose you there." Glycerin nodded and nearly knocked the table over in her rush to the kitchen. A minute later she returned with a key lime pie.

"I-I-I d-didn't m-m-make this. B-but the market had them o-out a-a-and the s-samples t-t-tasted so g-good." Her cheeks were rosy the entire time she served up pieces to everyone.

Blar looked at his slice. "I think I'm going to be officially happily miserable after this. Dinner was outstanding, Little Dancer. Someone is going to be a very lucky bastard some day."

Glycerin looked confused for a second. The light dawning on her face made Blar regret having said that. "Oh o-o-o-o-oh, no, I … I don't don't don't. Maybe? I don't … no, ahhhh!!!" She stopped trying and just sniffled as she stared down at her shaking hands.

Blar felt really awful. "I'm sorry, Little Dancer. I just think you're a really fantastic cook." Glycerin kept her eyes down but he got a brief glimpse of that little heart-stabbing smile. "I … I … I like cooking … for … p-people I … like."

Kpau's eyes widened but she said nothing. Tsika was fully invested in inhaling her pie slice and did not appear to notice Glycerin's remark.

Blar wiped his mouth with his napkin. "Okay, if the overfed slugs are ready, I'll lay out the plans for the next month."

Kpau responded with a belch worthy of a truck driver after day-old chili. "I've died. Go ahead." She slumped back in her chair and stared at the ceiling. At least Glycerin and Tsika looked attentive.

"Right. Okay. Wednesday, we ship our gear so we need to have it all ready to go. We'll hang on to Glyc and Tsika's guitars. Thursday we fly to San Francisco and taxi into town. I have us staying at the Edwardian Hotel in the Castro district. It is a quick walk to a live band club where a friend of mine has given us a Friday night booking. He'll have the rest of what we need to play but it may require some creativity. Low expectations, just fun and jamming. It's a coffee house, we can do some quirkier quiet stuff. I figured you lot wanted to sightsee and shop so Saturday and Sunday we can do Union Street and the Wharf or maybe Japantown."

Blar paused to make sure he had a conscious audience.

"Monday, we pick up the van and drive down to Monterey. We're staying near the night club we're going to play at. I don't foresee any problems at all with equipment there. The owner is a very good friend of mine. I think you'll like this part a lot." Blar smiled mysteriously.

Kpau wrinkled her nose and recovered from her food-induced coma. "Hey! Blar … that's Christmas Eve."

That insight stopped Blar cold. He had just assumed none of them bothered much with the holiday with no family.

Shit. Kpau and her ideas about family. Stepped into a ditch on that one. But Kpau is smiling?

"I think it'll be neat to play Christmas Eve with ... with you guys. See if your friend decorates for it, I like Christmas lights." Kpau's eyes went a little vacant after that.

Blar had a real strong feeling that most of Kpau's holiday memories sucked after losing her parents, so she clung to any good moments she could remember.

"I'll call and make damn sure that happens, little Chicklet. Lights for Christmas. I think ... I think my friend will have fun with that." Blar grinned and continued.

"Then Christmas Day we're kind of stuck for a bit, so I was just going have us hang out. She's very interested in meeting you all."

Tsika woke up from her pie haze for a moment. "She? Is this some old girl friend, large Bear?"

"No ... and ... yes ... it's ... complicated but I don't want to give it away. I really think you pirates will sync up well with her." Blar flipped his notepad to the next sheet.

"Anyhow ... after that, we road trip down to Big Sur, arriving at the 'Music of the Spheres Zen Resort' where our gear will be awaiting us. Rest, relaxation, and working until our brains and fingers bleed." Blar put his notepad down.

"Yay!! Blood!!!" Kpau waved her knife as she lay slumped in her chair – she appeared to be passing out from the food and drink. Blar figured he would be lucky if any of them remembered much of his speech.

- - - - - -

Later that evening, all four of them were piled on the couch with drinks in hand watching Blar's collection of his old band's music videos. Some of them were pretty outrageous, the remnants of the music video Golden Era. Kpau kept choking on her drink from laughing so hard. Glycerin was fascinated and kept shushing Kpau.

Tsika glanced at Blar. Apparently his expression was too obvious. "Whats the matter, Blar? You look … thoughtful? … reflective?" She curled up closer to him.

Blar shook his head. "No … well, I have been sort of thinking *'Here I Go Again'* but watching these – I realized I was completely wrong. Not the same era, not the same people, not the same at all. That band on the screen there, those were four very different people. I'm not the same person. I did a lot of stupid things then, I'd like to find new stupid things to do." He grinned and finished his drink.

Kpau burrowed into him from the other side. "Your drumming has gotten better, that's for sure. You got away with some rancid strokes on the tune in this video."

Blar examined the screen closely, "I'm pretty sure I was stoned out of my mind for that video. Erk, may we please avoid that chemical nonsense … a little?"

Tsika snuggled. "I'd like to think we're a bit too practical to get too stupid with things like that, large Bear."

Glycerin fluttered a hand at them to be quiet. She had not seen some of the videos Blar had of *Gothic Fire* and she was enthralled. The lanky brunette nodded her head and swayed as she watched. Blar was feeling far too warm and faded out between the two small bodies curled up against him.

- - - - - -

Blar's opened his eyes. It was morning. All four of them were still on the couch and the videos were still looping. Someone, probably Tsika, had gotten blankets during the night and they were covered under them. Tsika's legs were across his lap and she was laying back on the couch arm snoring softly. Kpau was curled up under his left arm with her hands clinging to his shirt. Glycerin's long legs were on the ottoman and she was slumped against Kpau.

Blar thought of his old band mates and how they would crash out like this. He wondered how Aina had dealt with three goofy hormonal guys as long as she did. He'd have to ask his old band mate to refresh his memory, and she was probably chock full of stories he didn't remember. Blar relaxed and fell back to sleep.

~12~ "Welcome to the Hotel California" – The Eagles

Blar and his troupe of feminine musicians stepped off the light rail express platform and strolled to the airport lobby under the large glass structure that covered the departure area. The weather had returned to its more typical pattern for winter – raining and just above freezing. The glass rumbled from the pelting precipitation.

Tsika had a nice rolling streak of blue curses trailing away from her as she walked. She did not like being cold. The petite waif had three glittering black shawls wrapped about her. Her black velvet dress caught the attention of passersby with its embroidered spiders and web patterns of stitching. Completing the eye-catching effect, her bright candy-striped hosiery peeked out from her skirt as she strutted. Blar admired how the leggings emphasized Tsika's prancing style of motion as she kept up with Glycerin's long strides.

Glycerin and Kpau seemed to be adjusting more amiably to the unpredictability of Pacific Northwest weather. Each was more lightly dressed. Glycerin had chosen a simple garb for the day; black leather jeans, slip on boots, purple button down blouse, and a leather jacket. Kpau had gone with a white motif, white slacks, white tank top, white hoodie jacket. The three women made quite a contrasting trio.

As they entered the lobby, Tsika began sticking tightly to Blar's ribs , huddling under his arm for warmth. He spent time watching Glycerin's public techniques, which he found fascinating. In this part of the airport, she hovered near Blar while using Kpau as an outer shield from 'all the people'. Blar wondered how the security process was going to go if the officers decided Glycerin needed special attention.

The band checked their luggage at the front baggage drop off. Blar was happy with the relative ease with which everyone got through security. There were two exceptions. One was Blar's top hat. It set off alarms thanks to some new metal staves he hadn't been aware of. The other was exception was that a TSA guard recognized Glycerin from her performance at Hans' club. On the upside, the officer knew she was shy and was extra gentle with her. When he lamented not being able to get a photo of her though, her embarrassment meter pegged out and she stopped functioning. Kpau had to lead her the rest of the way to the gate. As Kpau consoled the uniformed man, "She's happy but catatonic. That means thank you in Glycerin-speak!"

The weather didn't affect the flight other than some air turbulence encountered during the ascent. The band had one row to themselves but were surrounded by two families with little children who found the foursome absolutely fascinating. A little Hawaiian girl hung over her seat back enchanted with Kpau. They spent most of the trip double-winking at each other and playing finger games. Glycerin bashfully played the winking game for a few moments but then slept the remainder of the trip.

Across the aisle, Blar was staring into empty space the way he handled most airplane trips. He gradually became aware of a pair of small warm hands taking his hand and placing them on an enticing slender thigh. He blinked out of his trance and glanced at Tsika. An impish seductive grin and come-hither eyes brought him to full attentiveness. She started moving his hand further up her thigh under her skirt. This seemed both promising and alarming to Blar. It wasn't like it was a night flight in first class, no mile-high club was likely in economy. He leaned over to kiss her. Almost immediately, Blar was aware that his hat feather was being played with.

Blar straightened up and locked eyes with a pair of small amber eyes framed by jet black twin tailed hair. Not Tsika's eyes – the eyes of a much smaller near replica of Tsika peering over from the seat ahead of them. The little girl couldn't have been more than five or six but the similarity was astonishing. Tsika hastily took Blar's hand off her thigh and just interlocked her fingers in his as she smoothed her skirt out. She smiled at the little girl.

"Hi! You look just like me!"

The little girl nodded as she giggled and smiled. "You have pretty earrings!" She was admiring Tsika's silver and ruby spiders dangling from her ears. Tsika leaned forward and whispered.

"Do you like spiders? Yes? I do, too! I have one painted on my chest! Want to see?" Tsika unbuttoned the top three buttons on her blouse and held the shirt open just enough to show the little girl the elegant spider tattoo over her heart. She glanced over at Blar and winked at him as he admired the more erotic view of the spider's domain from his angle.

"I also have spiders on my jacket, see?" She pointed out the embroidered spiders on her clothing. "When you grow up, you can pretend it's Halloween whenever you want like I do! My name is Tsika. What is yours?"

The little girl blushed and answered softly. "My name, it is Ivana."

Tsika's eyebrows shot up. Blar heard Tsika say something in Russian to Ivana. Ivana lit up and answered in the same language. Blar sat back and watched a rapid-fire conversation between the two in, what was to him, incomprehensible Russian. Ivana handed Tsika a sketchpad and pencil. Tsika rapidly sketched out a cute spider on a lacy web as she chattered to the little girl. Tsika impishly signed her name into the pattern of the web. The little girl beamed and giggled when Tsika handed it back.

A mother's face appeared next to the little girl, seemingly about to apologize. However, she simply gaped at the sight of a grown version of her daughter. Tsika spoke to the mother in Russian and all three laughed. Blar was fairly sure Tsika had called her "mama" as part of some joke. A three-way conversation in incomprehensible Russian erupted. Finally, Tsika waved bye to the little girl and the mother as they turned around to sit down again for the remainder of the flight.

Blar stroked Tsika's arm. "Made a little friend there. If she frames that, it might be worth something some day."

Tsika lay back. "I made a memory, big Bear. Even if she loses the paper, she might remember the woman who looked like a 'big sister'. Her mother was amazed at our likeness, too. I'm afraid we have to delay when we deplane in San Francisco. Momma wants to have our picture taken together. Hope we're not in a hurry."

Blar shook his head. "No, I think I might want a picture of that, too." He kissed Tsika on the nose and settled in for a short nap for the rest of the flight.

- - - - - -

Blar dropped the last suitcase on the hotel suite floor. He had forgotten that most of the older hotels in San Francisco did not have elevators. Naturally, they had been assigned a suite on the third floor. Blar had lost his fellow mule Kpau to Tsika and Glycerin. The trio had immediately scattered to a boutique shop they had spotted right across from the hotel on arrival. Ah well, he figured he needed the exercise.

Blar looked around and realized his official First Error Of The Trip. Two bedrooms but only one queen-sized bed in each. Check the couch. Nope, none of them were sleeper sofas. Call down to the desk – no roll beds available.

He knew the logical adult solution, but that wasn't going to make it any less embarrassing. Kpau was going to have a field day teasing him about the situation. Blar threw himself on one of the beds and decided to think about it later. He immediately passed out.

- - - - - -

"Big Bear! My darling precious Bear! Need to wake up." Soft little voice and gentle kisses on the cheek. That was really nice. Blar opened his eyes and enjoyed the pale pixie's bright smile.

"Cripes, don't tell me I missed dinner." Blar rubbed his eyes while Tsika laughed.

"No, but you might want to brush your hair before we go hunting for food." Tsika looked around and smirked. "And, just so you know, the rest of the band has already noticed the sleeping options. Be prepared for merciless torture, sawdust-for-brains Bear!"

Blar groaned and lay back down. Tsika headed back out to the main room. She called back as she strolled away. "Move it, darling, the kids are hungry." Small pixie demon laughter followed, drifting in the air. Blar got up again and sat looking at his feet for a few seconds before forcing himself up and out of bed.

- - - - - -

The street in front of the Castro district hotel was an upbeat array of clubs, other small hotels, restaurants, and boutique shops. Blar corralled the women into a Thai restaurant -- he wanted something edible. There were going to be plenty of times where pizza was the only option and Blar preferred cultural variety. They ordered a pitcher of Thai beer and everyone picked a different plate for sharing. As they ate, Blar tried to ignore Kpau's innuendos, Glycerin's crimson blushes, and Tsika's dry witty sexual jabs about the hotel suite. Afterward, back on the street, Blar tried to redirect the chatter to something more productive and less focused on him.

"Lets go check out the night club where we're playing tomorrow. It's been six or seven years since I've been here and I want to scout out the place and the kind of audience we should expect." Once the women realized the boutique shops had closed for the evening, their resistance vanished. Blar made a call to the club's owner and they were able to skirt around the door bouncers. Kpau made the initial assessment as they observed from just offstage.

"Wow, Papa Bear. We're looking at young hipsters, aging hippies, and Dead Heads who missed the last bus. Are we going to mesh at all with this coffeehouse bunch?" Kpau had a twisted grimace as she analyzed the crowd.

"The owner, his name is Harvey by the way, just wants us to fill time and space. His original act spaced out on him – he's covering our hotel room. I can think of one song that will fit in here right off the top of my head." He grinned at Tsika, who looked perplexed and then blushed as she realized what tune Blar meant. "If we cover eclectic tunes not often played any more I think we'll be okay. I'll talk with Harvey in the morning while we're setting up and practicing. All of everyone's jazz and improv classes may be handy here. I do think we'll play the evening incognito so everyone dress down, eh?"

Kpau chuckled, "A four hour turgid dirge of a jam session!! How ... *Dead!*"

Glycerin snorted a giggle at Kpau's pun and then covered her face with her fingers as one of her power blushes bloomed on her face.

Tsika dryly retorted, "We'll just be *Grateful* stupid American blonde is not doing comedy."

Glycerin nearly split herself silently laughing at Tsika's terrible wit behind her hands. Blar simply winced and supported his tall shy guitarist as she recovered from her giggle spasms. They left via the stage door exit.

- - - - - -

They returned to the hotel suite uneventfully. Blar set his hat on the table just as the fun started. Kpau stretched and gave him a dangerous glittering smile before starting her torment.

"So! Who gets to sleep with Blar?! I could jump in front and call shotgun, but maybe rock-paper-scissors is more democratic!" Kpau smiled brightly at her solution.

Tsika giggled until she was coughing. Glycerin drew her legs up to her face in her chair and peered at the other two women from behind her knees in fascination.

"How about I sleep on the chair here and you three fight over – " Blar was cut off by a righteous Kpau.

"The hell! And have your back all messed up, old man? It'd make more sense for me or Tsika to take a chair for the night. We're small and featherweights."

"Now that'd make ME feel bad, Chicklet. And I'm not old. I'll sleep on the floor. That counters your bad back play."

Tsika growled, "Oh bullshit! Everyone here is grown up! Says so on passports! We shall rock-paper-scissors. Very adult solution." She batted her eyes innocently at her assessment.

Both Blar and Kpau burst out laughing. Kpau yipped, "Agreed! What a grown-uppy a way to solve it!"

Kpau stuck her hand out. Tsika joined her. They looked at each other, paused, and then both looked at Glycerin. Glycerin's face lost any hint of color as she realized what they were about to insist.

"W-w-w-w-what?!"

Tsika made a face at her. "Come on, Glycca. You're one of the adults, too."

Blar found this interplay between the three women fascinating. They weren't going to cut Glycerin any slack or baby her at all. He found himself hoping Glycerin would be spared. But such was not to be the case.

Glycerin lost – or won, depending on how one viewed the results. Blar was going to have Glycerin sharing his bed. Talk about mixed emotions. It wasn't like he was planning on doing more than sleep but he had rather hoped to curl up with Tsika. Poor Glycerin. She was just frozen in what Blar assumed was horror.

Tsika and Kpau appeared to have a glimmer they may have pushed Glycerin too hard. Both of them were biting their lips. Tsika coughed and spoke, "It is okay, Glycca. We were just teasing too hard. You don't – "

Glycerin's eyes flashed.

Blar had seen that look in Glycerin's eyes several times since he had first met her. She was getting mad at herself again. Good. He was seeing that look more often lately. She spoke softly.

"I-I-I can do it." She looked almost angry at them. "You two birds are j-just m-messing about with me. I-I-I think y-y-you rigged the g-game." Her angry look dissolved into a pouty sad clown expression.

Blar cast evil eyes at the two guilty looking goblins and took Glycerin's hand. "It'll be okay, Little Dancer. I'm too tired to care. We'll set things up however you like."

Blar gave the two pairs of puppy dog innocent eyes a very dry look. All they lacked were tinfoil halos. He focused on Tsika's eyes. Her expression faltered a bit and he caught what he hoped was a bit of regret behind her falsely angelic expression. Blar sighed, "Come on, Glyc. Let's go set up the room because I'm going to crash immediately. We have a long day and night tomorrow."

Glyc nodded and he led her to his bedroom, leaving the other two trying to make light of the situation as they trudged off to their bedroom. He stood with Glycerin at the foot of the bed.

"Okay, Little Dancer. You are in command. I'll do this any way that helps you feel safe. Do we sleep in our clothes with me on top of the sheets? Do you want to get in bed first? There's a dozen ways I've seen this done in old comedy movies. What ever keeps you unafraid is fine."

No answer. Blar looked over at her. He wasn't surprised she was blushing and looking at the floor. What did surprise him was that she was smiling that little smile he'd seen way back at the guitar shop. The precious smile that wasn't half-insane with terror but happy as a little songbird. She let go of him and covered her face with her hands.

"I … I … oh … um … y-you get r-ready and g-get in bed. J-j-just get under the sheets like n-normal. T-t-treat me like you w-would the o-o-others. I-I need to go g-get s-some things. Tell m-m-me when I c-can c-come in." She left the room in a single bound. A few seconds later, he could hear her and Tsika whispering to each other.

Blar decided he should stop over-planning or over-thinking how Glycerin might behave. He brushed his teeth, slipped off his trousers and shirt and put on his long gym shorts he wore around the condo. He got in bed and dimmed the room light for her benefit. Here we go down a rabbit hole.

"Okay, Glycerin. All clear."

He caught a brief glimpse of long beautiful legs, a tee-shirt, and shiny black hair as she jetted through the room to the bathroom. She must have changed in the other bedroom. He heard her brushing her teeth and the usual noises. A few minutes later, she peeked out from the bathroom. She reminded him of a mouse who knows a cat is on the prowl. She blushed harder and then slipped into the room.

Damn it, she is so pretty. She's wearing the same night garb she wears back home, that just tight enough tee shirt and those flannel short shorts. Did she have more than one of those tee shirts? Who still made them? I'm certainly not getting any royalty checks for them.

She made no eye contact but slithered over to the bed and sat down. Blar suspected Glycerin was moving fast so she did not have time to think about it. She sat there a minute facing the wall trying to control her fearful breathing sounds. Her hands were clenching the sheets and she twitched every few seconds. Blar was terrified of making a sound. He let her fight her inner demons. Suddenly, she swiveled, lay her head down on the pillow and pulled the sheets up to her nose. Blar silently applauded her. She had done it. This was probably braver than anything she had done, possibly in far more years than the short time he had been with her.

They lay there silently for a few minutes. He could feel her slowly relaxing and her breath getting deeper and more regular. Blar slowly reached for the bed stand lamp and said, "Good night, Little Dancer."

"W-w-wait?"

Blar stopped. Bomb squad defusing work sounded much less stressful as a second career.

"C-c-can you … you and I … just t-t-talk a m-moment?"

Blar could feel her trembling over on her half of the bed. "We can do that. Would you like to talk about tomorrow, what you want to do this weekend? Or, well we can talk about anything you want."

Glycerin was silent a moment. Just as Blar was wondering if she had fallen asleep, she hiccuped.

"I … I know I'm h-hard t-to be around … to d-deal with. You're s-so n-n-nice to me, w-when I know … it's … it's h-hard to b-be. Is it be-be-because you l-l-like Tsika?"

She certainly wasn't going for idle chitchat. How to answer her? He wanted to get it right. Exactly right.

"Well? It isn't simple, Little Dancer. We talked about this a little at the guitar shop. When I spotted Tsika, I had an instant physical attraction to her. I just have a liking for small, petite women. As I learn about her, I like the kind of person she seems to be. Then – I meet you." Blar paused to think about his next words. "When I say I have preferences in the way a woman looks, it doesn't mean I don't have a wide range of women I find attractive. You … you are … so beautiful, tall and slender. So graceful. You … you mesmerize me." Blar detected a small earthquake tremble from her side of the bed. Careful now. He kept talking.

"I want to get to know you, to learn about you, to be your friend. There's just something compelling about you. Part of it is your amazing musicianship, but part of it is just something that you radiate, a delightful personality under your shyness. You're mysterious, it intrigues me. I still don't know much about you but that's part of the fun of being with you – finding out."

Silence. No, not silence. Blar could hear her sniffling. He took a chance and looked over. There were small tears running from her eye down to her ear. His muscles ached because he wanted to give her a hug and he worried that would be a disaster. Blar wondered again what had happened to this girl. Glycerin's eye cut over and saw him looking at her. Surprisingly, she didn't flinch but she did start hiccuping as she spoke.

"Oh, oh no. I'm n-not up-up- … upset! Well … I'm ups-s-set with my-my-myself. I get so m-m-mad at mys-s-self when I g-g-get sc-sc-scared. D-d-don't think I d-don't know what p-people do for me. That's why I l-love them so-so-so much. I f-f-feel bloody smegging awful that I put them thro-o-ough so much. I w-w-want to t-t-tell you why-why … a-b-b-bout … m-me … us … ex … plain … but …. but ..."

She paused to take a few ragged breaths and continued. "It … m-m-makes me so hap-p-p-py to hear you say I'm n-n-n-not just a tag-a-long be-be-because of Tsika. I-I-I w-want you, Blar, to be pr-pr-proud of me. It means s-s-s-s-s-so much that you th-think I'm w-worthy to be here. And, Tsika is right – th-there's a lot of f-f-fangirl in that."

She paused to collect herself. "M-m-my i-i-idol Blar Umlaut thinks I p-play gui-guitar well!"

Glycerin made a happy little squeak noise. Blar couldn't stop himself any more. All the work she had put into getting all those thoughts out into the air and that little happy noise skewered his heart, he had to let her know.

"Little Dancer? You worked so hard just now. I can't stop myself. I'm going to give you a hug. Please don't scream or die." Blar turned to his side and wrapped her in his arms. He squeezed gently. That tall, slender body triggered memories of someone else he had held close long before in another age.

Surprisingly, there were no screams or death. In fact, he could feel Glycerin smiling against his cheek though she was trembling like an autumn leaf in a storm. Her fingertips were on his collarbone. Blar was pretty certain she was purring. They stayed that way for much longer than he thought his hug was going to last.

Glycerin's hands pushed him away. They were gentle hands, but firm. Her eyes had a glimmer of fear in them and she lost eye contact with him. "I … you … I don't think … likely b-better w-we should stop there. My precious Tsika. It was nice … I … I … I like you, Blar. You're going to be s s-so good f-for her." Shaky fingertips gently stroked his ear and cheek, then his hair before retreating.. "We sh-sh-should s-s-sleep now."

"Good night, Little Dancer. I liked this talk with you." Blar lay back on his pillow, but spent a while processing what just happened. Slowly he faded out listening to her soft breathing.

- - - - - -

Blar's eyes flipped open. Still dark, what had awakened him? Something heavy, oh! This is quite pleasant.

In her sleep, Glycerin had curled up against him and thrown a leg across his hips. Her arm was draped across his chest. Her head lay on his shoulder with her nose nuzzled into his neck. She had done the same thing when he had slept over at Hans' club with the band after the last performance. The practical part of his mind wondered if he was a substitute for some treasured body pillow she had left in Los Angeles.

Whatever the cause, it was certainly enjoyable to have her close and trusting him even if it was while she was asleep. Hopefully, he wouldn't lose any essential body parts when she woke up and panicked in the morning. Blar adjusted the blankets over her for warmth, then slipped his arm around her to stroke her back before fading back into sleep.

- - - - - -

Blar awoke to the sensation of fingertips stroking his hair. There seemed to be a lot of nice moments like that in his life lately. He opened his eyes expecting to see Tsika's aristocratic little face. Surprisingly, Glycerin's lavender eyes were what he focused on as she leaned over him. She was brushing his hair out of his face and arranging it. She flinched at his gaze, but stood her ground by the bed.

"I-I-I'm done in the loo, err, the b-bathroom. I-I-I'm going to w-wake the others." She started to turn away but then turned back and smiled as she whispered, "Good morning, B-Blar." Then she got an odd expression and left the bedroom, closing the door.

Blar decided to just not analyze that and got himself up. At least, he hadn't awakened to panicked shrieks, kicks, and punches. Or worse, a catatonic guitarist. What was today? Oh, yeah, coffeehouse club and weirdness to do. He rolled out of bed and trudged to the bathroom.

Okay, life has changed dramatically when the bathroom smells good. Lavender scent. Blar smacked his forehead. Duh! Her bath soap scent matches her eyes and makeup.

- - - - - -

After everyone was dressed, Blar inspected the troops and suggested a couple of changes. Mostly he pushed for toning down Kpau's glitter and glitz. He suggested she wear a vest over her bikini top to cover a bit more skin. "Kpau, we're emphasizing quirky, not rock star."

"Well, with me, they are getting 'surfer girl' no matter how I dress! But … grrrrrr! Rawrgh! Okay old boring prude! I'll turn my glitter knob down to five!" Kpau huffed off to make adjustments.

Glycerin was actually a bit racier than usual. She wore a form-fitting corset, topping off a naughty school girl look with her school cap, skirt, and boots.

Blar estimated that she would be a crowd pleaser with that and disarm possible sneering from the hipster crowd. He just smiled at her and nodded. He got that treasured little mysterious half-smile back as she gazed down at the floor.

Tsika. Well, she easily fit in with the Castro leather scene with her gear. Really, really fine in a sexy evil way. Anyone sneering at her would likely lose an important body part. Leather choker, laced up long gloves, sharp spikes everywhere – school girl demon dominatrix.

In the crossfire time, the women had a lot to say about Blar's outfit and it wasn't positive. Kpau was the loudest. "Really? We have to take you shopping and update you! You look like the Mad Hatter in a purple haze!"

"Why, thank you, Chicklet. That's exactly what I was looking for. I'm the psychedelic ring master for a three ring circus of feminine charm." That did not have the desired effect of placating the two goblins.

Tsika pranced up to Blar and toyed with his mustache, "Let me get my fucking whip, darling. We'll see about that 'master' bullshit." She smiled sweetly and batted her eyelashes as she swung her small hips in the walk away while Kpau and Glycerin giggled.

"Errrrrr, yeah. Okay, point taken. I'm painfully aware I'm not fitting in well visually. I'm trying to step over to the sorts of style you three like to wear. Obviously I'm not there yet."

Suddenly Tsika was back in his arms, cooing and stroking. "Is okay, Bear! We fix you up as we go along. Bear just needs us to help with some tweaks, am I right everyone?"

Blar had the distinct feeling he was having his head patted as a lost cause by the trio as they giggled agreement.

"Right. My future will have more glitter. Let's head over to the club and start trying to make something useful out of this so Harvey won't regret hosting our weekend here. One thing nice about this part of town, no one is even going to blink at how we're dressed as we walk over."

Blar grabbed his jacket, Tsika and Glycerin slung their guitar cases over their shoulders, and they were off to work. Kpau provided the musical theme music as they strolled towards the club, quietly singing a pornographic version of the old classic *"Heigh Ho"* march song from a certain old Disney film.

- - - - - -

Blar introduced the women to the club owner. Harvey was a tall thin mildly flamboyant man who gushed over the outfits "the girls" were wearing. Blar was treated to the amusing sight of the statuesque Glycerin cowering behind tiny Tsika during the introductions. Tsika slowly reeled Glycerin out in a clearly well-practiced move to at least shake the club owner's hand.

Harvey was extremely happy to have someone filling his Friday night entertainment. He sincerely tried to be helpful but he simply didn't have a working drum set that met either Kpau's or Blar's minimum needs. Blar told Kpau to be creative with anything she could find in the club "stomp style" – garbage cans, pots, whatever. He decided to take a couple of hours to hit up a few pawn shops and local instrument shops. Kpau attacked her mission with fervent glee. Harvey had someone bring them bagel sandwiches and coffee for breakfast as he tried to protect club assets from Kpau's imaginative scavenging.

By the time Kpau and Blar had cobbled together a working drum set, it was after lunch. Tsika had taken her own initiative and scrounged up sandwiches from down the street. Blar assembled a draft playlist and conferred with Harvey about it while the girls warmed up and checked out the stage sound circuits. After a lot of red ink and grumbling, Blar called a band meeting.

"Okay, Harvey thinks we'll survive with this. We're going to do a theme of 'Haight Ashbury Ironic'. A lot of dead people, long improv jams between each song. We'll open with *'Are You Gonna Be My Girl'* just for a splash, then some *INXS* starting with *'Need You Tonight'*. After that, we'll have Kpau vocal on the *B52s* tune *'Roam'* followed by her scandalous version of *'Our Lips Are Sealed'*. After those tunes on the list, we'll have a break there. We'll finish with Tsika's cover of *'Outside'* and then *'Gimme Shelter'* turning

Glycerin loose to jam out on the finish. I'm not going to waste any original tunes on an audience that may just spend the time chattering over coffee. Any comments?" They all looked it over. Harvey had wandered over to join the meeting and was looking over Tsika's shoulder.

Kpau wrinkled her nose. "Wow, that's pretty soft stuff except on the solos. How about this? Drop my *'Lips'* and have Tsika do *'Egyptian'* at that point. Then we add in *'Stray Cat Strut'* with a long jam. After that, I'll do a cover of *'Call Me'* before *'Roam'*. That's all stuff we've got a handle on and seems more like the ambience we saw last night. Serious retro '80s night … I should have worn more make up." The perky blonde smirked.

Everyone seemed agreeable to Kpau's changes. Harvey particularly liked her input and said so.

"Blar! Just send Kpau over from now on instead of you. She's much prettier to look at and I think she's smarter than you are." Blar laughed as he threw his hat at Harvey.

"Yeah, yeah, sure, sure – I'd worry about your lechery if you leaned her way." Harvey let them know he would feed them dinner before the show so they wouldn't have to go scrounging. That earned him a big kiss on the cheek and a hug from 'always-hungry' Kpau. The band spent their time practicing for the remainder of the afternoon.

That evening, the first road performance of *"It Really IS Rocket Science!"* went remarkably smoothly. The coffeehouse crowd reaction was decidedly mixed. About half the crowd seemed really entertained; the rest were at least civil or ignored the band. Tsika did get a remarkable reception from most of the audience with her vocal cover of *"Outside"*, an '80s composition created by a group called *Tribe* long lost to time. It was a catchy melody with poetically epic phrasing about unstoppable change and bravely facing an uncertain future.

Blar couldn't stop smiling during the elfin goth's performance. So much power and volume out of that small body. Tsika had great stage presence and projection, able to tightly focus a song's emotional content. Her physical moves and facial expressions seemed utterly natural on stage. As he watched her, Blar wondered if the little sprite had ever covered any tunes by Annie Lennox. There were parallels in their voicing would fit well. He silently filed some ideas away for Tsika to consider when they arrived at the retreat.

After the performance, the band mingled with the audience. Glycerin seemed to win the simple fan body count though she drove them nuts by clinging to Blar. She just kept flashing everyone her little terrified smiles. Blar computed that her fashion sense and exotic look was meshing with the eclectic coffeehouse crowd. It didn't hurt that her high caliber jazz improvisation skills during her solos had shut down even the most jaded chatter bugs in the crowd.

Kpau was running interference for Glycerin. Blar thought it was fascinating watching her manage the sphere around Glycerin. She "explained nicely" to everyone that Glyc was really shy but they could say hello one at a time. Kpau ran the queue and admitted each sycophant. Blar admiration for the blonde's bulldog persistence in protecting her constructed family grew.

He didn't feel totally ignored. Some of the older members of the crowd recognized him from his *Gothic Fire* band days. Blar used the opportunity to ask his old fans to spread the word that he had linked up with this new band. He told them to keep an eye out for their appearances up in Portland in the spring time ahead.

Blar kept glancing around for Tsika as the royal court for Glycerin proceeded. He finally spotted her in a small circle of new fans surrounding her at the bar. She seemed to be handling it quite regally. The flashing eyes, the smile, occasional touch – making each one feel like they were important. He hoped she was keeping an eye on going overboard. There was a fine line to maintain, crossing it easily resulted in creepy stalkers or worse. Aina could give the women plenty of tips and anecdotes in that department. Blar remembered he needed to call his former band mate and see if she had gotten a chance to look over the videos and materials he had sent. If things went as he hoped, she would likely jump at the chance to take them under her indie label.

Harvey was immensely satisfied with the results. "Blar, I got both music and buzz going here tonight! Your girls and their conversation are keeping the crowd here far longer than they usually stay. Who'd have thought that? Usually by now, they're off to the darker bars! Heh! Thanks for coming through for me!"

Blar gave Glycerin a gentle hug as she clung to him. She was managing to wave at a departing fan. "Harvey, I'm just happy this went smoothly for the women. They're pretty new at this and I'd like to get a few of these upbeat gigs under their belt before they hit the dive circuit where crowds can be rougher."

- - - - - -

Much later that night back at the hotel, no one made it more than a few feet inside before sprawling on some piece of furniture. In Kpau's case, her choice of furniture was the rug on the floor – face down on it. She mumbled into the shag fabric.

"Dunno which was more work, the music or the talking."

Blar deposited Glycerin in a chair and broke out some stout beers he had stored in the room's fridge.

"I didn't see anyone hitting the hard stuff, here's some liquid protein. Anyway, we've done the duty to pay for our hotel time this weekend. Harvey got a good deal with his Friday night, we got a place to stay for the weekend. Tomorrow, we can hit Union Street, Haight-Ashbury, and Japantown. Sunday we can do the Wharf – eat some seafood? How does that sound?"

Kpau already had her beer half finished. Glycerin and Tsika were sipping theirs much more slowly. Tsika blushed and coughed. "Um. Hey! Comfy darling Bear!" She wiggled her toes and shifted uncomfortably in her chair. "There is something this one would like to do that might sound kind of stupid." Blar and Kpau looked inquisitively while Glycerin giggled quietly. She apparently knew what Tsika wanted and found it amusing. Tsika squirmed more violently and finally blurted her dreadful desire out.

"I would like to go see Ripley's *Believe It Or Not* Museum!"

Blar just blinked at her. "You're … kidding. That old tourist trap?"

She nodded and fired up some impressively lethally cute eyes at Blar. "This pixie has never gotten to see such things! Can we?"

Kpau lay back down and snorted, "She didn't need to use the whip. The Princess of Darkness used the far more deadly puppy eyes. No resistance possible. I'm in! I love campy fun-house stuff."

Blar rolled his eyes and caved in. "Okay, I give up without a fight. Do you want to do ALL the touristy stuff on the Wharf? That'll kill the whole weekend. Hardly any time for clothing shopping?"

Blar had a premonition he knew the answer before he finished the sentence as he watched her light up.

"Yes! Oh, yes, big Bear! This pixie would love that! All the kitschy Americana! The sleaziness!" Tsika hopped over and landed in his lap, hugging him and demolishing whatever molecules remained of his resistance with big shiny eyes and wiggles.

Kpau rolled over and sucked the last drop of beer out of her bottle. "And three strikes, he's out. Come on, Glyc. Sleep with me tonight. You're a better pillow and the Princess gets mad when I thrash around too much in my sleep."

Tsika looked startled. "Wait .. what? Aren't we…? Rock-paper? Rock? … Scissors?" But Glycerin and Kpau made their escape to their room quickly and shut the door before she finished her babbling.

Blar watched Tsika. She actually seemed disconcerted and a bit alarmed even. Blar was not reading the situation well, he was too tired. Had something changed while he wasn't paying attention? Tsika seemed to realize the vibe she was giving off and apologized quickly.

"I'm sorry, Bear. You are not problem. They surprised me. They usually don't catch me off-guard like that."

Blar yawned and stroked the back of her head. "Kpau has all the subtlety of a wolverine on acid."

An uncomfortable silence descended as Tsika dropped her eyes. Her worried face began pinking up.

Blar was sympathetic. "It is okay. I have told you about a dozen times since we decided to take this path that taking things slow was a good idea. The *Rocket Science* project is front and center. It consumes so much energy. I'll give you the same spiel I gave Glycerin about sharing the bed. Any way you want to handle the sleeping arrangements is fine."

Tsika's shoulders slumped sadly. "I'm sorry, Blar. For all my bluster, flirting, and teasing, I'm kind of old-fashioned. Precious Bear, I want … I want the first time with someone to be important and special and right, not rushed or when we're tired out of our minds like right now."

Blar put his arms around her and held her head against his chest. "Really, it's fine. I can barely see straight at the moment. I'm just looking forward to curling up with you even if we're both snoring thirty seconds later."

Tsika's eyes widened. "I don't snore! … Do I? Is it … awful?"

Blar grabbed a twin tail in each hand and gently bobbled her head with them. "No! It is cute as hell! Tiny little noises! For god's sake, let's go to sleep." He grinned and kissed her nose. She raised her lips higher and gave him a long kiss.

"You're right, darling Bear. This energy rabbit's batteries are totally drained." Tsika did an acceptable impersonation of a yawning cat. Blar noted she still had her tonsils. He heaved himself up with her in his arms. "Kpau calls you portable, you know. I agree."

She giggled as he carried her to the bedroom and sat her on the bed. Blar couldn't stop yawning while he spoke. "Oh bother! I carted you in here but I suppose you need to get some stuff. I'm off to the bathroom while you do that."

- - - - - -

Twenty minutes later, Blar was half dozing in bed when Tsika tiptoed back into the room. Blar noted her taunting pronouncements about sleeping naked were more bluster. She had on a huge dark gray night shirt printed with black spiders. Her hair was unbound into her now familiar lovely unkempt fountain of long curliness. Tsika pranced over and dived under the covers to snuggle up with him, wiggling her dainty toes under his leg for warmth. She lay her head on his shoulder and looked up at him with tired, plaintive eyes.

"Blar? Are we EVER going to be not too exhausted, busy, or interrupted?"

Blar kissed her forehead and massaged her back. "If life goes like it did in my old band, there will always be too much going on, but at some point things will happen anyway. My band mates and I survived that. For a while anyway. I think this band will, too. Sweet dreams, soft and cuddly Tsarina." Blar chuckled and braced himself.

Sharp claws dug into Blar as he guessed they would. He had used her birth name. "I would KEEEEL you but I'm too tired and you're too warm and snuggly. You are on notice, Evil Bear. I will discover your true name and cast spells and curses on you."

Blar kissed her til she stopped struggling. Tsika draped against him, putting as much of her body against him as she could and making sure his arm was around her. A minute later she was passed out. Blar gently ran his fingertips along her body, enjoying the curve of her hips, her slender waist, the back of her thighs, and then resting his hand on her back. He could feel her little heart beating and soft breath on his chest. Lovely feeling.

Blar's last waking thought was how life was pretty good at the moment and he would never willingly go back to the financially secure crypt he had created before he met Tsika and her little group of misfits.

- - - - - -

~13~ "Sisters of the Moon" – Stevie Nicks

Blar wheeled the band's rental van up the entrance ramp onto the interstate highway leaving San Francisco. He was a bit less wealthy now despite having saved the cost of the hotel room for the weekend with their gig. Kpau, Tsika, and Glycerin had bags of souvenirs, shirts, funny hats, goofy sunglasses, and big stupid happy grins on their faces. Blar should have been irritable but the grins made it impossible to stay grumpy.

Merry Christmas Eve, you trio of little terrors.

He was either going to have to adjust his burn rate calculations or avoid any major cities with any entertainment. Blar wondered if he was being too much the curmudgeon. He wasn't that much older than they were. Only ten years. Really. Really? Some moments they seemed so young and child-like, other moments they had those mile-deep looks in their eyes, running circles around him in their thinking.

Things were starting to feel complicated. Blar had gotten a rash of clues in the last couple of weeks that Glycerin had a massive crush or worse for him. He and Tsika had purposely slowed progress down with each other. That was a mutual decision between the two of them to focus on the band. Blar had watched too many bands implode from internal drama, including his own first band. However, Tsika was obviously concerned that she wasn't "doing right" in their haphazard romance. Meanwhile, Blar was worried about damaging Glycerin's progress towards normality if he didn't respond positively to her. More worrisome, he found her endearing sweet attraction quite compelling.

He remained baffled at Tsika's encouragement of him moving closer to Glycerin. Was she using him as medicine or something? At least Kpau was on a stable plateau of acting as his buddy – daughter – little sister – flirt – succubus? What the hell was she to him?

Blar glanced up into the rear view mirror at Kpau's seat. She wasn't there. He used the mirror to glance over at Glycerin and saw the blonde's disarray of hair piled up against the shy woman's chest. Glycerin spotted his eyes and shrugged her shoulders in resignation, mouthing the words "my little dove" with a heartstopping smile.

Blar scanned the road watching the traffic, then glanced over at Tsika, who was riding shotgun. She had a pinwheel music-box device that played "Music Box Dancer", an instrumental briefly popular in the 1980s. She was turning blue in the face as she blew on the pinwheel to keep the music playing.

Too damn cute.

She noticed his glance and gave him a gleaming smile as she lay her seat back and put her naked feet up on the dash. She stretched her yummy slender alabaster legs out from her frilly skull-dotted skirt. Lethally cute -- but now Blar worried about pretty legs breaking if the airbag deployed. He told his brain to shut up so he could concentrate on driving safely. He was feeling really sensitive lately about the 'old man talking' label thanks to Kpau's torture.

Blar had a feeling he would be the only one awake in about half an hour. Fortunately, he had slept really well last night. Kpau had simply declared herself the Sunday night "Sleeps with Blar" winner by fiat. He wondered if she had plotted that to make sure Blar was well-rested. Kpau slept fairly solidly and without thrashing, except for one bad moment when a bad dream had bothered her in the night.

Blar had awakened to the sound of Kpau whimpering in her sleep and clinging to his chest. He had rocked her a bit until whatever night terror it was went away. She never actually woke up during the incident. He recalled Glycerin mentioning that Kpau ended up in her bed sometimes in the night. Blar hypothesized bad dreams were an ongoing problem for the fit little blonde.

San Francisco gave way to Redwood City, then to Sunnyvale. Now Blar really was the only one awake. He actually relished that – it meant fewer stops. He had originally planned on cutting over to Santa Cruz and taking the scenic Pacific Coast Highway down, but with them asleep he would merge over to the much faster Highway 101 and then jump off at Salinas over to their destination in Monterey. Blar hadn't told them but he was actually heading a little farther south towards Carmel for their Christmas surprise.

He was really surprised Glycerin hadn't connected the dots about his secretive plan for their Christmas destination, but she seemed oblivious. He guessed the stress of public traveling and just being around him was distracting her. The drive down to the peninsula was turning out to be quite nice. It was fairly sunny with cloud breaks and a soft chorus of female snoring. Blar put on some New Age jazz music to get into the right frame of mind for where they were headed. Ray Lynch and Deuter were two of his favorites. The percolating rhythmic melodies also blotted out the snoring.

- - - - - -

Blar pulled back onto the freeway after making a pit stop to purchase small meals for everyone. No one awoke during his drive-through. Blar had gotten suspicious looks from the window clerk as she surveyed the trio of inert feminine bodies in the van. So it usually went in his life. Blar ate his meal as he drove.

Blar was zipping down the highway parallel to the state beaches leading into Monterey when Tsika stirred. She sniffed the air and followed her nose. Picking through the meal bag, she selected a chicken burger and began munching as she took in the view.

"Are we there yet? Ha ha! I've never gotten to say that! Oh … that is pretty!" Tsika caught sight of the sandy dunes bordering the ocean. She picked at her eyes to clean her lashes. "Good thing you got a good night's sleep, Blar darling. Or did Kpau thrash you in the night?"

Blar shook his head, "No, just one little … bad dream."

Tsika bit her lip. "You are obviously understating. Her night terrors never seem to ever completely go away. She's never really said much about them. Just apologizes and brushes them off." They both stopped talking as they heard a big yawn from the back seat.

Blar grinned, "I think I'm getting good enough at this to know that's

Glycerin's yawn. Did you sleep well, Little Dancer?" He couldn't see her in his mirror but he could imagine the color transitions on her face.

"Y-y-yes! This... this lorrey van has p-plushy seats, and Kpau gets v-very warm when she sleeps."

Blar's silly grin transitioned to a warm smile. Each day she was stammering less when she spoke to him.

"Well, slap Kpau around! She needs to be awake for our arrival." Blar made a turn off the highway and they began winding through the streets of Monterey.

Kpau's eyes opened as she wailed, "Nooooo, no slapping! Use the soft cushions! But push all the stuffing up one end!" Kpau sat up and rubbed her eyes. "Ah! Monterey! Been ages since … I've … " her voice died away.

Blar looked in the rearview mirror at Kpau. He could swear there was a tear forming in her eye. She quickly wiped her eyes and just looked out the window smiling. No question about it, he could tell her "shields up" smile from a genuine one now.

Then Kpau pointed and wiggled more happily. "Oh, look! There's the Wharf! Food! Souvenirs!!!"

Blar flinched at that last word. "There is a restaurant there that I like. It specializes in squid dishes. Maybe we'll get a chance – "

Tsika had spotted Blar's grimace and tittered as she hugged her bag of San Francisco souvenirs. "I think we've been abusive enough of the budget, darling Blar. But aren't we supposed to be stopping near here somewhere?"

It was time to reveal some of his Christmas surprise. "I … I lied just a little bit. We're actually staying a little farther out. My friend lives on 17 Mile Drive and we're going to stay there. We're headed that way now."

Tsika's eyebrow cocked, "Your careful choice of pronouns and nouns is most disturbing. Okay, play your little game. I am just glad Christmas Eve will not include snow. It is blustery here but much warmer."

Blar wound his way through town towards Carmel, then took the turn onto

17 Mile Drive. He got out of the car briefly to speak to the guard at the gate before traveling on. As he drove, the women would drop their jaws and express awe at the multimillion dollar homes they passed. Many of the homes weren't even visible, just castle walls covered in ivy giving subtle indication of superfluous wealth within. They drove by a golf course fairway peeking out from the trees. That sight got Glycerin animated.

"Oh! G-g-golf! I remember … rem … da-d-d-dy … h-h-h-he t-t-t-took … me …." Damn it, her stuttering was back in full force. After that, she only mustered ragged breaths. He could see in the mirror that Kpau had taken Glycerin's hand and was stroking it. Glycerin had tears streaming down her cheeks but was silently stifling any other noises.

Had this been a terrible idea? It seems like I am mostly doing a splendid job of evoking deeply buried and painful memories. Jesus, what's going to happen when we get there?

His personal depression was interrupted by a small hand touching his arm. Tsika was watching him sympathetically. She quietly whispered, "It is okay. It happens at random to all three of us. Seems more often lately with all the stress we have been under. It's just how our evil little memories mess with us. We're happy happy and then pop! Smacks us in the face. Not your fault."

"Gods, I hope this goes well. It seemed like a great idea when I hatched it." Blar looked regretful. Tsika took his arm in both hands and squeezed it to comfort him.

Finally, he got to the gate he was looking for. It was open. Blar turned the van down the drive path. Behind the gate was a tight knit tunnel of eucalyptus trees. It was exceptionally clarifying. To the point, it was strong enough to sting nostrils.

Blar chuckled as all three women reacted loudly to the blast of scent from the trees I their own special way.

"Holy!" "Fuck!" "…!"

After a hundred feet, the trees gave way to open sky on a private road that hugged a short cliff that traced the edge of the beach. The sun had almost set, but there was still enough light to see the surf and the scrub-covered dunes. Everyone could see the twinkle of lights of a residence at the cliff top they were headed toward. Kpau stuck her head between the two front seats and peered at the small cluster of lights.

"Let me borrow a line from Tsika, Papa Bear. Fuck me to hell, this is a nightclub owner's house? I picked the wrong career path!" Kpau whistled long and low.

Blar smirked but remained silent and drove. Glycerin had restored her composure by now. She put her head next to Kpau's to see better. Soon enough, the van pulled up to the front entry way. The home wasn't huge by neighborhood standards but it was elegant, an ultra-modern split-level design. Expensive architects had been clearly involved. The side of the house near the ocean was largely made of glass. The women speculated as to whether it was a party room or pool. Blar said nothing.

"Okay, everyone just leave their stuff in the car. It'll be taken care of." They got out of the car and stood together looking at the house.

Kpau stared at the house briefly and Blar could swear an actual light bulb appeared over her goofy head. She struck an action pose, pointing her fist at Blar. "Ah ha! Now I see! It'll be taken care of! Dead giveaway! This is when we're drugged and we wake up later as sex slaves in the opium pleasure pits of Shanghai! I've dissected your little plan! You won't take me! Or maybe you will … seduce me and we'll see!" She leaped around Blar and jumped on his back, throwing her arms around his neck and growling in between giggles.

"So much for decorum! Get off me, you little ferret!" Blar pulled Kpau bodily over his shoulder and held her upside down by the waist as she wiggled and loudly enumerated planned acts of revenge in hysterical laughter. The other two women simply stood back and rolled their eyes at the roughhousing. He rotated Kpau and dropped her on her feet. She bowed and held out her arm.

"Shall we go to the ball, now, Mr. Bond?" She batted her eyes and stuck her tongue out.

"I'm more tempted to shove half a grapefruit in your face. Google that movie, little joker." Blar ruffled her hair up, then walked to the door. He pressed the door chime button. Instead of a boring buzzer, they were treated to an incredibly complex high pitched melody. Glycerin perked up. If she had cat ears they would have twitched to full alert. But she still looked perplexed. Blar let himself enjoy a slight smile.

A butler answered the door. Kpau said it. "Really? A butler? Well, fu – " Tsika clamped her hand over Kpau's mouth and smiled aristocratically at the butler. Blar shook his head in resignation, then smiled at the man.

"Hello, Alwyn. It's been a long time. I think I'm grayer than you now." Blar bowed slightly.

Alwyn bowed more generously, "Oh, there are elixirs for the hair that do wonder, sir. And who are the lovely ladies you've graced the doorstep with?"

Blar gestured as he spoke. "I'd like to introduce you to Tsika Tsarinkov, Kpau Angela Williams, and Glycerin Ping Wendham . Ladies, this is Alwyn Lewis, the house butler who serves our gracious host so well." Alwyn bowed to them but when he came up he was smirking at Blar and chuckling.

"Ah, very good sir. I detect you are still playing your little surprise. I shan't shatter the suspense. I will take care of your things in your motor car momentarily. Please come in." He backed up to let them enter.

Glycerin did a brave thing. She spoke directly to Alwyn. "Alwyn, is th-that a Ll-Llandrindod accent? I spent t-t-time at a boar-r-rding school n-near there. It … s-sounds famil-familiar."

Alwyn didn't even blink at her stammering. "Quite a good ear, Miss Wendham. But I've heard you have an outstanding set of ears and dexterous hands. I must break protocol and say that I'm quite excited that I may hear you play in person."

Alywn won the daily prize for making Glycerin blush the most with the color of red she managed on her cheeks. It was a happy blush but one might fear she would bleed from the pores. Her mouth moved, but no sound emerged at first. Then Glycerin hugged Blar's arm like a wary mouse as she stammered inarticulate happy noises as they walked.

The entry hall was austere but exquisite. Tsika's eyes scanned the contents. "Hmmm, Scandinavian themes. But I do see elements of Feng Shui and splashes of Buddhist thought in the styling. Someone has either done a lot of traveling or is very eclectic."

Blar simply continued to smile. Alwyn led them down the hall towards the glass end of the house. They could hear music now, electronic ethereal tonalities. The sounds contained complex melodies at just the edge of audible, interlaced with smooth deep tones.

Tsika actually figured out Blar's surprise first. Her eyes widened and she grabbed Blar's arm to pull him down to her. She whispered in a shaky voice. "Blar, this is wonderful. Let Glycerin go first. Please?"

Blar nodded and gently maneuvered Glycerin in front of him directly behind Alwyn. She was listening to the music curiously but still hadn't had any epiphany.

Tsika dropped back and whispered to Kpau. He could hear Kpau responding with a long "ooooo" sound.

They entered the glass area they had seen from outside. Alwyn stepped aside as they entered. The large solarium-style room turned out to be a musical studio. Electronics, synthesizers, amplifiers, and mysterious custom boxes were scattered everywhere. Intermixed with these elements was a thick garden of plant life: ivy, flowers, vegetables, and other edibles. There were also free standing sculptures of metal and stone, some of which had mobile elements that reacted to any breeze. In the center of all this rather random clutter was a complex array of keyboards and control banks. A woman sat at them playing, making the music they were hearing.

Glycerin understood. Her realization struck her physically as she stumbled. She was shaking and trembling. Blar could hear quiet shuddering little sobs from the tall gentle shy creature.

Tsika took the trembling woman's hand and patted it. "Yes, precious Glycca.

It really is her."

Blar wasn't sure what to do at this point so he simply said, "Merry Christmas, Glycca. Go say hello."

Glycerin let go of Tsika and took little halting steps. Blar could see her shoulders jerking now as the sobs got louder. The woman at the keyboards stopped playing. The sampled undertone tracks percolated away on their own. She stood up, turning to Glycerin with an excited smile – until she saw Glycerin's reaction. Her expression turned to sympathetic concern.

The woman was taller than Glycerin even without heels but the same slender build as Glycerin. In a mirror image sort of reflection, her skin was pale ice white, her hair was long, flowing, and completely silver. She was dressed in white with hints of ice blue that matched the color of her eyes. She could have passed for a Norse Ice Queen. Blar couldn't help a slight chuckle – his former band-mate had obviously wanted to make a big impression on the trio.

Blar could hear Kpau muttering beside him, "She looks like an elf from Tolkien. Too bright to look at."

Glycerin couldn't move her feet any more. She shook so badly Blar became concerned she was going to be unable to stand. The woman moved quickly to Glycerin, taking her into a supportive hug. Blar heard the same little dolphin shriek he remembered hearing the first time Glycerin met him. This shriek was longer and possibly higher. The silver haired woman gave Blar an accusing look.

"Bad bad Blar! You've nearly killed her! Come sit with me, little Glycerin. Come on, come on, sit with Aina. I've been waiting anxiously to meet you!"

Aina. Blar's former band mate from *Gothic Fire*, the keyboardist of Glycerin's daydreams about stardom. She cooed and cuddled Glycerin to calm the young woman. Aina eventually coaxed her to a bench where she sat Glycerin down and then sat next to her. Tsika followed them, almost in a trance herself, sitting next to Glycerin and stroking her back.

Blar heaved a sigh of relief. That instant of peace was interrupted as he found himself jerked down right into the upturned face of Kpau. Kpau grabbed him around the waist and hugged him. She was squeezing so hard he wasn't sure if he was being attacked again. She looked up into his eyes and squealed happily at him. She had a huge genuine smile and wet eyes.

"Papa Bear … if you never do ANYTHING else right the rest of your life, this made up for it. Glycerin … literally wouldn't be here without Aina and her music. You hear? Literally." Kpau watched the trio on the bench while still wrapping her arms around him. She whispered quietly to Blar.

"I'm going to tell you a little story, Papa Bear, but you act surprised if either of them tell you later because we don't like to talk about each other's past."

Kpau pulled Blar farther away from the other women. "Glycerin tried to commit suicide almost a dozen times before she was thirteen. You've noticed her scars, right?" Kpau paused to let that sink in.

"I'm sure they may brushed around how Glycerin lost her family, but that's just smoke and mirrors to keep her from having flashbacks. She was with hers like I was with mine. Her parents and her brothers, the whole family, was traveling the coastal villages in New Guinea. Her dad was in the British Foreign Service. Remember that tsunami back in the '90s that killed several thousand people? Before the big one in 2004? It hit them. It killed everyone in her family except her, the youngest. Her dad just barely managed to put her on the roof as the wave came in – the debris smashed the rest before they could get up with her. Glycca got to watch the whole thing from the roof. A little five year old girl."

Kpau paused again. She shuddered as if she was living Glycerin's story herself. "Little girl was stuck there alone for two days with the remains of her family down below. Snakes and other things covered the roof with her. Just to add to the trauma, the first men on the scene made a mess of recovering the remains before they spotted her watching." Kpau shuddered. "I've figured this out through bits and pieces over the years. Tsika says she was told it was almost two years after that before Glyc said more than a word. She just kept trying to kill herself. Somewhere in that dark hell, a little after she met Tsika, she discovered your band's music and especially Aina.

Changed her focus. Some of that self destructiveness shifted to music."

Kpau stopped to watch Aina stroking Glycerin's hair before continuing. "Tsika tells this part of the story better. Aina, her music, her solo stuff, the stuff she did with your band – Glycerin was fascinated with everything. She became obsessed with learning the keyboard but the big spaz couldn't sit still behind a keyboard. Lost her way again. She picked up the guitar entirely by accident stumbling around in the music lab. She just dove into it. And years later, that led to the amazing Glycerin you see today."

Kpau watched the trio on the bench. Aina was cooing and calming Glycerin. Glycerin was staring at a vision of her idol made real, trembling in disbelief. Tsika was running her hand up and down her friend's back. Kpau shook her head and continued.

"Tsika says Glycerin played her guitar every day, every spare moment. Hours and hours. She said she had only one option if she wanted stay with Glyc. That's when Tsika picked up bass guitar."

Kpau pursed her lips. "Tsika was, um, quite destructive in junior high I've learned over time. Strangely enough that tended to alienate people, leaving her friendless. Glycerin became kind of her princess to defend."

The little blonde went silent briefly. Glycerin was finally getting short sentence fragments out between ragged breaths to Aina. Tsika held Glycerin's hand, smiling at her big Mouse as the occasional tear ran down her cheek.

"Seriously, you could not have done any better, Blar. And hey, look! I got my Christmas Lights! The place is covered in them! I bet you told her." Kpau crossed her eyes. "Though, I am going to take a wild guess that Aina is quirky enough this place is always covered in lights year round." She looked at Blar out of the corner of her eyes as she smirked.

Blar nodded, "Yeah, quirky is right. The colors change with her moods but there's always twinkle lights. Aina did say she would make sure they were Christmas colored for you."

Kpau moved closer to the trio so she could hear the conversation, pulling

Blar along with her. Glycerin was rather animated now though she was still having trouble making eye contact with Aina. She couldn't seem to get words out fast enough now. Sentence fragments bounced around like steel balls in a pachinko machine.

"I tried to play k-keyboards … wanted t-to be like y-you. But … couldn't s-s-sit still. So … much … sitting! How d-do you d-do it? You … y-you were so pretty … and y-you're even prettier now! We look at my bloody hair … and our face … so desperately wanted … to be pretty like y-you."

Aina was transfixed by Glycerin, watching her move, speak, gesture. "Glycerin! You're absolutely gorgeous! We're like mirror image sisters! Light and Dark. We're both tall, thin, long hair, long fingers. You're so very pretty! But you are your own self! You have your guitar playing and – "

Glycerin interrupted her. Wow. Glycerin interrupted her. "I got so m-m-mad! I pushed the k-k-keyboards away. I … wandered … a-a-aaround the music lab … by myself. They left … me by myself." Glyc paused for breath.

"I … I think I w-w-wanted … t-t-to … c-c-cut … f-finish … finally d-do it."

Long pause while Glycerin glared at nothingness. Her face had a dangerous angry look to it for a second. Blar did not miss that Tsika visibly whitened. "T-Then … I picked up a guitar. … s-s-sharp … metal strings, long, sharp … I thought … maybe, maybe those could be used – then I strummed it. "

The deadly expression faded. "Pretty noises! I had h-heard guitar lots of t-times but n-never t-t-touched one. The frets reminded me of keys, b-but more expressive. And! And!" Now Glycerin began lighting up with a happier expression. "I could m-move around while I played! Didn't … have to sit still! And so … I practiced! Practiced so much. It li-lifted m-me away, away fr-from bad memories, just joy when I dance and play."

Glycerin seemed to wake up. She looked at her little twin-tailed friend beside her. "My poor little princess! My precious doll! She … she was … my only friend then. And … we are pretty sure I was her only friend."

Tsika blushed. Glycerin smiled tearfully. "She took up bass guitar just to stay near me. We loves her so much!"

No stammering at all.

Glycerin let go of Aina's hand and hugged Tsika. The little Russian lost whatever composure she had left and cried aloud now. Blar felt overwhelmed. All he had in mind was a little "fan gets to meet a rock goddess" gift. Instead, he had set the stage for something with far deeper emotional bindings.

Aina put her long arms around both Glycerin and Tsika. "And you're all here now! In my home! I'm excited! And I am amazed by the videos Blar has sent me! I want to jam and play with you guys!"

The silver haired beauty looked at Blar. "Blar? No option. You will all stay through the weekend here with me. My new friends? Your bad boy Blar fibbed a lot more than he's let on even now. There's no performance tonight or tomorrow – the club is closed over Christmas break. I'd like you to stay here with me, we'll play and have fun! Then we'll perform at my club this weekend. That's our big holiday celebration – a New Year's rockfest holiday weekend. And! I would like to sit in with you for that if you'll have me?"

Aina squeezed Glycerin and Tsika as she looked to Blar. "Hey, my Blar! This is almost like a reunion, isn't it? The two of us playing together? Meh, close enough for advertising! That's the hook we can use to celebrate the birth of your band at the same time!"

"I thinks that would be an excellent fusion of past and future, pretty Witch."

"Oooh, I'd forgotten you used to call me that. Still the bad Blar, my Blar!" Aina giggled, then moved her attention to Tsika. "Oh, my manners suck! I haven't said a thing to anyone else! This is clearly Tsika, Faerie Princess of Darkness my lecherous Blar keeps raving about. A beautiful sorceress who has bewitched him! I see why!" Tsika's cheeks turned downright rosy.

Aina shifted her gaze to Kpau. "The glittering bauble clinging to Blar's side has to be Kpau, the shiny and energetic Angel of Drumming." Kpau made gagging noises at Aina's compliment.

Aina gave Blar a coy look. "Blar! You had enough trouble with just me! How do you plan to survive THREE such sexy and tasty looking band mates?"

Blar stuck his tongue out at her. "Probably like the way you survived three big ugly metal head thugs. Hiding in a closet frequently. I have considered a monastery."

"Dumbass! I was meditating! Kept me from slicing all your fu-- ... all your throats in the night." Aina laughed and quickly clapped her hands. "But come on, you're probably all starved! Alwyn has already ninja'd off to gather your things and put your car away. Dinner is awaiting in the kitchen! Come on, come on. The Elvish Witch has food for her guests! Yes, Kpau! I hear very well! I'm vain enough to thank you for that compliment."

- - - - - -

Later after dinner, Alwyn was giving the girls a tour of the house and their accommodations. Blar stayed in the kitchen giving Aina a hand with the clean up. Some things hadn't changed. Aina was a busy little kitchen bug.

"So, where's Duane? I was hoping to say hello. Haven't talked to the bastard just for fun in ages! We're always just trading boring business babble." Blar handed Aina a stack of containers to put in the refrigerator.

"He headed out to Hawaii for the week to go surfing. Bastard figured he'd be in the way with a house full of music nerds." She had her head in the fridge trying to find a spot for the last container.

Blar wrinkled his brow. "He isn't still AFRAID of me, is he? How can I dislike a guy who's been so good to you?"

Aina laughed uncertainly, "No, no, he's not ... well, maybe he is ... a bit. You are still quite the rather ... imposing ... scary looking bandit." She stood up and closed the refrigerator door and wiped her hands on her apron, looking at Blar with a fond smirk. Aina arched an eyebrow and then pursed her lips.

"Okay, maybe I chased Duane off a little. It's hard enough to pretend to be angelic but with him around I just head straight to the gutter. Want to make a good impression! My first impulse was that I just wanted to see you and have some good times poking fun at the old pervert who had offered three little girls candy to get on the Magic Bus!" Aina looked thoughtful. "Not gonna poke too hard though. I see a much happier Blar. That alone is a wonderful present. More to the business point, I watched those videos you sent, the audio, the pics. They're good. Your little girls are really, really good. And now I've met them. I feel what compels you. They have powerful magic. Particularly Glycerin. You lucky idiot, you have stumbled onto something awesome in her. Stay the week. Perform this weekend. I want to spend a lot of time with Glycerin. The other two seem more solid and grounded. Glycerin is like a beautiful crystal flower – so beautiful just gazing at it can induce insanity but so fragile the same glance may crush it to dust. We want to protect that. Build some fences. Did you know?"

Blar took a deep breath and shook his head. "I know all three women lost their parents at an early age. The three of them are tightly bonded like a little family. They called themselves *The Lost Girls* before I tagged in. They still think of themselves as such inside the new band. *Lost Girls* is much more than a band name to them. I knew Glyc had a fear of men, that she stammered, that her music took her to her happy place, but not until tonight did I know about the suicide attempts or the tsunami story. I swear, I keep comparing this to bomb squad disarming work and that's no exaggeration. And yes, Tsika and Kpau seem to have a better lock on their demons."

Blar put a stack of dishes away and continued. "Well, you seem to be connecting wonderfully with Glyc. My first encounter with the Little Dancer, she actually got physically ill and passed out. You got a hug." Blar gave her an approving thumbs up.

Aina thumped his chest. "You were first contact with the pretty alien. And you're a big scary man. You made it easy for me, nimrod." She gave him an appraising look. "It's been too long since you were here. I've missed seeing you in person, Blar. Phones and mail just don't quite do it for me."

Aina took off her apron. "Ah well! You're here now! Give the Pretty Elvish Witch a proper hello hug and let's go find your little angelic strumpets of music. It's Christmas Eve. That was Kpau's wish you told me! Christmas Lights and being with her family. I'm adding in some presents for the little angels. My surprise!" Aina went in for a hug and surprised Blar by adding a kiss on his cheek. Aina led him by the hand as the two went in search of Alwyn and his tour.

~14~ "Happy Christmas" – John Lennon & Yoko Ono

Blar and Aina caught up with Alwyn's informal orientation tour as the butler led the trio of women downstairs. Kpau was excitedly flicking her head left and right as she absorbed the sights. She spotted Blar and Aina, squealed and ran back to the pair.

"Papa Bear! He's taking us to the pool. There IS a pool! And a hot tub! And a sauna! And an EXERCISE room!' Six A.M. Tomorrow! You and me!" Without waiting for Blar's response, Kpau raced back to the tour.

Aina arched her eyebrow and mildly glared at her former bandmate. Blar was having a lot of sudden epiphanies in the last few weeks. This one was the realization that Aina and Tsika shared many of the exact same facial expressions. Blar winced as he considered the old proverb about pairing up with the same personality over and over. Aina's lips wiggled as she poked an obviously uncomfortable Blar with her finger.

"Really? Really now? PAPA Bear? What was I saying about little girls and a Magic Bus?"

Blar shrugged in resignation. "Kpau loves a good torture. All will become clear as the week goes by, Pretty Witch. I'm not going to try and explain. Explanations would only get deeply sketchy and I would simply dig myself a deeper grave. Just watch and form your own opinon. You will anyway, dear woman."

Aina's melodic biting laughter carried easily down the stairs. Blar noticed that Tsika turned around to look back. Her expression was slightly – worried? Tsika masked it with a smile and a wave as soon as she saw Blar. He hoped that meant what he thought it meant. A little possessiveness about him?

The pool was small, more of a soaking pool with a view. Kpau was far more focused on the exercise room as she pranced around examining the equipment. Tsika and Glycerin were being polite for Kpau's sake on the matter as far as Blar could divine. Blar didn't think Tsika ever exercised and he had only seen Glycerin doing yoga stretches when she didn't think he was watching her. After a few minutes of Kpau's antics, Aina signaled for everyone's attention.

"I would like to offer desserts and drinks back up in the music room. It's still early this Christmas Eve. I have presents to give all of you!" Aina gestured back up the stairs as she spoke.

The three women simultaneously adopted concerned looks. Tsika spoke first. "Oh god, Aina! We don't have a thing to give you! Blar caught us off guard! Well, we have some silly souvenirs but – "

Aina waved her off. "Your present to me is letting me play music with all of you this week. Think of these as little gifts for setting sail on your big adventure." She turned to Alwyn.

"Alwyn, your choice! You're welcome to join us or not this week as you wish, though I suspect I already know the answer."

Alwyn smiled. "Thank you, madam. I intend to … 'hang out' for much of the week. I'm keen to hear what transpires musically. I'll jump ahead to the kitchen and make some preparations." He made his way up the stairs.

Aina explained to the others. "Technically, Alwyn clocks out after dinner so he can have his own life. Plus, I always give him the week between today and New Years off but over the years Alwyn has become more like a companion of the household and a friend. I would sell the house before I'd lay him off. I'm not sure what he would do without a house to manage. Dumpster dive with me I guess." Aina covered her mouth and giggled as she pictured that image.

As they walked back, Tsika sidled up next to Aina. Blar was not out of hearing range as he brought up the rear of the group but he let Tsika think he was. "Aina? Is this all yours? I thought Blar was well off but … this is amazing."

Aina smiled knowingly, watching Tsika dance around the question she really wanted to ask. "Don't fret, little sprite. My husband Duane of five years now shares my home with me. He's a smashing good copyright lawyer and we share a record label together. Blar played the part of giving me away at our wedding!"

Aina moved a lock of silver hair out of her face as she continued. "Duane is off surfing in Hawaii this week while I play with my new friends. Blar is rather protective and I suspect the big doofus still makes poor Duane a little nervous after all these years."

Aina put her hand on Tsika's shoulder. "Precious Tsika, I like it here. I make my music. I run my club. I love my husband. Blar and I are comrades, linked for life by our memories but I am not about to interfere with his life. I'd certainly wallop the crap out of him if he interfered with mine! I want to help. I particularly want to help your darling friend Glycerin find her way."

Tsika blushed at being so easily caught but said simply, "Thank you. I think this week is going to be a lot of fun. Anyone who helps my Glycca is a friend of mine."

Blar watched his Pretty Witch and Dark Faerie holding hands after that as they made their way to the music room. So, Tsika did feel a bit possessive of him in her odd way. That was nice to know. He could imagine how daunting Aina might look to the young woman. He still found Aina daunting after all these years.

- - - - - -

Alwyn had set out chocolate cheesecake and brandy for everyone. The treats scored swooning praise from Kpau who quickly scarfed down her first serving and drained her drink.

"Oh great Elf Sorceress! May this mortal pond scum have more cheesecake and brandy? You may sacrifice me at your convenience!" Kpau was on her knees holding her plate and glass out with her head bowed.

"Stop it, Kpau! You're embarrassing me!" Aina looked alarmed and amused at the same time. "The cake is right there and you can drink brandy until Blar has to carry your inert mortal remains to your bed." Kpau dropped her mock protocol and leaped over to the table, making drool noises as she cut and poured.

Aina shook her head in bemusement as she watched Kpau's antics. "You're each … so different from each other. Right! Let me get my little baubles for you. I hope they're appropriate. I'll be right back!"

Aina excused herself with Alwyn following her out, offering his own dry commentary. "Kpau's lovely lips make it clear more brandy is needed, or perhaps spiced rum worthy of a pirate. Give me a moment to raid the stocks."

Kpau had simply started finishing off what was left of the bottle by upending it into her mouth.

Blar ignored Kpau's debauchery and turned his attention to Glycerin, who had been floating on her own fleecy clouds since meeting Aina.

"Glycerin! So … what do you think of Aina as a mere human being? Rather than Aina the Nordic Ice Queen of *Gothic Fire*?" Glycerin was startled out of her glowing buzz.

The slender quiet beauty thought for a second. Blar watched her eyes. He had become obsessed with her eyes in the last week or two. When Blar posed his question and she was thinking, one of her pupils was dilated and the other contracted. When she began speaking, the pupils synchronized. Fascinating.

"I … don't know if there's a lot of d-difference. She laughs and s-smiles more. She … She feels more … like home? Motherly? But she's so … shiny and … wise sounding. She … she sounds like she's singing when she talks. When I think of the kind of home a r-rock star lives in, this home is what I think of – "

Glycerin's eyes widened and she began stammering harder. "Oh, Blar! I didn't m-mean … I mean … your place is wonderful … and-and you're so different than the Blar p-persona on stage. But! But! You're doing well, too! I-I like your-your p-place, our place … our … our home! We've n-never really had a h-home. J-just dorms and bunks."

Blar gave a hearty chuckle. "It's okay. I get it, Glycerin. You aren't hurting my feelings. I'll be the first to admit Aina's bets have played out far better than mine."

Blar refilled his glass before continuing. "I'm going to FIRST start a little speech by saying I have come to like you three very much. For me at least, whether we make more or less money seems secondary now. I am going to enjoy the ride. On the other hand, I'm not an idiot idealist. I did the math before gambling how this would play out. In addition to finding you all very amusing and dear companions, I've placed a bet with my life savings. A bet that *Rocket Science* can do as well or better than *Gothic Fire* did. If I lose the bet, I think I still win. Simply because I got to spend the adventure with you lot. Remember? It was either this path or me walking stupid yap rats in the park until they cremated me."

The smiles vanished. Crap. Bad choice of words. Kpau broke the pall with a very serious tone of voice. "You're getting up with me to exercise so that will be a long, long time from now. And we'll be watching your diet, too."

Blar knew she was being sincerely solemn but he started laughing and couldn't stop. "Chicklet, you're telling me this with a mouthful of cheesecake, cheesecake on your face, and brandy dribbles running down between your pretty boobs! You look like a slutty pirate crashing a tea party!" Both Tsika and Glycerin were choking on their drinks as they giggled at Kpau.

Kpau looked at them gleefully. "What? Do I look that bad?" She emptied the last of the bottle down her throat as she jiggled her boobs as she began dancing a pirate jig with the bottle as a prop.

Aina returned with packages and looked bewildered at the ruckus until she saw Kpau. "Oh my goodness! It's clear what moments you seized just now, little spark! They're all over you!" Kpau stood quietly like a small child while Aina towered over her and dabbed off the brandy and cheesecake. While that was going on, Alwyn returned with more brandy and bid the group good night after shaking his head at the scene.

Kpau clearly enjoyed the grooming repair from Aina. "That … brings back a nice memory. And I see presents!"

Aina nodded, "Yes. Okay, everyone! I made Blar try to describe each of you to me before I went shopping for these. I get to blame him if the gift is weird."

She smirked at Blar and continued, "Alwyn and I exchanged gifts before you arrived, so don't worry about him. Gift card for two to play at Pebble Beach makes his day." Aina had everyone gather close.

"First, I'm going to give Blar his gift. Just a little something to tie his old life and his new life together. To find new mistakes to make instead of repeating old ones." Aina handed Blar a small box with a nostalgic smile. Blar opened it and pulled out a small necklace with an amulet – a tiny silver Norse hammer carved with runes and intricate patterns.

"Blar made our thunder in *Gothic Fire* as the drummer. Now he has … a new partner to drum with. A young one! The old man might need a little more magic to keep up with the young spark!" Blar let Aina put the necklace on him and he kissed her on the cheek before grumbling.

"Seriously! Will everyone stop calling me old?! I'm in far better shape than most people my age! Thirty three! Only thirty three!" Blar couldn't help smiling as he groused. Aina pushed him back into his chair.

"Next. Little Tsika, who is even more a dark faerie of wonder than I imagined from her pictures." Aina handed a crimson-faced little Russian her package. Tsika opened the box and made a happy cooing sound as she pulled out an intricate finely crafted finger talon made of red tinted gold. She was ecstatic and alarmed.

"Oh my stars! This must have cost a fortune! Oh my god!" Tsika looked blindsided as she stroked it.

Aina was delighted at Tsika's response. "I noticed you had a silver one, Tsika. I like to wear them, too! And I thought you might like a blood-tinted one to go with your red bows and lace. You're the magic wielder in this adventure group, as I was with mine. You need artifacts worthy for that." Tsika put her new talon on her left index finger and happily curled it a few times to watch the joints articulate. Then she gave Aina a hug and sat back down, still as red as her gift.

"Glycerin?" The shy creature nearly jumped out of her skin at the sound of her name. "I had to think about you. Even after Blar's emails, you were still an enigma to me. You still are. So, this is … what it is." Aina handed the gift to Glycerin with special formality using both hands and bowing slightly. Glycerin automatically bowed as she took it.

Unwrapping the box, Glycerin made a small inarticulate squeak as she pulled out a small delicate necklace with a small carved dancing figure playing a stringed instrument. The circle around it contained inscribed kanji. Little gems were scattered about on it. Glycerin stared at the symbols a second before her face lit up.

"Ah! J-Japanese! *Ame-no-Uzume-no-Mikoto*" Glycerin bashfully continued, "It's … an am-amulet of Uzume – one of the … Japanese … goddess of mu-music and dance. S-Shinto spirit. I learned … about her in my Asian studies in university. My word! The l-little treasure is full of g-glitter!"

Aina smiled and clapped. "Yes! I'm happy you recognized it. Uzume, who with music and dance, coaxed Amaterasu the sun goddess out of her cave to return light to the world. I wasn't sure whether a Hong Kong Brit girl would know the myth. I suspect you're an incarnation of her in your own way."

Glycerin clutched the gift to her heart and mumbled her thanks unintelligibly. Blar took it from her shaky hands and put it around her throat. He could feel Glycerin trembling like a frightened deer as he touched the back of her neck while he closed the clasp. It took Blar a lot of effort to stay sane touching her. So lovely.

Aina took a breath. "And now, last of all, just because!" Aina's musical laughter echoed through the house.

"I KNEW the little spark would screw herself into the ceiling waiting her turn – Kpau. She was … actually the hardest because my intuition says she'd want something practical but I wanted to give her something beautiful." The tall woman grinned as she handed Kpau a small gift box.

Kpau had indeed worked herself up and was embarrassed at being so easily read by Aina. She meekly took the box and opened the wrapping. Kpau's face blossomed rosy red, the first time Blar could remember having seen her embarrassed.

"Oh … oh god, um … uh, help?"

She looked at Blar with some alarm, lifting the gift out. It was a mate to Blar's gift – a Norse hammer amulet. But instead of silver, it was made of white gold and obviously constructed so that the two hammers, if held together, could interlink. Blar got up to put it on her as she stood holding her hair out of the way with an appalled look on her face.

"Kpau, the runes describe Freyja, the goddess of love, sexuality, and battle. Valkyries swear allegiance to her, and she is the ruler of Folkvang, where warriors go after death. I don't really think I need to say a lot more. Protect your family, little one. You have a big lug standing behind you to help you do that now." Aina nodded her head at Blar. Kpau was completely speechless. She simply teared up and sat back down, curling up in embarrassment.

Aina stood up. "Right! I think it's been a big enough day for everyone. Everyone looks exhausted. Either that or I'm exhausted and projecting. So … I am going to ask for a rain check on a jam session for tonight. Let's off to sleep, because I want to spend Christmas Day jamming with you heathens 'til our fingers bleed. Then you can see for yourself that I'm just a grubby little musician underneath the stardust you seem to think I float in." She ruffled Blar's hair and then hugged each of the women before saying good night.

After Aina had left the room, Blar stood up and stretched. "Well! Everyone gets their own bed tonight. I'm off to thoroughly enjoy mine."

Kpau had recovered and stuck her lower lip out. "Awwwww! Didn't Papa Bear like having a different girl in his bed every night?" Glycerin blanched and became intensely interested in examining her feet. Tsika yawned as she walked over to Blar and just leaned into his chest face first. He massaged Tsika's head as he spoke.

"It was very ... educational, Chicklet. But frankly, once in a while it's nice just to lay face down and pass out without worrying about where I'm sprawled in the bed. Come on, I'm as bleary as Aina."

Kpau shook her fist, "Bah! Old people! Old!" Tsika and Glycerin stumbled on ahead. Blar lingered a bit looking at what Aina had done with her music room since the last time he had been there. Kpau tagged along with Blar, fascinated by the rat's nest of equipment herself. Blar watched the dark tanned woman as she squinted at the nightmare of electronics. After the other two were clearly away, Kpau bounded to Blar and lay against him with her back on his chest. She reached for his new hammer amulet and held it against hers so the interlink was obvious.

"This bauble may have just doubled my entire net worth ... jeezus. You and me! We really are a team, aren't we, Blar?" He put his arms around her and rested his chin on the blonde's head.

"I don't know what else to call it. But that will do for now. Bed time, Chicklet." Kpau nodded and they headed to their respective bedrooms for the night.

- - - - - -

Glycerin's eyes flickered open. Night sky? Stars?

Panic, mind-numbing panic. No, wait! We are not on the roof. We're not outside. We're not drenched. No creatures that want to bite us. Breathe. Just breathe. Focus. It is just a ceiling ... painted like night sky? Silk sheets, plushy pillows, extravagant comforter. Oh. Oh! We're in Aina's house. In ... Aina's ... home! It isn't a dream! Last night happened!

Glycerin couldn't stop the goofy delighted smile radiating from her face. She sat up. She was in Aina's house. The dim light told her it was morning, Christmas Day. Christmas at Aina's house. Glycerin rolled out of bed and stretched on her tiptoes. With her height, she easily touched the ceiling while she peered out the large bedroom window to check the view. Desolate beach and dunes, obscured by broken patches of sea fog. The sky was a thick cavern roof of dark clouds. The light gave the landscape surreal textures. The house seemed silent at first, but as Glycerin listened she heard soft noises from the direction of the kitchen. She quickly showered and put on her jeans and a tank top. She combed her bangs straight and then crept down the hall to the kitchen.

Aina is there. She is cooking! Cooking like we does! Humming and enjoying it! It appears she is making –

"Christmas Feast?" Glycerin said it out loud unintentionally. Aina turned at her voice.

"Good morning, Glycerin! Merry Christmas! Do you … wait, what would you like me to call you? Everyone seems to have their own special endearment for you." The silver-haired woman closed in and gave Glycerin a good morning hug as she spoke. Aina was warm and smelled of cinnamon.

"Um … you? Aiee … well? M-My friends call me Glyc for sh-short. M-Merry Christmas! Can … I … help? I can cook. Just tell me what you … n-need done." Glycerin was still blushing from the hug. She fluttered her hands as she spoke.

She … hugged us! I must have died long ago. That's it. That's the only-only way this makes sense!

Aina smiled. "That's a terrible way to treat a lovely name like Glycca – but okay! Glyc! And yes, I'd love for you to help me. You can start by chopping the crap out of those vegetables over there. They're for the stuffing. How did you end up with that other nickname? Glycerin? Or is that too embarrassing a story without wine?"

She handed Glycerin a glass of red wine and poured herself another. Glycerin fluttered her lashes and smiled. She muted the smile when it obviously alarmed Aina. The bashful girl knew she looked quite demented. She never could seem to smile properly so as not to alarm people. They always gave it away with their expression even if they played nice.

"No, ma'am. I … I can tell the t-tale. The … the bullies in boarding school g-gave me that name. I became rather adroit at s-s-slipping and s-slithering away from their clutches. It was … terrible for so long be-before our little doll came to rescue us. We-I just wanted it to stop, to be left alone." Glycerin reflected carefully on her memories.

How best to tell this without revealing wrong things? We don't wants to be medicated again or be put away!

"It w-was always bad. Then one day … Tsika came to my school. Her arrival … w-was like a bloody bomb. My little doll w-was so angry at everyone. She … broke things, hurt people. I was deathly afraid to go near her."

Glycerin stopped to sip her wine and stared at the ripples in the glass. "Then one day … one day … the bullies managed to c-corner me in the schoolyard. Tormenting devils, we ha-ha-hated them. They took my books and then … it … it got out of hand. They … were p-pulling at … my skirt. Dragging me … behind … the shed like dogs f-fighting over a … piece of meat."

She blocked thoughts for a second. "Tsika … Tsika saw what they were up to. I had no clue that some-someone so small could m-move so fast. She crossed the schoolyard. She had a cric-cricket bat … then the bullies were all on the ground … she-she was so fast. B-Blood everywhere … so much blood. The … s-sounds!"

Glycerin smiled grimly. "She said she'd k-kill them if they ever bothered me again. They knew she would, the look on her face was terrifying. She got detained. They w-were going to expel her. But I … I insisted on being with her. I stayed w-with her. Went to see her every day even though she terrified m-me. That upset the school to no end … I was their f-fancy top student … but I stood my g-ground! They were punishing the wrong one! They … didn't want to believe … that their old money royals might … try to hurt me like that. I thr-threatened lawyers. W-we transferred soon after that – together. We were never separate since then."

Glycerin started chopping the vegetables again, but then stopped briefly, looking at the reflection in her knife. "That's … the history of my n-nickname and … how Tsika became my friend." She looked at her reflection in the blade a second more and then resumed chopping.

Aina had watched her solemnly during the story. Then she softly smiled again. "The quote is if it doesn't kill you, it makes you stronger ... I don't really believe that. Sometimes it just hurts forever and you stitch it into your soul."

Glycerin paused to reflect on that and approved with a brief nod and a smile.

We understands that. We're just little broken bits stitched together ourselves, aren't we? Yes, you like her, too.

Aina resumed preparing the turkey and asked Glycerin to tell the band's story from her point of view. Glycerin described the trio's early halting starts after graduating, their attempts to run a business teaching music lessons, the erratic gigs, the eventual decision to move to Portland.

When Glycerin got to the tale of her first encounter with Blar, she couldn't avoid stammering harder. She related how badly the episode went from her perspective, how she had panicked, run away, thrown up. She mentioned Blar trying so hard to make her feel safe and not scared. Glycerin felt rather dreamy telling Aina the story about her big trip to the guitar shop, how Blar had protected her from strangers and how they'd escaped the news crew.

"It was scary, but a different k-kind of scary ... you know, an exciting scary. It was a bit ..." Glycerin felt the hot blush erupting on her face, "... a bit like being with a pirate. A movie pirate. Like Jack Sparrow."

Glycerin looked up from her chopping to see Aina giving her a strange look. Had she messed up the vegetables? They seemed okay?

"Did I c-cut the celery wrong?"

Aina blinked and shook her head. "No, dear Glycca, my dark haired twin. Your chopping is expert. Blar? Well. Blar. Out of those three protective big lugs I spent so many years with, Blar was the ... easiest to be around ... easy to get comfortable with ... easy to get fond of ... easiest to fall in love with." She had a distant nostalgic look. Glycerin had a dawning horror of what Aina was implying.

"No! No! Tsika! It's Tsika! I wouldn't do that ... no." Glycerin's chest hurt. Tears and hiccups started. Aina wiped her hands and hugged Glycerin until she calmed down.

"I'm sorry, Glycca. I pushed too hard. Are you okay now?"

Glycerin nodded while Aina blotted tears off of the tall woman's cheeks.

Why does it hurt so much when I try to talk about Blar and Tsika?

Glycerin started chopping again, faster. Aina resumed her preparation again. "Darling child, just keep your eyes wide open. Be honest with yourself and your friends, the people you love. Things ... can work out. Sometimes there's a creative answer for happiness."

Glycerin tried not to think, just chop. Thankfully, Aina changed the subject to music technicalities and the kinds of music each woman liked. Glycerin listened as Ainu described how she had shifted genre so many times, eventually to the point that Gothic Fire dissolved.

Glycerin stuck her lower lip out. "I ... I was grieved when Gothic Fire retired. But you, you k-kept making music. And later, sometimes I would discover little projects you did with Blar or Torsten. So that w-was always a nice surprise. But when college st-started I got so sodding busy I st-stopped listening to music for fun. I can't believe how ... complex ... your m-music has got-gotten."

Aina laughed, "I'm a latent electronic geek, I've discovered. Half my equipment I've made myself. What some do with acoustics I do with circuitry. I like to experiment with how complex and fast I can make a melody that the human ear can detect. Tones that mesmerize, that affect spiritual centers, induce awe. It's like a modern kind of magic power."

Aina paused to inject seasoning into the turkey. "But inside me, there still lurks a brash butt kicking rock priestess that lurches out on occasion. When I listen to your solos on guitar, I feel like I'm hearing a kindred sister – but what I excruciatingly plot and calculate, you just seem to call into existence without the motivation of thought. Like you're channeling something ... or someone." Aina gave Glycerin a devilish grin.

Glycerin flinched. Aina was far too close on target in some respects. "So,

Glyc. There's a bit of selfish in wanting to spend time with you. I'm hoping some of that will rub off on me and I can learn something."

Glycerin eyes widened. "You y-you w-want t-t-t-to learn-n-n, what I-I … from me?? … teach? … you?"

Aina looked at her with large sincere eyes, "Yes, I want to watch a master at her craft and see what I can snatch. Now, as your little bubbly Kpau says, we need to seize the moment … or at least this turkey. Help me get it in the oven, Glycca dear."

~15~ "Little Bird" – Annie Lennox

At roughly the same moment the turkey was being maneuvered into the oven, Blar awakened to someone bouncing on his stomach – straddling him as if he were a horsey ride to be precise. He didn't even need to open his eyes, it was obviously Kpau. She was in her exercise gear with a gleeful expression and a stellar case of bed hair.

"Get … up … Papa … Bear!" Kpau bounced with each pause and then leaned forward nose-to-nose with him. "Ex-er-cise Time!"

Blar spluttered and grabbed her wrists. He wrestled her while she whooped and giggled, then flipped Kpau and rolled on top of her. He pulled her arms up over her head on the pillow, pinning her in an exposed defenseless position. Kpau's face lit up and she flashed her eyes.

"Ohhhhh! You want THAT kind of exercise!! Oh, man! Wait! Wait! I get a safe word!" She wiggled seductively, wrapping her legs around his hips and dragging her heels up back of his calves. Blar's sanity took a major hit.

He put his weight on her, squeezing the breath out of her. "You goofy little ferret, one day I'll take you seriously!"

Kpau's face shifted to a very solemn expression. She relaxed against him and pouted. "I don't think I'd resist, Papa Bear. It might be what the big yummy bear needed right then. And we love to help!"

Silence as Blar looked in the little blonde's shiny brown eyes. Every part of him was sensitive to the feel of her body against him. Then she broke the silence with a petulant tone.

"But we do need to exercise. I don't think anyone else is up yet." She kissed his nose and then lightly bit it.

Blar released her wrists and, after laying on her a few seconds longer than he ought to have, rolled off of her and out of the bed. He held his hand out to Kpau. She took the offered hand and he hauled her to her feet. "Okay, Chicklet. Let me put myself together and I'll see you down there."

Kpau bounced and clapped as she bounded to the door. "Five minutes or I'm back with a wet towel to snap your butt with!" She vanished.

Now that was an odd moment. It only put more kinks into his murky understanding of what his relationship with Kpau was. She really seemed like she would have let him have what the back of his brain screamed for.

Stupid brain. I blame Aina. We're inside Aina's sphere of influence. There is something catalytic about being in the Witch world. It's deep behind the looking glass. Life has always been surreal around that woman.

- - - - - -

A short time later, Tsika opened her eyes and rolled over. She was luxuriating in the silk sheets and the extremely fluffy comforter, a small goth puddle in the warmth. The Russian faerie did not want to get out of bed. Tsika peeked out from under her covers. She could see out the window. She marveled at the blustery day on the beach, the patchy fog, wonderfully gloomy – and no snow.

Blar was right. It really was nice once in a while to have a whole bed to yourself. She rolled up in the comforter like an egg roll. Anyone walking in would see nothing but her hair, eyes, and nose peeking out.

Her ears perked up. She could hear Kpau carousing and roughhousing with Blar. From the sounds, they were obviously returning from exercise. Kpau was poking at Blar about his push ups and how he would do more if he let her lay under him. She giggled at their ridiculous bawdy conversation. Kpau was such a tease. The comradery also made her feel a bit lonely.

There was no arguing the matter. Blar was good therapy for Kpau and her maze of emotional shielding. She wasn't going to deny Kpau that, but Tsika dearly wanted to find something she could do regularly with Blar besides play music with him and help manage the band. Tsika knew she should start exercising as well. She was loafing on good genes and that wouldn't last much longer. Same for Glycerin, but at least her darling Mouse was doing yoga and tai chi. Even that was more than Tsika did.

Tsika forced herself out of bed and headed to her bathroom. A full length mirror presented her to herself. She appraised herself with a jaundiced eye.

Really. I am a skinny little waif. But I am no stick. I do have a figure. My boobs perk out nicely. Hips are small but curved. My arms and legs are too skinny. Bleck! There is hardly a muscle line to be seen on my tummy. All my gymnast muscle tone has faded. Ugh! What does Blar see? Is it my hair? My skin? My eyes? He seems fascinated with my hands and feet sometimes. It is just weird what some men like.

Stranger yet, Tsika had hints that Blar seemed to like a variety of aspects of different women. She had seen him slack-jawed more than once watching Glycerin from behind. Glycerin had a spectacular panther slink in her nice round butt and a mysterious grace in her movement that left even Tsika mildly aroused. She had also seen Blar trying not to focus on Kpau's breasts when she bounced around like a cheerleader. Tsika giggled at that.

Tsika knew if she ever wanted to have children, she needed to be in better shape to start with than she was now. She would talk to Kpau about it. She did not want to intrude into Kpau's bubble with Blar though. Tsika knew she was playing a balancing act on many levels.

Blar was therapeutic for her friends. He was good for Kpau, he was miraculous for Glycerin, and Tsika was certain she would be doing evil to her little family to be selfish about him. She loved them far too much. Nonetheless, it was making her insecure that there didn't actually seem to be time for her with Blar other than curling up for a few minutes or a trip shopping. Tsika winced. A wave of incredible anger and pain took her.

Someone … someone to hold me, to make the hurt stop. Make the lonely go away. Anger … lash out … no one there! Oh god! Slap myself! I haven't felt that psychotic murder rage since … since … in years! But I agree with Blar. The band project is most important thing. No matter what, hang together – make the band happen.

Tsika could smell cooking. She made a bet with herself that Glycca and Aina were in the kitchen together. That made her feel better. She had been listening closely to Glycerin's voice since they arrived. The changes were fast and wonderful. Blar was wonderful for having done this. She could hear Glycerin's voice and confidence evolving even in the few hours her dear

Mouse had spent with Aina. Tsika hummed forlornly as she put her clothes on, the hum evolving into an Annie Lennox composition about little birds leaving the nest, testing their wings.

- - - - - -

Blar approached the kitchen behind Kpau and Tsika as they padded down the hall together. The trio could see Glycerin and Aina were having breakfast. The evidence was also clear the pair of women had started their second bottle of wine between the two of them.

They were both giggling as Aina related a story about a tour disaster she and Blar had gotten into. They had gotten separated from the other band members during a rainstorm on a band tour of Thailand. Aina and Blar ended up spending the night in a rather desolate unoccupied temple shed since neither could find their wallets.

"He was trying to be chivalrous. I'd only really known the big lug a few months at that point. We were both dripping wet. I was freezing since I'm so skinny. He kept trying all sorts of ways to keep me warm … oh, everyone's here! Who's hungry?"

Tsika had stopped at the door by Kpau. Blar noticed Tsika's shoulders were extremely tense. He surmised the story Aina was relating was making the little Russian feel insecure or even inadequate. Blar put his hands on her shoulders and massaged. She immediately relaxed, leaning into his touch. What neither knew was the combination of Tsika's small body and Blar's large hands – his fingers were draped down over her breasts. It looked even more provocative from Aina and Glycerin's vantage.

Aina burst into giggles. "Blar, a little decorum! At least take her to the bedroom to grope her!" Glycerin's eyes had widened but then she burst into giggles. Tsika looked down at Blar's fingers and her lily white cheeks bloomed rose red. Blar jerked his hands away.

"Aina, your gutter mind hasn't dulled a bit, has it?" Blar settled for one hand massaging Tsika's neck. He could nearly completely encircle Tsika's tiny charming neck with his hand. She put a hand up to caress his hand as it kneaded muscles.

Glycerin waved her glass at Blar. She was hiccuping between every word. "Blar! She's so … f-funny! And she's cooking Christmas!" Glycerin rolled her eyes. "N-No! Feast! Christmas F-Feast! I've … been h-helping!"

Tsika leaned back into Blar and whispered. "Ah, a very tipsy Glyc. She is likely to be quite funny today, darling Bear." She squeezed his massaging hand. Blar noticed the squeeze was harder than seemed to fit the occasion and decided he should put extra quality time with her today.

Blar recalled the party over Han's bar in Portland, where Glycerin's drunken dance and impromptu song had entertained the group. He had missed that performance, having been downstairs helping with more food for the party. He decided to growl at his pretty Witch. "Aina, you seem to keep changing the plan. If my nose is any good, we're going to be utterly and happily miserable in a few hours and unable to crawl to our instruments."

Aina winked at him, "I'll take credit for the turkey but you are smelling Glycerin's stuffing magic. She's quite a chef!" Aina toasted Glycerin who retreated into bashfulness behind her curtain of hair. Aina already had moved on to lock her eyes on Kpau. The tanned blonde was roaming the kitchen with a scavenging look to her eyes. Aina took pity on the urchin.

"Top oven, Kpau. There are pot pies for each of you."

Kpau vibrated and grabbed a pad as she opened the oven. "Oh gods, the aroma! I'm already drooling. Everyone sit down!" Seconds later, everyone had their breakfast pot pie. Kpau was shoving large bites in her mouth and blowing as she burned her tongue.

Blar looked about the kitchen. "Looks like Aina and Glycerin have done everything. I guess I could clean up?"

Tsika quickly added, "I'll help you, Blar." Blar smiled at her but his concern was ratcheting up. He could hear an unusually plaintive insecurity in her voice. It was fairly alien in his experience of the little pixie to hear that tone from her. Normally, her confident demeanor was nearly imperial. No clue how to proceed.

Kpau looked up from her attempts to impersonate a vacuum cleaner. "Sounds like I'm open then. Does Aina want me to arrange the music room? It will take me a little time to set up a drum kit anyway. Or I could just help you and the Glycster drink?"

Aina and Glycerin both spluttered and laughed. They were very sloshed.

Aina nodded, "That sounds fine, Kpau! Both the music room project and the wine. I trust you with my stuff, but Glyc and I will join you to make it go faster. The turkey is roasting for another couple of hours." Aina reached for another bottle of wine to take with them.

Kpau smiled, "Good! I have a rule about not drinking alone."

- - - - - -

The last of the pot pie gone, Tsika and Blar were in the kitchen alone washing the cookware. The others had wandered off to the music room, giggling and drinking. Tsika was using a short step stool to reach the sink. She was washing and Blar was drying.

Blar wasn't missing that Tsika was standing as close to him as she could, brushing against him every chance she got. He enjoyed that. It let him admire her pretty neck, shoulders, and collarbone. She had tied her hair back into one large tail tied off at top and bottom. Amusingly, the result resembled a giant black raccoon tail but he wasn't about to point that out. It was too cute.

Blar was still concerned. The expression on Tsika's face was guarded. He guessed her closeness was part of her insecurity about Aina and maybe other matters he had been too dense to notice. Blar decided to take a stab at clearing the air.

"Little Pixie? You … well … okay, Aina and I certainly have a past but we're very much simply old friends now. I … well, you're … you're … who I, uh … it's you now."

Oh that was just flipping fabulous, Blar. Completely freaking spazzed the delivery.

Tsika put a frying pan up to her face, snorting and giggling. She leaned against him. "You're so … eloquent, big Bear. It is like Bear writes lyrics for a living or something. Oh wait, he does!"

The sarcasm and giggles were nice but faded out too fast.

"This isn't your problem, Blar. It's mine. I'm … actually kind of unpracticed at being with someone. I've had … two boyfriends … ever before you. One in boarding school. Darling lad put up with me so well … but he had to move away. It was so sad to say bye. The other was a short timer … in college. Apparently, I was … too difficult for that bastard. Too much … baggage for the prick. But you won't ever meet either of them."

Tsika took a long breath. "I am getting to stare at your past in the flesh … a past who obviously still cares about you and your friends. One who makes it impossible to not love her because she is trying her damnedest to help my most precious friend."

She stopped moving. Blar looked up from his dish drying. Tsika was staring out the window blankly and her lips were quavering. She seemed to notice him looking at her in the window reflection, rubbed her eye with her wrist and kept washing. Blar could feel her angst amplify and wished there was a valve to just bleed the pressure off.

Maybe this is a time just to be quiet and stand near her. Just … stay close.

Blar kept drying. Two pots were ready to be put away so he moved to Tsika's other side with each in hand. Blar considered Aina's cabinet organization. As far as he could tell, Aina kept pots on the bottom shelf so he bent over to store them down there.

He felt a light bump against his hip, then heard a simultaneous crash, followed by a string of lurid angry cursing. He jerked up and turned around. When he had bent over, his hip had clumsily knocked Tsika off her stool and over to the kitchen island. He was astonished but not because he was clumsy and had nearly hurt her.

His astonishment was from the expression on Tsika's face and her body language. The small woman was in a red boiling fury and she was wielding the frying pan she'd been scrubbing in a deadly manner. She was screaming and shrieking in several languages – at him.

"What in the fucking hell was that? God damn you! Were you trying to kill me, you pointless meat!? I fucking nearly busted my fucking face on the table, you *tā mā de yīwén bù zhǐ jīxíng er*! *Bespolezny byk*!! Fuck you to hell!"

Blar felt the whiff of air as the frying pan in her hands missed his forehead simply because he had straightened up trying to understand what was happening. The rage blast from her was shocking.

"God … damn fucking … fuck … you! I should cut you open! God … God … da- … oh no! Oh, no … oh, no! … oh … oh no, I didn't!! No! I didn't mean … didn't mean! Oh my god! Oh no!"

Tsika transitioned from homicidal rage to wide-eyed hysterical fright in mere seconds. Tears streamed down her face. She dropped the frying pan and started bawling out loud. Blar kept completely still, uncertain as to what he should do other than avoid any further swings.

"Darling! Oh Bear! I'm sorry! Oh, god I'm so sorry, so so sorry! None of that is true! You're doing wonderfully! My big Bear, oh god no!" She made a small terrified noise. "Oh … oh god! I've screwed up again! I … I … I … I'm afraid … I'm … afraid …!" Tsika's breath was too ragged for coherent speech now, her face covered in tears.

She ran. Blar dropped his towel and followed her. She was fast but she really had nowhere to go. Blar found her in her bedroom, curled up in the corner with her face buried in a pillow she was clutching. The terrified little pixie was sobbing so hard Blar feared she would crack a rib.

Blar got down and sat next to Tsika, gathering her up in his arms on his lap. She made minor resistance but he clutched her to his chest and stroked her back. Tsika wailed as she sobbed in despair.

"You … weren't supposed to … see that! Ever!" Tsika made an inarticulate wheezing noise. "No, no, no, nothing I said is true! I didn't mean to swing at … oh god! I might have hurt … didn't want to hurt my Bear!" Tsika's shoulders heaved as she sucked in breaths between sobs. Blar rocked her gently.

"My … big … sweet ... Bear, I think … I … might … might … l-lo-love … you. And I've botched it! I break everything!" Huge wracking sobs took her.

"This … this isn't good. This … this isn't … what we said … we'd … do. But I can't … help it. So … lonely! You. You're so … good to my friends. I love them so much. You're so … good to me … but … you hadn't … seen me … be angry. I'm afraid! I'm afraid! I break everything! I explode! I break things I love! It … I'm sorry, Blar! I'm sorry! None of that … is true! Oh god … I might have hurt you!"

She couldn't talk any more. All she could get out were wracked painful sobs and ragged breathing. She clung to Blar as if fearing he would physically run away.

Blar admitted being blindsided by the outburst and was still dumbfounded. Kpau and Glycerin had mentioned Tsika's explosive temper but had mostly laughed it off and rolled their eyes. He had seen little flickers but it had in no way prepared him for the intensity of Tsika's rage storm. What to say? He had no idea. Into the dark he went. Down a deeper rabbit hole.

"One. I feel terrible I knocked you down. I'm big and clumsy. I'm sorry. Two. I love you, Tsika. I have since that first night you were in my condo. The insane-for-you kind of love. I hope it becomes the more enduring kind as we learn about each other. Love is still ... that word … love … the word sucks. It is inadequate. It needs to be three or four different words. I love your friends. I love Glycerin. I love Kpau. Both of them, they're precious. You! You stop my heart like it was speared. All of you have become precious to me so fast. My heart hurts when I see any of you in pain. I feel awful seeing you so upset, little flower." Blar held her and kept rocking her slowly.

He took a breath.

"Tsika, I have to say this. This is as awful a time as any. You confuse me. I flirt with Kpau and you treat me sweetly and laugh at her antics. That's bizarre enough. But Glycerin … with Glycerin … you encourage … encourage so much … she's so sweet it's impossible not to … and I'm worried she ... I'm afraid she may be, she's already .... she's too fragile to say ...." Tsika put her fingers on his lips to silence him. They sat quietly for a moment.

Tsika kissed him and leaned her forehead on his chest. She was still shuddering but was breathing more easily. She swallowed hard before she spoke.

"Blar. My large Bear. You ... give my friends ... what they need most. That is what I want. That makes me happy. That endears you to me. So much! In just these short days, my Glycca has improved so much! That is worth anything to me! Bear, the only thing you could do that would make me really, really angry would be to hurt my friends. But ... you saw ... you saw a flash of the real me, just now ... I'm broken, too."

Bitter sobbing laughter.

"We're all broken misfits! We're the *Lost Girls*! We cling to each other in our storms, trying not to drown each other. You're ... you're ..."

Tsika stopped to push a small chuckle through her tears.

"You're like ... we found a life raft. A really big warm one. Such a nice ... easy to lo- ...." Tsika smiled sadly and wiped her eyes before burying herself in Blar's chest again. "I'm an emotional mess right now, all jangled up, I don't know what to do. I can't believe I tried ... to ... hurt my Bear! I thought I had gotten over those ... fits. I'm sorry I said and did those things. And I'm scared, scared of, scared of losing anyone. I'm so sorry you saw me like that. I don't ... want to ... lose you ... Blar? Please?"

Blar heard a click and looked up. Kpau was silently standing in the doorway. Tsika hadn't seen her. Kpau had clearly heard everything though. Kpau solemnly put her finger to her lips and gave Blar a thumbs up, then silently padded off. Blar took that to mean either the others hadn't heard the outburst or that Kpau approved of his words. Perhaps it meant both.

Blar squeezed Tsika until she squeaked. "Let's go back and finish the dishes. Then join our friends. They're likely to come look for us soon. If anyone asks, we snuck off for a kiss. One foot forward at a time, we'll figure it out and muddle along. Here's the kiss to make it honest."

Blar kissed her hard enough to make her gasp when he was done. Tsika hugged Blar hard enough he worried about his own ribs. They got up and headed back to washing the cookware, Tsika still sniffling but standing even closer to Blar.

- - - - - -

Christmas Day, a sunny afternoon that made Aina's music conservatory nice and warm. Kpau was at the mike, her salty voice resonating through the house. She was covering a tune by the group *Nickelback* about longing desires to be a rock star and live the high life. However, it was a version quite altered by Kpau to suite her own little eccentricities, quite seductive and outrageous – worded from a feminine rock star's view.

Tsika was laying down a slow funky bass line to complement. Her small hips and twin tails moved in metronome fashion, slow and steady, quite immersed in the sounds she was making with her bass.

Glycerin was watching them as she curled up on a plush chair. She finished off her wine glass, then covered her mouth giggling at Kpau's exaggerated posturing. Blar plucked out the minimalist melody on Glycerin's guitar.

Kpau detached her mike from its stand as she sung about joining the mile-high club on her own personal jet. She began slinking around Blar in an exaggerated seduction, running her fingers over his shoulders as she sang. Aina was covering her mouth, silently shaking in laughter at Kpau's clownish sexy antics.

Tsika strolled closer to the pair as she and Blar rolled into the power chords of the musical chorus. Kpau cut loose on her vocals, soaring through the chorus about having fifteen cars, huge homes, muscular men at call, and drugs on speed dial. As she did so, her voice spiraled into the thickest Texas drawl Blar could imagine.

Kpau dropped her stage persona and threw herself into a lounge chair laughing until tears streamed down her face. She clawed at the air in mock anger.

"I just can't get rid of my Texas twang!!! As soon as I get louder, I start sounding country!"

Aina shook her head sympathetically. "But Kpau, it disappears when you do that quirky talking style of singing, like you do for that *Freezepop* funk electronica tune you tried first. That was great! So your rocking voices are just in there hiding."

Kpau scowled. "Yeah, things certainly hide … in here." She pointed at her head with both index fingers.

The group had spent the latter part of the morning eating and jamming until they were miserable. They were continuing the jam sessions in the afternoon, trying out different ideas, styles, and arrangements. Earlier that morning, during one of the early breaks before lunch, Kpau had tagged Blar aside and taken him out to the patio deck. She was brief and to the point.

"Aina and Glycerin were outside enjoying the deck this morning. They heard nothing." Kpau kept her eyes on the ocean waves and horizon as she spoke.

Blar nodded. "Good. I'd hate to see Tsika have to cope with the idea that everyone in the house heard that." Blar wasn't sure what to call Tsika's meltdown yet.

Kpau bit her lip. "I haven't heard anything like that out of her since her freshman year at USC. The little vampire was having a phaser overload in the Financial Aid Office the first time I ever saw her. Glycerin, if you can imagine this, was trying to restrain her as Tsika was climbing over the counter intending to murder a financial aid officer. Needless to say, they fascinated me."

Blar decided to emulate Kpau in gazing at the horizon. "Well, it is easy to understand how the stress you three have been under the last few months can aggravate old wounds. But I have to state for the record, her intensity was stunning."

"Papa Bear? Thanks for not freaking out. Thanks for helping Tsika through it. Her ex-boyfriend in college not only dropped her like plutonium, but he wrecked her reputation by broadcasting the episode to everyone else. She was ostracized. She needs emotional support, not damnation." Kpau shook her head to untangle her hair.

Blar wrinkled his forehead. "Well, little moppet. Actually? I was completely freaking out. Being still, waiting, and watching is my default reaction to the unexpected. Sometimes I take a fist in the face for it. I almost took a frying pan in the head this morning but for luck – but more often the tactic works with a win-win solution."

Kpau laughed softly. "That's good to know if we get in a bar fight, eh? Glad she missed though I suspect your head is pretty damned hard. You're clearly too stubborn to run based on the amount of groping I'm seeing you two engaged in this afternoon! I guess we should go back in. Briefing completed, Papa Bear, sir." She grinned and saluted in mock military style. Blar didn't miss the fact her eyes didn't seem to reflect her smile. Her shields were up.

- - - - - -

The five musicians jammed without breaks the rest of the afternoon and evening. The remains of the Christmas Feast steadily dwindled as they grazed individually. By the time it was approaching midnight, Blar called a vote for bed time.

"Do we take a break and keep chugging along? We've almost got some song elements worked out for the weekend. On the other hand, the beds are singing their siren songs of sleep to me." Blar stifled a yawn.

Kpau bashed her cymbals and fired a few drum shots. A stick sailed through the air. "I have too much energy burning. Need to play!" Blar looked at her expression, it seemed a bit frantic. Now what?

"Okay, okay. Everyone else good for a couple more hours?" General head nodding made it unanimous. "Good. Right, I need caffeine and a stop at the 'loo. … crap … Glycerin has me talking Brit now."

Glycerin pulled her curtain of hair over her face and mumbled apologies while giggling. Alwyn, who had stayed the evening to observe, volunteered to get coffee and scurried off to the kitchen. Tsika and Glycerin scampered off to the dining room for tidbits and munchies.

Aina got up from her keyboard and stretched, "The 'loo … heh! … sounds like a fabulous idea. I'm off. Back in ten."

Kpau looked at Blar with a rather curdled expression. He motioned at a door to the outside deck. She went, he followed. They stood against the wall out of the night wind. Kpau watched the twinkle of city lights of Carmel in the distance for a moment.

Blar took her hand. Almost as small as Tsika's but rougher and more muscular. "Chicklet? Is it a good guess that you're completely stressed out, too? Do I need to put on kevlar for you?"

Blar got no warning of the incoming strike. Kpau grabbed his neck, pulling herself up to him. She put her mouth on his and her small, wet tongue fiercely explored his mouth. Her arms gripped his neck and one leg wrapped around his waist. She pressed her body against him, moving rhythmically as she kissed him. Fierce, wild, and dangerously exciting. Reality got timeless.

Just as suddenly, she released his mouth and buried her face in his neck. She was breathing hard and he could feel her heat. Then she looked up with painful eyes and an apologetic expression. Blar felt stunned – again. Twice in one day now.

"My god I bet you're a wonderful ride, Blar! … Sorry, Papa Bear. Blar. I … I needed … need … how do I … say this without sounding like a slut? I probably should have gone into town yesterday. I haven't been … with anyone since Los Angeles. The things in my head – they keep whispering louder, getting closer."

Kpau's eyes looked vacant for a moment. "Losing myself in the moment … helps … me keep the monsters away. Groping and roughhousing with you has been great, but it just … delays the monsters. I throw myself into everything ... hard. If I don't, they just wait until I'm weak and then they get me."

She was quiet for a moment. "I … I … make a great one night stand for the right guy. I don't want to get attached to them. No attachments. I just need to escape from thought for a few hours and sex is the best thing I've ever found that really works. Best medication ever."

Blar looked down into the little blonde's eyes. She looked back sadly, "Blar? Do you think I'm ... a ... a ... whore for being this way?" Just saying the word was wrenching to her. Obviously, the label had been stapled onto her in the past.

Blar gathered her into his arms. "Slut ... whore ... stupid words. Interesting how the words for active guys are completely different in tone, don't you think? I don't use those crap words. Aina calls them terms of patriarchy and misogyny. She goes on for a lot longer a rant."

He tightened his hug. "What I think? I think you have a coping mechanism for some horrific memories. I've noticed you do everything at full blast. What I think? I'm the last guy in the world to judge anyone with my history. There is some very specific terse language in those old books damning people who judge harshly. Forgotten by those who enjoy throwing stones."

Blar stewed on his next words. "I am going to say this – you prowling at night? That will worry me, Kpau. Every time you go out into the night, I will worry you'll run into a real monster and you won't come back."

Kpau lay her head on his chest. "I've ... been mostly okay since you joined the fun. I was hoping having you around would be good enough medicine. It really is helping but I'm far less certain now, especially after watching Tsika today. Just ... work with me here, okay?"

Blar stroked her hair a moment. "No one was exaggerating in the least when you, Glyc, Tsika, and ... what is her name? Ah. Sashiko. When you four decided to call yourselves *The Lost Girls*. But after today, I am worrying about our path. Even people with no baggage to carry have trouble with fame and fortune. But we're already on your roller coaster ride you want so much. The fewer secrets we have between each other the better we can manage things."

Blar paused briefly, "Eyes wide open. Right, Chicklet?"

"Okay, Papa Bear. Thank you. I'm glad you're dumb enough to stick with us!" Kpau grinned at him sadly. She looked up at him with those puppy-child eyes that did such a fine job of frying his circuits.

Blar let go of Kpau, ruffled her hair, and opened the door for her. They returned and finished the jam session as if nothing had happened. Blar coaxed everyone into the hardest rock and metal tunes everyone knew. He wanted to kill everyone's anxious energy with a large hammer. A few more hours seemed to be a good dose of that kind of medicine. Everyone was beat. All said their good nights and the lights went off.

Strange times.

~16~ "Rock Star" - Nickelback

The morning light streamed into Blar's bedroom between curtains he'd forgotten to draw closed the night before. Blar had almost forgotten what waking up to real sunlight was like after moving himself into his guest bedroom back in Portland.

Wait. Problem. No little frisky blonde is bouncing me like a horsey ride yelling to get up. Time to be alarmed after last night's little revelation?

Blar jumped out of bed, pulling his pants on as he jogged to Kpau's room. The door was open. He slipped in and relaxed when he saw tousled blonde hair peeking out of the comforter on the pillow and heard her soft snore. One leg was hanging off the bed and the sheets were a mess.

Blar observed the wreck of her bed and gained a sudden insight it might not have been a good idea to have Kpau sleep in a separate bedroom from the others. Night terrors and no one to rescue her.

Blar turned to leave Kpau be. He ran smack into Glycerin. The tall stealthy lass had slipped up quietly and was peering over his shoulder. She fell backward. Blar lunged to save her and Glycerin grabbed at him as they both wrestled to stay upright. The two of them shushed each other simultaneously while stifling laughter. Blar put on a more serious face and led Glycerin away from Kpau's door.

"Night terrors. The poor thing is so exhausted she missed her alarm for morning exercise. Think you can finagle Kpau into sleeping with you while we're here? She's been a little toasted recently."

Glycerin was clearly delighted with Blar's roughhousing with her. Blar knew she was sensitive about being treated differently. He had noticed her expression before watching him play with Kpau. However, as Blar filled her in, Glycerin's smile faded into her more often worn sad clown expression with those big doe eyes.

"Y-you're bloody right on t-target, Blar. I … I hadn't th-thought about that. She had been … getting in bed with m-me more frequent- frequently up in P-Portland. Right-o. I shall try t-to get her to come with m-me tonight."

Blar smiled at her. There were still vestiges of a Glycerin who sounded like she was drowning as she tried to speak but she had gotten so much better. Glycerin fluttered her lashes and blushed. That tiny smile returned. "Are y-you going to ex-exercise? Or would you, would you like to come with m-m-me for some breakfast? I … I was headed … that way."

"You sound much more appealing, Little Dancer. Besides, it'll give Kpau something to yell at me about. It will just add to her certainty that I'm doomed without her managing my health." Blar winked at Glycerin, who covered her mouth and giggled. Lovely lavender eyes peeking over long fingers. Heart failure commencing right now. Blar took a silent action item – stock replacement hearts.

They joined Aina in the kitchen where she was already starting up a pitcher of coffee. The aroma of caramel mingled in the smell of coffee as the machine percolated. The light shining in through the window seemed to assure a sunny if cold day ahead.

"Morning to … both of you? Blar? Oh? I thought this time of the morning was the Little Spark and Papa Bear kiddie hour!?" Aina winked at Blar. She clearly wasn't going to entirely let go of the idea of tormenting him about his Magic Bus ride for 'little girls'.

"Chicklet seems to have wiped herself out. She didn't sleep well last night. She may be really late this morning." Blar started some toast. Glycerin pulled out eggs and ham as Aina handed her a frying pan.

"Well then, Glycerin," Aina wiped her hands on a towel, "Want to go shopping with me today? There's a couple of fashion boutique shops that specialize in women built like the two of us. Human giraffes! I think you'll be excited!"

Glycerin got sparkly eyed as she cracked eggs. "Y-yes, I'd love that! It's always so dodgy shopping! The bloody stores j-just seem to think someone m-my height is as wide as I am tall."

Blar marveled again at the quality improvements in Glycerin's speech since meeting Aina. It seemed like it really was improving by the hour as Tsika had claimed. Magic.

Aina glanced at Blar. "Think you guys can amuse yourselves today? We'll probably be gone til about three or four."

Blar nodded. "Is this going to be stage clothing? If it is, it can come out of the band's equipment budget. Otherwise, it should come out of your personal account, Little Dancer. We don't want the tax people to eat us alive." Blar was mostly making a joke but Glycerin was still a difficult read about whether she had gotten his humor or not.

Glycerin nodded bashfully, "I know, B-Blar, I'll k-keep t-track."

Aina huffed at Blar, "If I, the Elf Witch, see something darling for my beautiful moppet, I might just splurge on her myself! You're not the only sugar daddy here! And I'm a witch! Witchcraft on you!" Aina pounced, spraying Blar with a large puff of powdered sugar from a shaker.

Blar growled in laughter as he grabbed at the shaker while Aina shrieked happily and dodged his hands. They wrestled each other for the implement. A large cloud of powdered sugar filled the kitchen air and coated them both.

Glycerin sat down, pulled her knees up to her eyes and peeked over – enthralled at the horseplay. Both Blar and Aina stopped in a comical wrestling lockhold to look at Glycerin quizzically as the cloud of sugar billowed around them.

"It … it is bloomin' fascin-fascinating to watch my wonderful idols being so bloody silly! Right in f-front of me! In a regular k-kitchen. And … and me … about to eat breakfast with them and I'm liv-living with them." Glycerin's eyes teared up as she considered her situation. "Like I'm one of them. Like I matter! … like I matter!"

Aina moved to hug Glycerin and stroke her hair as the young woman cried. "Little magical child, you're going to run circles around us if the wind blows the right way for you. For better or worse, I think you're going to BE one of us."

Aina sprang her trap and dusted Glycerin with a spritz of powdered sugar.

Glycerin happily squealed and tried to wave the cloud away as she rolled out of her chair and dodged. Her eyes were glittering more than the powder floating in the air. In seconds, the entire kitchen was a cloud of powdered sugar as she slithered and danced to dodge Aina's sugar dust attacks.

Blar's breakfast was one of the finer moments in his life later recalled, watching Glycerin eat with them. His guitarist was tearfully happy and vibrating as her hair and shoulders shimmered with sugar dust. His only concern was that she might not ever clean the powdered sugar off.

- - - - - -

Tsika had likely rolled out of bed just as Glycerin and Aina drove away to head into town for their shopping trip. Blar encountered Tsika in the hall where she stood peering around with a perplexed expression. Blar grinned at her clothes – barefoot with black shorts and a black midriff-baring tank top festooned with small hearts and skulls. Those little hips, that waist, and cute navel had his heart pumping harder.

"Good morning, Blar. Where is everyone? Are we … alone?" Tsika leaned against Blar with her face buried in his chest. She had developed quite a fondness for doing that. Blar certainly didn't object.

"Not quite, pixie. Kpau is face down in bed. It looks like she not only stayed up too late, but she had a bad night."

Tsika looked up at Blar with a sad face as he continued. "Glyc said she'd try and steer Kpau into sleeping with her for the rest of our visit here."

Tsika smiled, "Sometimes I think Glycca looks after us more than we do her."

Blar played with the petite woman's twin tails, twirling them as he spoke, "From what I'm seeing, each of you is always doing your part for the others. Each of you believes you're essential to protecting your family. I'd say you're all correct and that's a good thing. Feeling needed is healthy. Follow me and I'll warm up some leftovers for you."

Tsika retrieved her hair back from Blar and adjusted the small skull festooned red ribbons holding each tail in place. "So where are others? House seems unnaturally quiet."

"Aina took Glycerin to some boutique shops in Carmel. She says they specialize in tall, slender women." Blar watched with interest as Tsika's face shifted through several emotions. Her porcelain doll face was alarmed at first but then that shifted to forlorn before finishing with a thoughtful look.

"I understand why Glycca would be excited. Both she and I have a hideous time finding clothes! I can sew but I just don't have the tools now to make my own clothes. We sold everything starting up the music studio. I'm on the minus side of dress size zero – they just never have anything and when they do I have to roll it up or cut it!"

Blar smiled as Tsika began ramping up into a grand rant. Her hands were punctuating words as she waved her arms and stomped back and forth in front of him.

"But Glycerin is in total hell! She's like, a size six in the boobs, a size two in the waist and never mind finding pants long enough for those legs. The regular stores only sell things with waist bands all three of us could share at once!"

By now, Tsika was circling Blar, stomping and gesturing. Blar could imagine little skulls and lightning bolts dancing in a cloud over her head. He couldn't stop the expanding smile on his face.

"At least Kpau has some luck in the Junior department! She likes glitter and doesn't mind if it has Hello Kitty on … you're laughing at me!" Tsika started kicking Blar in the shins with her bare feet. "And these are size four feet, mocking Bear! God damned stores don't even carry size five most of the time! They send me to the kid's department!"

"No, no, I understand! Its a beautiful rant, I'm just applauding!" He only dodged every second or third kick from her elfin feet, letting her land soft blows as he backed into the kitchen. "Okay, delicate flower, you need to stop so I can get your food in the microwave."

Tsika growled and poured herself some coffee. She sat in a chair; it was not designed for her - her feet didn't reach the floor. She swung her legs back and forth as she sipped.

"Maybe we can set you up a seamstress shop in the office back at the condo. Sewing equipment and whatnot – we'll see when we get back. That actually sounds more useful than what we're doing with that room now." He got a growling grunt for that proposal.

Blar was looking out the window at the sunny blustery beach. Idea time. "Hey, pixie, do you like to fly kites? The weather looks very kite friendly today. Aina usually keeps a small squadron of them in the entry way closet."

He turned to see Tsika hugging herself and smiling. She noticed his gaze and the smile vanished into a blush. She looked away from him. "I … I suppose so. That would be some small change of pace."

Blar crossed his arms and focused on not laughing. "I'm pretty sure Aina also has sand toys. Want to build a sand castle? That would be a change of pace."

Tsika lost any pretense of haughty disdain and lapsed into an innocent child-like expression. "I've … I've … never built a sand castle before! I'd like that. A lot." Blar decided Tsika wasn't actually very good at playing a snooty aristocratic princess. It also bothered him that she had grown up and missed doing so many things so basic to childhood.

"Well, snarf that up and I'll go hunt down everything. It's sunny but a bit cold. Wear stuff you don't mind getting wet. We'll meet at the front door when you're ready. I'm going to let Alwyn know that Kpau is still in the house."

Blar walked down the hall and looked back. Tsika was still swinging her legs but hugging herself and rocking as she smiled. Blar decided he'd take that as having 'done good'.

- - - - - -

Kpau's eyelids popped open. What the hell? Daylight? She poked her head out of her comforter and blearily focused on her cell phone. Nearly noon.

Nearly noon! What the fuck?

"Why didn't Papa Bear wake me?" She huffed and growled until she looked at her bed.

Oh. My bed covers look like hell. The monsters came last night. Blar probably looked in on me and computed I should be left to sleep.

She pouted momentarily but then hopped up to shower. Afterward, Kpau threw on a ratty pair of jeans and a tee-shirt. She padded down to breakfast. The house seemed very empty.

A note from Blar on the table. Breakfast for her in the fridge. Thanks, Papa Bear! Glyc and Aina are shopping. Wow, that sounds like it would be fun to watch. Those two tall creatures with their slender limbs and the way they move like giraffes together. Gorgeous.

Kpau's eyebrow arched as she read further. Blar and Tsika were out having a play day on the beach. Kpau stood on her tiptoes and peered out the kitchen window. She spotted two kites in the sky near the ocean waves. Tracing back from the kites, she spotted a big dot and a little dot. The little dot seemed to be running back and forth a lot.

"That … is so sweet. Be careful, Papa Bear, I'm getting very very fond of you."

Kpau finished eating and explored the house. She could hear Alwyn down in the garage. It sounded like he was woodworking. She had always wanted to try that hobby. She thought about bouncing down to see but, well, it was Alwyn. She didn't dislike Alwyn but she just felt kind of uncomfortable interacting with him. The kind of money his profession represented just seemed alien to her. Tsika and Glycerin moved in those circles far more easily with their international family backgrounds. Not too many butlers where she was from. Cattle, on the other hand … yeehaw.

To the music room! I'll practice! That's the ticket!

Silence greeted her. Kpau tried to practice several different pieces but she'd fade out on each after a few bars. Over and over she would end in silence.

More silence. Kpau suddenly realized Aina almost always had music playing throughout the house. It was off. Silent. Kpau had no idea where the home audio system controls were.

Silence.

Kpau sat tapping her feet in the silence. Her breathing took on a ragged edge.

No. Stop it. Shut up! Go away!

She kept wiping her eyes. She heard her lungs rattle, then wheeze. Damn wheezing. Fucking smoke. Stupid memories!

"Crap! I … I need, I need to do something. I could go down to the beach … no. I can't! Tsika needs her time with the guy. She gets so little. I need … damn it! I told him I'd try not to … it's hard … crud. Sorry, Papa Bear. Damn it. I don't know what else to do. This always works for me. Nothing else ever has."

Kpau trotted to the kitchen and looked for guides to the area. She felt focused now. Make a plan. She found an area tourist entertainment guide and scanned it. Finding several potential destinations including Aina's club, she popped out her smartphone. She checked out likely candidates on Yelp for reviews and locations.

"I wonder if Alwyn would loan me a car. Meh, probably not. I don't have car insurance now."

Kpau trotted to her bedroom and changed clothes. Something snazzy. Some sparkle but not lurid. Skirt. Definitely a skirt. That's the ticket. Some cleavage. Got it. Let's go upscale. Now, call a taxi and rock on.

Thirty minutes later, Kpau left the house and walked up the road to meet the taxi at the gate.

- - - - - -

Blar and Tsika returned to the house drenched and covered in wet sand. Tsika's hair glittered with sand. Even her eyebrows sparkled. They'd fallen in the ocean several times as well as rolled in the sand. Tsika was dancing around Blar excitedly.

"Oh, Blar, thank you! I've never been tide pooling either! All the starfish and urchins and creatures! I hope my pictures of the sand castle aren't blurry, it was hard to tell out there!" Tsika stopped suddenly as she looked at Aina's beautiful home and smacked her forehead.

"Blar! How are we going to get to our bedrooms without making an utter mess of the house? We're covered in beach! Eww. A piece of seaweed!" Tsika had already undone her hair ties and was extracting the wet leaf out of her hair. That marvelous mane of curly hair blowing in the breeze made it hard for Blar to concentrate on what she was saying.

Blar realized he had indeed goofed tactically. "Well, derp me! Normally, I'd say we go down to the entrance by the pool. But I bet that's locked. Maybe Kpau's up?" Blar opened the door, called out and rang the doorbell a few times. No answer. He looked over to the garage area. The garages were closed. He listened. Silence.

"Well, I can't believe Kpau can't hear you with all that bellowing, Bear. Maybe her and Alwyn went on an errand?" Tsika had her sandals off and had peeled off her jacket. Blar stood with no clue about how to proceed.

Tsika audibly sighed and took an an authoritative air. "Blar, just strip down to something minimal here and we'll just bundle our wet clothes and dash for it."

"Right, sounds like a plan."

Blar stripped down to his jeans and bundled his clothes up. That wasn't going to cut it. His jeans were drenched and filthy. He tried smoothing the water out of them without much luck. Seawater drizzled out of the hems. Maybe there was a garden hose somewhere?

Blar looked up and was struck dumb. Tsika had stripped down to her bra and panties, bundled up her stuff and was futilely using them for visual shielding. She blushed furiously under Blar's wide-eyed stare.

"I … I … shut up! I don't want to get Aina's beautiful carpet muddy! Why are you looking at me like that?"

"Because, uh … because you're so damn beautiful." Her blush intensified and spread all the way past her collarbone. Blar grimaced and stripped off his jeans, squeezed them out, rolled them up and added them to his bundle. Tsika kept getting more nervous as she glanced up the driveway and prodded him to move faster.

"Okay, Tsika. Let's go. Be careful on the marble floors." They entered Aina's house, Tsika leading the way in her hurry. Blar reflected that he was scoring a wonderful viewing experience, but he wasn't about to point that out.

He just enjoyed the scenery. The way her butt shifted as she walked was tantalizing.

If they were casting for a small vampire interpretation of Snow White, Blar would recommend Tsika. Moonlight skin, raven black hair. Goth-themed black lace on her lingerie, of course. He had simply assumed she was small in all measurements she actually had a nice little figure. Elegant. She was a striking contrast from her friends.

Kpau was tanned, toned, and muscular – a surfer girl build. Glycerin had her Asian features coupled with being tall and slender. But Glycerin wasn't a stick figure either, there was definitely some presence in her hips and bust from her Brit genes. Three very different examples of beauty that Blar felt lucky to have as band mates. At the moment, however, this view had every scrap of his attention.

His lovely view of the alabaster pixie lasted all of ten seconds and then they split off to their bedrooms.

"Tsika? Meet you after we shower."

"Well, obviously. Duh! Stupid-head!" She shouted from her bathroom. She already had her shower started.

- - - - - -

Blar's shower complete, he stepped out of his bathroom and executed an immediate u-turn back into its refuge. Tsika was sitting on his bed. She was extremely nervous and crimson faced, wrapped in a large towel and apparently nothing else. She was looking at her toes and hadn't seen him. She looked absolutely gorgeous to him but he needed to think first.

He stared at his reflection. It was obvious what Tsika had in mind, she regularly worried out loud that she should consummate her relationship with him. She wanted to "be a naughty girl for him" as Tsika put it. Was that really a smart idea now? He growled quietly. Kpau would tell him he was sounding old, to enjoy the moment. But Blar felt off-balance after Tsika's emotional explosion the prior day. It had informed him that he didn't know her as well as he thought.

Well, it would be cruel to put her off. The little sprite at least deserves a cuddle, no matter what. It was pretty brave of her to be out there and vulnerable like that. Let's put our gym shorts on. Here we go..

Tsika panicked almost immediately when she saw him. "Oh … oh, darling Bear, maybe this wasn't a good … maybe it wasn't … I should go." She started to get up.

Blar blocked her, put his arms around her and lifted her onto his lap as he sat on the bed, careful to keep her towel in place. "It's fine, Tsika. I just want to sit and hold my dangerous beautiful little faerie a moment." Tsika gave him a small scared little smile.

Reminds me of Glycerin. Crap, stupid brain. Don't do that. Never ever do that. Treat each as their own unique self. Add to my list of eternal personal rules. Do not compare women. Just enjoy them.

Blar kissed her forehead as he ran his fingers along Tsika's back, tracing her bare shoulders and the ridge of her spine. Tsika shivered and tilted her face up to kiss him. Blar gently stroked her throat as they kissed and then traced just under her collarbone line using his index finger. To Blar's utter surprise, that unlocked the little princess.

Tsika relaxed and lay back in his left arm. She put her hands on his hand as he stroked her and kissed her throat. Her breathing got heavier and she pulled her legs up onto the bed.

Blar kissed her mouth again and repeated his trace along her collarbone. This time he slowly traced down to her armpit, continuing down the outer line of her breast. Tsika was panting, soft shallow breaths, her eyes locked on his. She pulled his hand now towards exciting destinations. The towel slipped open.

He brushed his fingers under one lovely little breast and was rewarded with an alluring erotic noise from a pretty mouth. Her legs stretched out and relaxed, offering ... then they both heard the front door open. Aina and Glycerin were calling out as they entered the house. The two shoppers were back from their expedition.

Tsika rolled her eyes and hugged Blar fiercely, muffling a shriek into his neck. "Fucking god damn me to hell, I am cursed! Now am going to be on horny pins and needles the rest of the day, you bastard. Lemme go, I gotta move quick!"

She scampered away but not without Blar getting a glimpse of a very cute pale derriere. She stopped at the door and turned, striking a tiny goddess pose, her towel just barely covering the minimums.

"Blar? Thank you for today. I really had a good time with you. I'm going to call today our first real date." She flashed a happy smile and then she was gone.

Blar grabbed some jeans and a tank top to throw on while he willed himself to calm down. Somehow Tsika was quicker, she was already dressed and prancing down the hall to Glyc and Aina. Now it was time for him to see what the pair of swans had purchased on their expedition.

- - - - - -

Before Blar rounded the corner he could hear Tsika squealing in delight.

"Oh ... My ... God! Glycca! That ... is ... spectacular!"

Blar completed the turn to the entry hall – and his brain shorted out. What was left of his mind noted that Tsika had been waiting to see his reaction and she was stifling laughter behind her hands.

Glycerin. She had her back to him. The slender brunette was wearing her thigh-high buckle and lace leather boots that regularly teased Blar's sanity. That wasn't the problem.

The problem was that above those boots were a new pair of lavender shorts. They were extremely brief and might as well have been painted on her glorious body. Blar didn't consider himself much of an "ass man" but he already had the opinion that Glycerin had the most gloriously perfect slinky butt and this just amplified its perfection. The new shorts were playing peekaboo with her mesmerizing crease line between butt and thighs. Just as enthralling, the top of the shorts stopped at her hip line accentuating her slim waist. A couple of inches of bare skin further up, her new blouse took over coverage. It was a matching color of lavender, clingy on her body. The sleeves were shredded to the shoulder, exposing the extensive tattoo art on her arms.

But then Glycerin turned around. Blar was really having trouble breathing now.

The blouse neckline was a v-neck, deep cut almost to her navel so it framed her snake tattoo that curled from navel to collarbone. It wasn't a wide decolletage so it played coyly with the viewer, revealing just a hint of her breasts. Big doe eyes and a Mona Lisa smile let Blar know how excited Glycerin was about her new clothes.

The design was brilliant – an outfit that appeared to show a lot of skin without actually doing so. Aina had left with mousey Glycerin and returned with a rock star.

Aina grinned with a devilish smirk, "I think Blar just gave his review. He may need CPR."

Glycerin was looking at Blar with concern now. She walked up to Blar; that walk, those hips, the large innocent eyes, her pouting lips, moving close enough to smell her scent. "Is it … too much, Blar? D-Do you not like it?"

"Gah!" Blar gasped, "I love it! I can't take my eyes off you! I should have known what Aina would steer you toward given what she used to wear on stage. Let me grab for a strand of sanity. I see several sacks behind you, looks like a good haul of clothes." Tsika was digging through them and making little bird noises admiring Glycerin's new goods.

Blar gently tousled his guitarist's hair. She beamed and blushed. "I-I'm really glad you like these. I got several colors of everything." Blar decided it was wiser in front of the others not to say it was the body they were draped on that made all the difference.

He scrambled for a change of topic. "Okay, I guess we should start practice. Are Alwyn and Kpau back?"

Aina looked puzzled. "Alwyn's car is gone. Kpau went with him?"

Blar shrugged. "I assume so. Neither is here. Hopefully, they won't be too much longer."

Tsika was punching on her cell phone and looked up at the group. "I sent Kpau a text. Aina, can you text Alwyn?"

Aina shook her head. "He doesn't carry a cell phone most of the time. Says they just distract him. Ah well, come on, Glyc, lets hang your treasures up."

- - - - - -

"Blar?!" Aina came running into the music room where Blar, Tsika, and Glycerin were working out some musicality kinks. "Alwyn is back! Kpau didn't go with him!" Aina was distraught.

Tsika put her bass down and picked up her cellphone, "Still no response to my texts and voice goes straight to voicemail." She put her phone down, her shoulders sank as she sighed.

Glycerin just sat on her stool and looked glum. Blar grimaced as Aina looked back and forth at them. "Blar! Should I call the police? What's going on?"

Blar looked at Tsika and Glycerin. Neither seemed inclined to talk. Time to clear some air.

"Aina … Glycerin is not the only broken *Lost Girl* in the group. I got some warning this might happen yesterday."

Both Glycerin and Tsika looked at Blar with startled expressions.

"These three call themselves *The Lost Girls* for very good reasons. In Kpau's case, she is running from horrific emotional pain, monsters in her head. I don't know exactly but surely related to watching her family die. She gets night terrors, she hates silence, and she's drawn to any activity that snuffs out thought. These two women here know more but they seem to feel like it isn't their place to talk about each other. I have a suspicion we left Kpau alone in the house and it got too quiet for too long. Her stress levels have been high since we left Portland. She was trying to keep me posted. I think, I think it's a good idea we should all have our emotional demons in order before life gets complicated."

Tsika's mouth was wide open. "Blar! I'm … impressed you've ferreted out that much from Kpau."

Blar heard a sniffle. Glycerin was crying. "You … you brought me here to … help me?! I just realized it. Not … just because it was on the way and you wanted to see Aina. To help broken me. Like I matter! You think … I matter. Thank you." Glycerin curled up in her chair, covering her face with her hair. Tsika sat down with her to hug her and stroke her back.

Tsika sighed, "While we're airing our closets out … I might as well cough up mine, too. Most darling Aina. I have a … I have … temper control trouble. Oh, fuck it. Truth is I'm a walking nuclear bomb. Rage fury. Violent. Really violent. I was on a path that would have ended with felony murder and jail before I met my Mouse. Dear Glycerin is probably the most normal of the three of us. Years of therapy and this is the best it gets."

Tsika let go of Glycerin and picked up her martini. She slugged the contents down her throat, slammed the glass down and growled.

"Aina darling, Blar was being polite. Kpau uses sex, alcohol, drumming, exercise, anything strenuous – to self-medicate. Especially sex. She's out prowling. Some guy will get the night of his life and then never see her again. We love her dearly but sometimes I want to just beat her senseless because we always worry when she does this. We get to worry a lot. I thought it had faded after college."

Aina shook her head sadly and looked at Blar. "Why does it seem so often that being really good at something is connected to some terrible cost."

The silver haired woman gazed sympathetically at Tsika and Glycerin. "All three of you young women took up music to ... to deal with terrible memories among other things. Those memories, in some powerful way, help create great music." Aina sighed, "My history seems minor in comparison but it whacked me pretty good. When I was younger, I was terribly insecure – Blar knows – I didn't believe anyone when they told me I was good."

She sat down and furrowed her brow.

"Hell, I thought *Gothic Fire* only hired me because they liked my ass! I certainly didn't keep it locked away from them! I shared it with everyone in the band! I had a paralyzing case of Imposter Syndrome, I thought I had simply borrowed or stolen everything. After we got famous, I still didn't believe I was any good. I took drugs ... lots of drugs. I was in rehab several times. The drugs messed me up bad, really bad. Once Blar had to haul off and slug me I was so out of control."

Glycerin looked horrified and glanced at Blar fearfully. He was studying his boots. Aina continued, "Biggest love-tap I ever needed, dear Glycerin. He still grieves about it."

Glycerin's expression softened and she retreated behind her curtain of hair.

Aina threw her arms up and waved them around. "Well, this isn't a self-help counseling group. Work is better therapy. All I'm trying to say is it is possible to work through your baggage and do great things. For now, I'm going to wring my hands and worry about little Kpau. People are pretty nice here, but we do get a lot of transient folk I can't vouch for. Oh gods, I'd just die if anything happened to her!"

Glycerin looked vacantly glum for a moment and then took a deep breath, "Let's play ... s-something loud and n-noisy. It w-works for Kpau. She likes that."

Six loud and noisy hours later, Blar noticed his phone blinking and sat down to check it. A text message from Kpau.

"me ok rly sry papa . monsters . bback morn rly sry pnsh me thn :("

He looked at the others. "Kpau. It's Kpau. A text. She seems to be safe for now." Blar punched a message back to the prowling blonde.

"be careful, we love you little rock star"

Blar realized Tsika was peeking over his shoulder at his phone when she hugged him from behind.

~17~ "Life in the Fast Lane" – The Eagles

Breakfast the next morning was a bleary affair. Coffee was the most important dish for everyone in the kitchen. When Tsika wasn't drinking her coffee, she was inhaling the steam. Aina looked like she had stayed up worrying all night. Glycerin kept pacing as she sipped her coffee. Blar kept checking the time as he grumbled out loud.

"Kpau texted she was on her way. I hope she's ready to hit the sticks fast because we're burning practice time and Friday night is roaring up on us."

Glycerin was at the sink peering out the window. She was keeping an eye on the road leading up to the house. She perked up and squinted, "I see … I see a car coming. It's not a taxi, though. Oh! It is … a Porsche!"

The others were too bleary to get up. Blar could hear Tsika blowing bubbles in her coffee. Glycerin kept reporting as if she were a scout on patrol. "It's stopped. I see Kpau! She has some sh-shopping bags. She's talking to the driver and she … oh!" Glycerin blushed and sat down. Tsika nearly choked on her coffee as she giggled. The little woman's laugh was acidic but her eyes were looking kindly at Glycerin.

"Come on, Glyc! She's going to say bye-bye to the guy!"

They could hear the front door open and the sound of bags crinkling. Kpau appeared at the kitchen doorway holding several clothing store bags. She was sporting a new outfit. A sleeveless blouse with a bright pink tiger stripe print. She had coordinated that with a black skirt embroidered with a large pink skull and crossbones emblem. The ensemble was decorated with quite a few belts, bangles, and dangles. Kpau had accomplished that appearance of ambiguity again that she seemed to excel at – jail bait or legal? Either way, she looked the sporty little pirate to Blar.

Her voice was a heavy contrast to the perky picture. Meek, tired, and worried. "Hi, guys. I'm sorry I forgot … to … leave a … note."

Blar, Aina, and Tsika remained silent with chagrined expressions. Glycca had a pained expression. No rocket science required to know the tall alien beauty hated it when her friends were annoyed with each other.

Kpau stared at Blar for a brief moment as he squinted at her with one raised eyebrow. He really didn't know whether he should yell at her for scaring them or just move on with the day's business. Her shoulders slumped and she dropped her gaze to the floor. She turned and stepped briskly down the hall towards the bedrooms. Blar critically examined the empty space where Kpau had stood seconds earlier.

"Tsika? I thought you said she comes back upbeat. That did not appear … upbeat." Blar drank the last of his coffee and put his dishes in the sink.

Tsika was befuddled, "I don't … think … anything bad happened. But no, she's never acted like that before. She looked … sad. Usually, it goes like 'gosh-I-f'd-up-about-leaving-a-note-sorrrrrrry' and we make fun of her the rest of the day."

Aina chewed on her bagel and waved it where Kpau had been standing. "I thought … well, I wasn't going to jump down her throat in front of everyone for making me worry. I'll wait 'til later. She left me a little off balance just then." She looked at Blar inquisitively.

Blar threw his hands up, "Fine! Fine. You're all looking at me. I'm gonna go chat with her." Glycerin cringed slightly. "No, Little Dancer. I am not going to yell at her or lecture her. I just need to get some bearings. It throws me off that you two seem confused about how she acted so I want to talk before I react."

Blar ambled down the hall to Kpau's bedroom. Her door was open. Blar took that as a good sign. Kpau was sitting at the room's vanity table staring at herself in its mirror. Vacant eyes.

"Hi, Chicklet." No response. "Looks like you went shopping."

Derp. I'm Captain Obvious today. Come up with better noises.

"I really like your new outfit with the pirate motif. Ah! The stripes match your drum kit! It's very Kpau. Was that a result of me calling you a pirate the other night?"

She nodded glumly but kept silent. Blar kept watching. Kpau's glum look deteriorated into a full pout and then advanced to a tear dribbling down her cheek. He came on into the room and sat next to her on the bench; joining her in examining her reflection in the mirror. Now Blar was lost, had something really bad happened to her?

She sniffled, her eyes squinted, and then the tears started streaming. She coughed and reached for a tissue. A couple of loud nose blows later she threw the tissue in the trash pail and wrung her hands in her lap.

"You're supposed to yell at me, Papa Bear!"

Kpau's shoulder's drooped and her face took on a tragically sad expression. Blar was a little bewildered but figured he had just a few seconds before outright bawling ensued.

He put his arms around her and pulled her head against him. Kpau muffled her whimpers into his chest as he rocked her.

"Aren't … aren't … you to going … to yell? Don't … you … care?"

"Precious little pirate. I do believe you're beating yourself up far more thoroughly than I could. I am not your parent. Don't want to be your parent. You're an adult. I'd like to think I'm your friend. I am just extremely glad you're safe and back with us. Tsika and Glyc told me you usually come back upbeat and they don't have to say anything. They are confused and have no idea why you are upset I'm clueless myself and I'm worrying something bad happened out there. Talk to me, Kpau."

Kpau was making small pitiful whimpers. "It … your … fault, Papa Bear! I spent the whole time … thinking about you and how you'd be mad or … or … disappointed in me. And then … I come back and I get … oh hey, nice shopping?" She looked up into his eyes with a painfully hurt look.

Blar rocked her and patted her back. "I get it. Listen, I was really angry at first but right now I'm just glad I get to hug you again. You did give me a good warning that you were edgy." Blar picked up a brush and started combing the results of the wind out of her hair.

Okay, small lecture. She seems to want that. Raise the voice just a little.

"Look! We're all grownups here! You are one of three who are just a little newer at the label. It's not like you need permission from us to live your life. Just keep us posted! So we know not to drag the river for your body! We thought you'd gone with Alwyn somewhere. Hours later, we realized that wasn't the case. You weren't answering your cell. Naturally, we were worried you'd fallen off a cliff or some other awfulness. There was some serious relief when you finally texted me last night!"

Blar put down the brush and wrapped his arms around her, putting his lips to her ear. "The one who is going to yell at you is Aina. When she figured out you were missing, she was crazy distraught and nearly useless. I thought she was going to throw up she was so anxious. You're in her home and Aina has a sense that she's supposed to protect people she invites into her home. She kept going on about sneaker waves and sand cliffs. And then when she thought you might be prowling, she wrung her hands about murdering psychopaths who dine on little blonde girls. I'm pretty sure she didn't sleep last night."

Kpau burrowed into his chest as if to hide. "Augh! I didn't even think about Aina! I just figured … she was all about Glycerin … and … wait … you mean, I'm going to have a Mama Bear yell at me?"

Blar nodded and thumped her forehead, "Yes! If you're looking for martyrdom, I think she's going serve you up to her pagan gods and then hug the remains. Heh ... Mama Bear ... I like that." Blar had an evil amused expression as he chuckled.

Kpau smiled through the tears. "That's … kind of nice. I'll never forget the way she cleaned me up the other night. I … don't have many nice memories like that."

Blar massaged her head. "Aina has had too many years of practice dragging barf-encrusted drunken band mates out of dumpsters for a bit of cheesecake and drink to faze her."

Kpau reached for another tissue and wiped her face, smearing her makeup. "Crap … that didn't help." She got a cleanser wipe out and began cleaning her face off.

"I … I went to the wharf first, you know, where all the shops are. That's really as far as I got solo." She leaned against Blar.

Blar was hesitant, "Um, Kpau, you don't have to tell me – " Kpau softly elbowed him.

"Shut up. It … matters. Just listen. You don't have to say anything." Kpau took a deep breath.

"I wandered around the tourist area. Some nice guys, some jerks, the usual. A few tried to pick me up, but for some reason they weren't the type I wanted this time. It was weird because usually that kind passes my minimum requirements easily. I usually end up with beach boy types, fluffy and lots of energy." Kpau tossed the wipe and put her hands on Blar's shirt, clinging to it.

"Then I found a crystal shop right at the front of the wharf. It was great, lots of trinkets, lots of neat little figurines, little dragons, wizards. There was a man in there shopping, he seemed nice. Suit, shoulder bag, professional looking but not stodgy, ya know? I struck up a conversation, helped him pick out some gifts for his wife and kids. He was in town from Toronto for a software conference, been traveling international for months. Hadn't been home in even longer. He went shopping with me for clothes, he was actually helpful … helping me choose a lot of what I bought. We ended up going to dinner … to a pub … to his hotel."

She paused. "He wasn't the usual kind of guy I tag up with, I couldn't figure out why he was attracting me. It didn't hit me til I woke up this morning and was watching him sleep." Kpau was silent for quite a long time.

"He reminded me of you, Papa Bear."

Kpau shifted uncomfortably. Blar suddenly felt adrift but said nothing. "He was a big guy … like you … and lean … like you. A fair bit older than you though … maybe forty? Very mellow. He loves his wife and kids dearly. He spent a lot of time talking about them. He was just really lonely, been away from home for months overseas in India. I became the fix-it fairy for his loneliness. It was a mutual fix-it – he was very kind and gentle. I never felt nervous. He actually … made love to me, not just crude sex. Very sweet. He made the monsters go away, back to their caves." Kpau softly smiled at the memory.

Kpau took Blar's hand in both of hers and squeezed it. "Okay! Okay? Hey! Please, I'm not getting weird. I'm not saying anything. But something feels different. I don't know that I'll need to … well, whoa there. Not gonna be stupid and say something I have to take back later. I just may not need my escape valve so often. I just want you to know, Blar, you've gotten in my head – in a good way. But nothing else! We're buddies!"

Blar kissed her on the temple. "I appreciate that … I think."

Kpau dropped her gaze and smiled. "I saw you two on the beach yesterday flying kites. That was so sweet, Papa Bear. I bet Tsika had a terrible time telling you she had fun."

Blar found his bearings again. Drinking buddy Kpau had re-appeared.

"At first, yeah. It took some careful nudging to get her to relax. The last part was nearly a tragic comedy. I regret to admit our date was interrupted before I wanted it to be over. But I loved it … long overdue. There seems to be quite a lot of things Tsika has never done. I'm going to have to learn a lot more about her because I'd like to do them with her – and I'm betting you won't just fill me in."

Kpau reacted in mock horror, "Noooo, my lumbering friend! That would be cheating! You have to play the game and solve the puzzles! I admit I have noticed you really have triggered an advanced challenge dual prize game. Awkward. Just full of land mines. No advice on that because I don't know the answers myself. All I'll say is I'll help where I can. Gotta keep my princesses safe and happy."

Kpau almost looked thoughtful. Blar stroked her hair.

"Great. Maybe I'll just practice my music all the time and never speak. Okay, Chicklet. Don't wait too long to take your medicine from 'mama bear' Aina … and, um, do me a favor? Be SURE and call her Mama Bear to her face? That's an order." Blar couldn't stop an incredibly evil grin from spreading across his face. Kpau began laughing.

"You ARE a bad man! You're going to drag Aina onto the Magic Bus, eh, Papa Bear? Yeah, yeah, sure, sure! I listen. I've heard her little sharp jokes about the Candy-van Man Predator! Yes, sir! Mission accepted!"

Kpau swung her legs up and over his lap. Blar received a big hug from her and then she was scampering off. "Ah haz more clothes to show the girls! And I want to see what Glyc got!"

Blar was relieved. Kpau was remarkably resilient or a great actress, probably both.

- - - - - -

It was about an hour later that Blar got to admire the results of Kpau's mission. He was in the music room tuning the drum kit. Aina came storming in looking for blood. His blood preferably.

"You! You had something to do with that! She wouldn't say, but I know you!" Aina pounded on his chest. "I'm not old! Not that old! They're not much younger than me!"

"Yes, pretty Witch. You're not old! You're not any older than I am!" Blar knew that clinched his guilt but couldn't resist. Aina grabbed his shirt and tried to shake him with little effect. He couldn't help laughing as she flailed at him. Finally, he wrapped his arms around her. The flailing subsided in a minute or so

"Welcome to the Magic Bus, Aina. Keep your hands and feet inside during the ride."

Blar held Aina close. Held her close for a good minute more before they mutually let go of each other. Aina had a sad nostalgic smile, "That was then and this is now. Good times though, Blar."

Blar nodded with a smile as he ignored internal regret. "More good times ahead, just different paths. So! Was Kpau sufficiently mortified by your scolding?"

Aina made a funny face and shook her head. "I think the little spark actually enjoyed being punished by me!"

Blar scratched his mustache, "They all lost their parents really early. It affects everything about them. That's why I'm always floundering. I flip back and forth between being their friend and some kind of crappy substitute for a parent. Kpau really cherished having her messy self cleaned up by Mama Bear the other night. I didn't suggest anything. She named you that all on her own – so you did it to yourself."

The beating and cursing started anew. Blar just smiled. He didn't bother dodging this time. Just like old times.

- - - - - -

The next day's practice was grueling. One more day remained before they would relocate to Aina's club. The schedule was going to run from noon until three in the morning every day through New Year's Day. Four performances; each one to be more elaborate. Aina wanted them to focus on fun music for the customers, specifically dance, rock, techno, upbeat. Her theme was upbeat optimism for the new year. *Rocket Science* wouldn't be the only band there. Aina's club had three venues and there were two other bands scheduled, but she planned to rotate the groups from stage to stage each day.

The five musicians were slamming their way through a rendition of a melodic metal tune when Glycerin cried out in pain. One of her guitar strings had snapped and caught her hand. There was blood.

Blar found himself shoved into an amplifier. Tsika had smacked his chest with her bass, her version of a handoff as she raced to go to Glycerin's aid. The lanky brunette was down on her knees and crying. She held her hand away from her as it bled. Tsika grabbed a sweat towel and was blotting at the wound to check the damage while cooing at Glycerin.

At the same moment, Blar was discovering that Kpau did not have the makings of a paramedic. The little blonde was green-faced and nauseated after seeing the blood. Blar was having to help keep Kpau's head between her legs as she curled up near Glycerin.

"Good gods, Kpau, keep your head down. Tsika, how does Glyc look?" Blar rubbed Kpau's back as she gagged.

"She got lucky, Blar. It'll sting but it's only a scratch on her hand. Must have hit a healthy capillary though. Quite a lot of blood." Aina had sprinted off and returned with tissues and first aid kit which Tsika gratefully made use of.

Blar caught Glycerin's attention as she whimpered and sniffled. Her tears had subsided. "Ever had a string break before, Glyc?"

Glycerin nodded. She returned her eyes to watching Tsika tend to her. "A lot of them, until I figured out the brands that worked for me. This is the first time I've ever bled though."

Blar was taken aback. Glycerin hadn't stammered at all. He could tell Tsika had noticed it as well. She looked mildly awed at her best friend and then silently returned to her bandaging.

Glycerin insisted on returning to practice immediately after Tsika was done mending her. It took Kpau quite a while longer to get over being nauseated. Aina brought the little 'collateral damage' a sports drink and sat with her until Kpau returned to her normal color. Blar refrained from cracking any 'Mama Bear' jokes. They needed to focus for the rest of the day and he didn't want to waste any more time.

By the time Blar called for bed time, everyone was just about burned to a crisp and getting cranky. His final clue they were done for the night – Glycerin. His sweet, shy Mouse snapped at him during a discussion on timing. She had never said a cross word to Blar before. Blar took that as a healthy sign for her, but also as a sign that it was way past everyone's bed time.

- - - - - -

Friday morning. Blar had finished his exercise hour with Kpau. She opted to go for a run on the beach to finish out her morning routine and burn energy. He showered, dressed, and headed to the kitchen. The kitchen smelled like breakfast, everything was cooked and ready to eat. He found Glycerin sitting at the kitchen table. She was curled up in her favorite sitting position, her legs drawn up to her body with her feet on the chair. She was resting her chin on her knees intently perusing her music notes. On seeing Blar, her face bloomed crimson and she averted her eyes from him. Blar was too fuzzy to think much about it and headed for the coffee first.

"Good morning, Glyc. Looking forward to setting up at the club today?"

Glycerin said nothing. She put her notes down and focused on him with her sad doe eyes. Blar sat down with his plate of food and coffee and started eating. "Did you cook this? This quiche is damn good."

"Y-y-you aren't … m-m-mad at us … at me?" She looked like a pathetic puppy, one that shredded a pillow and is awaiting certain punishment. She kept peering at him over her knees as she hugged her bare legs. Blar was mostly processing her distracting flannel short shorts she often slept in and a loose pullover.

Blar kept adding two and two in his head and getting 'long delicious pretty legs' for an answer, so he squinted and cleverly asked, "What?"

"L-L-Last night. We … we yelled at you! We said … s-s-s-something mean!" She wiggled her toes nervously. This was also highly distracting – he found her feet very sensual looking with their long slender toes. What was wrong with his mind this morning? He must be more tired than advertised but his mind was completely agog over the lovely little sexy treasure at the table with him.

"Wait … need coffee before this make sense. Exercise did not help my brain this morning." Blar drank some of his coffee as quickly as he could. "Okay, let me think. Last night. Um …"

Glycerin's eyes flashed in anger, "D-Don't treat me dif-dif-different than the others! When you need to be m-m-mad at me, be mad at me!" She seemed really hurt by her notion that he was cutting her extra slack.

Blar was still disoriented. He felt like he must have missed a page of script in the play. Then his brain lit up.

"Oh! I remember now. You called me a 'bloody dunce' when I suggested, oh well, it doesn't matter what I suggested." Blar couldn't stifle a chuckle. "Hell, Glyc! We were all so tired we were going backwards. No, no, I didn't call it quits after that because I was mad at you. That was just a signal to me that it was bedtime. When even my precious sweet Glycerin is biting my head off, it is definitely way past bed time!"

Glycerin seemed confused or disappointed by that explanation. "Oh. I s-s-spent all night thinking ... you aren't m-m-mad at me at all?"

Blar ate another bite of quiche. Were these women just used to having others mad at them? "I was mad at you ... last night, for about thirty seconds. You have to work a lot harder if you want me to actually stay mad at you. Sorry, Glycca. I just don't tend to stay mad. I don't like being angry. My enemies list of people to destroy for a hobby is pretty short and I think most of them are dead anyway."

Blar ate more quiche. "Besides! Your quiche destroys evil on contact! This is really good!"

Glycerin looked at him skeptically. "I still think you are bloody well treating m-m-me special. Please don't. But I'm glad you l-l-like my quiche. It has shiitake m-m-mushrooms in it." She smiled a little at that.

While she was speaking, her feet slipped forward until the balls of her feet were exposed as they hung off the edge of the chair seat. Blar failed his internal dice roll check for impulsive behavior. He reached down and stroked the bottom of her feet. Those lovely soft arches. The results were far more explosive than predicted.

She managed to shriek and giggle simultaneously as she tipped over backwards in her chair. Her right leg flung out straight up, almost upending the table and missing his face by a mere whiff. Blar lunged forward both to keep her from falling and to stop the launch of the table. She grabbed his shirt in panic, he lost his balance. His chair skittered away. After that events were hazy.

When the room stabilized, Glycerin was on the floor on her back. Her notes were everywhere. Blar was supporting the back of her head, having barely stopped it from cracking on the marble tile. To make that critically important catch, he now lay between her legs and on her chest. Her hands were gripping his shoulders and her right leg was wrapped around his legs.

There was a long silence except for the sound of hard breathing. He lay on top of her, neither moved.

Blar spoke first. "Um, yeah. I had no idea you were that ticklish, Glycca. Sorry about that, it was an impulse I didn't think through. Are you okay?"

Glycerin nodded breathlessly. "I can call you a bl-bl-bloody dunce now, right?" Blar nodded. Glycerin lay there looking up at Blar. Her eyes seemed really large and they were doing their little pupil tricks like crazy. She kept breathing hard, but now a very subtle quite devilish grin creeped into her expression. Blar was suddenly thinking of a couple of nights past when she had curled up on him while she slept. He felt really good laying on her. Really nice.

"Bloody d-dunce!" She shyly giggled. "Blar, um, quite … it is quite ruddy n-nice but a little heavy?" Blar scrambled up and offered her his hands. Glycerin pulled herself up with his help. "Well! Hee! I guess that certainly qua-qualifies as treating me like the others. Regular r-rugby!" She blushed. They restored the kitchen furniture to original positions, recovered the food items, and gathered her notes up. Blar poured coffee for himself and for her. They both sat back down and Blar resumed eating while Glycerin resorted her notes.

"How's your hand today, Little Dancer?" Glycerin put the wounded hand out mutely and let him inspect it. He took her hand in his hands.

Damn, my brain is massively curdled today, even her hands are sexy. Too bad the keyboards didn't work out for her – she has enormous span with her long fingers. Of course, that makes them excellent for guitar as well. The cut seems to be mending, good idea to leave it exposed this morning.

"It doesn't look like it's in a spot that will hamper you, Glycca. But keep me posted if it starts to bother you, please. We can always do some playlist tuning." Blar held onto her hand and stroked the knuckles.

He looked up – right into Glycerin's eyes up close; she had gotten nearer to inspect the wound as well. She blushed but didn't flinch away from his face. Blar suddenly became very aware of her lips.

Augh! Stupid brain! Time to shift gears. Smile and let go of the hand! Good. Now stand up, idiot.

Glycerin seemed to regain her composure as well. She also stood up. "Blar? I'm headed to the music room. I want to do some warmups before we start, okay?"

She stretched. A lovely stretch that blew a few safety breakers in Blar's head – he couldn't look away. Glycerin took a deep breath, reached over and brushed his hair out of his eyes, turned and walked out of the kitchen. Blar gave in and adored the view of her slinky butt swishing hypnotically as she walked away.

"Bloody dunce is right. In spades today! Focus, idiot!" Blar poured more coffee into his cup. Wait, the tall beauty had lost her stammer again. Wow. He should ask Aina what they had been talking about on their own for the last few days.

Blar decided that right now he should go check on Tsika. Now. He made a silent bet that the little princess was still face down on her pillow. Blar wondered if he needed to talk to Tsika about Glycerin and what was happening. He decided against it for the moment. Tsika was still on edge emotionally about Aina – though Tsika seemed to like Aina a lot. He wasn't sure Tsika needed to worry about her best friend right now as well. He should make time during the retreat, get recentered, everyone on the same page.

Blar reached Tsika's bedroom door. Closed. He knocked softly, "Hey, Pixie. Are you awake?" Blar thought he heard a mumble so he stuck his head around the door as he opened it.

Face down on the pillow, comforter up to her neck, and her wild spray of dark hair draped on top of the comforter. "Mmmmmmmmergh, go 'way," squeaked the bed's occupant.

Blar considered about a dozen lovely ways of waking her but most seemed to have the likely result of massive pain resulting for him. He opted for crawling onto the bed next to her. He lay his head on the pillow next to her and just watched what he could see of her face.

One eye slowly opened at him. Tsika turned her head so that he got to see two eyes and the rest of her face. She slowly mumbled, "Pervert. Sneaking into a girl's bedroom. Gonna have your way with her now?"

"If I weren't completely dressed, I might consider that. As it is, I may just grope you."

"Can't. I'm in my impenetrable Shield of Comforter." She smiled in supreme confidence.

Blar dove one hand under the comforter intending to tickle her. He aimed where he thought her ribs were. Tsika shifted to dodge him and instead, he unintentionally cupped a pert naked breast in his hand.

Blar's first thought – no clothes, she is quite possibly completely naked under the comforter.

Second thought – sensation is extremely pleasant, her breast fits in my hand perfectly. So soft and strokable. Want to taste it.

Third thought – I have done a bad possibly fatal thing.

Blar blushed and jerked his hand to release her. Tsika grabbed his wrist with both hands keeping his hand on her softness. She turned almost as red as her favorite lipstick.

"Pervert Bear! No, I'm not going to do some stupid comedy knock-you-to-the-moon slapstick because I know you didn't mean to. Besides. I … I have been wanting you to touch me for weeks now." She looked away. "They're not … too small, are they?" Tsika arched her back and put her hands on top of his hand as he caressed her breast. Her eyes closed and she shivered and whimpered in pleasure.

"They're absolutely perfect, little sultry princess." Blar traced the captured breast with a finger. Tsika's breath caught and her legs twitched. She kept shivering as he drifted his hand down to her tummy. Tsika let a soft moan escape her lips. He kissed her nose, her mouth, her throat.

"God damn you, Bear. I bet we have to get up now." Tsika was trembling and breathing heavy. Blar sadly nodded. Tsika sat up and smacked him hard with her pillow. She repeated the assault. He grabbed her arms.

"I'm sorry, little goddess. Your blows have no effect. You've already delivered me a mortal blow with your natural beauty." Tsika looked down; her comforter had slipped down when she sat up. Her perky breasts had nowhere to hide. She dropped the pillow, jerked free, and crossed her arms over her lovely distractions.

"Evil bastard! You have to take responsibility for me now! You've seen me!" Mock anger and hint of smile from the coy delicious goblin.

"Errrr, I think I'm already WAY past that line in the sand. But I'll make my exit so you can get dressed. Hurry, Glyc made some powerful quiche that kills evil on contact. I'm pretty sure evil little goblins will burst into flame but you can try it anyway." He pulled the comforter back over her and scampered out of the bedroom dodging a barrage of pillows and the sounds of high-pitched growling.

Good. I think that got my focus back … for now at least.

~18~ "Du Hast" - Rammstein

The band completed their morning rehearsal and were in the middle of having last drinks in the large music room before packing everything up to relocate over to Aina's nightclub. Kpau was sitting at Aina's keyboard throne marveling at the sheer number of buttons, slides, keys, and pedals that made up the command console while Aina tried to explain it all to her. Blar and Tsika were sharing a bench by a small ivy garden, the little Russian chattering to Blar about a planned shopping trip in Monterey as she stroked his arm.

Glycerin was draped across a lounge chair looking up at the ceiling. Blar was half-watching her as he tried to follow Tsika's chatter. The tall Brit had an expression he had recently learned meant she was psyching herself up to say something important. Part of the look included staring at the tip of her own nose while chewing on the inside of her cheek.

"H-H-Hey!" Glycerin paused to see if anyone had heard. "Hey. What about … what if … I know we have … but …." Glycerin's determination wavered as her face reddened. Blar silently cheered her on. He was guessing it had something to do with the performance coming up.

Aina moved to Glycerin to encourage her. "What, dear child? We're listening."

"I … I know we've already got a p-p-playlist for tonight. B-but it seems … it seems … not right. Wonky somehow. W-w-what if … could we … we … do the *AC/DC* t-t-tunes we know as a tri-tribute show? J-Just tonight? Do the other playlist tomorrow? The tunes are s-s-so easy for me I don't have to c-c-c-concentrate at all, we'd only need one … one run through, it's fun music to play and hear … and it'd be easier on m-my hand."

The truth at the end, thought Blar. Her hand hurts. She had let him push her too hard. However, that last revelation went unheard by the others because they were excitedly talking now. Aina was suspiciously making the most noise. Blar had a hunch she had encouraged and coordinated with Glycerin beforehand. It was likely Glycerin had asked her how to bring the subject up.

"Glycerin, I love that idea! Especially if you wear that darling naughty Brit outfit with the hat, skirt, and bikini top! With your lovely tattoos, the audience wouldn't be able to forget you." Aina clapped her hands as she spoke.

Faux innocence. Nailed it. There had been collusion with Aina. Blar knew he had already lost the debate. Tsika was standing now and she was being drawn into the excitement.

"Yeah! Is great idea! I can wear my new leather catsuit! Hard rock queen, no survivors!" She swished her hip towards Blar and purred at him.

Kpau spun around in Aina's piano stool. "This sounds appealing. I can strip down to my pirate skirt and my lingerie! Hush, Blar! Such a prude! It's black with pink trim – can't tell it from outerwear!"

Blar threw his hands up. "Obviously, the pretense at debate is over and we're choosing outfits. I guess the message is that I have been over-managing. Sorry about that. Thanks for the entertaining method of feedback."

Glycerin got up. She walked over to him with her slinky hips in full gear, pouting lips and seductive doe eyes. She had obviously been practicing. Again, Blar suspected Aina had been busy. Even with his cynical opinion, her sultry approach messed his head up anyway.

"B-b-blar, you aren't over-over-over … m-m-mana- … managing! Uh, it's just that I l-l-love y-your gravelly s-singing voice on those songs. It f-f-f-feels so lovely with m-my guitar!"

That little awkwardly executed seductive praise vaporized his remaining resistance. Blar wondered how many times Glycerin had practiced that at a mirror. Out of the corner of his eye he spotted Tsika. For just an instant, an honest expression leaked out of her – helpless inevitable sadness. Blar knew he was dim and slow at times, but a light bulb flashed in his head. Was Tsika intentionally throwing herself under a train for Glycerin's sake? A small part of Blar wanted to shake the daylights out of the small woman. He had some say in these matters!

Blar quickly tugged on Tsika's belt, pulling her into his lap. "You win, Glyc!

You win! Say, Tsika? What's this leather catsuit you mentioned? I haven't seen it." Tsika smiled nervously and batted her eyelashes as he stroked her ear. Blar hoped his diversion was enough to stroke Tsika back into a more secure zone.

"Darling Bear, I don't always wear bows and lace. You've seen some of my leather. You'll like this one. But you don't get to see it until we're dressed for the show."

Blar's attention seemed to get Tsika perky again. Blar glanced at Kpau, who just quietly rolled her eyes at Blar. Apparently, she thought him amusingly clumsy at juggling everyone's fragile feelings. Aina had a smile but the expression in her eyes was opaque. No doubt doing her own data collecting and appraisals.

"Okay, okay, let's get moving. *AC/DC*, it is. I'll need a bottle of scotch for my voice to last the night." Blar set Tsika on her feet and got up. An impulse told him to reward Glycerin for her efforts so he patted her butt. He got a startled happy squeak from her and a double bonus prize of a stifled giggle out of Tsika.

I'll just not even look at Kpau. She's probably collapsing in laughter at my expense.

The band packed up the equipment and instruments they would be using at Aina's club. Alwyn had brought the rental van around front for Kpau and Blar to load. The general vote was for eating lunch down at the wharf after everything was stowed away at the club.

Aina directed the women to bag up their performance clothing because they would have a dressing room. This went over tremendously with the young musicians – the idea of their own dressing room was foreign to them. The trio raced off to get their outfits.

Finally, Blar was able to settle into the driver's seat and put the vehicle in drive. Alwyn wished them luck as they pulled away, saying he would keep his cellphone handy in case anything was forgotten.

The vehicle accelerated up the driveway as Kpau launched into an *a cappella* version of her mangled girly rewrite of the Nickelback tune, 'Rockstar'. By the time the vehicle hit the public road, Tsika had joined in with her lower pitched edgy voice. Blar could hear Glycerin humming quietly. One more stanza and Aina had joined in with her husky voice.

Blar desperately tried not to listen to the words. "God damn it, Kpau! You're infesting my head with your twisted lyrics! I'm going to sing the wrong lyrics and have to fend off the men afterward instead of any women!"

The four females broke into laughter. Kpau, sitting behind him, ruffled his hair and giggled, "Don't fret, Papa Bear, you've already got your hands full handling the little harem you got!"

Aina choked as she held her ribs laughing along with Kpau.

Blar noted distinctly less laughter from the right side of the car. His mirror-check revealed both Tsika and Glycerin looking out their respective windows with embarrassed expressions. What had Kpau said about land mines? Seemed like she had triggered one herself. Kpau took up her singing again heedlessly. It wasn't long before all four women were at it again. Fame and fortune, hilltop houses, fancy cars, and the desire to be rock stars in four part harmony.

- - - - - -

The van drove past the glittery front plaza of the multi-faceted nightclub. It was simply named in a fancy font: Aina's. The complex was a rather large two story structure located right on the hotel and conference center district avenue. Aina informed them that there was also a basement floor – giving her room for three venues. She had taken a former shopping mall that had gone bankrupt during an economic downturn and converted it, betting that her ideas of entertainment right in the middle of a heavily used West Coast conference center would do well. It had paid off handsomely for her.

Blar pulled around to the loading dock, following Aina's directions to park off to one side. Club staff unloaded the van for them, leaving Kpau feeling underutilized. She ended up hanging onto Blar's arm as she watched.

"Okay, Papa Bear. It feels weird having other people do stuff for me."

Aina grabbed Kpau away from Blar. "Come on, Spark! I'll give you guys the tour first and show you where everything is. Then you can start setting up for your rehearsal. Since you're doing an *AC/DC* tribute tonight, I called our effects guys to set something up special."

Aina showed them her club from the customer's perspective first. They roamed through Aina's *Gothic Fire* museum, the dance floors, the arcade, the restaurant, and the bars. Then she took them on a backstage tour and finally to their dressing room.

The young women came to a halt. The dressing room door had been decorated with the band name and their logo. Tsika spoke softly, "Wow. Almost feel like professional now."

Blar scratched Tsika's back, "Seriously, Tsika. There are thousands of good bands out there – the ignition is usually when someone believes in you and supports you. You three are getting a kickstart from people who got a kickstart themselves when starting out. We had our own mentors."

Kpau straightened up, "Three? We four! We plus Blar. You're just playing two roles in this epic ride!"

Blar patted Kpau on the head and looked inside. "It's a good thing I'm wearing my performance clothes. I don't think I'd actually want to be sharing that dressing room with three frantic *Lost Girls*." He was awarded three punches in the arm for his verbal jab. Blar smiled, even Glycerin had punched him.

Kpau's face lit up. "Hey, are we really *Lost Girls* now? We're found. We're the *Girls of Rocket Science!*"

Aina grinned, "I hope you know what to do with rocket fuel, Kpau. Last thing to see – your stage for tonight."

The stage wasn't huge but it had plenty of room to mark off Glycerin's radius of whirling dance and guitar work. Aina took Kpau by the arm over to the drummer station where a technician was finishing up some work. He looked up at Aina and gave her a thumbs up with a smirk.

"Little Spark? What is the first tune you're doing tonight?" Aina had a devil's smile brewing.

Kpau eyed Aina cautiously, "We're doing the *AC/DC* title 'For Those About To Rock, We Salute You'."

Aina nodded and continued, "What musical instruments are missing?"

Kpau blinked, "Cannons. Artillery pieces. I compensate by stomping both bass drums at once, double pedal"

Aina pointed at the floor. "What's that?"

Kpau looked down. "A large shiny … red … button."

Aina had a wicked smile going now. "Step on it."

Blar was certain the kaboom the button triggered was heard outside on the street. Immediately following the kaboom was a Kpau war whoop that probably was heard all the way to the beaches.

The boom certainly rattled his innards. Much more importantly, Blar suddenly had all lovely seventy two inches of Glycerin in his arms, princess rescue style. She hadn't made a sound when the thunder-boom ignited. She had simply leaped completely into the air and into his arms. She weighed a lot more than Tsika and Blar couldn't avoid staggering. Tsika had her hands over her mouth snorting and laughing at the two of them.

"T-T-That was … bloody unexpected. Sorry, Blar." Glycerin slowly slid back down but kept a grip on Blar.

"No problem. One of the few things I'm good at, I think. Catching women in mid-air."

Aina was holding Kpau back from pressing it again. "Wait! Wait! We want it to keep working, Kpau! I don't know how many times it will work! There's also going to be some pyrotechnic but my tech guy is still working on that, little Spark!"

Blar shook his head. Aina loved special effects and seemed to be getting quite attached to 'the little spark'. After that piece of entertainment, the group retrieved their equipment off the van and stowed it. Blar wanted lunch. He insisted on visiting his favorite restaurant on the wharf. It specialized in squid dishes and he especially liked the fried squid and chips.

One meal and three more bags of souvenirs later, they headed back to the club for rehearsals. Rehearsing was a mildly grueling affair. The new surroundings were putting the young women mildly off balance. Silly mistakes were being made though they were compensating quickly. Midway through rehearsal, Blar signaled for a break.

"Okay, the goblins and Glyc should put their costumes and stage makeup on now. I'm set to go other than asking someone to bring a hairbrush back with them." All three women looked at Blar and then looked at each other. He got a very suspicious three-part-harmonized "Sure, Blar!" as they left for their dressing room.

- - - - - -

Their return appearance was quite impressive, especially Tsika. He really had not seen this outfit before. It was black leather with red leather trim. Red leather lacing marched the whole length of her arms and legs as it tightened the leather up. Her shoulders were bare and her neckline exposed enough cleavage to display her black widow spider tattoo over her heart. The most unusual part about the outfit was the tight leather slacks. Tsika almost never wore pants. That alone got Blar's attention since it hugged her legs and cute rear tightly. The result had her projecting the demeanor of a high fantasy action princess, or perhaps a sexy nemesis of Batman.

Kpau looked like a cute glitter pirate heading to the beach. Her 'skull and bones' black mini, boots, and black bra with pink trimmings coordinated with all that exposed tanned skin. As a drummer, Blar knew she had a practical reason for keeping her torso and arms as bare as prudent. Her tan was starting to worry Blar. Was it natural? Make a note to find out. His inner curmudgeon worried about long term effects of radioactive tanning. That initiated mental echoes of Kpau telling him he was old.

Glycerin had done a sexy combination of her beloved laced thigh boots with her old boarding school plaid skirt. That was topped with something he hadn't seen before: a bikini top with UK flag markings. The remarkable thing to Blar was the large quantity of skin the fairly modest big Mouse was exposing. Every tattoo that he knew about was in full display. The outfit screamed naughty British schoolgirl anarchist. Perfect for grinding the music of *AC/DC*, especially with her boarding school cap on her head. It was difficult not to be hypnotized by the swishing of her pleated skirt when she moved.

The trio had brought him a brush as he had asked. And a makeup kit that he had not asked for.

Kpau made him sit while Glycerin brushed his hair and Tsika applied eyeliner and shadow. She touched up his mustache and hairline. "Idiot Bear! You just fade out on stage under the lights. Aina says she always had to tie you down to get you made up. She said the other guys in *Gothic Fire* never gave her near the trouble." Blar grumpily allowed the grooming and eventually rehearsal resumed.

At one point, there was a pause as Tsika and Kpau began arguing over a bass and drum riff combination. Blar announced he would get some colas and asked Glycerin to help him carry them back. The pair made their way to a refrigerator for performers in the backstage hallways. While Blar was deciding on the choices, he hip bumped Glycerin to get her attention. Treat her like the others. She squeaked happily at his rough treatment.

"Little Dancer? Are you okay performing with that skirt? I know Aina has been filling your head with advice, but she has a flamboyant carefree idea about what happens on stage and what the audience gets a glimpse of. You got pretty upset when Tsika told you about flashing the audience back at Hans' club."

Glycerin broke into a satisfied smile. "I made ch-ch-changes!" She lifted her skirt. Blar gaped. She lifted it without a second thought. Instead of the boring white briefs she'd worn back then, she displayed black string panties. Much more discreet under stage lights but, good gods, those legs! Long tasty legs all the up to her hips. Nice curvy hips. Slinky round butt. It wasn't that he hadn't seen all those lovely assets but the presentation knocked him breathless.

Glycerin blinked, "What, my Blar? Tsika always checks me gear before … me … um, oh my! Oh dear!" Her eyes got wide, she let go of her skirt, and made an unearthly shrieking noise. "Sorry! So sorry! I … I … wasn't … I wasn't thinking … just automa- … at boarding … school inspection!" Her words wove around an unearthly bizarre shrieking sound as she trembled.

The panic radiated from her. She turned to run, but Blar blocked her. She made a magnificent attempt to slither by him but the hallway was too narrow. Blar threw his arms around her and cooed in her ear as he gently rocked her. He paid special attention to the nape of her neck, stroking it as he whispered calming sounds.

Damn it, she had been doing brilliantly until just now.

He ratcheted up, patting her back with some force, like he was burping a baby. Solid thumps on her naked shoulder blades. "It's okay! Glycerin! Glycca! Shhh! It is okay. You made my day just now. You managed to boggle the hell out of me. You have amazing fabulous legs! Be proud of them! You just forgot I was a guy for an instant, didn't you?"

He smiled as kindly as he knew how as he kept hugging her. Glycerin shifted mood suddenly. She responded with fire in her eyes, pulling him against her body and enveloping him in an embrace.

"No! I think about you being a guy all the time!" She blinked. "Wait! … That's not … what … yes it was! I meant that! No! No, it wasn't! Yes?!" Blar thought it was always fascinating to watch someone's face as their mental gears shredded into dust.

"Shhhhhh! Glycca. Music. You and me are going to play music. With your friends. We're going to have fun. You're doing really well. Really so well."

Blar kept patting her back, slow and steady like a bass drum. She lay her head on his shoulder. He could feel her relax but he could also feel her confidence leaking away as she clung to his body.

"I … thoughts we was g-getting b-better. We g-g-guesses we was just fooling ourselves." She sniffled.

"Wrong. Dead wrong, little dunce. You are amazingly better! Your stammering! It completely vanishes sometimes! I've lost count now in the last week. You call me bad names! You change the plans. You're not just a shadow of Tsika anymore, you're standing side-by-side with her! I am damned proud of you! So proud! You just keep swimming! Just keep swi- oh fuck me to hell! Kpau has infected my brain with her damn movie quotes!"

Blar threw his head back in mock despair.

Glycerinbroke into laughter. Her laughter was surreal. It had a quality to it that always left Blar feeling like he had fallen down a particularly bizarre rabbit hole. Possibly demented, not quite normal. But she was laughing and her eyes sparkled. She hugged him, holding him tightly against her. This was the longest full body hug she had ever given him while awake. All Blar's brain could muster was the smell of lavender and the feel of soft skin.

"Thank y-you! My Blar! I keep getting re-reminded how nice it is … to know you and … know you're my friend. You're … you're … the first man … the first bloke … I've ever … f-f-felt safe with. I'd let … let you … do … let you do … I would." She stopped talking and blushed so hard Blar worried about her bleeding out her pores.

Time to save her from what she was about to say.

"Come on, Dancer, let's take the drinks back before those two goblins eat each other. Two drinks each, maybe we won't drop them."

- - - - - -

The pair returned to find Tsika and Kpau still butting heads over the way each wanted the bass and drums to interleave. Blar sat down and watched after setting two drinks down next to the debating goblins. His intent was just to watch how each behaved when they disagreed. He refused to intercede. Glycerin sat next to him and curled up in her chair, sipping her pop. Blar was very aware that she was leaning against him. She was nearly in his lap. Her physical contact was cute, like a school girl too shy to actually demonstrate affection. Blar warily added it to his growing worries about the internal dynamics of this little band.

He did not want to be a point of contention between these two friends. Blar was now painfully aware that he found both Tsika and Glycerin deeply desirable and fascinating. The dilemma had been bumping around in the dark part of his brain even before they had left Portland. Blar felt it was only ethical to stay focused on Tsika. He had chased the little pixie in the snowstorm back at the beginning after all. But the little Russian made that complicated. Tsika had essentially drafted him into helping her with Glycerin. No, that wasn't right – he himself had felt compelled to be part of that project from day one. Tsika was totally focused on helping Glycerin move to normalcy, apparently at any cost to herself. Blar glimmered a new thought, wondering if Tsika focused on Glycerin to side-step her own problems.

Goblins are still arguing. Sip my cola more slowly. Glycerin is warming her hands on my arm. Best let her.

Quandaries abounded. Telling Glyc to back away would almost certainly decimate her budding self confidence, possibly leaving her worse off than before he'd met her. Tsika would be both crushed and blame Blar. But letting Glycerin get closer to him was building tension in Tsika. The little pixie was caught between her intense desire to help Glycerin and her own desires, leaving her fragile. Couple that with her tremendous unresolved anger problems and Tsika could implode. Blar did understand Tsika's feelings about Glycerin. The woman cast an awesome enchantment spell. It had Tsika and it was ensnaring him.

Kpau's mine field analogy was astute. He'd fallen into this sticky web just from wanting to romance a little pixie and help her get her rock band on it's feet. Just muddle along. Try not to hurt anyone. Try not to be miserable.

How Buddhist. I'm doomed.

The soft drinks seemed to calm the dueling goblins and they came to a compromise. Blar stroked Glycerin's arm to signal it was time to get up. She squeezed his hand as they got up to join them and the rehearsal continued.

Just before dinner, they called the rehearsal good. Nothing else to do before the show. Glycerin and Tsika opted to go fangirling and visit Aina's *Gothic Fire* museum for a closer look. This left Kpau and Blar on their own. Blar suggested the arcade and Kpau was gung ho on the idea.

"So, Kpau, you pick the game – as long as it isn't *DDR*. No *Dance-Dance-Revolution*, nope!" Blar was scanning the play area. He didn't recognize half the games. He wasn't surprised. It had been ages sinces he had been in one.

Kpau stamped her feet. "That was my first choice! You're not a bear today, you're a badger! A honey badger!" She looked over the choices. "We'll start old style for the old honey badger. Air Hockey!"

The hyperactive blonde wasn't stellar at the game but she made up for it in exuberance. Blar was not oblivious to the fact he was getting a fair number of jealous glares from younger guys who were ogling her in her stage outfit as she bounced about chasing the game puck.

"Hey, Chicklet. It occurs to me that your friend from the other day might be at the club tonight. That conference is still going on." It had the desired effect. Kpau missed the block and Blar scored a goal.

"You did that on purpose, dork!" Kpau flipped her middle finger up at him. "If you must know, when I was trying to impress him I let on that I was a rock star and he should come watch tonight so he'd know I wasn't just blowing bullshit. I don't know if he'll show up or try to say hello or not. I mean … Bill is married and all. I certainly don't want to get him in trouble. Ships in the night and all that."

Blar blocked a ricochet shot from her. "Well, if he does, don't be afraid to drag him over. I'm automatically fond of anyone who keeps my little Chicklet safe."

Kpau completely missed the disk and Blar scored again. She was managing to combine a glare and a smile with wet eyes. "Sure, sure! Hey! I lost! You're an evil cheater, Papa Bear. I challenge you to that racing simulator over there. I haven't driven in ages!"

- - - - - -

It was time. The announcer introduced the band as they entered the stage. The applause and whistling was acceptable. Blar deemed it a decent welcome. There were a few cries of "Blar!", "Woot! *Gothic Fire!*" and fair smattering of exclamatory remarks about the sexy women onstage.

Blar silently pointed at Glycerin, who opened with a melodic metal solo under a single white spotlight. She didn't even move much, just glared at the audience as her fingers flew. The chatter stopped as she crushed them with the sounds.

Good girl! Got their attention. Where does that magnificent glare come from?

Glycerin shifted into the opening bars of their opening piece, a familiar driving repetition of chords opening a classic song. A fair percentage of the audience recognized it quickly and started cheering. The rest figured it out when Tsika and Kpau joined in with cymbal and power chord followed by their driving musical lines. Counting down silently and then Blar's gravelly roar welcomed the audience in his lyrics and Glycerin launched herself into the air across the stage. That sealed the deal for the audience – long jump meets music. Blar made a note to either put the instruments on wireless or get a much longer cable for Glycerin. She had nearly outjumped the guitar's cable length.

By the time Kpau triggered her cannon simulation boom switch the first time, the crowd was at capacity. With all the bodies in the room, Blar wondered if the technicians had overdone it. The sound pressure was palpable. Glycerin visibly flinched on the first boom even though she knew it was coming. In contrast,Tsika was wearing quite the demonic grin and she drove the pace with her bass flicking. Kpau was so into her performance that Blar worried she would start using the boom switch as her bass pedal.

- - - - - -

During Glycerin's solo on the fourth *AC/DC* tune, "*Moneytalks*", the lacing on her right boot burst, snapping free during one of her gyrations. Without missing a note, she wiggled and kicked off the boot. The audience found this remarkably sexy, giving Glycerin wolf whistles, cheers, and a few "take it all off!" roars. To her credit, she played through it, blushing away with one bare naked leg. She coped by playing to Blar, her eyes on him. After the song ended, Blar leaned over and whispered to the strange beauty.

"Want to break now and fix it?"

Glycerin shook her head, "No, my Blar. I'm fine. S-stick to the sch-schedule."

Blar loved the way British women said 'schedule' with the silenced 'c'. They played on.

Just before break, Blar spoke to the audience. He couldn't quite let the old-fashioned patter to the audience go. Screw it. Like chatting on stage.

"Greetings, Monterey! As the announcer said, *'This Really **IS** Rocket Science!'*. Some of you know me from some other band a few years ago, my name is Blar. I want to thank my long time friend and former band mate Aina for giving us the space here tonight. But the people you should really be interested in are these three rocking women who crank out the music!" Blar paused a second to let the crowd respond.

"First, the pale beautiful leather faerie, Tsika on bass!" Tsika flicked out a jazz bass riff with a high kick as the spotlight hit her.

"The energetic glitter bug, Kpau on drums" Kpau executed a crash-bang reminiscent of the Muppet drummer Animal – complete with growl and flying locks of hair.

"And someone you probably noticed immediately, our whirling dervish on lead guitar, Glycerin!" The spotlight hit Glycerin. For a brief instant, Blar could see terror in her eyes but then she gave the audience that heart melting half-demented smile. She executed her own high kick to the side with her bare leg and delivered more notes on her guitar than Blar thought could possibly exist in the span of a three second interval. Every time he thought he had heard her top speed on a shred, she dashed the idea to dust the next time. The audience went nuts. Really good girl.

"They're all USC grads – so if there are any Trojans in the audience, Fight On!." There was a short pause because it turned there were Trojans in the audience. They wanted to hear them to do the fight song. Glycerin obliged with a very short rapid metal version of the tune. The Trojans in the audience cheered so Blar assumed she had done something they recognized. He had no idea what it was supposed to sound like.

"Okay, we're going to take a short break. Back in fifteen minutes. The bar and concessions are that way." Blar cut the mike off. He leaned over to Glycerin and whispered, "Go repair your boot. Aina's just offstage to help."

Blar stroked the side of her thigh. "Very sexy leg by the way." Glycerin giggled delightedly at his touch and danced off, leaving Blar watching the flick of her skirt. He felt a tug on his belt.

"Hey, darling Bear! Pixie wants a drink." Tsika slipped herself under his arm.

"Have I said enough times how sexy that catsuit is?" Blar traced her collarbone with his finger.

Tsika purred, "You're just used to seeing me in skirts or shorts. But I'll be happily stroked. To the bar, scrumptious Bear." She spoke more quietly. "Thank you, Blar. Thank you for being so sweet to Glycerin. There's nothing I love more than seeing her happy."

Doom on me.

- - - - - -

Blar and Tsika had their drinks in hand and were mingling at the bar while Glycerin was off repairing her boot laces. Kpau had vanished for moment, presumably to get her own drink. Tsika was getting many requests for autographs – Aina had made program notes with a picture of the band and left stacks of them around.

"Blar? Why are rabid fans not asking for your autograph?" Tsika sipped her drink as she waved bye to a fan.

"Oh, even I can answer that one. You're sexy hot and I'm not. They're undressing you in their head. Signing the pic gives them a legit reason to stand close and memorize the tasty smell and looks." Blar stretched and grinned.

"H'okay! Right! Now should take shower thinking about that. Ewwww, Blar!" Tsika looked as if she had inhaled pepper dust. "Oh! I see Glycerin! And a small pack of fans behind her. She's not quite running but I can see her hyperventilating. Faster, Glycca, faster!" Tsika waved to her friend.

With Blar and Tsika protecting her, Glycerin felt comfortable enough to sign autographs along with Tsika. Blar thanked them and kept mentioning their collectible quality. He never could quite turn off his business degree in his head – everything was a market opportunity.

"Hey, *Rocket Science* mates! I got someone for you to meet." Kpau's voice, rising over the crowd noise. Blar, Tsika, and Glyc turned to see Kpau and an obviously distressed older man in a suit. He was about Blar's size and build, but obviously older. Blar chuckled. She had the poor schmuck by his arm with both hands and was dragging him along.

"This is Bill, my buddy from the other day. Bill, this is Tsika, Glycerin, and Blar. I told him he could have a pic taken with us. Ya'll don't mind, do ya?" Kpau blinked at them with puppy-child eyes. Tsika and Glycerin simply gaped. Apparently Kpau never brought her kills home to show them. Blar stepped up. "No problem at all except we need a camera. Do you have a camera, Bill?"

"Um, yes, my iPhone?" He was clearly nervous. Probably best to sideline the humor ideas.

"Kpau, go get a staffer to handle the camera." Kpau lit off. Tsika and Glyc announced they were off to refill their drinks and would return promptly. This left Blar and Bill alone for a moment. Blar gauged the gentleman before speaking.

"Look, Bill. Don't be worried. We really are grateful someone like you was who Kpau tripped across. You kept her safe and looked after her. That's what we care about. Thanks."

Bill relaxed just barely. "I really wasn't planning to come but she sounded so earnest about being in a band and I guess I just wanted to see. She really is quite a drummer and the group is great. Weren't you in another group about ten years ago?"

Blar nodded. "Yeah, along with Aina, the owner of this club in fact. We called it *Gothic Fire*."

Bill raised his eyebrows, "Ah, I remember now. Aina was very pretty back then."

Blar smiled, "She's still pretty. She's going to sit in and play with us for New Years Eve if you're still here. You might even see her roaming around doing club business. Six foot high, very slender. Bright silver hair. Ice blue eyes. You and I both have good taste in women."

Bill's nervousness returned. Blar tried to be calming. "Hey, really. You are safe. I've traveled most of my life, Bill. I know how rough it gets on the road. Kpau said you had kids. How old are they?"

Bill looked a bit distressed at Blar's topic change. "They're both teenagers. High school."

Blar avoided the easy jab that Kpau wasn't a lot older than that. He just laughed, "Maybe pics with us will increase your cool factor with them. Like I said, you're safe. In our history, you bought us drinks during a band break if they ask how you got the picture. If things break our way, it will be quite a collector thing and you might have to endure posters of us in their bedrooms. You got to meet the *Rocket Science* people before they were world class. Heck, I still have an *Evanescence* photo of me taken with the band back when they were *Gothic Fire's* opening act. Now they're a world act." Blar held his glass up. He and Bill clinked their glasses together.

Kpau returned with a staffer at about the same time Glyc and Tsika came back. Pictures were taken. The staffer had the photos printed for them behind the bar. The foursome signed the hard glossy copies. Kpau signed her signature with a small heart where the "a" would go.

"Okay, we're running late – back to the show, young ladies. Bye, Bill. Safe travels." Blar took both Tsika and Glyc in arm and escorted them off while Kpau said goodbye to her fling.

Tsika looked past Blar at Kpau and her transient sex interest with a jaundiced eye as he hustled them off. "You were awfully nice to him considering he had his way with YOUR little Chicklet. Not jealous at all?" She clearly thought ill of the gentleman and the bizarre emphasis implying Blar's ownership of Kpau snapped an overwrought cable in Blar's head.

He was feeling mortally fatigued after all the emotional juggling the last few days. His mental gears stripped some teeth off and Blar lost his cool.

What the hell are Tsika's rules of this game? Fuck her friends? Don't touch them? Stroke their tits? Bite them? What?!

"Jealous? What the fuck? I was appreciative that Kpau didn't hook up with a torturing cannibal! She doesn't belong to me! I just care about her! I care about all of you!" More restraints snapped in his head. "I'm getting completely mixed signals here, Tsika! Are you jealous of the time I spend with Kpau?" Blar tripped farther into the mine field. He got louder.

"What about Glyc? Do you want me to just fu- ... I'm confused here! What the hell do you want me to do?!"

Crap, why am I blowing up like this? Dangerous ground, especially in the middle of a performance. But I don't have anywhere I can see to tiptoe!

The color drained out of Tsika's face. She seemed fatally struck, as if realizing she had tripped into a pit of broken glass. She swallowed hard and spoke plaintively.

"No, Blar! No. Being jealous would be terrible of me. Really terrible. Want my Gly-! Want us all ... I want ... I want you ... I ... I just don't want to be alo-- ... never mind! Was wrong! Was wrong thing to say! I am sorry!"

Glycerin said nothing. Just kept her eyes straight ahead as they walked. Blar could feel an abyss of depression starting to flow from the shy woman. Blar felt awful. Awful in both directions.

He kissed Tsika's forehead and put his arms around her. "No, I'm sorry. I'm really sorry. I'm confused and stressed. I'm sorry, that really wasn't ... crap, I just care about all of you. I'm just stumbling in the dark. I want to do the right thing. Just trying to do the right thing." He squeezed Tsika. Glycerin put one hand on Blar's shoulder and her other on Tsika's neck. She squeezed both of them and whispered.

"Come along. You pair are my best friends, almost my only friends. Let's go. Play music? Have f-fun? Right? Spit spot?"

Both Tsika and Blar weakly nodded in agreement and drew Glycerin into their sad little hug. They all knew they had work to do. Blar guessed his flaming blowout had been a reality check to the fantasy. A bit of the new had gotten scuffed off and the harder work of making relationships endure was starting. He hoped he hadn't permanently nicked it so soon.

~19~ "What Doesn't Kill You" – Kelly Clarkson

There had been a lot of silence off stage after Blar's flare up. The women had been professional. The practices ran smooth and the performances had been energetic with lots of smiles. But Tsika, since Blar had snapped at her, had excused herself to her room or away in some fashion, even eating at different times. She was avoiding everyone, even her precious friend Glycerin.

Sunday morning. Aina jerked Blar out into her garage for a private chat on the matter.

"Blar, what the fucking hell is going on? Glycerin acts like she's in god damned mourning, Kpau is down in my exercise room beating the fucking crap out of my equipment, and Tsika has gone batshit recluse. Then they all put on their god damned masks to practice and perform. Very professional but very fucking unhealthy!"

Blar was drinking straight from a bottle of scotch. He was grimly amused by Aina's language. Her mask of motherly purity had been dropped in her consternation. "Some of it is my fault. I bit Tsika's head off Friday night when she made some weird jealous remarks about how I was handling Kpau's affairs. I had been dancing my head off trying to keep things stable and then I blew up. The mixed signals from her … well, I apologized but damage done."

Aina smacked Blar on the head with the rolled up magazine in her hand and pointed it at him. "Yes, Blar, I know that didn't help but I'm feeling kind of fucking helpless and bitchy without knowing more." She poked him in the chest sharply with one end of her improvised punishment tool. She did it again.

Blar sighed, "Look. You know when I got into this, my base motivation was romancing the goth faerie and helping her to get her band moving. It has exploded into so many other things. Me being used by Tsika … no, that's not right. I silently volunteered to help her … as a lever for Glycerin to grow into a functional independent person. I've even sucked you into this project … though I think you understand now what I feel here with these three people."

Blar pulled at his hair in frustration. "I suspect repairing Glyc is the single most important thing in Tsika's world. More important than the band. More important than any relationship she and I might have. She does seem as interested in me as I am in her, but it's complicated how she expresses that."

Blar took another drink of scotch and continued.

"My guess? Tsika is tearing herself up inside with conflicting goals. She's got this life goal of helping Glycerin, but the little pixie has her own desires of band and family. Then she has anger problems she buries. She's possessive of me ... heh, she worries when you and I flirt. But when I flirt with her two friends she gets weird. The more I get entangled emotionally with Glycerin the better Tsika treats me – that confuses the bloody damned hell out of me."

Blar sipped his scotch. "Mashed in with that, Tsika seems deeply insecure about her desirability and I get these little hints of fear and jealousy at odd moments. Other moments, she's giggling her head off and a happy bird when I'm all over Glycerin. It's really freaking complicated, and that's before I consider her rage storms. I don't have a clue about the basis of those other than it is related to her loss of family. At times I get the sense that Tsika worries that Glyc will leave her if she doesn't depend on Tsika any more. Kpau tells me Tsika had no friends before Glyc. None whatsoever. Completely alone for years. Tsika is so focused on her first friend that she's avoiding addressing her own traumas."

Blar paused to collect his thoughts as Aina stood quietly watching him. "Meanwhile? Glycerin ... damn, if I tell her to cool her jets, I'm worried I'll wreck her confidence. Her progress is very fragile – I've seen it crack easily."

Blar took a deep breath. "And, here's where it gets really insane. Beat me to a pulp with that newspaper now, Aina. Because I deserve every damned whack as hard as you can muster. I don't WANT to tell Glycca to back off. I'm ... I find ... I ... I deeply enjoy Glycca. It is total nirvana being close and having the shy creature feel safe and comfortable with me. She's utterly hypnotic. But that is so not fair to Tsika at all even though the little twit encourages it because she sees Glyc getting better."

Blar took another drink. Aina still hadn't moved.

"Short summary of that rat's nest of a rant is I'm just doomed. Completely flipping doomed. And I have no idea how I could have avoided it. No idea how to manage it. I refuse to run away from it. Running away would qualify as what I consider immoral."

Aina stared at Blar for a moment longer. "Well! I'm impressed. You are a much more self-aware Blar than you were when you, me, and Torsten were having our own drama back in the day. I could be an acidly bitter bitch and say 'told you so' but your predicament ... is only similar to our little ancient tragedy in body count."

Blar brushed Aina's hair out of her face. "I don't want to end up in a repeat of Aina's Choice. Right now, I'm not sure whether Tsika is mad at me? Or mad at the others? Or if she's afraid she's going to explode in a rage storm and drive me away? I've seen one of her rages. They are impressive. She is quite correct to worry about really hurting someone, even killing them. I need to ... I don't know ... I guess I need to just go stand by her and keep standing by her until something happens."

Aina poked him once more in the chest and then kissed him on the cheek. "Good boy, you're learning. I'll go girl-talk with Glycerin and Kpau. See what I can glean and patch things there. Yes, Blar. I'll talk to Kpau. Somehow Little Spark and I have bonded. I've given up, I'm her Momma Bear. She'll listen to my advice."

Blar chuckled and handed Aina the whiskey bottle. She took a long sip and then sputtered and coughed. "How the hell do you drink this rotgut like that? I'll stick to wine. Anyway, off you go. I'd like to get past this before New Year's Eve so we can blow the cruft out of our minds and start afresh in a new year. There's a path to happiness for everyone. I assert there is. I say so!"

Blar quietly padded down to Tsika's bedroom. She wasn't there. Blar stood and thought a moment. She wouldn't be downstairs. Kpau was down there. Glycerin was in the music room, he could hear her playing her guitar. She was stretching the sadness of a mournful blues tune authored by Stevie Ray

Vaughn.

Blar remembered – Aina's house had a top floor, or rather a small partial floor. At the top of the stairs was a small circular stair that went up into an eagle's nest. The nest was a single octagonal room about eight feet in diameter with bay windows all round, meant for whale or storm watching. Blar made his way to the foot of the circular stairway. It was metal so there was no way to sneak quietly. He put a foot on the first step. It creaked.

"Please don't … should stay away. I want to be alone." A quiet, plaintive very sad little voice. Right, found her. Now the tough part.

Blar kept moving up the stair.

"Seriously! Fucking go away! … Glycca, is that you? … Glycca?" The amount of painful sadness in her voice made Blar's chest hurt. There was a lot more buried inside eating her than just his bitchy crab moment the other day.

Blar stuck his head up into the room. Tsika saw him. Her eyes got wide and she flipped around on the bench under the window. She curled up and stared out the window. "No, Blar! Don't. It's not a good idea … please?"

Blar kept moving anyway until he stood in the center of the room. Tsika was trembling. "Please, Blar. Not a good idea. You've seen what I am capable of … please?"

Blar stuck his hands in his pockets. "I'm just going to sit here. I'm not going to talk. If you don't want to talk, that's fine. If you want to talk, yell, scream, whatever, that's fine. I just … want to sit by you." Blar sat down on the adjacent bench. He watched her shoulders as they trembled. Damn, he wanted to just put his arms around her. With Aina, he could just hug her until she was better. These women were much more complicated.

Blar turned and watched the ocean. It was dark, blustery, and rain spattered the glass. He just sat and listened to the weather. About five minutes passed. He was finding it rather meditative. Blar just settled in and tried not to fall asleep.

Unexpectedly, he felt a small warmth next to him. The window glass reflected the back of a small head with two large sprays of curly black hair sprouting out of it. He could hear her breathing irregularly. Then two small, dainty hands touched his arm and clung to his sleeve. Tsika spoke so quietly he could barely hear her.

"Fuck you, big Bear. I was practicing for being alone again. You're interrupting."

Blar gently put his other hand on the hands clinging to his sleeve. "Why are you practicing for something we're not going to let happen?"

He could feel her hands shaking. Tsika sniffled, "Because I'm going to break everything. I always do, no matter how hard I try not to. I'm even …," she heaved a sob, "I'm even going to hurt Glycca. And then there's … nothing … no one. No one to hear me, no one who will answer … or hold me."

Blar couldn't stand not doing something. That was her inner pain. Abandonment. Being abandoned by everyone she loved.

He shifted around and scooped her into his lap and hugged her. She whimpered, "You should never have followed me in that snow! I'm bad news! I hurt people! I'm not sure I know how to stop!"

"Little idiot, the first words I ever heard out of you were a lurid string of curses when you were mad at the world for trying to kill you. I wasn't exactly unaware that you were a small angry thunderstorm. As for Glycca, I'm pretty sure she'd die for you. She's down in the music room in mourning because you won't talk to her. She thinks you're not speaking to her over something she's done to hurt you."

Blar stroked her shoulders. "You are beating yourself up when you should be angry at me. I'm the one that over-reacted. I should have just fired back with some witty joke, we would have laughed and moved on. But no, I picked a wretchedly bad moment to reveal how confused and frustrated I've been."

Tsika crossed her arms over her chest and lay her head on his chest. "I'm afraid of getting mad. I … am … afraid. I don't control the anger, I just set everything on fire. You were right, I made a shitty remark. You're just doing what I want you to do … and love you for … helping and loving my friends. I can't be selfish about you. That's wrong of me."

Blar started rocking her. It made him feel better at least. "Seriously! It is okay to be selfish about what you want sometimes. It sounds like you just don't have any practice setting your power knob between zero and eleven."

Tsika couldn't stop a tearful little giggle at the old Spinal Tap movie joke about superior volume knobs.

"You three women have held together many times when one of you needed saving. From what I've heard, you're the one who throws herself under the train most often."

Tsika furrowed her brow, "Kpau has been telling you stories, I guess."

Blar rubbed her brow with his fingers to smooth them out. "Just a few. Glycerin has mentioned some, too. But your little blonde guard dog is pretty fierce about trying to cover the angles. She wants this to all hang together."

Running his finger from her brow to her nose, Blar then traced her lips. He then lightly stroked her throat and bent down to kiss her. He kissed her deeply, exploring her pretty mouth as her whole body relaxed. She took his hand off her throat in both of her hands and pulled it down to her breasts, dragging his fingers across each one as she arched her back. She pressed his hand against her spider tattoo where he could feel her small heart beating. She opened her eyes and looked into his.

Tsika took a deep breath, "I think … I think I'm a lucky bitch to find someone like you who is too stubborn to have good sense and run away. I have a really black heart beating there. You keep doing what is good for my friends. We will do this together. It may get rough sometimes. But I am stubborn and crazy. Maybe Bear is also?"

Blar kissed her again, "I'd escalate this but there's a big Mouse downstairs who needs a big hug from her beautiful doll. And a puppy-eyed Kpau who needs a pat on the head … and a needed hug for a worried Momma Bear. You should grit your teeth and go get it over with."

Tsika sadly smirked, "We have one fucked up bizarre family, don't we, Blar?"

Blar squeezed her, "Like Kpau says, it's broken … but good. Still good."

- - - - - -

Sunday night's performance was going to be a short evening, so the band was dining on a stew Aina and Glycerin had made for lunch as they planned out the Monday night New Year's Eve performance. Blar wanted everyone doing vocals at the center mike at some point during the first part of the show. The second half of the performance was going to be a metal rock tribute performance, rowdy and fun, good to bring in the new year.

Blar lifted his pencil from scribbling notes and pointed at Kpau, "Chicklet, you've got a few songs under your belt now. Which two would you like to sing?"

Kpau buzzed her lips as she thought. "From what we're saying, the first half seems to be leaning … nostalgic? … memories? … past times? I'd like to start with a rowdy "*So What?*" just to fire them up and then … sing that *JoanOvArc* tune, '*Sisters*' … dedicate it to my little Babble." Kpau's eyes watered up. Shields down.

Glycerin silently took Kpau's hand to hold. Kpau wiped her eyes with her free hand and then her smiling shields went back up. "Yeah, that's what I want. It's loud and noisy so that will mask any drippy feelings I might be having."

Blar said nothing, just nodded and added it to the list. Babble had been Kpau's nickname for her only sibling, the little sister who had died in the car wreck along with Kpau's parents. She had never explicitly mentioned her sister to Blar. Glycerin had told him about Babble during a late night chat about Kpau's night terrors.

Aina came back in the room with a tray of wine, scotch, and glasses. She set it in the center of the table and took a seat. "Progress?"

Blar nodded, "Yes, I think so. We're opening with your guest segment mini-concert. It ends with the piece you've all discovered you like, "*Outside*", you introduce us, and then you can sit back and drink til I sling your comatose body over my shoulder and bring you home."

Aina stuck her tongue out at Blar, "That's what parties are for, brazen hooligan, so you can drape me over your shoulder at the end of them." Everyone laughed, including Tsika – though her laugh was tinged with a nervous giggle. Blar stroked the pixie's thigh under the table and she patted his hand.

"Okay, we've got Tsika doing a Jett/Benatar medley, I'm doing my *Tartarus* composition ..." Blar couldn't help a small grin and winked at Aina. The two of them had discussed this next moment extensively in secret.

Here we go. "So! Little Dancer …?"

Glycerin, who had been daydreaming, stiffened up and her eyes got quite large. She squeaked. No wonder Tsika called her Mouse, such a cute noise. Blar wasn't even sure how she made it. "Whaaaaat? Um, I have all my guitar solos w-worked out for all the pieces! I'm s-set!"

"We'd like you to sing something, Glyc. I've heard you sing at least three or four tunes you could do easily on stage." Blar put his pencil down and put his hand out to her. Glycerin slowly took it as if his hand were on fire. She was already hyperventilating. Aina put her arm around Glycerin's shoulder.

Tsika spoke up. "Glycca … we will be right with you. Just look at the lights, pretend you're cooking or in the shower." Blar's surprise suggestion had made the little goth visibly twitch but she was getting onboard.

Glycerin's eyes were little purple strobe lights she was blinking, contracting, and dilating so fast.

"I … I … I didn't know anyone heard me! I thought I was whispering! I can't … just can't!" Breathing fast and nearly shrieking. Blar squeezed her hand tighter.

"Glycca." He used her real name. That got her attention. "I think you need to try this and I think you CAN do this. One song! Right before break. Then you can go back to guitar. Don't you know you've been singing on stage already? You've been joining in on harmony for the last week!"

Evidently, Glycerin had no idea she'd been doing that. The remaining color in her face vanished. For about ten seconds she just stared at Blar as he watched each pupil dilate and shrink independently. It gave the impression of the two eyes having a silent argument. It was possibly the weirdest thing Blar had ever seen but Glycerin just seemed to be doused in the weirdly alien.

Tsika used her cooing voice she used often to settle Glycerin as she took the trembling brunette's other hand. "Glycca, why don't you do *Stronger, What doesn't kill you*? Come on, shout at the fear. You can do it. I've heard you do it."

Glycerin's eyes synchronized and she sniffled, "O-O-O-Okay … I'll t-t-t-try. F-F-For you, Tsika." Blar sighed, three steps forward, two steps back. Stammering like a jackhammer now.

"I'm going to give you an escape clause, Little Dancer. If you're so rattled it affects your playing, we'll skip it. But really, you have a beautiful voice and it would just be sad if no one got to hear it except us." Blar stroked her long fingers and intertwined them with his fingers. Glycerin blushed down to her throat and fluttered her lashes at Blar with a terrified little smile.

"And-d-d-d, for y-y-you B-B-Blar, I'll t-t-try for you." Blar felt silently awful about playing on her crush but he really wanted her to try.

Glycerin poured herself some scotch into her glass over the remains of her wine. She sipped it and choked, her eyes watering up. "M-M-My goodness, bl-bloody hell! H-h-how do y-you and K-K-Kpau drink this stuff? Is th-this why y-you two are s-s-so barmy brave?"

Everyone giggled. Glycerin forced another sip down. Blar snagged the glass away from her while the tall exotic wonder coughed her lungs up.

"Glyc, I won't say you can't find bravery in a bottle – but shelve that thought til we're closer to the performance or you'll be the one I'm slinging over my shoulder before the show starts."

Glycerin nodded meekly. Her foray into the new world of scotch had a rapid effect on the color of her face.

"I'll be … bloody careful. J-Just a f-few to pivot into slosh, and then Bob's Your Uncle! Blooming brilliant, right?"

Blar instantly found himself dearly wishing Glycerin would drink a little more often, her British slang was so freaking cute. Her face was red but now it was as much from the whiskey as embarrassment. She slouched in her chair as the scotch pooled in her skull.

The discussion continued as they tuned their plans for the performance. Blar slowly became aware there were long slender toes slipped up inside his pant leg against his ankle. They weren't moving but they were there.

Glycerin was doing it again – the kind of moves a junior high girl might make if she had a crush on someone but was too shy to directly confess. Blar thought it was sweet and also a little sad. Her social skills were so far behind the curve. Given her past, he supposed it should be a miracle she had any skills at all. Blar adjusted his leg so she wasn't having to reach so far. She didn't make eye contact but her expression was priceless as she realized he knew. Now she was too terrified to jerk those lovely toes away.

Blar kept talking as if nothing was going on. He let her just quietly stew in embarrassment for about twenty seconds. Then he silently rescued her by getting up and getting some ice cubes for his glass of scotch. Glycerin straightened up in her chair, but she kept her terrified mousey expression.

- - - - - -

Later after the meeting, Blar rounded the corner in the hall and walked right into his lovely lead guitarist, who nearly hit the ceiling in a jumping panic. She looked in about ten directions at once and fluttered her hands.

"I-I-I didn't m-m-mean to … um, stick my f-f-foot, um ..." Blar could see tiny tear droplets on her lashes. He put his hand behind her neck and drew Glycerin close to her, whispering in her ear as he stroked her neck.

"Shhh. I'm not stupid, Little Dancer, I think you're lovely and I'm attracted to you, too. No, there's no clear path here. You love Tsika. She loves you. I adore both of you. I am going to be as caring to both of you as I can. But none of us want to hurt each other or the band. It's a long way to the top if we want to rock it and we need to help each other."

Glycerin had gotten really still when he drew her into his arms, like a cat basking in a warm lap. She pressed her cheek against his neck. "I … I … know. If … if I can … at least do this … cuddle with my Blar … it'll be okay."

She took a deep breath. "Thank you. It's still … kind of amazing to me … that you even look at me. I never … never want to hurt … Tsika … never."

"Neither do I, Glycca. Nor do I want to hurt you." Blar let go of Glycerin and held her hands in his, squeezing them. "Just keep swimmin- … god dammit, I did it again! Freaking fish movie and Kpau's brain worms!"

Glycerin's eyes widened. It was the same Kpau movie quote he had blurted by the soda pop machine at the club while consoling her. She started giggling. She giggled so hard she snorted. It was beautiful to hear.

"Oh, bloody hell! That was an unladylike noise!"

She snorted again as she giggled. "Bollocks! I'm off to the bloody music room to practice before I fart or something!"

Glycerin darted in and brushed her lips on Blar's cheek and ran. She left him standing in the hall stunned by both the kiss and the burst of undamaged speech. He wasn't sure which was more amazing.

He stood there in disbelief until two small hands grabbed his belt and shook him from behind. Blar turned around and grabbed Tsika by the waist. He hoisted her up in the air as she giggled and shrieked. He settled her in one arm. She put her arms around his neck and put her lips to his ear.

"I don't know what you said to Glycerin just now but I have never heard her laugh that hard or that long. Don't tell me, I don't want to know. I just know the sound made me so very happy." Tsika kissed his ear.

All Blar could think was about how utterly screwed he was. He did not want to repeat history but there didn't seem to be any emergency exit for the ride he was on.

Doom on him.

- - - - - -

The Sunday night performance was short and sweet. Aina had predicted a slower night and it was indeed lightly attended. The software conference had left town and the locals were having their own parties before the Monday night club bash. The band was back at Aina's home by eleven in the evening.

Blar brushed his teeth, glaring at his reflection in his bathroom mirror as he moped on the recent massive changes in his life.

I haven't dated anyone since Aina decided to go her own way because Torsten and I were ass hats about her. Now, in the space of a month after ten years of isolation, I have living with me three women, two of whom are the closest of friends but who seem to have their eyes on one target. Me. Whee fuck. Male fantasies are bullshit. In real life, it is maddening and scary when you actually care about people who love you.

He was simply terrified that he might hurt either of them. Not just because he loved them, but the emotional fragility was alarming. All he could do was juggle and rely on their friendship for now. And pray. Maybe one of them would get a roving eye and solve things for him. Blar began to regret setting up the Big Sur retreat now. They'd be essentially alone, the four of them, for a month. There would be other guests and staff – but the way the Zen Center was set up, it wasn't designed for much socializing.

Doom on you, Blar.

It was late but Blar decided he needed another drink. He opened his door and ran right into Kpau as she sauntered down the hallway. She was in a splendid teddy lingerie sleepwear. Pristine white. She wore white a lot. Blar refrained from any parlor psychology games on Kpau's frequent use of pink and white in her fashion choices.

Try not to drool, moron.

Kpau looked up at Blar. She was embarrassed but it was quickly obvious that it was the pillow in her arm she was embarrassed about, not her outfit. She was headed to Glycerin's room.

"Good night, Chicklet. You're sleeping much better now, right?" Blar messed her hair up.

Kpau punched his arm and then punished him with her puppy-child eyes. "Yeah, Papa Bear … I could come sleep with you, ya know. I don't make very much noise. Welllllll, it depends on how good you are and what you touch!"

More punishment as she propped her pretty breasts up with the pillow and what Blar had to concede were hot fuck-me eyes.

"You really know how to torture my head, little Chicklet. Off with you."

Kpau blinked at him, then giggled quietly, "Night, Papa Bear, maybe some other time." She pranced off to Glyc's room. Now Blar really needed a strong drink.

He ran into Aina in the kitchen. Thank goodness she was at least in a decent house robe, though it was loosely tied.

"Ah, the big doofus is here for a nighty-night drink? I'd forgotten how much a band of musicians could put away in alcohol. No! No! Don't even say it! You're not allowed to offer money – you're my home guests and you brought old Aina three new friends."

"You are not old! Stop that!" Blar poured a scotch, then decided to add ice. "Duane is a lucky bastard to have snared such a sexy witch. I give thanks he caught you and keeps you happy every time I see you. I salute him."

Aina leaned against Blar as she sipped her wine. "Well, I'll salute you for apparently juggling your love life to something stable – though my intuition says you're just deeper in the quicksand. Glycerin was awfully happy tonight for having been told she has to sing tomorrow night."

"I gave Glycerin some … acknowledgment of what's happening between her and me … and the idea we would work together to make sure nothing evil happened. No one wants to hurt anyone. I think … hope … that's what is different here. Those two women love each other. They love each other so much. I don't even know if it's healthy or not. Love? Codependence? Is there a difference? I'm a business major, not a psych major."

Aina put her lips to her wine glass and sipped. She was evidently much farther along in her drinking. Blar knew he sucked on catching signals but she sure seemed to be radiating pheromones at him. She leaned close until she was nose-to-nose with Blar. "As long as someone isn't getting the raw end of the deal, it doesn't matter. Love shouldn't be a selfish thing. Everyone deserves love, you handsome idiot." Aina kissed him. He could smell her perfume, she hadn't changed it. So many memories with this woman.

Aina put the glass down and took Blar's glass from him and set it down. She turned to him and pressed against him, her head on his shoulder. Blar put his arms around her and his hands on her behind. Aina purred and licked his neck. He kissed her ear, then the back of her neck.

"My Blar needs a time out, maybe? One last time? For old times and memories? There won't be time or place after this. We each have our own adventure we're on now. Different paths for each of us."

Blar could feel his self-imposed blocks crumble. "You … will never be just a time-out. I … I'm stupid. I can't turn away. You'll always be my pretty Witch. Memories won't let me." He kissed her as she led him to her bedroom.

Tsika yawned until her tonsils were cold, stretching her petite body. Her toes poked out of the comforter. Cold! She curled back up under her comforter until she resembled a wary snail with a spray of hair for antennae.

New Year's Eve! Party time! It will be good day!

Brushing her hair out of her eyes, the young woman peered across the room through the window of the bedroom. The weather outside looked to be shaping up to be an overcast but dry day. Still not as warm as Los Angeles but much better than wretched snow. Tsika had tossed her robe off in the night so her naked skin was enveloped by the silk sheets. It was a yummy feeling. Tsika promised herself to set aside some money for her own silk sheets when they got back home.

Dainty lips smiled at the sound of that word. Home. Tsika was getting comfortable with thinking of Blar's condo as home. She missed the coziness of that setting already. Just her, Blar, Glycerin, and Kpau sharing daily life. And Blar was turning out to be someone who wouldn't run away. It made her heart pound.

It was funny, they'd only spent a couple of weeks there before hitting the road but the place had quickly imprinted itself in her mind. Tsika had not had a real home since she was a small child, only assigned lodgings, dorm rooms, and bunk beds. Temporary shelter. It felt a little vulnerable to admit that sort of thing bothered her.

Some of Tsika's hair had wrapped around her neck in the night, tentacles gone wild, so she began unraveling the mess. So much time it took to deal with her mane of hair. She had thought about cutting it off a number of times, but it so defined her in some ways she had always tabled the notion. Her hair was full of memories of her father.

Tsika had dim happy recollections of her father brushing her long hair when she was little. Her daddy also liked to hold her twin tails at their base and gently shake her head when he was lecturing her. Somehow Tsika knew intuitively that her father was only disciplining Tsika at her mother's command. Tsika knew she deserved occasional punishments back then, she was a mischievous little imp but nonetheless she was daddy's little princess. Tsika rolled over onto her back as sharp pangs of loneliness began poisoning those memories. Tsika sadly silently beat her memories back into the darkness.

Blar certainly loved her hair. He played with it all the time. He liked to wiggle her head with them like her daddy had. Blar let her know he liked to walk behind her and watch her hair sway like twin clock pendulums as she walked. Tsika blushed recalling the first time he told her he was enthralled by the way her hair tails framed the swish of her little hips.

Jeez, stupid bitch! Quite likely double-plus ungood idea to analyze conflation of daddy memories and Blar. That moves head into creepy zones. Stupid brain psychology. Damned therapist would love that. Eww.

Tsika decided to defer her morning shower, makeup session, and hair brushing routine in favor of heading straight down to breakfast. She couldn't stop herself from applying some black eyeliner and lipstick as a temporary measure. She selected a pair of ragged jean shorts and opted for staying barefoot. She finished by tying a white blouse up, not even bothering with the buttons so her midriff was bare.

Not like there's a lot of bounce to me anyway. So it goes! I am pinup for special tastes!

Tsika peeked out into the hallway. Quiet. She crept down to Kpau's room and found it empty. No pillow though. She smiled at the clue and moved on to Glycerin's room. The lanky brunette and the blonde were curled up together under their blanket, deeply asleep. Kpau was face up snoring softly with her mouth open.

Ooh, that meant no exercising with her and Blar! Maybe Blar could be lured and entrapped!

Tsika softly padded down to Blar's room. It was unoccupied. She pouted. Tsika wanted to curl up with him. A little pang of insecurity arose but she growled at it until it went away. She hated that needy feeling – so childish.

Maybe he's eating breakfast. Tsika grumbled as she wished he would have come gotten her.

She heard the clink of flatware on plates and conversation in the kitchen. Blar and Aina were talking.

"I still can't believe I passed out! My head touched the pillow and I was gone! I am getting old!"

Blar laughed. "You're just overloaded by all these people infesting your house and you trying to be a perfect goddess mother for them. Really, you ought to just relax and be yourself."

"Oh, shut up! Missed my chance. Probably forever." She sighed. "So it goes. Here's my printout of the day's schedule for you. See if you spot any screwball stuff."

Tsika was a little fascinated as she stood there listening to the two. Blar and Aina by themselves. Glycerin would be taking notes and vibrating in excitement. Then she stuck her tongue out as she stood in the hall shadows. Tsika had hoped for just a little Blar time to herself but that was just stupid.

I'm a childish idiot! It is just a couple more days! Then we drive down to Big Sur and our retreat where it is back to just the four of us! Almost a month to get to know more about each other without distractions!

Tsika couldn't stop feeling a little inadequate and nervous around Aina. She knew it was a stupid feeling, Aina had been totally supportive of them all, especially her dear Glycca. On the other hand, it was abundantly obvious to Tsika that Aina and Blar had a really deep enduring love for each other. She didn't begrudge her large Bear that but nevertheless – it made her feel small and vulnerable.

Tsika took a deep calming breath and walked into the kitchen with a bright smile. Blar and Aina were eating breakfast. Aina was looking over the local entertainment newspaper. She waved at Aina. "Good morning, Aina!" She kissed Blar on the temple. "*Доброе утро*, large Bear!"

Blar wrapped an arm around Tsika's bare waist and pulled her onto his lap.

"This … this is what the little pixie looks like without all her Victorian or metal goth finery – a wild sprite of the woods sporting this spectacular fountain of raven-colored curly hair."

Crap! He just punctures my shields like balloon! Blush erupting.

Tsika was purring at the feel of his hands on her waist and his breath on her neck – whatever anxiety she had melted under his touch.

Aina laughed as she watched Tsika obviously liquifying. "I'll get your breakfast for you, wild nature sprite! I think you've been captured by a fascinated giant ogre! Coffee, dear?"

Tsika wasn't playing hard to get. She was thoroughly enjoying Blar's cuddling. "Thank you, Aina. Yes, coffee please. Black." Her head rolled back onto Blar's shoulder as he kneaded her shoulders. "It boggles me that the ogre acts like this. I am lacking makeup, my hair would scare Medusa, and I'm wearing ragged unkempt grubby clothing. No packaging, no decoration. The man has no good sense. Nothing at all to be fascinated at."

Aina rolled her eyes as she set Tsika's breakfast and coffee down at the table. "Oh, come on, Tsika! You're the very essence of a small enchanted fairy Russian princess. You could be covered in mud and he'd still be doing that!"

That praise caught Tsika off guard momentarily and made her blush again. After a few neck nuzzles, Blar set the elfin woman in her own chair to eat and got up before Tsika could think of a reply.

"You two beautiful creatures, I'm going to excuse myself and head to the music room. I've got a drum rhythm in my head I'm compelled to check out. Then I may go rattle the cages of Kpau and Glyc if they still haven't moved. Busy day ahead." Blar gently arranged Tsika's hair to be out of her way and headed down the hall.

Blar's sudden exit threw Tsika completely off balance. She was alone with Aina. She ate quietly as the silver-haired woman read the paper.

Aina chuckled, "I think the reviewer can't decide who to drool over the most between the three of you. He didn't mention Blar at all. Outside of the sexual adoration, he does write that you women projected a lot of dynamic hard rocking energy on stage. That's good. You don't want to just be a pinup musician. I hated it when all the critics talked about was my legs. I mean, yeah, I was nearly naked sometimes on stage but it was PART of the performance, not the whole performance!"

Tsika smiled. She felt the same way. She kept eating, hoping it would mask her nervous jitters. Aina was watching her with catlike eyes.

"Tsika?" Startled, Tsika jerked reflexively and dropped her fork onto her plate. Aina patted Tsika's arm.

"Dear darling Tsika. Please relax! I feel really awful I make you so nervous! I want you to know I think Blar is a lucky bastard to have found you. You need to know I think that! Blar was just fading away before he found you! I got more depressed every time I saw or talked to him. He's so alive now!"

Tsika blinked as she stared at her food. Damn it, don't get all wet eyed.

"Tsika, Blar is precious to me. He always will be. We have a lot of memories together – both good and bad. I'm happy he let me meet you. And Kpau. And especially Glycca. I'd be really happy if you would consider me a friend. I want to consider you precious friends as well."

Aina had a pleading sound to her voice. Tsika wondered how many friends Aina actually had. Both Aina and Blar seemed to have a lot of acquaintances but very few real friends. Tsika knew what that was like.

Tsika pushed what was left of her egg around and smiled softly. "Well, as far as Kpau is concerned, you are inside our fortress. You've passed her guard dog test. I know that because she named you her Mama Bear. That's her way. And Glycca, she's had two of her gods become mortal just to be friends with her."

Aina was silent with an expression Tsika couldn't quite decipher. She wondered if she'd said something wrong from the way Aina kept staring at her. Then Aina reached over and stroked Tsika's curls. "So much curl and length! So strong and thick. My hair just thins out if it gets any longer than it is now. Your hair is just so gorgeous."

Aina sighed. "I know you perceive me as kind of threatening to you. Old band mate, old lover, unavoidably scary. I'd certainly be wringing my hands! But I really want you and the other Rocket Science women to succeed. I want to support you all – especially you, Tsika. Blar cares about you so much. I want him to have some happy in his life. Try to remember that even when you want to throttle the grumpy idiot."

Aina smirked as she said 'throttle'. Tsika got her message that being infuriated with Blar wasn't a rare event and wasn't unique to Tsika's experience with him. Tsika suddenly needed to talk to someone, anyone – even Aina. Her shields crumbled. She started to wring her hands and felt her eyes tearing up. Everything started to spill out.

"I'm fucking it up! I feel trapped in a mess of my making! Nothing! Nothing is more important to me than Glycca getting better. But … I don't know where that leaves ME afterward! I don't know if Glyc will still want to be around a psychotic bitch like me. No one else ever wanted to before her!"

Tsika started hyperventilating and sniffling. "I don't know! I pushed them together … Glycca and Blar … may … they may be already … I did it because I saw her getting better! I want my Glycca to be unbroken!"

Tsika cursed herself silently. Damn it. I'm going to cry. No. Stop it!

"I was alone before Glycca. And I may be alone again at the end." Fuck. Stupid tears.

Aina scooted over and put her arms around Tsika, rocking her and stroking her head.

"There's a lot of unspoken awareness among you three, of what's happening and the dangers. Each of you is more on the same page than you may think. But you all love each other so much! I can't believe how much! I think … I think there's enough caring between you all to figure it out."

Aina took a long breath and stared into nothingness. "Tsika, listen to my story. Please. It might help."

A tear was dribbling down Aina's cheek before she even began. "Back in the days of *Gothic Fire* ... my band was a rowdy hedonistic lot. No rules. I ... I was the band harlot I guess. That's a nice polite way to put it. Their muse as well as a band mate. I slept with everyone. But as time went by ... I fell in love with Blar ... AND with Torsten. Asgeir was always a loner so there was never a problem with him. But Blar and Torsten – I wanted them both. I had no idea what to do. I was barely into my twenties! I couldn't bear hurting either one. They were initially wonderfully civil about it – but over time they starting fighting. Often over stupid things. They wouldn't confront the situation directly. They were just college buddies, not life friends. It finally ... well, I did something. I confronted it. And ... and I broke it!"

Aina lay her head on the table. Now Tsika found herself stroking Aina's hair.

"I said I wanted to share, to have them both. There wasn't any reason we couldn't set our own rules. They couldn't handle that option. They were too ... conventional! I couldn't believe it! My wild crazy lovers were conventional under it all! Torsten lamented it would have been better to have left the situation unspoken. It finally got so bad, I had to make a choice. I was watching two people I loved who had been dear friends unraveling – so I left. I left the band. I left them. Not over music differences but to escape pain."

Aina's face was a waterfall of tears. Tsika dimly noticed her own eyes were streaming tears as she listened and kept stroking that lovely silver hair.

"I didn't talk to any of them for several years. Then I found Duane. Such a sweet guy. I started making music again. I started talking to them again. Little steps. Blar first. Then Torsten, though by then he had moved to Norway. Distance is tough to overcome, even now."

Aina stopped to take a few calming breaths. "Blar finally met Duane. It went well! The big lug gave me away at our wedding. I think Duane's still scared of Blar though. My sweet bastard walks on broken glass around me for fear Blar will crush him if he makes me cry."

Aina took a deep breath and sat back up. She wiped her eyes with a kitchen towel. She wiped Tsika's face as well, embarrassing the pixie with the motherly gesture.

"I'm telling you this because I don't want to see that bad ending happen again. Not to people I love. Make other choices, find another path, think outside conventional ruts. We're not normal – we're musicians! All of you, keep your eyes wide open, trust each other, talk to each other. Please." Aina fell silent.

Tsika reached for the bottle of scotch on the table and poured it into her coffee, more scotch than coffee. She swallowed as much as she tolerate in one gulp. "That … is a lot to absorb. But thank you. That, that helps. It tells me I'm not totally crazy in some of my own thoughts about what to do. About how to proceed. And I really appreciate you telling me. Blar doesn't say much about his past outside of what Fan Girl Glyc could recite. He says he wants to focus on the present."

"Tsika, no one outside our little circle knows that story, I trust you to keep it that way. I don't mind Glyc or Kpau knowing but no one else. My pain is not the world's business."

Tsika nodded and finished her coffee scotch in one gulp. She coughed and sputtered. "Usually … Kahlua … Ugh. I won't even tell Glyc this unless I think it's the only card left. But I will say … I think Glycca and I are a different situation. I love my Mouse. I'd do anything for her. But I just want a few small things in life for myself, too. I don't want those needful things to collide. I think I need to play music now. Loud."

Tsika helped Aina clean up and they headed to the music room. Aina took Tsika's hand as they walked. They could hear Blar experimenting with a drum rhythm, starting and restarting. Blar looked up as they entered the room. Tsika hid a smirk as she watched one of Blar's thick eyebrows arch up warily as they closed in on him. He got up and met the two women.

Tsika glanced up at Aina. The tall Witch winked at Tsika. They both kissed Blar on the cheek at the same time, Tsika stretching up and Aina bending down. Tsika enjoyed putting Blar off balance and it was kind of fun knowing Aina did too.

Blar hesitantly put his hands on each one's shoulder. "This is either really good or I've just been marked for assassination."

"Hey! Hey! What's this?! No fair! My turn!" All three turned at the sound of Kpau's voice. She and Glycerin had just entered the room. Kpau took off in a run and threw herself into the air at Blar. He defensively caught her in his arms, staggering as he absorbed the load. Kpau planted a huge French kiss in his mouth. She followed that by affecting a totally innocent bewildered look as Aina and Tsika reacted.

"Bad little spark!" "Ewww! Kpau!" Tsika and Aina supported each other as they giggled hysterically.

"What?! What?! No one told me there were rules!" Kpau slipped down from Blar and went to her drums. "Augh! Papa Bear, you've moved things! My rules say you ask me first!"

Glycerin hung back, abashed and rotating through various shades of pink. Tsika watched carefully, gauging Blar's expression at her dear Mouse. Blar seemed hesitant, but then rolled his eyes in resignation.

"Come here, Little Dancer. Everyone else has slobbered on me now, no sense in you getting left out."

Glycerin's eyes darted from Blar to Tsika and then to Aina. She tiptoed towards Blar with slithering grace, her eyes radiating caution. Hesitantly, she put her long arms around his head, her slender fingers touching the back of his neck as she drew him in. Now she reminded Tsika of a rabbit stretching towards a carrot in a trap. Her lips finally touched his, lingered a bit, and then she drew back with a terrified expression as if she had been caught red-handed.

Everyone in the room was blushing, including Blar. Tsika felt like her face was on fire. But watching Glycerin also had the effect of Tsika deciding to set course for realms she'd never considered before. It could work. It was important enough to her to make it work.

"Jeebus Crispy, Glyc! You should have told us to leave the room first! That was so erotic I'm all sweaty now!" Kpau gleefully bashed on her drums and cymbals. "But enough of that. Okay! Let's play!"

- - - - - -

The band and Aina ran through their final rehearsal over the course of the next few hours. Finally, the quintet gathered their stage clothes, instruments, and equipment to load the van. Once they arrived at Aina's club, the effort of setting up, doing sound and light checks, and more rehearsing took up the rest of the day until six in the evening. That left everyone a couple of hours to kill before show time.

Food was a high priority. More importantly, Blar had finally given Glycerin 'permission' to start drinking before the performance. He and Glycerin were loitering at the central bar while Kpau and Tsika hunted up food for the foursome. Aina had vanished to handle club management duties.

"Simple drinks, Glyc. No sugar-sweet nonsense with ten ingredients." Blar handed her a rum and cola. Glycerin nodded as if she was taking cues from the master of a cult.

"I'll only d-drink whatever y-you hand m-me, Blar. I don't know b-b-bollocks about m-mixed drinks. I tip mostly wine and b-beer." She sipped it. "Oh, this is q-q-quite brilliant. Scrumptious!"

Glycerin quickly downed the drink to Blar's surprise. He got her another.

Blar considered explaining again that he was just giving her instructions, not acting as her gatekeeper for drinks, but gave up on the notion. The shy creature was going to stick close to him all night anyway.

Tsika had privately told Blar earlier that as much as she would love to have him to herself for New Years – it made more sense for him to tend to Glycerin so the statuesque beauty could get through her performance. The curly haired waif hoped out loud there would be a balance of 'Tsika time' down at Big Sur – but she really wanted Glycerin to successfully sing center stage when her turn came.

"Little Dancer, I haven't heard you complain about the new guitar at all. Is it still working out for you?" Blar decided to distract Glycerin for now. The second drink was already half gone.

Glycerin's tongue was slowly licking a dribble that had worked its way down the outside of her glass. She seemed unaware that she had Blar transfixed at her sensual act. She gazed innocently at him.

"I ori-originally thought the upper p-pickup was bomb, but when I leg it through a ripping n-note spray, it spirals into a dog's d-d-dinner."

Blar stared at the doe-eyed beauty. "I may need subtitles before the night is over."

Glycerin cocked her head to the side like a curious bird and tried again. "The upper pickup n-needs a hand up be-because it's all sixes and sevens on a scrumptious shred."

Blar dimly interpolated she was saying the upper sound pickup on her guitar needed to be swapped out for something that didn't smudge the notes together at the speed she shredded notes on solos. The booze seemed to be activating her native home girl dialect. Full power British slang, uniquely Glycerin style. There may be moments when he would just have to nod pleasantly when she felt eloquent.

Wait, where had the rest of her second drink gone? Okay, she did need a gatekeeper on drinks.

Blar wondered if the tall creature had just enough meat on her to have one more. Tricky questions time.

"Um, don't take this personally but how much do you weigh? For deciding how much you should drink?"

"Posh, not a b-bother, love! We w-weighs almost thirteen stone with yummy foods in us! No use pre-pretending we is like our weightless little doll! All me tall bones and meat a-a-adds up!" Glycerin looked brightly at Blar, if a little unsteadily.

Stones, eh? Cute British girl slays American with adorable charm, exotic eyes, and incomprehensible units of measurement. Film at at eleven.

"Um … that's … how many pounds? Gah, I used to know absurd unit conversions."

"Oh! Sorry, love!" She scrunched up her face. "One hundred seventy pounds-ish? We've gr-grown a little extra in the tits and bum since we were a bl-bloody teen. But we weighs less when we is nakey!"

She blushed as she sloshed down the last of her drink. "Our h-handsome Blar wields us like a str-str-straw rag doll when he manhandles us. We l-loves that feeling, makes us f-f-feel petite."

Blar stifled laughter. Her adorable aura was filling his chest with a burst of utter happiness talking to her. It just felt nice having her able to do what passed for friendly chatter with him.

"Would you like another rum and coke, pretty little girl? ... or do you want to try something else?"

"I think this is brill, my dashing liar! Anoth-nother please. I'm already f-feeling a little squiffy." She was touching him almost every time she spoke now. Her inhibition locks were crumbling.

The flush on her face was not from shy embarrassment now but from the alcohol. Blar had noticed that before when she drank. He knew some Asians had an allergic reaction to alcohol – the symptom was a flushed red face. Glycerin seemed to have that feature, thanks to her mum's genetic input. It meant she couldn't ever deny having had a drink. She'd be lit like Rudolf on a foggy night.

Tsika and Kpau returned. With pizza. Blar grimaced. The two goblins took one look at Glycerin's now shining face and burst into giggles.

Kpau punched Blar on the shoulder, "Fast work, old Bear. She's all yours! Dare her to take her clothes off now!"

Blar put his hand on Kpau's mouth. "Not now! We have a show to do. This is apparently pretty tricky to gauge. And no one told me her face lit up when she drank. I just now put two and two together!"

Tsika smirked, "She was bright as a light bulb at the party over Hans' club. You were just too smashed yourself to notice. Here, Glyc! Have a pizza slice to sop up that booze."

They stood at the corner of the bar to eat their pizzas. Aina came by to check on them.

"Really? Really?! I have this lovely restaurant down the hall and ya'll are snatching my grease traps from the arcade concession?" Aina wrinkled her nose.

Kpau glanced curiously at Aina before defending her food noisily. "Nmph, dis fm goomph stubbf! Look! Gator and garlic! Just like home in Texas!"

Aina assessed the blonde dryly, "You're going to need to be hosed down, Spark. You're a grease fire hazard. Are you going to need some tummy antacids, Blar?"

Blar ripped off a hunk of pizza with his teeth. "No, our health agreement is they can have pizza night once a week. More only if it's the only choice. I'm looking forward to the hippie food at the retreat."

Aina shook her head, "See you food heathens backstage. I have more boring managing stuff to do." She made her way out of the bar area.

The foursome finished their pizzas. Kpau took the platters away while Tsika checked Glycerin's laces and buckles. Blar admired Tsika's skirt while the little pixie groomed Glycerin. It wasn't exactly rubber but it was some stretchy material with a side slit all the way up to her waist and tied with red lacing. If there was a thong bikini under it, she'd hidden the strap quite well.

"Have I said that's a racy little skirt, pixie?"

Tsika pinched his nose. "Yes, single-minded Bear! About a dozen times since I put it on. I get it! Large Bear want to unlace me and do unspeakable things to my defenseless body!" She pulled Blar's head down to her level and pecked him on the cheek. "Glyc, keep him distracted so he doesn't try to undress me on stage. We are not live porn band!"

Glycerin furrowed her brow, "But ... the only way I know to distract Blar ... is to ... let him ... have at ... to me." Blar was pretty sure she was blushing under the alcohol flush and in any event that was an amazingly immodest response from her.

Tsika seemed to be quite relaxed with Glycerin's idea. She snickered, "Well, with all those buckles and straps, the concert would be over before he got very far with you, my Mouse." She stretched up on her toes and kissed Glycerin on the cheek. "See you two backstage! Kpau has challenged me to one more whacking-of-the-moles. Game is new to me! It proves to be great fun to beat the crap out of those things! Very invigorating!"

Blar did not fail to notice Glycerin's expression. She seemed to be ogling Tsika, watching sultry hips swish as the little Russian made her way back to the arcade area. Her expression was dreamy. Blar filed that observation into memory as he gave her a nudge. "Do you want to go watch them, Glyc? Probably is great fun to watch two wild goblins smacking the crap out of plastic mole heads."

Glycerin giggled into her drink and then got quietly solemn. "No, it's … nice to 'ave you to me'self for a moment." Her eyes widened and her ears blushed. "I … that … didn't … no!"

Blar put his fingers on her lips. "Look. Look, my pretty girl. You don't have to freak out and deny your feelings every time you say something true. I like spending time with you alone, too … as well as each of the others. You're all very important to me."

Glycerin looked at Blar as if she was searching for something. Then she edged closer and stared down at her drink. Blar shook his head in resignation and put his arm around her back. She snuggled under his arm. Happy.

"Bravery in a bottle, Glyc. Don't get dependent on it. Even without a drink, you're so much braver than that day I met you back in Portland."

Glycerin stared glumly off into space as she answered. Her voice was strange, not her usual pitch. Blar had heard her speak that way once or twice before but it was quite disconcerting to hear, like she was doing an impression of a small child. "We weren't bloody brave at all before our little doll came. Not even brave enough to properly finish what the waves … meant to happen … jump down to my … join them." Blar could see tear drops on her lashes. He put his lips to her ear and whispered.

"You have people who love you now, Little Dancer. Kpau needs you a lot.

And it may sound weird but Tsika needs you desperately, more than you need her I think." Blar lightly kissed her temple and she shivered.

"Do … do you … do you need … me?" Her regular voice he was used to hearing again. A long slender hand gently clung to his shirt. Brave question. Blar thought for a moment. He wanted to answer clearly.

"I can no longer imagine anything without you. There would be a huge hole in my life now without you. So … yes. I need my Little Dancer. That's a little different than being dependent on you, but I think it's important."

Glycerin was silent for a moment. "I … I watch your music vids on my comp. And then I w-watch you in real life. So d-different! I … I idolized the scary Blar and the e-ethereal Aina on those vids but I think I like the r-real Blar and Aina much better. Both so kind and I feel safe with both."

Glycerin looked around to see who was about and then kissed Blar. Not just a brush of the lips, a firm insistent kiss. Blar responded to her lush lips. Glycerin wasn't expecting his response. She twitched slightly.

"I … shouldn't have done that, Blar. I'm gormless, a nutter, sorr – " Blar put his fingers on her lips again.

"Be honest. We don't necessarily act on all our feelings but that doesn't mean they aren't there. Like I said in the hall yesterday, I care for you. I also care about Tsika … Kpau … I still care about Aina. The strings that bind me are unique to each one, but they tie me firmly to them." Blar hugged Glycerin, he could feel her warm breath on his neck.

"You've had three drinks. That's probably half a drink more than was good. Lets go do final sound checks on the instruments and mikes. The goblins will hopefully keep an eye on the time and join us eventually."

Blar asked the bar for another rum-and-coke to go and the pair made their way backstage. Once there, Blar had Glycerin sing a few vocal tones into the mike to make sure the sound board memory had a setting for her voice. He watched her strap her guitar on.

Between her sexy leather thigh boots, her slinky hot pants, her new shredded blouse, buckles, straps, and her triangular flying swoop of a guitar – she looked deliciously hot and that wasn't even factoring in the dark bangs framing her brooding purple eyes, the sad clown makeup, and her pouting lips.

Posters. Got to remember to have posters made of everyone in the band. They will adorn the walls of the rooms of young males everywhere. Blar gave up hoping for Tsika to arrive to refocus him – he took Kpau's advice. Just enjoy the moment. Right now, Glycerin filled his brain.

"Ow."

Blar broke out of his trance at the lanky lass's annoyed cry. Glycerin was trying to reach behind her neck.

"Blar, I think I've g-got my hair all besnaggled into this bloody s-s-strap and it hurts."

Blar walked around behind her. The strap was a leather weave affair. It looked cool but was stupid for just the reason Glycerin had discovered. Glycerin detached the guitar and laid the instrument on her stool, leaving the strap hanging from her hair over her shoulder. Blar commenced extracting her hair out of the strap while doing as little damage as possible. Such strong silky hair.

As Blar worked, Glyc stood very still. It was a bit obvious, she was engaging in another school girl behavior. She had all her sensors extended wanting to experience his every touch. His touch on her neck, her shoulders, her back. Blar wasn't under any illusion about his mood. Her sensuality was engulfing. He found the situation extremely erotic. He got the strap free and dropped it. She didn't move. Blar knew he was about to do something there was an excellent chance that he would regret.

Blar very gently put his fingers on the skin of her hips where they peeked out the top of her shorts. Glycerin shivered and leaned against him with her back. She was tall enough her head lay back easily on his shoulder. Blar kissed her throat and shoulder. Her pert breasts were at full alert, just barely covered by her deep cut blouse. He dropped one hand from her hip down to the back of her thigh – more bare skin. Soft. He stroked it and her breath tipped into panting. His other hand drifted across her exposed tummy just below her navel. It trembled under the touch of his fingertips.

She seemed to come out of her trance and her eyes flicked open. "Oh! We should … that's … prob … probably … too much. We should get ready, we should." Glycerin turned around, her eyes wide, not with fear but just very alert. Her pupils were flickering fast, like twin sprockets on independent motors.

"You're right, I'm off base now. I … it just seemed … right … just then. Yes, I agree, working is good." Blar took a deep breath. Glycerin squeezed his hands and then went to her guitar.

They continued their sound checks until Tsika and Kpau arrived. Glycerin had been nervous but Tsika's arrival had amplified that mood into jittery panic. Blar felt badly, but then he had an epiphany on how to fix it. It used to work brilliantly on Aina when she was all wound up and he already knew Glycerin was susceptible to his solution.

"Hey, Glyc! Come here." Glycerin approached him cautiously.

"What, Blar? Is something amiss?" Glycerin's eyes were wide and she was sweating bullets.

"Yes. Hold still." Blar took Glycerin's guitar off of her and set it down. Tsika and Kpau watched curiously. In a flash, Blar put his hands on Glycerin's slender waist, gripping her tightly and lifting her into the air. He jiggled and tickled her until she was shrieking, laughing, snorting, giggling and gripping his arms.

"EEEEEeeeee! Blar! Stop …. sto- … put me … Aieeee! … my blouse! It's … oh my god!"

Her long legs were flailing, she giggled hysterically, her hair was flicking and flying. Blar was smiling peacefully as he held high in the air the chaos he was creating.

Tsika and Kpau were riveted, standing frozen, eyes wide open, mouths agape. Then the two smaller women started laughing and giggling as well. Blar finally set Glycerin down – completely disheveled and in the throes of a major wardrobe malfunction.

Glycerin shrieked, "Blar! What were you thinking! Oh, my god! Are you blooming off your trolley?! I'm nearly nakey – Aieee!" She spotted her blouse malfunction and quickly re-taped her blouse to her chest. The frazzled woman looked up to see Blar and the two goblins nearly incapacitated with laughter.

"Feel better now, Little Dancer?" Blar crossed his arms.

Glycerin was pouting fiercely, but after a few seconds she fluttered her lashes. In a meek voice she answered, "Yes, that was a lot of fun, actually. But I nearly wet myself! I thought you had gone wonky!"

She looked over at the two goblins with a betrayed look, "And you lot!! You just clapped and cheered! Jolly good fun watching him undress me!"

Blar looked at Tsika and silently mouthed the words, "Hasn't been stammering at all." Tsika smiled.

Kpau jumped up and downed and clapped, "You should make that a weekly, no, a daily event! When she least expects it!!"

Glycerin looked horrified and edged away from Blar, picking her guitar up as a shield.

"You're safe … for now, Glyc. You just looked way too tense. Better?" Blar stuck his thumb up with a querying smile on his face.

Glycerin nodded. She giggled in a mildly demented way with a surreal oddly lusty expression in her eyes.

- - - - - -

Aina appeared shortly afterward with a small crew carrying her keyboards and unidentifiable gizmos of her own design. "Hello, all, sorry I'm running a bit late. Boring management stuff attacked me."

Kpau watched closely as the men assembled Aina's station. "Have you ever named some of these things you've built? Like Mr. Tentacle Monster there?"

Aina screwed her face up. "I think, unfortunately, that's going to be its name from now on. I can't get that out of my head now."

Blar took Kpau by the neck. "Get away, Chicklet! The poor guys can't focus with you leaning over them. I don't want Aina to explode because something was cross-wired." The little drummer girl blinked at the hopeless pair of technicians ogling her, stretched, grinned and danced back to her drums.

Once Aina's gear was powered up, the other band members made sure they were tuned in with her gear. Aina was running a synthesized digital loop of bubbling harmonies in background while she checked her settings.

Once again, Kpau was over at Aina's station, fascinated as a ferret by shiny objects. "That sounds like a little army of spiders playing tiny bongo drums. I'm feeling a bit obsolete."

Aina stretched and yawned, "Don't worry, Kpau. Nothing will ever replace a young attractive woman banging the crap out of drums with the energy of a bonfire."

Kpau grinned while Aina scratched her head like she would have done to a puppy. Blar grimly pointed at the drums and Kpau grumpily stomped back over to her drum kit stool. The stage had screens that concealed them from the gathering audience but they could hear the rising murmurs. The overhead speakers were playing recorded music to warm up the crowd.

Aina grinned, "Imagine the day when you have a live opening act for you instead of canned music. Work hard so I get to see that happen, okay? Two minutes until the announcer."

- - - - - -

The announcer did his job properly revving the crowd up. Aina only performed live at her club a few times a year so the crowd was already excited. Knowing Blar was in the house just increased the amplitude with the buzz of a minor *Gothic Fire* reunion. The word on the street about the mysterious *Rocket Science* Girls wasn't hurting either. Aina had put them through a quick photo shoot and plastered the conference district with posters of each woman enshrouded in fog and dim lights. Blar had been listening to the bar chatter before the show. There were good vibes brewing.

The canned music faded and the screens retracted. The light engineer flashed the stage lights simultaneously as Tsika, Glycerin, and Aina flattened the audience with a power chord to open the first piece. The crowd recognized Aina's classic signature music immediately and a cheer went up.

- - - - - -

Aina's set went really smoothly. She didn't dominate the stage, making sure everyone got their own moments in the spotlight. The young women loved playing with her. She closed with a favorite classic of hers before moving away from her keyboards and standing center stage. She transitioned from that into a piece both she and the *Rocket Science* girls discovered they shared a love of, a tune called *'Outside'* written by a band lost in the '80s.

After the powerful tune ended, Aina began introducing the new band. "I really appreciate everyone showing up for old Aina and Blar! I love you all! Now I think you're really going to enjoy the rest of the evening. Blar has found us some smashing new talent. They're about to go into hiding for a month to write original music but right now it's a party night! For that, we're going to cover fun tunes we all know to rock in the New Year!"

Aina paused to let the mildly drunken cheering fade somewhat. "I'd like you to meet Tsika, Kpau, and Glycerin, part of the new band – *It Really IS Rocket Science!!* I think you'll be delighted!" Aina spun and danced off the stage in the stylistic manner that had generated her 'silver witch' reputation. Kpau stood up from her drums and helped Blar adjust the drum settings for his size. They had gotten their swap out down to a science with some Kpau customization of her kit.

Kpau. She pranced and twirled to the mike, waving at the crowd with a huge infectious smile. Blar loved watching her antics. The blonde puppy just loved the attention of the crowd. The band started off with a funky danceable *Freezepop* tune, *Less Talk More Rokk*. It had a rising crescendo duet opener between Glycerin and Tsika that started slow and then shifted rapidly up into maniac speeds. Coupled with the light show the engineer was pumping at the crowd, the results set the mood for an energetic raucous party.

After that, Kpau rolled into a raunchy tweaked version of Pink's battle anthem tune 'So What?'. The crowd loved that, especially with Kpau romping out into the crowd. To close her part of the show, she paused to dedicate the song *Sisters,* a hard rock lament, to her little sister. Blar had let her insert that piece against his best instincts for scripting a sequence of songs. He let it slide for both emotional and practical reasons. Practically, it had a strong fast finish and kept her songs in a single set. That minimized the time needed to reset the drums when he and Kpau swapped out. Emotionally, it was good for Kpau. She streamed tears for the entire song but kicked it out of the ball park as she rocked the finish hard.

Time for their big risk of the evening. It was Glycerin's turn. Blar spoke into his drum mike, "We've badgered our guitar goddess into trying her voice at the center mike. It's her first time, so be gentle." There was some lecherous chuckling and giggles from the audience. Glycerin made a face at Blar as she took her guitar off.

Kpau picked up her own guitar to take Glycerin's place, one the platinum blonde had scrounged out of Blar's dungeon. It was a clear Lucite Fender guitar, a limited edition. Kpau had selected it not for the sound but because "they can see that I'm not wearing much behind it!" Kpau remained stubborn in her belief she wasn't a fabulous guitarist. She substituted enthusiasm and glitter for skill.

Glycerin took a roundabout path to the mike, keeping to the shadows as she slithered between the lighting engineer's futile attempts to put a spotlight on her. Blar could hear her gulp as she stepped into the spotlight focused on the center mike. Tsika whispered encouragement and moved a little closer to her tall friend. Blar silently approved when the lighting engineer seemed to sense Glycerin's mood and softened the light, mixing the surgical white with a muted blue.

Blar found himself wondering what Glycerin's body language was going to be like as she sang. Static rigor mortis? Stevie Nicks twirling? Florence

Welch? Glycerin was a little taller than Florence, who liked to jump and scamper all over the stage in her capers with her band *The Machine*. He was completely clueless. He had literally only seen Glycerin singing solo in the kitchen, wiggling as she cooked and unaware he was watching.

Glycerin coughed as she whispered into the mike, "All right? Mates c-call me Glycerin? Just … just a mad d-dodgy tart who has … been told she can warble. Uh, if-if you get arse over tit about me, I'll b-be gobsmacked."

The crowd cheered, though Blar doubted more than two or three of them had the slightest idea what she had said. Glycerin looked in every way doomed, a deer in the headlights of a freight train. Even with the drinks in her, Blar could sense sheer terror blossoming in the fragile creature. He sighed, ticked off the beat, and Kpau started the opening musical phrase, a simple fast pick strumming. Tsika came in with a slow metronome bass note.

And – Glycerin sang.

She was soft at first but the more verses she forced out, the more volume she put out. Like other singers who stammered when speaking, her speech impediment completely vanished when she sang. She had a throaty voice that depended more on volume than octave range but at times she would shift in and out of much higher pitched whisper singing. That twist in her voice provided a sexy surreal hook that dragged the audience in.

Blar could see the sound engineer actively tuning his board to compensate as the exotic lass shifted up and down in octaves and volume. She began to move as she sang. Blar wanted to see the video later. The way she moved her lanky arms and legs while she stood between the two small goblins flanking her just made for a fascinating visual feast. Her movement was slow and deliberate, gracefully reptilian and hypnotic.

Blar already knew she was graceful dancing with her guitar, but his brain kept serving up snake metaphors to label her movement. Slithering and coiling around the mike, there was an edge to her stage sexuality, a gangly not quite awkward body rhythm. It was endearing and riveting. The audience loved it – both sexes. The women in the audience seemed just as enthralled. Glycerin radiated imperative waves of command that demanded 'cuddle me, protect me, worship me'. Blar knew a Japanese slang word for that feeling: *moé*. She had *moé* in spades, a cult priestess of *moé*. Her audience had no chance to resist it.

Glycerin's voice faded away as her vocal performance ended. Blar counted almost five seconds before the crowd erupted into cheers and applause. They wanted more. Glycerin had blown her mental circuit breakers though. She was welded to the spot with a terror-stricken smile. Blar got up and gently took the mike from her. Aina jogged over from her keyboards to put her arm around Glycerin.

Aina whispered in Blar's ear. "Gonna stay and play in your set. Protecting our crystal flower right now."

Then she led Glycerin offstage hugging and congratulating the stricken lass.

"Okay, you hooligans. We're going to take a fifteen minute break and then start the loud part of the party. Get your head banging gear on. Those who remember Aina's metal days will be pleased. I thought she was going to spend the rest of the evening getting soggy drunk but she wants to join us while we damage the damned walls with sound pressure! Headbanging in fucking fifteen!"

- - - - - -

By the time Blar got backstage, Glycerin was surrounded by Aina, Tsika, and Kpau. They were all crushing her in a group hug at once. Glycerin was blinking and wringing her hands.

"I don't even re-remember what I s-said! Didn't I bodge the song?! Was I-I-I even in tune?!"

Blar took her hand and squeezed it. "You can watch the video later. It was brilliant. Awesome."

Glycerin hiccuped, "V-V-Vid? Someone m-made a v-vid? Oh, I can't! Can't … watch … I'd just die!"

Tsika stretched up and pinched Glycerin's cheeks. "Big Mouse! You can watch it with a bag over your head in a dark room by yourself! But you should watch it."

Glycerin shuddered. "I just d-don't think I can do that very often, Aina."

Aina patted her back and straightened Glycerin's hair. "You'll do fine. Just go for it once in a while … for me, okay? It might get easier!"

Glycerin nodded. She bent down and hugged Tsika, more for her own comfort than Tsika's benefit. Kpau danced around to Blar.

"Blar! Blar! Hee hee, that sounds funny when I repeat it. Blar! Hey, Papa Bear, did I do okay on guitar?"

"Well, you didn't fall on your ass this time. Work on your basic skills and less gymnastics, eh?" He stroked Kpau's head while she purred.

"Meh, me and strings?! I need all the special effects and distraction I can muster! I should just play naked!"

Blar put his hands on Kpau's shoulders and mildly shook her for the hell of it. Kpau just happily droned that rhythmic noise children make while parents pat their back.

"Okay, goblins. Potty breaks and water drinkies. Then back to the stage, we have another half of a performance to do."

Tsika and Kpau escorted Glycerin away, both of them chattering happy noises to Glycerin as she slowly nodded. Aina and Blar stood watching them vanish around the corner.

"Didn't break the sweet thing that time, idiot. Slow and easy, steady braking. She's magnificent to watch, Blar. I was almost as drugged as the audience."

"Yes. She is a drug. A wonderful drug. Constant exposure may be fatal. I'm doomed."

"Bullshit! Your dancing is better this time, stupid darling dork. And I don't think your band mates are stupid like you were. Hey! Hey! No touchie! Augh! Bastard, you haven't changed at all! Augh!" Aina shrieked and giggled as Blar lifted her off the ground and tickled.

- - - - - -

Blar spun around as he held the mike stand upside down in the air. He was singing of video vamps and kinky lovemaking. The band was in the middle of *Def Leppard*'s *"Pour Some Sugar on Me"* when the announcer waved at him with a signal: one minute to midnight. The band shorted the piece and gathered by the center mike. Aina stepped up in front and shouted.

"Thirty seconds to midnight! Grab someone to snog the daylights out of! Hopefully someone you know! Or make a new friend! Experiment!"

Blar realized he had a diplomatic dilemma, the nice way of saying he was in a jam. His first impulse was to kiss Tsika at midnight, but he honestly wanted to kiss all four friends.

Sigh, I'll just have to go down the list. Someone is going to feel slighted no matter what.

Blar reached for Tsika – she surprised him by twisting his hand into an judo hold. That was when he realized all three *Rocket Science* women had a grip on him. They were steering him to Aina. She was oblivious to the commotion behind her as she counted down from ten seconds to midnight.

Glycerin tapped her shoulder. Aina turned and found Blar pushed right up into her. Blar swore Aina surpassed Glycerin's best for the shade of crimson that blossomed on her face.

"Wait! Ah! NO! There will be pictures!" Aina babbled but Glycerin used her hip to bump Aina into Blar just as the siren sounded.

"Right, Aina. The goblins have spoken. I'll be gone, you can explain to Duane. Happy New Year!" Blar put his arms around Aina and kissed the daylights out of her. She didn't struggle very much. By the end of it, her long fingers were snaking up through his hair the way they had so many years before.

Then Blar turned and snagged Tsika. She had been enthralled watching them, an easy catch. He picked her up, turned her sideways and went after her like a harmonica. He kissed her mouth, her eyes, her neck, her spider tattoo, and even landed one kiss on her navel. Lots of satisfying shrieks, especially on that last nibble.

Kpau was next. The wide-eyed shrieking blonde tried to run but he cut her off at the drums. He slung her over his shoulder head forward and took his kiss upside down as she giggled and growled.

Last. Glycerin. The brunette had frozen like a rabbit hiding in tall grass during his other attacks, but suddenly came to life as she realized she was the next target. She jumped to the side, slithered, spun, and dodged. She was good but then she tried to hide behind Tsika. That proved her undoing. No luck for her as Blar got a finger on her belt and pulled. Glycerin squealed and shrieked.

"No!! Not in front of – ! Augh! My pants! B-Blar! Inappropri – !

To use Glycerin's own slang, he snogged her brilliantly. She didn't even bother to struggle once in his trap. She went limp as he had his way with her lovely mouth. After a few seconds, her tongue softly responded to him. Then her arms encircling his neck. Afterward, Blar hauled her along with him, her feet dragging the floor as he enjoyed reviewing the results of his revenge on the trio of women.

Aina was on her knees laughing hysterically. "Blar, watching that might be worth the crap I'm going to get from Duane when the gossip rags post the pictures half the crowd took! Bad naughty goblins!"

Kpau and Tsika were helping each other repair their wardrobe malfunctions, still shrieking in mock indignation and giggling. Glycerin pulled herself upright using Blar as a set of handholds. She got nose-to-nose with him. For an instant, all Blar could see was erotic horny purple take-me eyes. Her breathing was rough and sexually ragged. Then she fluttered her lashes and blushed as she focused on his collar. Blar had a sudden insight the bashful mouse might like her lovemaking rough. Good grief.

Glycerin whispered huskily, "We've got two more bloody hours to play, Blar. I suppose we should do a smashing good job of it. Right? Happy New Year, love."

~21~ "Free Ride" – Edgar Winter Group

Blar planned to get up early to enjoy their New Year's Day. His first glimmer of awareness was that he had failed to achieve that goal. He was face down in his bed with something small and warm curled up on his back. He didn't recall Aina having a cat. He turned his head to the side and opened his eyes to a jungle of curly black hair. The hell? There was daylight leaking through the tangle. Blar took a guess it was mid-morning.

Tsika was on his back, fast asleep under the sheets with him. Blar made the educated guess that she had snuck into his room at daybreak with some cuddling in mind and simply passed out after getting warm and comfortable. Now how the hell was he supposed to turn over? It really was like having a cat fall asleep on him.

Blar lay listening. Aina's house was silent. Likely no one else was up either, everyone sleeping in after the party performance they had given the night before. A day earlier, Aina and Glycerin managed to slip time in during rehearsal breaks to cook ham, stuffing, mashed sweet potatoes, and other goodies for New Years Day. Everyone looked forward a lazy goof off day. Blar stopped grumbling and reckoned sleeping in was not a bad thing this particular time.

He lay still. Tsika's small heart beat beneath her breasts against his back. Her breath flickered the hairs on the back of his neck. It felt really soothing. She had her house robe on but it was open and loose on her. His back was enjoying a considerable sampling of the silky skin belonging to her warm little body. Blar really wanted to turn over. So close and yet not happening. Not that he could really do much with her this late in the morning. They would have an audience in no time.

Blar thought about the previous night at the New Year's Eve performance. After midnight, they had provided a two hours of expertly executed entertainment for the crowd. He was satisfied with that. Somewhat alarming in a pleasant but dangerous way was the spectacle of Glycerin's behavior on stage.

Blar had never had someone playing a guitar try to seduce him on stage before. She had been, as she put it herself, awesomely snockered. It made for great audience showmanship. At some points the audience was transfixed by Glycerin. She pranced, slithered, brushed against Blar, batted her eyes at him, even once licked the air at him with her tongue. Amazingly drunk. The crowd loved it.

Jesus Christ on a stick, it made staying focused on the music difficult.

Blar had consciously tracked his time to make sure he spent as much time interacting with Tsika as they played. It was a tricky dance. Tsika hadn't seemed upset or put out by Glycerin's antics, but she adopted a peculiar blank expression when Glycerin was doing something particularly sensual – like she was trying not to think about it.

He hoped Tsika realized Glycerin's aggressiveness was mostly 'bravery in a bottle' but it would take some rugged denial not to grasp Glycerin's intentions were quite different from Kpau's goofy clowning around with him.

Tsika murmured and adjusted her head. Blar took that opportunity to flip over while keeping her body on top.

There! Wow. She feels nice. Really nice. So nice I'm not relaxed now. Guh, I want the little creature so bad!

Blar slipped his hands inside her robe and ran his fingers from her shoulder blades slowly down her back.

"Mmmmmm, brg bmm wrm … mmm." Half-awake now. Blar smiled as he put his hands on her hips and pulled her up to kiss her mouth. Sliding her lovely body up his stomach, skin against skin, that woke her up.

"Mmmm, Darling Bea … oh god! Where's my robe! I'm … I didn't mean … it's too late in the morning. We …" Tsika looked pathetically sad. "I wasn't trying to tease you. I just fell asleep because I got warm."

Blar was feeling a bit aggressive though. He spread her robe wider and shifted his hands from her hips to her behind up to her shoulder blades, pressing her tummy and breasts against his body. She whimpered in pleasure. He kissed her shoulder. "You're a delicious little breakfast, pixie."

Tsika's cheeks lit up. "I'd call you an evil bastard but I put stupid self in this situation. God damn me! Feels good against you, my horny Bear."

Tsika lifted up on her elbows, gripping his shoulders with her hands. She brushed her soft breasts across Blar's chest, softly whimpering with pleasure. Blar moved his hands under her armpits and lifted Tsika a bit further, exposing those delightfully pert breasts for Blar's appreciation and attention.

Kissing and nibbling her breasts elicited a string of ecstatic moans and then a loud shriek from the pale pixie as she threw her head back. Her moans were loud enough but the shriek was spectacular, the sound of a wild forest creature wanting to couple with her mate. Tsika turned bright red and grabbed Blar's wrists, scrabbling to sit up and tying her robe back up.

"Oh shit! Will never hear the end of it if Kpau heard that! I'm sneaking back to my room pronto. God damn you -- I want you to take me so bad, Big Bear. Must settle for breakfast though. Five minutes, in the kitchen?" Tsika was breathing heavily. Her flared nostrils and dilated pupils weren't hard to decipher.

"Off you go, delicious pixie! Ninja time. Quick!" Tsika silently scampered out of his room and Blar dressed. He grinned though – Kpau had guessed right. It seemed Tsika really was a very noisy little lover if her switches were stroked right. Blar found that notion very promising and desirable.

Once Blar had made himself presentable – jeans and tee shirt – he quietly made his way into the hall on bare feet. He peeked in on Glycerin. Dead asleep, only her silken black hair showing … and a Kpau leg hanging out from under the cover on the other side of Glycerin's bed.

Good. That was much better than two whispering women giggling about Tsika's erotic love noises.

Blar got down to the kitchen and started coffee. A minute or so later, Tsika appeared. She had tied her hair into her characteristic twin tails but Blar was attentive to the clothing she'd chosen. Tsika didn't often run around stripped down at home. Typically, she was fairly modest – not a lot of skin actually showing other than some strategic exposure. She had gone for the wild nymph look again this morning. That was twice now she had done that to him. A simple blouse, unbuttoned but tied in a knot at her solar plexus, a pair of cutoff jeans and bare feet. She looked for all the world like an errant underage farm girl turned vampire. Blar decided Tsika was purposefully going to torture him for the whole day in retribution for his bedroom aggressiveness. Pleasant torture but torture nonetheless.

"Big Bear, good morning!" Little cute liar. "I know we're eating lunch in a few but want me to scramble up some eggs while you fix toast?" Her words did not match up with what her face said she wanted.

Tsika lay her hands on Blar's stomach, then jammed her fingers under his waistband and tugged at his jeans. She arched her back to emphasis her nipples were still at full alert under her shirt. Blar put his hands around her bare waist and lifted her onto the counter top. Tsika's eyes radiated excitement. Her lips parted seductively. He went in for a deep kiss. Tsika pressed up against him, putting her arms around his neck and her legs around his waist. Blar tasted her mouth, neck, ear, and then returned back to her hungry little mouth. Tsika pressed herself against Blar and raised her legs, pushing her heels against the small of his back. She gently rocked her pelvis against him, pressing against exactly what she wanted as she purred. She started to moan more vigorously as Blar pressed back.

Tsika opened one eye, then shrieked next to Blar's ear. "Aina! Uh … we were fixing … break … fast."

Tsika's crimson blush went from her face down into her blouse. Blar chuckled as he turned sideways and shook his head as he grinned at Aina. He kept his arm around Tsika's waist with a finger in her navel. He planned to touch the little pixie a lot today.

Aina's expression reminded Blar of Kpau – a wide-eyed completely insincere innocence.

"Yes … breakfast! I see! There's more room for that kind of preparation on the dining room table, you know. It's quite sturdy! I've tested it!" Aina chuckled as she grabbed herself a coffee cup. "I didn't know I was walking into a crime scene. Goodness, Tsika, you make me feel ancient! I thought Kpau looked like jail bait but you win the Grand Prize. I couldn't pull that look off when I was fifteen much less twenty-something!"

Tsika darted her eyes around. Blar was pretty sure he had never seen the little Russian as pink as she was right then. "Glycerin says the same thing. She'd get so mad when we were sixteen and slipping into pubs! They'd card me and they'd just let her pass … and we both had fake ID cards."

She slid off the counter and put her arms around Blar's waist as she huddled under his arm. Blar's forehead wrinkled. "I am having real difficulty imagining Glycerin in a pub setting."

"Precious Mouse would play darts. Everyone learned pretty quickly that she was mostly mute and shy. It was rare I had to defend her. Usually the rest of the pub would beat the crap out of anyone who scared her."

Aina chuckled as she headed for the refrigerator. "Well, if you two have breakfast covered, I'm going to get the ham into the oven to warm it up. I think my kitchen is large enough to be a 'three butt' kitchen."

Tsika giggled, "Is that a real phrase? Measuring a kitchen by butts? I like that. Sounds very American!" Aina handed Tsika the eggs and started taking out lunch items. The kitchen bustled with activity for a few minutes as the three went about their tasks.

The petite Russian finished seasoning the eggs in a bowl and set up the table. "See Blar? No hellfire this time! The vampire CAN cook without kitchen bursting into flames!"

Aina looked puzzled but let the cryptic remark pass. Blar just grinned and silently mouthed the word 'later' to the tall woman.

Tsika wiped her hands on a towel. "I'll go wake up – "

Tsika was interrupted by Aina, who had an inspired mischievous grin. "Wait, Tsika! I want to wake the kids up! Can I? Can I?"

Tsika wrinkled her brow. "Sure? Go for it. We will listen for the screams."

Aina nearly ran out of the kitchen with glee in her eyes.

"Big Bear, what was that about?" Tsika looked to Blar who was reflectively stroking his mustache. He thought he had a pretty good idea.

"I'll … Remind me to say what I think when we get on the road tomorrow, okay?"

Tsika looked solemn, "Okay, Blar." About thirty seconds later, Blar and Tsika heard screams, giggles, and shrieks from the other side of the house. "H'okay! Mission is accomplished. Your pretty Witch was successful, Blar."

Blar nodded thoughtfully, "I would say you are completely correct."

- - - - - -

Kpau sat the table with a napkin stuffed in her tee shirt. She gazed at the roast ham with drooling avarice.

"I can't decide whether this reminds me more of the Who-ville feast in the Grinch story or the Norman Rockwell image at the end of *Lilo&Stitch*!" She really was just barely avoiding drooling on herself.

Blar sipped his scotch and pursed his lips. "Great! Now I have this image of Kpau with a Cindy Lou Who hairstyle but with Stitch's maniacal laughter."

Glycerin snorted as she tried to suppress a giggle. The tall exotic creature had awakened with a minor hangover from her neophyte drinking experience but was already mostly over it. Blar looked at the lanky brunette with some interest.

"So, Glycerin. Do you … remember much of last night?" Blar watched her seize up and flinch in response. Blar suspected he was about to watch Glycerin try to lie her way around the matter.

"I … I remember … d-drinking. Rum and cola! It was tasty." She blushed and shyly peered at Blar through her lashes.

Ah, she remembers some things. There's a wild little creature lurking inside all that fear and terror.

A sudden gleam came into Glycerin's eyes that Blar noted Kpau clearly noticing. Kpau leaned back and rolled her eyes while Blar waited for Glycerin to power up to trying a witty reprisal. Glycerin's lips formed a classy pout. "Um … uh … everyone thought we were the dog's bollocks. And! And! My Blar tried to t-tear my clothes off. Twice. In f-front of everyone. I remember."

Aina's eyes widened as she stifled wine from shooting out her nose. "Twice!? I only remember once! Bad Blar! No restraint at all!"

Blar was laughing hard enough to choke on the biscuit he had just bitten into.. "Ok! Ok! Touche, Little Dancer. I was just trying to embarrass you a little. You win, I'm embarrassed! Wait. What are the dog's bollocks?"

Kpau was clapping, "Usually she falls on her face when she's plotting a witty bit. Maybe she's finally found someone dim enough to skewer, ha! Blar, I think the dog's bollocks means cracking splendid … or something like that. Best not to translate literally, I think."

Tsika was mashing peas into her baked sweet potato and eating the result. "Do we have any special plans today after this?"

Aina shook her head, "Not that I know of. I was just thinking a nice quiet afternoon of tabletop games or video games." She giggled, "I have the game *RockBand* if you're interested."

Tsika, Kpau, and Glycerin all shook their heads. Kpau said, "The drums drive me nuts and the streaming notey things actually make me a little nauseated. The one time I saw Glycerin try it, she broke the guitar – one of those pro guitars. The owner was not happy." Glycerin scrunched down in her seat.

Tsika chewed on a piece of ham as she considered. "Nyet. This one only likes the karaoke part of it. I did hear it does vocal harmony now though. That might be fun if we run out of ideas."

Blar took another large bite of ham himself. "I'm fine with tabletop games or shooter vid games. The weather is too crappy to do any beach combing." A mild storm had rolled in while lunch had been set out. The driving rain, wind, and occasional thunder had put a rainy day mood into everyone.

Aina snapped her fingers, "Oh! I have the videos from the performance! You can watch your stage performances!"

Glycerin faded to a darker shade of pale. "Watch myself? I've .... only seen myself a few seconds playing guitar back in uni."

Kpau was enthralled with the idea, "I wanna see!! I've never seen myself singing. Just bashing away on the drums. Guess I should check for squirrel shots at the drums too, huh."

Glycerin screwed up her face up, "When were you shooting squirrels ... what?" Kpau whispered in her ear and Glycerin turned a lighter shade of red. "Oh ... my word ... what a strange expression!"

Blar didn't know about the others but he was enjoying the hell out of the meal and the company of the women. This was the happy family moments of being in a band that he loved. Just people who cared about each other having fun together.

- - - - - -

The five of them were playing the board game *Settlers of Catan*, or as Kpau called it – "Sheep and Wood". Kpau had more fun making raunchy statements than actually winning.

"I have sheep! Who has wood for them?! Gimme!" One of her more printable lines.

Tsika completed her move, adding a segment to her road. She then caught Aina's eye, "Hey, are we going to get to see Alwyn before we leave? Kpau and I did spot him at the club yesterday. We said hello, but he was in a hurry to meet someone so he just waved in passing."

Aina smiled as she executed her turn, dropping a new village on the board. "Yes, he should be back early tomorrow before you birds are up. He's seeing to a lady friend in Monterey today."

Kpau got a funny look on her face, "For some reason, I never thought of butlers having girlfriends. I guess I thought they just stood in a closet when they weren't around. Yes, it was a stupid notion. Just never thought about it before. And she's never given him a hard time about spending so much time alone with you at the house?" Kpau did a comedic leer at Aina

"Well, Duane is usually here so it's more fun when we invite her over for an orgy – I'm pulling your leg, Spark, you can pick your jaw up! She is quite nice, we've had her over for barbeque on holiday!"

Blar rolled the dice and won control of the thief, which he used to ruin Kpau's resource production. The blonde drummer growled and squinted at him. He grinned before turning his attention back to Aina. "No chance of Duane being back before we leave, eh? I did want to say hello and introduce him to these maniacs."

"No, he's not flying back until Friday. And yes, he has seen the photos of you 'snogging' the daylights out of me onstage. They're making the gossip news headlines already along with grim pictures of an angry Duane culled from god knows where and airbrushed. I loudly blamed you three evil goblins." Aina stared at her game cards, not liking her choices. "You might like to know there are pictures and video of Blar ravishing you naughty girls on stage making the rounds as well. They're quite hilarious. According to several gossip rags, Blar had a nervous breakdown on stage and sexually assaulted all of us. Duane says he's sorry he missed the action and the squealing. I told him I would save the private video." Aina giggled mischievously.

Blar sighed. "I guess we're starting to edge into the public view outside of Portland. So it goes. Free advertising of the annoying kind. It will be interesting to watch them overload on you one day, Kpau."

"Just gotta keep twisting their brains around, Blargle. I plan to make Miley blush from the gossip I generate!"

"Duane is-isn't r-really mad, is he?" Glycerin blushed. Blar chuckled. She was probably thinking her hip bump that sent Aina into his arms was stage center in the video and photos.

Aina spoke in her motherly voice. "No, Glycca. I won't tease you. Duane knows how the whole gossip game works. He's anxious to meet you guys sometime – especially Kpau! The dear bastard is kind of an inveterate joker himself."

Blar eyed Tsika as she started her turn. She was looking at her cards with annoyed expression. She did not have the greatest poker face in playing board games.

Kpau suddenly straightened up in her chair, "I need to move around! How about a round of DDR after this? Dancing for points! Drinking game! I saw it in Aina's stash of video games!

Blar flinched, "Ah, you all have fun. I'll watch.

Tsika smirked, "Yeah, I bet you will, lecherous Bear. I say he has to take his turn." Blar was voted down four to one, not even Aina was going to let him off.

"I'm a terrible dancer. You'll be psychologically scarred, I'm warning you." Blar realized he had missed a chance to build a road on the game board during their distraction. Damn.

- - - - - -

The dance game went as painfully as Blar had promised it would. Tsika actually apologized for making him dance. Aina just laughed and Glycerin covered her eyes. Kpau's helpful insight was that he should take his clothes off, then no one would notice how badly he danced.

On the other hand, watching the women dance was quite pleasant for Blar. Tsika danced like a gymnast or ballerina no matter what the music was. Her hair tails substituted for the long ribbons they used.

Kpau danced as if she was cheerleading and admitted she had actually been a cheerleader in high school.

Glycerin had to be badgered to dance in front of Blar but once she started, she moved in the same quirky slithering way she had moved when singing. It had a kind of tribal ritual mystic feeling to it. Blar found it quite compelling. She would make a riveting high priestess for a cult.

Aina had come from the Stevie Nicks school of twirling and her own stage performance history. She was smooth and fluid as she spun. Blar opined silently that Glycerin might evolve to those kind of moves over the next ten years. He found himself wondering what things would be like in ten years, what would happen, how the band would evolve, would there even be a band?

He was disturbed in that reverie by Tsika crawling into his lap and curling up for a neck rub. "You're zoning off into space, Blar. What is the moody bear thinking?"

Blar didn't see any point in hiding what he was thinking. "Just thinking about what the band might be like in ten years."

Everyone came to a halt. Kpau had a horrified look. "I try not to think about what things will be like next week! Ten years! That's like … forever!" She stared hard into nothing. "I'm clueless. What did you envision?"

Blar decided he was getting into dark deep water. "Reply murky. Ask again later … maybe ten years from now."

Aina twirled on the dance mat with a gentle smile. "Too many possibilities. Even this witch can't divine it."

Tsika and Glycerin just sat silent with crimson faces. Blar figured they had some ideas they weren't sharing with the crowd. He thought about Tsika's occasional little slips about wanting a daughter some day. Time to divert.

"Hey, pretty women, lets play something that doesn't embarrass me. Who's up for *Call of Duty*? We'll rock-paper-scissors and the fifth gets more snacks.

Blar lost the challenge. He wasn't too upset, it was kind of fascinating watching Aina and Glycerin versus Tsika and Kpau. The melee full speed ahead goblins were slaughtered by the camping snipers every round of the video game.

- - - - - -

Later that evening, Glycerin did manage to survive the video performances of the band and of her singing at center-stage. She peeked over a protective pillow she clutched. The big mouse tried to make herself as small as possible as she watched herself in the video. The images were quite sensual. Onscreen Glycerin was extremely sexy as she came onto Blar while she played guitar. Blar could see her eyes darting over to Tsika and back to the screen. Glycerin wouldn't make eye contact with him at all. Wasn't hard to decipher she was worried.

Blar thought Glycerin needn't have worried much. Both Tsika and Kpau had gotten fairly sloshed during the video gaming and were just laughing their heads off at the images of Blar being seduced by Glycerin on stage.

Blar couldn't detect any concern on Tsika's part at all – this befuddled him. Tsika was sending such mixed signals. Blar supposed Tsika just really loved Glycerin that much and didn't view any designs on himself as a competition. Her mood on the matter seemed to have stabilized in the last few days. It simply didn't seem to be bothering her now.

Blar looked to Aina but her expression was just reflective. She would occasionally remark on stage positioning or give Glycerin advice on timing her interactions with Blar or the others to create a musical conversation. Very professional of her – except for the small fact that Aina was laying on the couch upside down with her legs over the backrest and her head hanging off the seat cushion, giving her an inverted view of the videos.

- - - - - -

Late night in a silent house. Everyone had retired for the evening. Blar woke up feeling dry in the mouth and padded down to the kitchen for some water. He rounded the corner and found someone sitting at the kitchen table. Not quite correct. The woman was asleep with her head on the table. At first, in the dim light, Blar thought it was Aina but realized quickly it was Glycerin. He got down on one knee and got close to her face. Blar just really liked watching her sleep. No fear, no terror, no embarrassment – just a relaxed beautiful face.

Blar didn't want her to wake up all twisted up in cricks, so he put his hand on her back and patted her. "Little Dancer … Glycca … time for bed."

Her eyes opened. Blar could see the momentary disorientation, panic, epiphany – all in a flash. There was also that effect he never failed to be fascinated by – the odd mismatched dilating of the pupils. Each eye would shift independently. It remained the oddest thing he'd ever seen eyes do. The most unexpected thing to Blar was that the more Glycerin improved, the stronger the effect got instead of fading.

"Oh! Hullo, my Blar. We cames for a d-drink and we w-were just thinking, we was." Her big doe eyes peered into Blar's eyes and she raised her slender hand to stroke Blar's hair.

"I was out-out-out of line at the club. We-I hope … nothing is amiss with Tsika."

"No, Glycca … I think she's just fine. Really happy. It didn't seem to bother her at all. Some moments it seems to please her to no end when you assert yourself. Me? I'm the one in a dither and I'm just going to have to walk the tight rope. I'm not going to pretend I'm not attracted to both of you. It's just that I care about both of you and I don't want to hurt either of you." Blar stroked her back as he spoke.

Glycerin got a vacant expression. Blar watched with fascination as her pupils engaging in their independent twirl of dilation.

"Tsika … she was f-first. Y-You followed my lit-little doll. It isn't cricket."

"It's more complicated than that, pretty flower. Tsika encourages me spending time with you. She's so focused on helping you … normalize … get better … to be happy. That makes her happiest, seeing you happy. My feelings matter, too, as confused as they are." Blar kissed Glycerin's forehead.

"Even … even b-back at Han's … she pushed aside m-m-my worries about you and us. She told me to f-f-focus on the band." Glycerin stuck her lower lip out as she spoke.

"Sounds like good advice. You know I care about you, that I care about Tsika. Heck, Kpau and I care about each other in our weird perverted way." Blar grinned as Glycerin suppressed a snorting giggle.

"Tomorrow we hit the road, Glycca. We absolutely need to focus on the music. Writing songs, tuning what the band is. Three weeks of that. Then I have a spring time tour set up in Portland and Seattle … and I have an idea for the summer that I'm not going to talk about until I've got some firm leads – it'll be exciting if it pans out." Blar ruffled her hair as he whispered.

Glycerin's eyes were shiny. "I k-keep saying I'm gl-glad I met you, but I am. I love my Tsika. This band is her dream. I'd die for her … really. We'll … be okay if we work hard and care f-for each other."

"Come on, sexy, we need to go to sleep. Aina is going to take forever saying goodbye tomorrow."

Glycerin turned a shade of red when he called her sexy that Blar could spot even in the dim light. He stood up and held his hand out; she took it and stood up. Glycerin darted in, kissed his cheek, and hugged his arm. Blar led her down the hallway and they split up for the night.

- - - - - -

Morning. The van was packed, the sun was peeking through the clouds, and everyone was standing in the driveway. Aina was not handling the goodbyes well. She was teary-eyed and kept hugging everyone, especially Kpau. The little blonde's shields were a wreck, she was just streaming tears. Blar's premonition that it was going to go like this was certainly panning out.

"B'bye, Mama Bear! I wish you could go with us." Kpau clung to Aina as a small child might.

"Little Spark, we all have our stuff we have to do. You have to get on the Magic Bus and I have to go back to work. Plus … my Duane will need tending to when he gets back."

That morning Duane had called Aina to admit he had broken a leg while skiing on Mauna Kea in Hawaii. He was flying back on crutches. Blar had been nearby for that hilarious phone call. She had berated the poor guy for nearly twenty minutes and then cried in worry about her husband after she hung up, using Blar as a large tissue.

Aina bit her lip. "Spark, can … may I … may I visit the Magic Bus on occasion?"

Kpau looked at Aina as if she'd spoken heresy. "Well, yeah! You're Mama Bear! Family! My family! You have to visit us and we want to see you!"

Blar winced as Aina disintegrated into a cloud of tears. "I'd … I'd … love to be … family. Thank you, Kpau."

Tsika hugged Aina. "Thank you. Thank you for helping Glyc. Thank you for everything you've taught me." Aina nodded as she wiped her face and kissed Tsika on her forehead.

Glycerin didn't say anything. She was in the throes of a hiccup attack and sniffles. She just hugged Aina silently and held tight to her for a long time. Blar was certainly sympathetic to all the emotion but he felt like he was drowning. No getting around it though. He had really meant for this bonding to happen. Aina was going to be a very good mentor to the women and he knew she would treat them fairly if records and albums started to happen.

Blar hugged Aina and kissed her lips. "Bye, pretty Witch, I think you did good. I'll be in touch about the summer plans, okay? I'll keep you … well, what am I saying, you lot are all connected a dozen ways from Sunday on the Internet and cell phones. Aina will be lucky if she isn't buried in girl chatter." Aina shook him by his coat in mock anger.

The band took their seats and Aina waved as they drove off. About the time Blar hit the highway, Kpau popped up from her moping at having to leave.

"Hey, Papa Bear! Aina acted very weird when I said she was family. What's up with that?"

Before Blar could respond, Tsika looked up from her e-book. "Yes, Bear, also – you said there was something you'd tell me about Aina when we got on the road."

"Well … " Blar stayed silent for almost a minute.

"You remember Aina told you she had drinking and drug problems during the *Gothic Fire* band days? Well … at one point … we discovered she was pregnant. It didn't go well. The pregnancy failed, badly enough she … well, Aina can't have children. So … you saying she's family and calling her Mama Bear … that goes really deep into her."

There was a long silence. Blar looked away from the road to see all three women silently crying and wiping tears off their faces.

Tsika blew her nose, "Blar … that's … so …sad. Who … who was the father?"

"Dunno, pixie. We chose not to find out. Torsten and I just felt like we both were and left it at that."

Tsika's cheeks grew even paler if that were possible. She just sat quietly in shock as she stared out her window.

Kpau was just bawling now. "I feel like … I need to … go back and hug her the rest of the day."

Blar smiled, "No, no. You did good … Spark. Everyone wipe their eyes and don't feel sorry for Aina. She got just as much good out of your visit as you guys did – I think you all just earned yourselves a very determined protective den mother and someone we can rely on with the business of making music. You guys put her squarely in the Magic Bus."

Blar added some speed to the van, steering towards the Big Sur and their music-writing retreat.

- - - - - -

~Continued in Volume Two~

It Really IS Rocket Science
"Surfing with the Alien"

acknowledgements

Forces from superficially unrelated directions drove the creation of this book, the first in a light novel series.

I have long been a fan of classic romantic comedies of the Cary Grant and Audrey Hepburn variety. I grew up on Saturday afternoon movies on television that ran classics from the 1950s and 1960s. Some elements of this story are an homage to those classic jewels though with contemporary twists.

I am also a casual fan of Japanese anime, the genre that covers absurd comedies, romances both dramatic and funny, and slice-of-life character studies. When I write, I enjoy taking archetypes and tropes out of anime and twisting them around to fit into Western stories. They become little Easter Eggs for fans of the medium to enjoy. One thing that drove this series was the tendency of anime and manga to end the story right when things start to get interesting – after the characters declare their attraction for each other.

Finally, the characters who populate this story have lived in my head for thirty years or more. I have used them in tabletop role-playing games, online virtual multi-player worlds, and video games where you create characters to adventure in a world. They needed a home with their own story. I wanted them to have a place where they wouldn't be forgotten after I've given my last performance and left the building.

I'd like to thank those who provided crucial feedback as I floundered in the night on each chapter. I credit my main goblins – Stephanie Schaefer (my editor) and Corinn Heathers (an author with her own stories), and a few that contributed heavily but prefer to remain anonymous. I also got useful feedback from a small squadron of beta readers, many of whom I only know by their online names. As in the *Matrix*, their names online are what they say they are – but they are real folks who cared enough to give me feedback and that is appreciated.

I also thank Pat Benatar, at least indirectly, via her auto-biographical *"Between a Heart and a Rock Place: A Memoir"*. Most music biographies, to be blunt and crude, are several hundred pages of drugs, ego, and repetitive sex.

They are boring. Hers was one of a handful that were different. It discussed the business, the politics, the corruption and hassles, the romancing, the adventure on the road, and how to raise a family – all while being a rock star. I also credit David Byrne's book, *"How Music Works"* and Donald Passman's *"All You Need To Know About The Music Business"*, an essential guide for real bands starting out in the modern music industry.

As noted, "Rock'N'Roll Fantasy" is the first volume of a series. The first book of any series is always more difficult to make exciting. The author has to construct a universe and define the characters while propelling the story. I decided I had done something right when my beta readers were anxious to dive into volume two (currently in final drafting).

At the moment, I have enough raw story for four volumes and have storyboard outlines that go out much farther. Rock on.

Credits
The lovely model gracing the front cover of some editions of this book goes by the professional name of Elisanth. She's an alternative fashion/fetish/cosplay model and does spectacular work. Visit her website at http://elisanth.com. She posts much of her work on Facebook at https://www.facebook.com/model.elisanth. Go! Enjoy her mad skills! Obligatory note that her site contains some adult imagery that might be problematic at a workplace. Just fair warning.

Channels
To keep up with the latest releases, new volumes, and just some of the antics that go with writing stories, follow these links:

Facebook: https://www.facebook.com/bhbranham

Twitter: https://twitter.com/BHBranham

And more channels in development (gotta write story sometimes).

27815254R00195

Made in the USA
Charleston, SC
22 March 2014